Praise for SINFUL FOLK

"A pilgrim tale worthy of Chaucer, evocative, compelling and peopled with unforgettable characters artfully delivered by a master storyteller." —Brenda Rickman Vantrease, best-selling author of *The Illuminator and The Mercy Seller*

"An exquisitely written historical thriller, told by a brave and charismatic narrator who will twist your heart-strings with her story from the first page to final startling revelation. An amazing novel based on a truly fascinating, unsolved mystery of the Middle Ages." —Karen Maitland, best-selling author of *The Owl Killers* and *Company of Liars*

"Brilliant, insightful, unflinching and wise. This spellbinding mystery will keep readers turning pages until the last sentence. Remarkable." —Ella March Chase, best-selling author of *The Virgin Queen's Daughter* and *Three Maids for a Crown*

"Suspenseful, page-turning mystery of a mother pursuing the truth. . . . Every reader will come to love the brave and intrepid Mear, a most memorable character in a most memorable story." —Jim Heynen, award-winning author of *The Fall of Alice K.*

"*Sinful Folk* is a work of art. Miriam's story is a raw, brutal and passionate tale, but her story touches the reader because it's a timeless story—a wonderful portrayal of medieval life." —Kathryn Le Veque, best-selling author of *The Dark Lord* and *The Warrior Poet*

Books by NED HAYES

Glossolalia: Speaking in Tongues (poems)
Coeur d'Alene Waters

SINFUL FOLK

Interior illustrations by Nikki McClure
Book design by Sara DeHaan

Campanile Books www.CampanilePress.com
244 5th Ave, Suite N-242, New York, NY 10001
United States of America

Publisher's Cataloging-in-Publication data

Hayes, Ned.
Sinful folk/Ned Hayes.—1st ed. in the U.S.A.
p. cm.
ISBN-13 978-0-9852393-0-5
1. Great Britain—History—14th century—Fiction. 2. Historical fiction.
3. Suspense fiction.
I. Title
PR6064.073M57 2014
823.'92—dc
222006024710

Printed in the United States of America

FUL FOLK

A NOVEL OF THE MIDDLE AGES

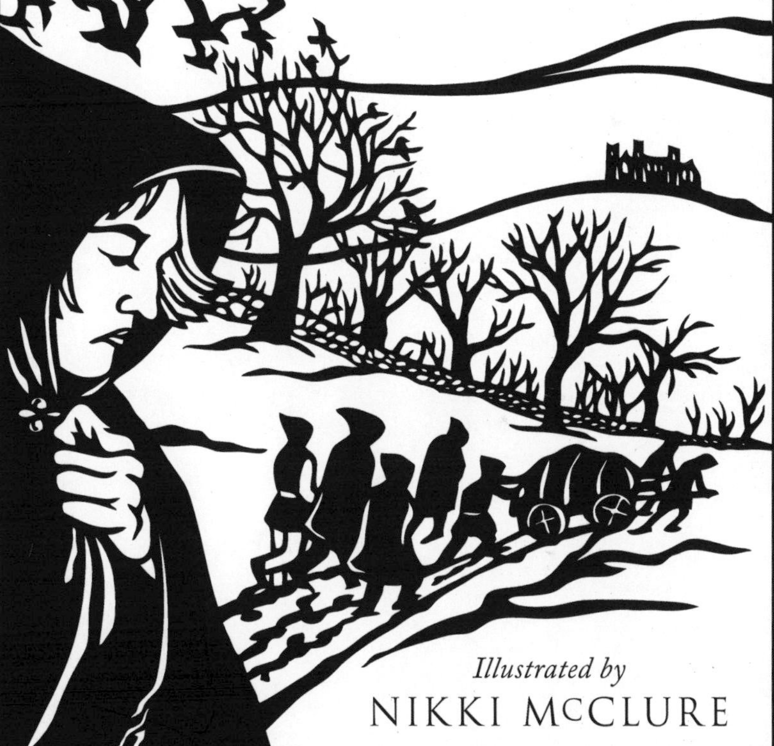

Illustrated by
NIKKI McCLURE

NED HAYES

Pray for us, we sinful folk unstable....
My child is dead within these two weeks,
Soon after that, we went out of this town...
Up I rose, with many a tear trickling on my cheeks

—Geoffrey Chaucer,
The Canterbury Tales

A CURIOUS incident is brought to our attention from the year 1377. In December of that coldest year in the medieval records, the village of Duns in the northeast of England suffered a great tragedy. Five of its young boys were burned to death in a house fire near the center of the village.

As was common with many tragic events in that century, it was supposed the Jews were to blame. Yet all Jews were destroyed, forcibly converted, or expelled from England by order of the Crown, some fifty years earlier, in 1325.

Although most English peasants at that time had never traveled during the course of their lives more than twenty miles from the place of their birth, five men from the village of Duns loaded the charred bodies of their children on a farm cart and journeyed over two hundred miles to London. The Court record states that the villagers went to present the bodies to the King, and to demand justice against the Jews.

The historical record is clear on these few facts. History does not record any further details about the incident—neither the motivations, intentions, nor experiences of those who undertook this arduous journey are noted. Not a single person from the village is identified, not even the guilty party.

—Miria Hallum,
The Hollow Womb: Child Loss in the Middle Ages

LITURGY OF THE HOURS

Lauds	Aurora, the dawn prayer, to greet the day
Prime	Early morning prayer, first hour, about 6 a.m.
Terce	Midmorning prayer, third hour, about 9 a.m.
Sext	Midday prayer, sixth hour, about noon
None	Midafternoon prayer, ninth hour, about 3 p.m.
Vespers	Evening prayer, at the lighting of lamps, 6 p.m.
Compline	Night prayer, before retiring for sleep
Matins	Vigils or Nocturns, during the hours of night

BOOK 1

CHAPTER 1

IN THE END, I listen to my fear. It keeps me awake, resounding through the frantic beating in my breast. It is there in the dry terror in my throat, in the pricking of the rats' nervous feet in the darkness.

Christian has not come home all the night long.

I know, for I have lain in this darkness for hours now with my eyes stretched wide, yearning for my son's return.

Each night that he works late, I cannot sleep. I am tormented when he is not here—I fear that he will never return. I lie awake, plagued by my own fears of loss and loneliness.

But my fears have never come to pass.

So on this night, I tell myself that the sound I hear is frost cracking, river ice breaking. I lie to my own heart, as one lies to a frightened child, one who cannot be saved.

All the while, I know it is a fire. And I know how near it is.

First, I could hear shouts and cries. Then there was the sound of rapid running, of men hauling buckets of water and ordering children to help.

A house burns.

Yet always I fear to venture forth, for my fright has grown into a panic that gibbers in the dark. *What if someone started this fire to burn me out?*

What sport would they have, watching a mute moan as she turns on the spit?

A crackle and hiss in the distance. A heavy thud, and then the roar of an inferno. *Where is Christian? I must go, I—*

Scrambling out of the straw, I rush to the door in my nightclothes. Then I remember poor Nell, who died last spring.

I do not forget her agony.

I blunder in the darkness, fumbling for the fireplace soot. I smear the smooth edge of my jaw, marking with trembling fingers a hint of beard on my soft upper lip and my chin.

Always, I must hide my true face.

As my fingers work, I grip hope to me, a small bird quaking in the nest of my heart. Desperately, I mumble the words of a prayer from my past.

O Alma Redemptoris...

My sooty ritual is perhaps my own strange paean to womanhood. Like Theresa of Avignon, that spoiled heiress of the French throne, who shared my vows at Canterbury, the world will see me only as I intend. It is a type of vanity: if I cannot be a woman, I will be as ugly a man as I can muster.

And in this ceremony, my dread subsides. My fingers stop trembling. I think clearly for a moment. Even now, perhaps Christian is one of those who carry buckets of water to fight the flames. Christian will be fine. He is strong, vital, alive. He is mine, and I am his.

All will be well. I repeat it in my head like a rosary. *All will be well.*

Then there are harsh shouting voices outside, men rushing toward the burning building. "Trapped!" they shout.

Now I quake with dread, for I am not finished. I should wrap my bosom tightly, bind the feminine shape of my body into that of a eunuch. But I lunge for the door, my bosom unbound, my heart full of fear for my son, and fear for my own flesh.

Even as my heart belies me, I pray that this fire is nothing. Nothing to do with my life, my secrets.

Across the village square, the largest house—the home of Benedict, the weaver—is consumed by flame. Every piece of wood smokes and bends in the fire. The roof seems supported not by heavy timbers, but by ropy masses of blazing smoke.

It is the home where my son is an apprentice.

The smoke chokes and claws at my nostrils and my throat. The roof catches in a roar of flaming darkness. The crowd churns in turmoil, seeking to save their village, their children.

Not one of the villagers pays the slightest heed to me.

I am an old man to them, and a broken, mute one at that—wiry as a starved mule, leathery with long labor. It is rare that any in this village look beyond the wrinkles and the rat's nest of chestnut-colored hair to see my face.

Tonight, I force them to see me. I seize each of their faces with my gaunt hands, turning them, staring quickly into each pair of wild, frightened eyes. Here is that layabout Liam's frightened pale face and red beard. He looks for his son too. Across the way is a boy wrapped in a cloak and hood. My heart lifts—is it Christian?

But when I meet that boy's eyes, they are black as night. It is only Cole, the orphan. I see my friend Salvius, the blacksmith. He runs past, throwing water on the flames.

Then I see Tom, who hangs back in the crowd. I clutch at him, wanting answers, but Tom pushes me away, his wide-set, cowish face full of fear.

I turn. I pull down another man's hood, and it is bald Benedict, the weaver who owns this house. He gives me a dark glance and pulls away, to lift a bucket of water.

I grasp a short man next, small Geoff, the carpenter, with the squint. "Where's my boy?" he shouts in my face. "Where is he?"

I turn about again, I seize on every person, look into every face. I hope for only one boy, I search for his blue eyes. My son.

Christian.

Is this really all the living folk we have? Frantically, I count on my fingers. All the women accounted for and most of the men.

Only a few are not here: Jack, whose foot was trampled by a cow, and Phoebe, who is about to give birth. Benedict's wife will be with her this night—Sophia is the closest we have to a midwife now, now that Nell is gone.

That accounts for three. *But where are the older boys?*

Desperately, I search each of these villager's faces again and again—going over old ground—until they push me away.

Men and women shout their children's names. "Breton! Matthew! Stephen! Jonathon!" The large boy who belongs to Tom. The son of the carpenter. Then the second son of the weaver. And the eldest son of Liam, the woodsman. But there is only one name that echoes in my mind, and no one shouts it aloud. My son, my only.

Christian— Christian— Christian—

The house falls half apart, split wide, a timbered carcass steaming and cracking in the winter frost. Salvius is always brave: he leaps up onto the smoldering threshold and uses a beam to batter in the smoking door. Then Liam steps into the smoke, wrapping his arms in a wet cloak.

I push my way through the milling villagers to see Liam and Salvius emerge, dragging out a charred body. Then another, and another. Five, in the end—all the missing accounted for.

My tongue forms his name, but I cannot speak a word. Instead, I give a cry—that meaningless animal groan that is my only language now.

The flames rise again, the west wind gusts strong across the heath, a demon roaring as it takes the building apart. The crackle is that of hell itself. The men run frantically with buckets of water to save the neighboring crofts.

The five bodies lie on the ground, black as broken shadows. They stink now of death. Burned flesh, scorched wool. It is a nauseating stench, yet despite myself, my mouth waters at the smell of flame-roasted meat. I am always so hungry.

A bit of metal glimmers faintly below one charred head. It is a thin silver chain. *Is that my chain? My boy's neck?*

I am pierced to the root then, all of my veins bathed in a liquor of terror.

CHAPTER 2

THE DAY IS almost upon us, the houses and trees silhouetted by a faint blue light in the east. The burned croft is a smoking wreck, embers steaming in the dawn.

The wind dies now. In this winter, we have had several unfortunate fires, but this is the worst yet. The crowd slows its frantic work, as the danger fades.

Now I can hear them: the cries of children, the sobs of babes in arms. No doubt those cries were all around me for hours in the crowd. Yet I had ears only for one cry, and that cry never came.

The bodies are surrounded by their families. These youth were our bleak earth's brightest, our highest roll on Fortune's wheel.

I go to the dead. They are blackened and unrecognizable, each boy stretched out like a penitent against the raw earth. *These are other children, not mine, not mine.*

But I reach out my hand, I cross them with the holy sign. My mouth moves silently in the rhythm of that last rite, although I have not a whit of faith left in me.

If I still believed in such fictions, the souls of these innocents would be trapped in limbo for eternity. A cold God to condemn children to such punishment. And *my* blessing means nothing: we have no priest in this village, no sacrament of burial, no sacraments at all.

The world blurs as my eyes go wet.

A voice calls my name loud. "Mear!" I turn, blind and terrified, covering my tear-streaked face. Liam's voice is strained and hoarse. "Mear. Ah, Mear, there is no shame in tears. All of us have lost."

Liam is the poorest man in the village, and we have lived side by side so long that I have wondered if he and his wife Kate see through my soot-stained skin to the woman underneath. I stay apart from him as much as I can, but always he talks to me, despite my silence.

Most of the villagers act as if I am of no more importance than a beast. No one here ever pays me mind. There are few who know I am alive. I prefer it that way, for I want to be invisible.

Yet I would have taken my child and left long ago except for this man, Liam, and my friends Salvius and Nell. Salvius needs me at his bellows and his smithy—he values my labor and my friendship. And Liam at least helps me laugh.

But Nell—poor Nell—she is gone.

Now Liam puts an arm around my slight shoulders, holding me as I sob. There is no laughter in him after last night. His green eyes are full of water, and his red beard trembles.

"Oh, Mear, thank you for blessin' their souls."

Who else has seen me bless and cross the dead?

But Liam does not care that I make the sign reserved for priests and nuns. He mourns over his son, and then he turns to look at another body, close at hand.

"I think here's your lad. Seems to me it has to be him. He was the last one I brought out—the tallest and the furthest from the door."

And when he says this, I cannot pretend any longer, I cannot wish away this hard truth. The silver chain glimmers faintly in the dawn light—it does not lie. I fall to my knees. Here is my beloved, my son.

Liam bends down to his own firstborn son, burned and blackened on the ground. A groan comes out of the stricken father, an anguished sound to shake the earth.

Now the crowd swells and crests under the whip of a mad grief.

Tom is slavering out some half-remembered tale, a demonic vision. "This is the work of those who killed the Christ. They are cursed—infested with the devil's seed! They drink children's blood in the night!"

Everyone knows this is the third terrible fire we have had this winter. This time, it was Benedict's weaving house that burned, and some in the crowd move toward his family.

"Why were the lads here?" cries Geoff, the carpenter. "Why were they burned?"

"I didn't do it!" Benedict's voice is strained with fear. "They gathered at Vespers, I tell you the truth. They were only here to work on the grand tunics for Sir Peter of Lincoln."

"Where were *you* then?" shouts Liam, choking back a sob. "It's your house!"

"I was with my wife!" Benedict sweeps his hat from his weathered scalp and throws it on the ground. "I took Sophia 'cross the valley to see to Phoebe's birth."

The men stink of rage, like a pan of smoking oil before it catches fire.

"You're a liar!" says Geoff to Bene, pushing toward him through the crowd.

"Goddammit, I lost my son too," Benedict shouts. "I wasn't even here!"

Hob, the alderman, affirms that Benedict returned late, at Nocturns hour.

Most times the crowd will listen to Hob, but today they will not be stilled. Women scream at Benedict and his family, wanting his blood in payment. Small Geoff rushes at Benedict, to hurt him.

But Geoff can't get through the crowd drawn tight around Tom, who bawls out the sordid details of his imagined witchcraft. The Star Chamber, the White Tower, evil stories of Old Gods and black fairies. And that ancient villain, the Jew.

"Every child knows who does dark deeds in the night," shrieks Tom. "Every child knows we suffer now in this world because of that crime against our Lord Jesus Christ. Jews did this!"

Ripe nonsense. But the villagers want so desperately to believe there is a reason for this loss.

Tom tells them that there is a root out of which murder grows, a seed that can be plucked. The fires come most likely from an old chimney catching, or a load of hay that catches spontaneously. Yet no one has died from the previous fires. This time, the villagers want a cause, a goat to tie the blood to, an empty vessel to fill with hatred and bludgeon with their loss.

"The Jews!" calls Tom again.

There are a few of Jewish blood here—I know who they are, even now, years after they converted. *How long will it take the crowd to remember and find those who once were Jews in this village?*

"Damn the Jews to hell!" someone in the crowd shouts. "Make the Jews pay!"

No one notices when I rise from the ground and stagger to the smoking ruin. My mute questions will find no answers in gruesome children's tales. I know what will tell me the truth— the bare reality of the boys' deaths. I push through the crowd to the place they died.

What power held the door so the boys could not flee the rising flames?

With my foot, I stir the warm cinders. The door broken by Salvius lies in pieces, smashed flat. But there is a knot here, an unlikely twist of the rope that I must examine.

I can see now that this was the rope that held the door tight closed. I pick at it, pull out pieces of a rope still stretched taut across the doorframe. I have seen this curious binding once before. But no fairie tied this knot. No errant ghostly Jew. It is a triple knot, tied fast across a half hitch. It crumbles to ash under my probing touch.

"Trial by water," wails Tom. "Trial by fire. Kill the traitor Jews, save the innocent!"

Liam taunts Benedict. "Don't you know a Jew? Did you burn the place for her, Bene?"

"We are all of us the traitors to our children! Every man in this village," cries Benedict. "Every man stands accused, every one should suffer trial by water, I tell you. Every one of us!"

"Who do we drown first?" Liam's face is stained with tears.

"Hell, I know you did it," screams Geoff at Benedict. "You killed them. Drown yourself in the pond first!"

The people surge back and forth, panicked. My heart thrums, fear shrinking my bowels, quivering through my pulse.

The quarreling men bring back to me the chaos of my dying home village many years ago, when I made that last promise to my mother. I can picture the hands moving from gestures to fists, from sticks to sharp sickles. Quick as a breath.

"That's enough!" Hob's deep and lordly voice finally stills the milling crowd. "The blood of these innocents cries out, as our brother Tom tells us. Their souls plead for vengeance! I agree. But I tell you, drowning—or near drowning—half the men of this village won't bring our children back to us."

The crowd murmurs affirmation.

"What will bring them back is justice!" shouts Hob. "And there's one seat of justice here on earth."

"Kill them Jews," mutters Tom again. "Kill 'em now." But the crowd ignores him this time.

Hob cries out louder. "We will take the proof to our King!"

"To the King," echoes Salvius. His masterful tone is a herald's cry that cuts through the chaos. Salvius leaps onto Benedict's cart that stands near at hand and finds a common cause with the crowd. "Come, my friends, we will seek the King's justice!"

Some in the crowd move at this—the men who shouted loud against the Jews now lift the lifeless bodies from the ground.

Benedict and the orphan, Cole, load the body of Benedict's son onto the cart. The boy's corpse lands with a sodden thunk.

Geoff pushes past me, muttering. "If I cannot kill a Jew here, at least I will go with my son, Goddamn them, and tell the king what I think of his damn'd protection against Jews, much good it did us."

Liam lifts his own son's cold body. He places him gently on the straw in the cart. "I'll go with you, my boy," he says to his son, and shakes with weeping.

The wind blows a hard gust. There is a simmering argument in the crowd. When the harvest failed and the belts tightened in this starving season of ours, most were left too weak to search for food outside the village. *How can any of us take a journey now?*

My friend Salvius waves away the questions. "Yes, yes, we've got enough food, and we're taking strong men only. We'll make it all the way to London, by God's bloody Son!"

As the light bleeds into the sky, the feeling of the crowd shifts with it. The hunger for this journey jumps back and forth between the villagers, like the heat of a flame passing between them.

Geoff protests, his voice a thin reed of reason. "We should take them to somewhere close-at-hand. The Abbot at the Cluny Monastery—it is close on the King's road."

Salvius skillfully whips them all forward, turning them all toward a journey as a great beast is turned with a small prod.

"The Jews!" the crowd cries. "We seek justice against the Jews—and we will take this proof of their crime all the way to the King. The Throne will judge the Jews!"

The men bellow loud, they swear on their children's unburied bodies, they will go and find the truth. Hob and Benedict shout themselves hoarse, promising justice to their clans. I turn away—I cannot keep up with the arguments that shudder from the crowd. None of their moans and barks is worth a spit in the wind.

I look at my son, and I sink into grief. When they come to get the body with the necklace, I do not let go. I close my eyes, I can hear them all around, their voices a cacophony.

"Why do you hold on, old Mear?"

"Let the body go."

"He is the father."

"Show him pity. He canna speak."

Tears leak out of my tight-shut eyes. *I want my boy.* My soul is tied to his sweet body, the one stretched out as a tortured savior. I can feel his burning through my flesh, the choking smoke is in my own lungs. I will burn with him.

But however much I wish it, I cannot take myself out of existence. I open my eyes once more. My body still breathes, my heart pounds ignorantly in my bosom.

I will not let him depart from me. I will heal him, I think desperately. *I will care for his wounded body until he is well again.*

The men lift his body onto the cart.

They are taking him away. There will be nothing left to me. Not a body, not a token, not a grave.

I lift my face, stained with ash and tears. A baying sob breaks from my throat.

Years have passed, almost a decade, since I made a sound that the villagers could hear. Now, all turn toward me. Even the men loading the bodies on the cart heed me.

I make a motion. I will come with them, wherever they are taking my son; I will go too.

Tom points at me and mumbles more of his cracked vision. "Let 'im come along! Mear here, he'll find the truth, I tell ye. The angels done foretold it."

People look away from Tom, shaking their heads. Few believe that I understood the debate of the morning and all the decisions that have been made. No one believes that I can make the journey.

I stumble back to our tiny cruck house—wattled and daubed by Christian and me. I bind my bosom firmly this time and I pack what little I have. After the poor harvest this fall, there is no food for me to bring except one old loaf of dark bread and some dried mutton. I put on the tarnished silver chain that matches the one my son wore;

and I search for but cannot find my ring. I have had it for years, but it is not in its hiding place under the hearthstone now. My heart plummets at this loss, but it is too late. I do not have time to hunt for it further.

I seize also the sheepskins and furs that make up our bed, and a small pot of soot, for my face in the night, and that is all.

When I return, Hob has ordered supplies from the meager stocks of the village. He asks for sacrifice from families here to sustain the men on the open road, and his appeal is met despite the larder houses that sit empty after the terrible autumn and the poor fields that yielded nothing. Geoff piles up wood and tinder; Benedict loads straw and fodder into the cart. Liam has brought an axe, while Salvius sends Tom the miller to retrieve the last remaining sack of flour from the mill.

The villagers are like the swallows I watched as a child at a cliffside near the sea—gathering, arguing, a swarm of rising fervor filling them. I remember the flock of birds moving as a mass—breaking, re-forming, ragged at the edges.

Finally, a few brave souls know that it is time to fly.

The men put their shoulders down and push against the cart. Every person in the village wants to touch the wood of it, as one would touch a baptized child. The outstretched hands seem to hold it back for a moment, and then, with a loud heave and the crack of breaking hoarfrost, the wheels roll forward. The shifting crowd gives a hollow cheer and surges in a mass.

It is a confusion of purposes. The cart is leaving the village, but at the same time, it is as if the whole village is going with us. There are dogs and small children underfoot, and mothers are wailing, their ululations echo against the trees.

The small children of the village who trail the cart are beginning to know that those dead are not coming back. The realization of their loss blanches them white—grief giving their cheeks and chins a gray pallor, corpse-like in this light.

Salvius leaps again upon the farm cart, his handsome face distorted by grief as he stands tall. His hair catches the dawn light, bright as wheat chaff. "We will not stop until we see the king—until we claim his protection and his justice. Our children's bodies will testify to the murder. We go to the king in London!"

"Aye," agrees Hob. "We take the bodies to the king—we seek justice, not vengeance!"

"What's the diff'rence?" shouts Geoff, and the crowd roars its approval.

There is one elation at the prospect of traveling, of going somewhere so far away it is almost mythical: London. The women pull the children close, keeping them away from the cart and its dangerous journey. Several stand up to Hob and Salvius and begin to badger their men to come home. They question Hob and Salvius openly, doubting this accusation against ghostly Jews in the forest, these will-o'-the-wisp murderers. Hob and Salvius do not deign to answer them.

For the spirit moves the men, just as it moves the wing'd creatures and rough beasts. I think of our first parents—Adam and Eve—as they staggered away from their paradise, thrust out of the garden by an avenging angel.

We are at the edge of the village commons now. After this point, we cannot turn back. We must find out who did this.

I am already weary, yet as I struggle to catch up with the cart, I know that I am really going because my son is going. I have no one else. My whole life is contained in that tortured, blackened husk. My child.

Where else would I go, but with him?

CHAPTER 3

STARS STEAM AWAY as a pale sun rises, hot coal dropped in a watery sky. Light seeps across the forest as the reedy shrieks of wood fowl echo in the trees.

The valley where our village of Duns rests is surrounded by forested hills. The path from our village to the King's Highway is no road at all; it is a crooked line of mud rutted with cart tracks, a rough trough where the dirty snow is stabbed through by the hooves of feral sheep. To the east, that faint track leads up through the forest until it reaches, finally, the open country and paths that lead to other places.

The flock of villagers around the cart thins now. At first, as we approach the last house of the village, it appears Hob and Salvius might be heading for the open ground of the graveyard, but then the cart passes that turning. Hob is taking us beyond the bounds of the known world, aiming for the White Road, the King's Highway.

Sophia, Benedict's wife, calls out to us. "Without a noble blessing, you lot take your lives in your hands!"

I know she is right. Peasants should have a tunic from a Lord of the Land, to show his blessing on our travels. Except for Benedict and his family, the others here do not have my knowledge of how the world works. I do not know if half of them have ever set foot outside the forest around our little vale.

These men have set, grim faces. They push on despite the warning. They are the fathers of the missing, and this drives them onward. And always, they look to Hob for direction.

Hob is sinewy and grizzled and humorless: sharp-eyed as a blackbird and possessed of the false merriment of one as well. Veins make ridges and valleys on his forehead and the backs of his leathery hands. Like maps, the lines on his hands point to destinations unreached.

Hob urges us on. The others need a leader as they stumble forward, nearly blind with grief. Near the front of our pack is stoic, brooding Geoff, the carpenter. His eyes remain as dull and remote as ever, but his hands move constantly now, touching the cart, his side, his hat. It is as if his hands are puppets on a string, plucked by someone else's mind. Beside him is that layabout Liam, his bright red hair all awry, his lips moving with silent words I cannot hear, curses or prayers.

I am surprised to see both Liam and Geoff continue with us. Both of them are poor and aimless in their ambitions. They have naught with them for the journey, but—like the other men—they ignore their womenfolk and push forward.

The women like Sophia know the truth of adventures like the children's crusades, when people—young and old—wander from their villages onto the open road, trusting in God's providence, often to their own perdition or ruin. So the women collect the old, the infirm stragglers, the random children, and the feebleminded. Those too weak to go should not be pulled into the current of our passage, enticed down a path with no certain end.

One who does not need their help is Tom the miller, bullheaded and massive, who seems to move the cart almost by himself. His arms are heavy with muscle from the millwheel, his hands horned with calluses. Yet despite his brawn, his mouth is still full of those empty blustering words, those accusations. I think he talks so he won't have to think.

The thinking is done for us by Salvius, the blacksmith, the kindly one who gave me the wood to build my hut. He looks back for me from time to time. He looks back perhaps also to find his ward—young Cole, the orphan—who Salvius says he did not see this morning.

Salvius does what he can to encourage us, even as he looks up and down the trail. Cole has not yet been found, even among the dead.

Benedict, who owned the burned weaving house, is trying to push the cart, but at every step he is pulled backward by his wife. He shakes Sophia off time and time again, and in the end, she simply staggers after him, crying, no longer pulling at his coat.

I pass her slowly, my feet already wet and painful, weighted down by my solitary bag of rags and oddments. At this point in the morning, as the others fade away, Sophia is the only woman in the village still with the cart. I wonder if she is afraid of going back to the village alone. She is known to have Jewish blood—even though her family converted when she was a babe in arms.

As I pass, Sophia turns to me, her face wet and heavy with sorrow.

"Ol' Mear, this is a pilgrimage for fools—you can't go on this journey." She takes my arm gently. A few of the men nod in agreement, and look away.

But I lift my hands, I make gestures as forceful and angry as I can, trying to show them that I need to be with my son.

Still, she pulls me back toward the village. So I make a sound as only the mute would make. This time, as loud as I can muster: a keening howl.

There is an argument, Sophia's voice high and strident, the men shouting back. Hob comes to us, muttering blackly under his breath. He sees my agonized face and makes the final decision. "Let 'im come. His only family lies here dead, isn't that enough for ye?"

Salvius and Benedict push the cart ahead while Hob is separating Sophia from me, so Salvius misses when Geoff speaks up. "Aye, Salvius is going too, even though young Cole is back in t' village."

When I am free, I push myself forward and I go to Salvius, I pluck at his sleeve, and Salvius follows me. I point at Geoff, and Geoff repeats what he said, and explains further: "Sure, I saw Cole this morning, with water for the fire. He's alive, in the village, I tell you."

Salvius starts with surprise, and then he wraps his own cloak around my shoulders for the road ahead, wordlessly thanking me. He takes his belongings from the cart. He will go to find Cole.

"Take 'er with you too, won't you?" says Hob. He points at Sophia, who is marooned in the road, standing like a weeping statue. Her beautiful black hair is caught by the breeze and whips around her face. Her white skin seems paper-thin in this light, and her eyelids flutter, as if she is caught in a terrible dream.

I think it is more than grief that keeps her here. Her incessant need, her grasping desire, is to own or hold onto all that she can. She always wants to hold the reins, to have what she cannot keep. But for the first time, Benedict is pushing on without her, disappearing around the bend ahead, and she does not know what reins to seize.

Gently, Salvius takes her hands and turns her back toward the village. Sophia walks in a daze, but she will be safe with Salvius escorting her. Her face shines with tears as she stumbles backward, past us and down the road.

I see them go, and something quails in me, a cold thing turning across my grave. I am worried about us traveling on the open road without Salvius's sure confidence, his clear purpose, and his lordly manner. He directs men as few others do. We may be lost without him.

✠

Fog lifts in the valley, rising as mist through the bare-limbed trees. Far below lies the deeping combe with our village in the heart of it.

My whole world for nearly a decade has been contained in that place—and now the village of Duns looks so small. I hold up my hand, form a circle with my fingers. The distant village, wreathed in mist, seems a child's plaything that I can hold in my own hand.

A great fallen yew with nurslings jutting evergreen from its broken body lies near our path. This is the very place at which I first saw the village ten years ago. The line of trees here on the ridge is unchanged, as if I came here only yesterday.

I waited in the quiet vale of Duns far too long. At first, it was a refuge, where I could hide my tracks and recover my strength after the vicious attack that drove me from my home and my books. Then I met Nell, and she gave me sanctuary, and in that comfort of her friendship, I remained for years.

Last spring, after Nell was killed, I knew the village was no longer safe: my haven was gone. But I had only a few months to wait until Christian was ten years of age, and then he could claim his birthright. One winter more and then we would have left together.

But now my son is gone—alone, without me—where I cannot follow until my ending comes in its turn.

Breathing deeply, I try to still my fear as I stare down at my wet feet in rags trudging through the snow. I step onto the sunken, snowy track, and I move beyond the fallen yew. Past this point exists a world—a life—known to me years ago. Ahead of us on the King's Highway is a monastery, where lives a monk who spent much of summer beside me as I held my babe. He scribbled constantly, writing down the stories I told him. I wonder if he is still there.

Would any remember me now at that monastery on the road? And what of Canterbury Abbey far away? And the Court?

Do any remember my name, after all my years of silence and obscurity?

The cart rocks to a halt just before the crest of a long hill. The heavy weight of the bodies has sunk the cart deep into a rut, and a wheel sticks fast in slush and snow. Ice welds the cart hard to the hillside.

"Heave ho," shouts Hob. "All as one, push together. Now!"

The first thrust from our shoulders doesn't budge the cart. Not a bit.

Benedict glares at Geoff and me. "Come on, even you weak ones there, you push too!" Geoff the carpenter, stares back at Benedict. He still holds resentment toward the man whose house burned.

Hob puts his shoulder down. "Come now, men. Heave ho! Can't you move it?"

But Liam mocks him, making a half-born attempt at a joke. "Oh yes, Hob—it's me who's holding it back. If I'd just lift my li'l finger, you'd move, you would."

There's a faint whisper of chuckling, but that dies quickly. No one dares laugh out loud at Hob. And these are our boys we carry.

Liam and Benedict push at the stuck cart. Hob and Tom lean their bodies against the heavy wooden wheels.

I come to the cart and take hold. I peer inside, I shuffle through the straw, trying to find more answers. The chaos I see slowly resolves into sense, like letters read in a forgotten language.

The bodies of our boys are thin and weak from the poor harvest this fall: I can see their bones. Yet these boys are clad in heavy cloaks and warm furs. They are wearing the most lordly clothes possessed by their families, as if they wished to make themselves look better than they are. These are the best garments of their meager homes.

The threads and fur are burned and tattered, so I know for truth that they wore such clothing to their deaths. Even as I flinch from the sight, that firm fork of logic seizes hard. *They were in a house, not on the road. No one had planned a journey, that I knew of. So why were these dead boys wearing furs and cloaks?*

The cart does not move, despite our efforts; instead, one wheel sinks deeper into the snow.

Hob bends down and digs with his hands. He barks hoarsely at us in his commanding tone. "You lot, find summat to wedge it out—branches, wood, straw—anything to get this wheel out."

Reluctantly, I leave behind the puzzle of the boys' clothing. We step into the forest and spread out, trying to find spare wood.

Sound carries far here in the trees. Snow slides off a heavy oak as some creature shuffles through the woods, and ancient branches snap. Out of the corner of one eye, I see the flash of colored feathers. It is a yellowhammer, black eyes flickering in a hedgerow, tiny breast plumped out in golden livery, streaked with colors rich and brown. It was calling in its winter song:

> A little bit of bread and no cheese—
> A little bit of bread and no cheese—

Moments later, the bracken flutters and the slight shadow of the bird darts into the woods. Deep in the forest now, I hear a low voice that wends back and forth, whispering in secret. It is one of our party. I edge my way closer, stepping quietly so I can hear.

"Why were they together that night?" In this close copse, I can hear the whisper louder by some trick of the woods. "It's a lie, I tell you—they're lying to us!"

It is the small carpenter, Geoff, speaking with a dour look.

I have always found him distasteful. Perhaps it is but the memory I have of Nell whispering to me of his father: a man who defiled his own son. On that man's deathbed, she said, there were running sores on his flesh, the price of Gomorrah. Nothing she could give would help him, and no one believed the rumors of him.

And she was killed for it.

Geoff, now a man himself, has his father's choleric looks. He bears the same harsh voice, the same dark flickering eyes. I wonder if his father's desires run in his mind, in the blood.

Geoff is speaking to Liam as they push their way through the woods, searching for loose branches. "Our lads were takin' a journey—they were dressed in warm cloaks an' furs!"

Geoff has seen what I saw.

But Liam isn't listening. Instead, he interrupts before Geoff can speak again. "You've got to promise me to tell no one of my crime.

You know what I did. Benedict knows it too. But keep my secret, an'—" begins Liam. Then my footsteps through the rotten snow, and a branch cracks.

I tumble forward out of my hiding spot. Liam starts with sudden fear. He drops the wood he has collected.

But I stumble forward, keeping my face incurious, even while my heart churns. *What secret?* I wish Salvius were still here, to find the truth of this. He would know what to do. *What crime does Liam conceal?*

When they see it is only me in the snow, they pick up their wood again. Liam nods his head in greeting, gives me a wink. "Mear knows the truth of all things, dontcha know? Pity 'e can't talk."

Geoff grimaces. He stoops and lifts a pair of twigs out of the thin snow in this copse. "An' I'll ask you this—why the rush to get on the trail at first light?"

"Aye, an' we have no blessing for the open road."

"Why does that matter?" says Geoff.

Liam grimaces. "Without that, we can be taken, dontcha know? Any man can kill us."

I am surprised that Liam knows this. He is right that we have no sanction from the Lord of our County, Sir Peter of Lincoln, for this journey. And without an embroidered Lord's tunic, or some such blessing—some holy writ of Church or King would serve—we are prey, subject to any man's whim or greed.

"How do you know?" Geoff shakes his head.

"I've been out here before. I've seen it happen," whispers Liam. And this is a surprise to me too—for years, I have thought Liam was born and bred in the village of Duns.

"There's a liar here somewhere," continues Liam. "After all, the house with boys in it was tied shut, from outside. Salvius and I had to break the door to get the bodies out."

The knot. I have a sudden vision of the boys pushing helplessly on the door, striving to get out as the knot holds tight. Smoke overwhelmed them. My eyes fill with tears.

Liam rips a branch from a small tree, his hands shaking with anger. "Before this journey is done, I tell you, I will know why they were gather'd together. Why did this happen?"

"I blame Benedict," says Geoff. "It was his house, and the first fire this winter where someone died. I don't believe his story of the boys weaving—not for a moment. Here's my guess—what if the boys were seeing his wife already?"

My heart sinks. Sophia, even in her fathomless need, would not seduce boys so young, would she? Liam gives his face a sardonic twist, a leer that makes his grin unseemly. My skin goes cold at that look. It makes me doubt him more. Liam always has been at the bottom of the village bounty, scraping the dregs. What if his need finally broke him and he took vengeance on his betters?

A loud bellow echoes from far away, on the other side of the hill. It is Hob's voice. Liam and Geoff lift their heavy load of branches, and we start back.

The skewed cart lies like a foundered ship in the drift of snow. I take my turn digging wearily at the frost-hardened ground; then I reach down to rub my painful feet, and I see a boy in a hooded cloak. He stands on the other side of the cart, pushing alongside us.

For a moment, my eyes are bewitched. I see Christian standing alive and hale again. That moment lasts a long breath, and then it is gone.

The boy's hood drops off his head.

Raven-black hair. Sunken coal-black eyes.

It is only Cole.

He is Salvius's misbegotten ward, the orphan. But he is here alone. Hob talks to him, asking of his "Uncle Salvius."

I cannot hear all they say, but it seems Cole was in the woods and found us on the trail. He points at the cart, gesturing toward his dead friends. Hob's face is hard and untrusting.

Cole has the curse of lying and of theft. Few folk trust him, least of all Salvius who often must punish him for his many misdeeds. And Cole's face is etched by the scars of ringworm. Such marks are said to be the mark of a devil or a witch, and those scarred are mocked and called by names, so as to torment the devil inside. I do not know the truth of it. I do not concern myself.

He is a gangly, overgrown orphan boy from the edge of the village, the one some whisper was abandoned by his own mother. Perhaps they said the same about my Christian.

In fact, Cole once helped me watch my son. He is a little older than the boys who died but always he drifts toward those younger than he. For Cole has a wandering stammer, and no one treats him as a man. His weak voice is the last echo of the tenderness I once saw in that lad.

Cole says he sought us out, hoping he would find Salvius here, wanting to honor his dead friends.

I think that Cole is like the other children—he will spend the heat of this winter day walking with us, but he will fade eventually, when he wearies of the hard track and the heavy cart. In fact, even now, I can see a few of the other children in the valley below, wandering back along the switchbacks toward the distant village.

"Cole can come with us," says Hob. "It's too late in the day to send for Salvius."

"Let's go back ourselves," says Geoff. "You're right. It's late—I'm damn'd tired."

"None of us are going back!" Bene seizes Geoff's head with his great weaver's hands. He turns Geoff, forces him to look up at the trail ahead. "Look at the tracks, I say, look at them!"

We all stare at the hillside. The virgin snow is spattered with bootprints that go out of sight.

"We're followin' the villain, can't you see?" says Bene. "The tracks are—"

Geoff wrenches his head out of Benedict's grasp. "To hell with yer tracks! My son is gone—he ain't comin' back."

"Push on," calls Hob, and Geoff's complaints are ignored. The cart tilts forward this time and out of the ditch. Red-haired Liam and I both hold now to the branches of the whippletree in front, guiding the way forward.

Hob moves behind me then, goading us to the work. He spits on the ground and slaps our shoulders. I am the only one to follow his gaze and glance behind us. He is staring into the distance, along our backtrail.

Deep in the vale, a large puff of steam or snow punches into the air. A rider. I watch closely. Some group of people—another cart—follows along the adjoining trail, but I cannot see them in the trees.

Hob touches Benedict's elbow and whispers low. Benedict's cheek twitches, and he scratches anxiously at his bald scalp. Hob glances back again, then he shouts loud, urging more miles before nightfall. I put my shoulder to the cart.

We are pushed onward by the force of their will.

CHAPTER 4

THE DAY WANES until the sun is caught once more in the net of the darkening sky. I struggle ahead of the cart now, into the tracks.

"Stay back," calls Benedict. "Come back to the cart!"

But I pretend the wind covers his words, that I cannot hear him. Ice cuts through the canvas rags on my feet, but still my curiosity compels me. I pretend to stumble, and I fall to the ground so my face is close to the trail.

The marks of boots and horses are here. That is true.

But the tracks go the wrong direction. There is no bootprint going out of our village, no horse going toward the deep woods. No one fled. Instead, some strangers came into our village. Three men and at least two horses, by the look of the prints. But who?

Our village is small, and we should have seen them, unless they came in the night.

"Come back, Mear," Hob calls out. "The bandits may be ahead."

I now know we chase no bandits, no Jews, no villain here at all. Yet from their vantage point, these footprints are unseen, and rapidly the steps are disappearing in the thawing snow. In less than an hour, it will not be possible to see which direction they came from, even up close. Soon, the truth will melt away.

Christian would be asking for answers; even in his youth, my son had a penchant for inquiry. Always he wanted to stretch his wings. *Why am I trapped in this village? And why can't I go to Lincoln town this spring with the lads? Why not? Why?*

Always asking, Socratic in endless examination, until finally I would throw up my hands and shake my head in mute exasperation. In the night, he would murmur his questions to me again, and then I would answer as best I could, whispering back what I hoped was true. I imparted to him all I could of my secrets, of what my mother taught me.

I also gave him the tools of inquiry and debate. I murmured like a night animal, teaching Aristotle's endless coiling logic. In my ear, I can hear him now—repeating back to me the secret lessons, his sibilant whisper in my ear:

Every art aims at some good end. The end of the art of medicine is health; the end of shipbuilding a vessel; the end of strategy in battle that of victory; the end of economics, wealth. The ends of master arts are preferred to subordinate ends… for all things aim at a good end.

I clench my fists until the skin whitens and the knuckles crack. Anyone among us has seen so many die over the years—wave after wave of death sweeping in like a tide that strikes all, haphazard. The good, the bad, the virgin, and the harlot: no one is spared, all go rose-spattered with plague lesions. I see no sense, no judgment before doom strikes. Death takes us all with the black malady or the sweating sickness, or the white blindness or the winter croup, or the crops failing or bitter water in our mouths.

There is no justice to such deaths, and there is no sense.

But this fire—the flames that burned our boys—these few deaths were an act of malevolence. Someone intended this. There was a judgment made, an evil act. And in this, it is for sure and certain that there is a soul at fault. Someone can be blamed for these deaths, if not for all that came before.

I look down at the wrong-way tracks. I squint, wishing I could read more from this trail. I will find out what I can from the signs I do see. I will know the truth.

What was your good end, Christian?

The cart comes closer. Benedict throws off his hood and shouts at me for abandoning my post. He says without my guidance, the cart nearly went off the trail. At this, Hob glares at me too and curses under his breath, as if I am a wayward child. But I pay them no heed.

There is a stab of pain in my side. My limbs are weak as water, for I have not been able to eat much this winter with no food in the larders or the mill. And now my feet and toes feel each lump of frozen mud. I am not that young Miriam who once climbed these hills with a babe in her arms. I am old and tired now. My legs burn with effort, but still I persevere.

Hob watches us all closely, as if he wants to be sure no one will go ahead again, and he goads the men harder to push the cart up the long hill before sundown.

Hours later, as evening shadows surround us, the hillside finally flattens, and the path opens out into a hollow encircled by boulders. Beyond a last steep embankment is the King's Highway. We will camp here for the night before gaining the highway.

I collapse into a drift and lie there nearly insensate.

Through my fog comes Liam's voice. "God's wounds, Mear, you look weary enough for Death himself to dance with. Why dontcha shove off your pack—'ave some water and a bite o' mutton. Tom there, he's already lightin' a fire to warm your bones."

In this makeshift shelter between boulders and under overhanging snow, Liam lays pine boughs and bracken over cold ground. I let the flow of his voice settle me onto the branches as he wraps me in a fur-lined cloak. Then he uncovers my numb feet, examining each inch of whitened, cold skin.

"A hard nip of frost, but they haven't gone to rot yet," Liam says. "But there's a cut on your toe too—you'll want to watch it close."

I open my eyes and look at the campsites in this ravine. There are six of us, and only five spots out of the wind. Even Cole has found a place. He puts his bedroll under the cart.

There is not a place left for me, it seems.

Liam has seen the same. "Well, I've got to tell you, Mear—there's naught left for another body out of the wind, is there? Would you have in mind to share mine own mansion?"

I stare at him. I am so weary that I cannot find the humor, and my friend Salvius never jokes like this.

Liam speaks again, his prattle lifting my spirits. "There's no roof, of course. No walls either, I'm afraid to say. And I must admit to a certain breeziness in the night, but I 'ave my standards, I'll have you know!"

He wags his finger in my face. "I'll warn you now, ol' Mear, with that wild life you lead, you can't be bringing your brewmaids and your wenches around here! An' there ain't no cows to warm the place either. But hell's bells, you've got *me*—and what a cowish girth I bear." He grips his belly and grimaces broadly.

Liam goes on in the same fashion, and by the time he finishes, I am bent over with laughter, the sounds coming out of my mouth a hacking hilarity.

I am astonished I am able to laugh at all. Then the chuckles turn into broad guffaws, and I find that my cheeks are wet, my eyes leaking wildly.

Tears stream down my face, grief melding with mirth in some wild witch's brew that brings the fact of Christian's death deep into me. He is dead and gone; I am alive and able to laugh. This is the truth of it, and nothing I do will change it now.

Our camp is in the lee of a slab of rock jutting from the hillside. The outcropping looms over us, thick with snow-covered moss.

Geoff sidles into our campsite. He takes Liam's ear and whispers urgently. "Lookit this—my son had this with him." Geoff opens his clenched hand. Inside is a small carved wood animal, that great bird that nurses its young on its own flesh. A pelican—a symbol of the Christ—and it is scorched by flame.

"What is that to you?" asks Liam.

Geoff digs his foot deep into the snow. He cannot meet our eyes. "It was the first lovely thing he ever made."

"A memory," says Liam. "An heirloom of his house."

"Why would he take this to Benedict's house?" says Geoff. "Why take something so precious to our family? Was he going away from our village? Were they all leaving us?"

I have a niggling thought in the back of my mind that there is something here that ties Geoff's son to my Christian, but I cannot think what it is right now.

Christian was not leaving me, my heart says loudly, so that I cannot hear that still-small voice in me saying something true and painful.

Now Liam is telling his tale. "I saw in the cart that in my son's hand was the stick he uses to walk the sheep over to the Hartvale meadow. His walking stick."

"An' you weren't going anywhere with him."

"You know I can't leave the village." Liam's eyes slide nervously from side to side. "If the King's officers found me out here... I'm only on this journey now because my boy is dead, and I... I could not leave him."

Geoff nods. Curiosity eats at me, a poison that makes my skin crawl. *How much do I really know of Liam?* I raise my eyebrows at him, I grunt, but the two of them don't pay me mind.

"Where were the boys going?" hisses Geoff. "I don't believe for a moment that Benedict had them weaving—every time he says it, his eyes belie him."

"Do you mean to accuse Benedict of doing something with them?" Liam seems taken aback by the insistence in Geoff's face.

Geoff whispers. "Ayuh, Sophia was suppos'd to be in that house that night. An' what if Benedict was jealous of his own wife? What if he—?"

Liam sighs wearily. "Foolishness. What about the other fires? And why would Benedict burn his own house? Why would Bene—?"

There is a sudden, loud laugh. Benedict has stepped into our campsite. In fact, he almost strides onto my bedroll. He claps Liam on the back "What's that you say— 'Why would Bene—'?"

"Nothing," mutters Liam. "Just talk. It were nothing."

"Nah, tell the truth." Benedict gives that laugh again, a forced jollity.

Geoff stares with the bloodlust of the accuser and raises his voice. "You tell the truth, Bene! What journey did you plan with our boys?"

Hob and Tom come closer when Geoff shouts. Benedict stares back and forth between the men, his face flushing slowly red. "The truth?"

"Yes," says Geoff. "Tell us, why were the boys there, at your weaving house?"

Bene breathes out, a long hiss. "I do not know why they died."

Geoff shouts again. "Goddammit, Bene, you know why they were there—I can see you do! Why were the boys there at your house? Were they seeing your wife?"

Now the blood drains out of Bene's face, his skin white with rage.

"Wait, wait," says Liam. His hands move nervously. "That's not what we meant—"

Benedict makes fists, his fingers clenching and unclenching. "Then speak plain. What do you mean?"

Geoff does not falter. "Sophia—she saw more than one man, as you well know—and I just want to know, did she see any of the boys in her chamber, did she—"

Benedict brings his great weaver's hand up. Faster than I could have imagined, his clenched fist strikes Geoff's face, knocking him flat against the ice.

The winter air seems to freeze as Geoff falls. A stray snowflake hangs in the air. Bright blood spatters from Geoff's broken lip onto the white snow.

Benedict roars, a sound that has words in it I cannot decipher until after it is all over. "You damn'd scut-worms! Ah lost my own son—my *son*—an' you lot still accuse my wife, my own Sophia. She lost him too, you know!"

Benedict glowers in rage. We look away in shame.

"You there," Bene points at Liam. "I can turn you in, you know. There's still a reward—in gold—for poxy bastards like you."

"I know," mutters Liam. "Please..."

Liam scurries back from Benedict's rage. I huddle into my bedroll.

But Bene has turned away from him. He glares, bloodshot and bellowing, at all of us. Only Tom holds his gaze. It would seem Tom has nothing of mortification in him, but I see a catch in the corner of Tom's eye before he locks his gaze, as if he must force himself to do this. It is as if an actor's mask drops over his whiskered face.

"Right," Tom says. "The boys had naught t' do with Sophia. She's a pure one." His tone is sincere, though the pupils of his eyes move ever so subtly back and forth.

Liam scurries back from Benedict's rage. I huddle into my bedroll.

Benedict turns from Tom. He seizes Geoff, like a cat shaking a trembling, torn rat. "Goddam you, my wife *is* pure, ah'll have you know—pure as the feckin' driven snow!"

Benedict whispers thickly as blood drips down Geoff's face. "Say it to me. Say it!"

Geoff's voice shakes. "Aye, Bene. Sophia is pure."

Benedict drops him to the snow. The anger washes out of him as rapidly as it came. He seems spent now, exhausted by his rage.

Bene is not a man familiar with emotion—he is the one who coldly calculates the odds. I have seen him in the village, running games of chance against the day of harvest—the next throw of dice, the next shot by a bow. He gives the winners their take without feeling, and takes the loser's coins without a care. But Benedict bet awry when he married Sophia. He wooed her knowing she had been a Jew, thinking her family had gold buried.

In the end, there was no gold, no dowry, nothing for him except the big weaving house that just burned to the ground and Sophia's ever-wandering eye. She seeks for something everywhere—something Benedict can't, or won't, give her.

There is an emptiness in her heart that can never be filled, a bottomless longing that causes her to hunger for affection and devour every scrap of kindness. Whatever you give her is never enough.

She has even seized on me at times—mute Mear—for conversation. For when she seizes me, I touch her hand, I look into her eyes, I watch her face, I smile when she speaks. And Benedict never does these small things.

Now Bene talks quietly, his voice hoarse. "Tha must see, these lads were not on a journey. They had naught for the open road. *My boy*—" Benedict's voice breaks.

A bird calls, distant and wounded. The woods are still as death. Quick steam huffs in and out of Geoff's open mouth.

Hob steps forward. "Enough of this shite. Look to the campsite—we must be ready for the night."

And with that, the dangerous moment seems past. We gather wood and help Tom build his fire. As I pick up spare twigs and dried bracken, I wonder how far our sounds penetrate into the black forest, and how far our shouts echo along the White Road. Anyone approaching along the road could find us here.

Supper is roasted pork we brought from the village, and warmed snow. After we have licked our fingers clean, we edge closer to the fire, heads cocked toward the whispering wind as it brushes the treetops. Night birds warble, and small creatures rustle in the snow.

Benedict digs in the straw of the cart and brings out a half cask of cider. Tom and Bene guzzle long before they share with the rest of us. The apples were squeezed in the summer and fermented all the fall. I gulp a mouthful, and the taste of it is bright and bitter on my tongue. My head goes dizzy after a single swallow.

Hob has the knife out that he used to carve our dinner meat. He passes the cider and doesn't take a sip. Instead, he painstakingly strokes a whetstone across the edge of his blade. "The road tomorrow could be dangerous. Bandits and the like."

The cider goes around the circle again, and we lean closer to hear Hob speak again. "We must stick together, that's our only hope. We will get to the monastery, seek the Abbot's protection, demand justice for our loss."

Hob's knife scrapes harshly on the stone. "We few from the village are nothing in the greater world, you understand. We could be taken for chattel, for labor, even for killing sport."

"Aye," Tom agrees, his words already blurred by drink. "Captur'd by witches."

Liam laughs aloud. "Oh, Tom, if you're fear'd of witches, you can sleep in my bed, with smelly ol' Mear." The other men guffaw, but Tom continues, the cider giving him a pompous certainty.

"They say if you creep along the right valley in the dead o' night, 'round the dark o' the moon, you'll hear them witches a-singin' an' a-chantin'."

Yet this time when he speaks, there is something in his tone that gives us pause. There are some who believe to speak of a thing is to summon it into the world, and Tom speaks with such conviction.

We become so quiet that the loudest noise is the sizzle of burning tree sap.

The darkness around us presses down, as if to listen. The music of the wind rises and falls with the swirls of the snow, the creaking of the sea of branches in the darkness above us. Liam takes a long swallow of cider, and even the sound of it splashing in the cask unnerves me.

"Ah think there was more than one of them witches in our village. Ah saw them once, dancing, deep in the woods," says Geoff. He pushes the words out carefully, drink slowing his speech.

"There was one we know for sure," says Benedict. He takes the cider from Liam and spreads his hands apart, to make his point. "She was a strange woman—kept herself apart."

"Nell," says Cole. "That was her name." And as he speaks, there is a loud and distant moan, one tree moving against another. I can't tell how far away the sound is, or which direction it comes from. Sound travels strangely in the wildland.

"You hear that?" Geoff says. His eyes gleam in the light of the coals. His whisper is coarsened by fear. "What is it?"

Eventually the wind dies, and young Cole goes into the bushes to drop his pants. He returns and wipes his hands with dead leaves.

"There's someone following, on the hillside, on the open road behind," says Cole. Geoff turns from the fire and climbs up onto a stone, to see our backtrail.

"Whoever follows is not from our village!" Benedict says. "Ah think they might be—"

"There's no one behind us," Hob says shortly. "You all are pie-eyed drunks. Go to bed." Hob spits on his whetstone and keeps sharpening his knife, louder now.

Yet one by one, each of us steps away from the brightness of the flames and looks up at the hillside where the faint track winds back and forth.

"Look," says Tom. "The moon's got a fairie circle 'round it."

All of us turn our eyes higher, to see the three-quarter moon floating in a fog-flecked winter sky—glimmering around that uneven globe, an ethereal silver circle.

"More snow coming tonight, that means," says Liam. "A heavy fall of snow."

"Aye," Benedict agrees. "The new snow will cover our tracks, but it won't cover our cart. If there's someone coming, we should get ready for a fight, dontcha think?"

"Nah, there's no one there," Hob repeats calmly. "Who would be out from the village, in the woods?" Bright sparks shoot out as Hob rasps hard at his blade.

I look back at the dying fire. Cole has not moved with the rest of us to gaze up at the moon overhead, at the clouds rapidly moving in. Instead, he still scans the hillside, his mouth nervous and twitching, firelight flickering across his anxious face as he pulls aside his hood. In the faint light, I discern a faint burn on his neck, something red and unhealed, a touch of ash and pain. I see a tremble in his fingers, wide fear in his eyes.

And it comes to me that Cole knows of that night. It beats in me, in my blood.

Cole knows.

CHAPTER 5

FROST CRACKLES ON the sheepskin as I push it away, white plumes of breath rising in the faint light. For years, I have arisen at Lauds, before dawn: in this hour, the deep darkness of the sky is touched with royal blue.

The landscape has changed in the night. A vast shroud of snow drowns every feature, the unceasing tide sweeping over the land, covering the path and the campsite.

Under the new snow, our campsites are hidden, like the holes of vermin, buried among the rocks and drifts. Above us now, the high hill is peaked with an overhang of snow that curves like a butcher's blade above our hollow.

I move toward the cart and sweep away the fresh snowflakes that lie on my son and his friends. And there, in the morning light, I see a flash of silver that catches the sunlight—the chain on my son's neck glimmering from the straw.

Drawn by that brightness, by the need to see his face, I push aside the straw. I pull aside the sackcloth that covers the boys, and I fumble at the rope tied across the cart.

Then a shiver runs up my spine. For the rope is looped with that strange triple knot tied fast across a half hitch. It is the same knot that was tied across the door of the Benedict's house. It was this knot that killed him.

The one who tied this knot might be here. He must be traveling as one of our company. *Who?*

My fingers tremble, but I slide the curving snake of that triple knot apart. I turn the bodies of our boys, blackened and charred. And here, on this one neck, is the silver chain that marks my son.

I touch the chain, and then I see a new surprise. Strung on its slender length is the ring I told Christian he must never take from our little house. I had noticed the chain, but I had not seen the ring. Christian took an heirloom of our house—he is wearing that great token of his father's love.

When I left Canterbury Abbey, I took with me everything my lover had given me, most importantly this ring. I took it from the abbey for my newborn son to have when he was grown.

At the last new moon, I told Christian of it, finally, when he had nearly reached the age of ten. I unearthed it from the small birch box in which it had been hidden all those years, and I showed it to him. The ring was his by heritage, the only token of his father I still bore.

My heart tells me the truth, but I do not want to hear it—*Christian took the ring from our croft because he would not return. He meant to leave our village forever.*

A cry comes up my throat: I choke it off unvoiced.

Now I wonder if it was right of me to stay hidden in the village all those years, wanting to protect my son from the world, sheltering under Salvius's gentle care. For all those years, I had not even taken a daylong sojourn to discover if the Earl or Edward won their clandestine struggle, or if any knew of Christian's birth.

Admittedly, my boy's life in Duns had not been much. He grew strong from work, he learned the secret lessons that I taught, but he couldn't claim what was his by birthright.

He would have gone to claim this birthright. *Oh, my son—Christian.*

Now perhaps in death, Cristian's true name has been taken from the world. But I still live, I still breath, I still know.

I unfasten Christian's chain and remove the ring. I place it ever-so-carefully on my own small chain, close to my heart. Then I refasten his own silver links around his neck, letting him keep one of his last possessions. I will give him the silver chain, even when he is buried in the ground.

Yet I grip the ring in my hand, my heart pounding. I must hold this tight. It is the last sign of my past, the last token of who I once was.

✠

Our fire is almost out now, the large heap of wood we gathered the day before nearly devoured. The men hardly stir in their sleep, the sound of their breathing deep with the residue of drink. The rotten aftertaste of cider is still in my mouth as well.

But I am sober this dawn, and cold, so I pile dead bracken and fresh wood on the fire. The bracken smokes, and we need more firewood, so I push my way through the snow toward the trees.

My thoughts turn to my companions. I have seen much through my ten years living with them, but now it seems I may not know the truth of these men. Any story is an ocean whose tide begins in a place I can't know, and my life is but a moment in that flood, my part in it only a mote in the flow.

Before I came to this village, these men and their families had a long history. They had generations to build up resentments and grudges, and stories that trickled down through the years, which allowed them to know each other in ways I will never know. For my village—generations in the building—it all disappeared when I was a child, wiped out by the plague, the last remnants of my people scattered and lost.

What do I really know of these men from the village of Duns? As I stagger through the drifts, the threads of logic weave together into suppositions, accusations.

Geoff did it. That small man with the dark and gnomish face, the uncertain expression. He was a weak boy, the butt of jokes when he was a child. Even now Geoff cannot shake the fear that he is still mocked behind his back. There were reasons for the teasing. That is an old history, full of rot and pain, and I know but half of it.

What if Geoff took his pleasure with boys, just as his syphilitic father before him? Could he have tied the house shut, set the fire, and burned them to their deaths? What if Geoff accuses Benedict to conceal his own crimes?

I come back down the hill with an armful of wood. The fire smolders hot with dry twigs. Smoke rises. Dawn strokes the horizon with an edge of steaming brightness.

I think of the several fires in our village: who lit those? And why?

And then, why would the boys gather together? Perhaps to speak of their fear of Geoff? But who would be afraid of that man? He is small and frail and he and I are all too often discarded from manly work, because of our light frames.

Maybe it's Liam. He told Geoff he hides a crime. I spend my time serving Salvius's smithy and doing what I can to curry favor with Benedict, not with such a poor woodsman. Despite this, I thought I knew Liam well, with his fox-like face and his fringe of red hair, and always he seeks to ally with me.

They still call Liam "young 'un," and it is not because he is particularly young—he is older than half the men. They call him that because he came to this village a mere fifteen years ago, marrying into the village. His father and his grandfather and generations before him did not live here. And I imagine the men do not trust him, because he is still an outsider.

What would Liam do in fear of his own life?

And what of Tom's vision? Tom is an unlikely prophet, with his wide-set, staring eyes, his mad speech and his great oxen muscles. But what if, for once, Tom's eyes had seen aright?

What if there was indeed a Jew who wished revenge for the killings fifty years ago? Someone who saw his family die and came back to put a blood-curse on our village for the crimes of the past? There are still Jews concealed—what if one held a grudge?

I shake my head. I do not believe it. Tom's vision of Jews in the night is but a faint and uneven sketch: there is no truth in his fantasy of sacrifice and sorcery.

Then again, what do the men know of me? I am an old mystery to them and an outsider as well, even after all these years. If someone discovered my secrets, I would be the one accused. I am bound by silence, but that would not prevent them burning me as a witch. I have dreamed that death far too often, grinding my teeth in the fetid darkness of my little hutch.

Do they suspect? How long will it take for the men to accuse me? I wish again that Salvius was here. He has always upheld my manliness, trusted my strength in gathering wood for his smithy. Salvius is always my truest friend, my first defender. There is no falsehood in him.

Liam and Geoff, though, they worry me. I shake my head. Secrets and lies.

I trudge to the top of a hill, where the wood is dry. From the forest, we are invisible.

Yet now I can see that our camp has been revealed to anyone who travels on the open road. I have revealed it by making a smoky fire. From our campsite, a black line of smoke rises tall from the hollow, a beacon against the aurora light. I must get dry wood now, not wet, and damp the smoke.

Why were the boys together? If the murder was aimed at the village, as some rude crime aimed at all of us—or as some sacrifice to a pagan god—then someone would have had to gather the boys together. They would not have gone willingly if they knew the true purpose of their gathering.

Benedict says he had gathered them because he needed all their nimble, small fingers to move the warp and woof. He had a great set of weavings due for delivery at Lincoln.

But could he have told a tale to us? Bene the weaver is always jealous of Sophia, and always he seeks to hold her for his own. His sunburned bald head always seems worried for her. And because he has remained faithful to her—despite her many small betrayals and cheats on him—that has made me respect bald Bene despite myself.

For there is much to dislike in Benedict. He still conceals the fact of the boys' intended departure from the village. And I know for certain that they meant to travel away from us: the truth is with the boys.

The chain around my son's neck, and the ring. Liam's son's walking stick. Geoff's son, who carved a pelican, took that heirloom of their house with him.

It was a secret journey, to set out in the night—only Benedict knew the truth of it. And like our travel now, I doubt anyone had a lord's blessing. Not them. Not us.

And even now Benedict does not tell the boys' secret.

Hob, the dark-haired alderman, has some hold on Benedict, for often I see Bene's hands tremble with fear as he looks at Hob.

Could Hob have tied that triple knot? Hob has always been our leader in the village, but why now does he drive us forward with such fervor?

And why would Hob have any cause to burn them up in the night?

Cole knows. If I gain his trust, if I find a way to worm my way into his heart, he might tell me more of the truth. I know he saw something that night.

I kneel on the hillside to gather dry twigs. Something catches at me, a distant sound. In this late morning, frost thickens on the wind; snow is gusting down.

Already the new-fallen drifts are hardening under a crust of ice.

Yet that fearful promise of cold is not what brought me pause. I wait, I listen. These hours are as silent and pallid as the inside of a whitewashed tomb.

Someone moves in the camp. I look down. It is Cole, pissing in the snow. Then he sees me, he finishes, and he strides slowly toward the hill on which I crouch.

I push the fresh snowflakes out of my face and peer again at the horizon, squinting against the faint dawn, my eyes tearing in the cold. There comes a faint sound, the cry of a lost winter bird. Then I see them, a shape of men on horses.

The uncertainty in me resolves into a knot of fear in my belly, a churning mass of dark apprehension. I duck quickly into the hollow, but I know it is too late. They have seen the smoke. They know there is someone in this corner of the snowbound world, someone with fire and with food.

Cole comes up into the trees, close enough to touch. I take his shoulder and push him down into a small ravine so we cannot be seen. I look at the distant figures, the moving dots of men on horses, growing visible even in the scrim of falling snowflakes.

I point and show Cole with my hands how open we are to eyes on the road, how vulnerable to bandits.

As I turn to slide back down the lee of the hill, Cole speaks: "We must tell Hob."

CHAPTER 6

I TRY TO WAKE the men, but they still lie heavy with drink. Tom and Liam don't even move when I push at them. Benedict and Geoff stir when I thump their chests, but that is all. Bene still has his arm wrapped around the empty cask.

Hob did not drink the night before, but we cannot find him—he is already out of his bedroll, and we do not know where he has gone.

Snow is falling down from the sky now, but I cannot wake the drunken sots.

So I quickly strip all I can find from the men's beds. The best furs, the solid boots, the packs that hold all of our food and the heaviest cloaks. These things we push deep under the straw beneath the boys' bodies on the cart.

Food and good warm clothes are always the first to be taken on the open road; only after those things are gone will the bandits search for weapons and for gold.

I grip tight my ring. Those many years ago, this talisman was concealed next to the flesh of my tiny babe when I fled from the Earl and his men.

Quickly, I conceal it in the same place now. I lift the chain with the ring over my neck, and give it back to him, pushing it under Christian's corpse. A splash of snow over his blackened body, and the ring is hidden again.

Then I stagger back up the hillside with Cole to check on the approaching men. From behind a brace of trees, we peer out to see a small troupe. Yet no glint of armor, no heraldic flag. Steam rises from the horses, their sides flecked with frozen foam.

We are near the top of a high bank, made higher by ranks of white drifts that overhang the hollow. From here, if we slide the wrong way, the weighty drifts might collapse: I am careful not to disturb the crest. We were fools to camp so close under the overhang.

I look up into the slowly falling flakes. Bare black trees quake under the mass of the heavy snow.

Three riders lead the charge, well fed and well armed, surmounting the hill astride heavy horses. The largest rider is a swarthy man who holds a notched sword with a rich hilt. He holds it with pride, for it is the band's only true weapon. The others bear staffs and pikes. More than common ruffians, but do they work on their own, or has some lord hired them?

The mounted men rein in their piebald and uneven steeds.

"There must be a hollow ahead," says the swarthy man. "That's where I seen the smoke come from."

"Rabbit holes," says another. "Coneys in a trap." He has a sallow face streaked with a violet birthmark. And a bare red stump at the end of a sleeve, where a hand should be. A thief.

His horse shies back as it scents us behind the bushes. The man's darting eyes move toward our hiding place. I duck lower, behind a fallen tree.

"They think to hide the merchandise," the swarthy man says. He gives a harsh laugh. "Try to escape their due—but we'll get our five men out of them. They can't hide forever."

The sallow-faced man replies. "I don't believe a word of the story they told in the village."

Behind them, a strange cart with mismatched wheels comes into view. It is topped with a type of pen with bars and shackles. I have seen the like before: this cart is a cage for serfs who have escaped their masters, for criminals who avoid their lords. These men work to retrieve lost servants. I have heard rumors that when those servants are not found, they take another man's serfs—as slaves—to fill the number they have lost. They take who they can find.

I look down at our concealed camp. I push my hands down into the stinging cold and slide backward, motioning to Cole. He slides down the hillside toward the fire. Soon I can see him in the campsite, striving again to wake the men.

Then, on the edge of my sight, a shadow moves. Someone is hiding there, watching from the trees.

I flinch back: I am discovered. But it is only Hob, our leader. He must have seen me watching on the hillside.

Now Hob comes toward me, striding tall and confident. He puts a big work-coarsened hand on my shoulder.

"Don't worry yerself about them men on the horses," he says. "I'll take care of 'em. No need to tell the others. Not yet."

So I wait there alone in the trees as Hob half slides, half walks down the long bank of the hill, away from the overhanging danger of the drifts. Soon he is far below the trees, out of sight of the men. For a moment, he is out of my sight too, behind the last tall drift. Then he barrels his way through, and now I can see him moving along the base of the hill.

The men on horses are casting about for the source of the smoke they saw earlier, but the thin fumes are hard to see in the brighter light. In the fresh sunlight, mist is rising in thick waves from every outcrop and stone and tree. The earth itself seems to be melting into smoke.

"Hallo," calls Hob. He comes toward them like an apparition rising out of the fog. The men draw their horses back.

"It's the merchant," says the swarthy man finally. "It's Hob!"

"Come back with our gold then?" says the man.

Hob speaks, but I cannot make out his words. The other man with the birthmark guffaws. The rest of the men join him in laughter, and for the first time I fear for Hob. These men seem to know him, but they do not mean him well.

"Look, my friend," says the swarthy man. "You made a devil's bargain, an' there ain't no way out of it."

"They're dead, I say," Hob barks at them. "Heaven help me, those boys are gone to God."

The large man on the horse glances over at his birthmarked friend, to see how much of this he buys. But the sallow man has a sneer on his face.

"Come now, Hobby boy, where are they then? Where did you hide 'em?"

"I'm telling you the truth," Hob repeats. "Those lads are—"

The swarthy man holds up a hand, stops Hob's voice in his throat. "I told you lot what to do, an' how to do it," he says. "Keep your plan a secret. None to know."

The man with the birthmark urges his horse forward, pushing Hob back against the snow wall. "But no, bastard had to tell someone, an' now they're all gone. Runned away, am I right?"

The swarthy man sits back—he shakes his head sadly, as if bemused by man's perfidy.

"Where's our gold, Hob?" barks one of the other men. "Where the bloody hell did it go?"

Hob shakes his head nervously. He no longer seems tall or confident. Against the men on their horses, he is a supplicating child.

"Spent it, no doubt," says the one-armed man. He leans forward and his horse rears suddenly, so that Hob cowers down in the snow to escape the hooves.

"My partner," Hob says loudly. "My partner, he—"

"He has a partner!" The men guffaw again, but there is no humor in it. "Oh yes, that's a new one—a partner who took the gold an' ran for the castle!"

Who is Hob's partner? It is Liam? Is it Benedict?

"We've got the gold," Hob blurts out. "Back at the village."

Once more, Hob's words are cause for mirth.

The swarthy man bellows at him now. "An' if we were to go back to the village, what would happen there, do ye think? No, no, my friend, you're stuck with us here. An' we want the goods. We paid for it, an' we want 'em."

"But I'm telling you, they're gone," Hob bleats.

"Loosen yer tongue, Hob. It'll do you good," says the swarthy one. Suddenly, Hob flinches back and yelps in pain. Something is bright red on the skin of his cheek, and his shoulder is now bare. A moment later I hear the crack. A whip, moving too fast for me to spy.

"Tell the truth! Where are they, eh?" bellows the swarthy man. "Where the feck are they hiding?"

Hob does not reply, and the whip crack comes again, and again.

I watch a moment longer, from my hillside combe.

Then I slide backward, moving down into the camp, out of breath. Cole runs up beside me.

"Mear," Cole mutters in my ear. "Where's Hob? I've got to tell Hob what happen'd. I was there that night, and I saw—"

The whip crack comes again on the other side of the hill of snow, and there is a sudden high shriek. The sound of horse hooves are on the hillside.

Desperately, I lean close to Cole, wanting him to speak. But he is silent, his face white, as we hear screams of pain from the other side of the slope.

The horse hooves are coming nearer every moment. Cole whispers in my ear, but he does not speak of the fire now.

"I will run," he says. "I will be a lure for those men on horses, I will take them fara way from our camp."

I shake my head. *No.* But Cole does not listen; he has in mind to be a hero.

Cole runs. At first, I struggle after him, trying to pull him back. But I cannot catch him, so I turn the other direction and climb the rise through the trees.

Finally, after a hard climb, my head crests the rise and I can see and hear the men on their horses again. The swarthy man is bellowing, "Find the rest of 'em, wouldja? They have to be here somewhere! Where's his feckin' partner?"

The men look around at the woods, spurring their horses onward, while the birthmarked one uses a pike to shove Hob into the cage, as one would move a cow into the stocks. The other horses trot forward slowly.

With Hob secured, the birthmarked one canters up to the large man. He squints into the sunlight. "If we find 'im, do we take the gold back from 'im too?"

The swarthy one drops his jaw in mock surprise. "I'm surpris'd at you, Dirk, sure I am. You'd take back your payment, given in proper business, after you have the goods?"

Again, the men laugh. The swarthy man cuts the laughter short. "Dirk—best be quick 'bout it. Take us over the top of the hill."

I slide hurriedly down into the campsite again, my hands sinking into the stinging-cold snow. The white hillside quakes with the sound of hooves.

The overhang casts a shadow over our camp. The new-fallen snow has created an overarching heavier lip above us in the night, a looming threat. The words of the men on the other side are muted now, swallowed by the snow. Here, close-at-hand, I can hear tiny ruptures, cracking and creaking. Quaking in my heart, I step under the shadowed curve.

I can see that Tom's bedroll is too close to that heavy knife-edged kerf of snow. I seize his legs and lean backward. Halfway out from under the overhang, Tom's face twitches now, his fingers fumble for his covers.

"Bloody 'ell, gerroff me!" Tom's eyes open, still bloodshot with drink. He shouts at me. "What are you tryin' t' do?"

Benedict raises his head uncertainly. He looks at the sharp edge of the overhang, then turns his head toward the sound of the pounding hooves. He stands and staggers forward. "Where are they?" he says to me. "Have they found us already?"

But Tom pushes me then, and I fall into the thick snow. As I claw back to my feet, Cole slides past—he is running toward the cart, but I have no time to find what he is doing.

"Get 'way, you daft bugger," Tom shouts at me.

"Did they track us?" Benedict says. "Are they here?"

Liam finally stirs, moving like a sleepwalker. I seize his chin and turn his head to look upward. I point, my finger trembling. Above us is where the danger lies now.

A wave of sound ripples along the edge of that ocean of snow. A faint crack, the crumble of mortar, and then a sudden ripping crash. A vast cathedral collapses around us, long pillars splintering to bits, cracking apart into massive snowballs and frosty dust.

Liam moves quickly then, scrambling out of the way.

I am thrown forward, my feet churning wildly in the surf of roiling white.

The riding men surge into our campsite now, their horses slowing in the deep drift rolling from the overhang.

The snow has covered most of our cart, and the riding men do not stop there. Cole lunges out from underneath the wheels. "Damn you to hell," he brays. "Bastards!" A horse rears back, and Cole seizes the large man's sword. He dashes madly for the woods.

Cole runs like a hellion, using the sword to balance as he skitters across packed snow and fallen ice. The swarthy man spurs his horse ahead.

Cole is the rabbit, leading them away.

Then the hillside goes, a snow-packed promontory as thick as my chest breaking off. I turn to run, but something cold strikes me in the back, rolling over me without pause and flattening my face into the stinging ice. When I raise my head, I can see blocks of frozen snow tumbling past, rumbling across our fire pit. One great chunk lands on the cart, which trembles from axle to whippletree. Now it is entirely concealed.

Cole will escape, I think. *Cole is away from here. But he knows what happened that night.*

Then another blow strikes me in the back. I stagger, and another comes and another. The sounds I hear change now as I'm pushed deeper underneath. My eyes flicker open. *If Cole dies, I will never discover—*

I swim desperately upward as falling ice shudders over me. I struggle to breathe, thrusting my face toward a tiny dot of light. My limbs are encased in frost, and it clots tight around me. I beat my bloody fists against soft and suffocating walls until my eyes close dark in dream.

CHAPTER 7

TEN YEARS AGO, at Michaelmas, the early autumn hours were fading into dusk. The day was dying slow. I had fallen off the straight and narrow into a place of harsh rocks and broken brambles, like the story of Satan falling from heaven on Saint Michael's Day. But I had fallen from no heaven, and those who pursued me were no angels.

Someone wished me dead and silent, and my lover's heir with me; they had proved it already. But my head whirled with questions: *Did the Earl of Hereford succeed in his plan? If I went to Court with my son, would fortune change? Did Edward love me true?*

I have never yet found answers to these riddles.

On that long autumn day, I stole a monk's cassock and cloak from the Cluny monastery, rosary beads and all, using the shapeless brown cloak to conceal my womanly figure.

I hacked my auburn hair down to a nub and shaved a tonsure on my scalp. Yet my disguise was thin, for I carried with me that tiny mewling creature borne only by a woman. My babe, Christian.

Yet I had spent a season at that monastery before I departed in my monk's stolen garb, and my caution had faded. After I went on the open road, I nursed little Christian openly in the woods, my monk's robe pulled down, my breast displayed for forest creatures to see.

Then the flap of a bird in a bush, and the crack of twigs under stealthy footsteps. There was someone watching me from the trees. A faint shape and shadow in the wind, a stirring in the leaves. I gazed into the dappled dark, wondering at the watcher.

I was facing away from the road when they came.

I heard them first. The sound of horses in the distance was a vast thrumming like a swarm of distant angry bees. Then I turned and saw them.

They rode over the crest and achieved that stretch of the King's Highway in the blinking of an eye. Four of them galloped down the center of the road, horses lathered, heraldry whipping in the wind of their passage. I remembered the men who shot my carriage full of arrows, who killed my guard. I knew how quickly they could strike.

To this day, I do not know if these men were the Earl's liege men or if they were other messengers entirely. I do not know if they would have killed me, or galloped past.

I did not wait to find out.

I ran. A path seemed to open before me into the woods, some small track to a little town, a forgotten village.

I sensed the watcher—keeping pace with me in the thickening forest, maneuvering silently through the clasping vines, the slapping branches and heavy windfall logs—close to me at times.

Then my poor left foot betrayed me, catching on an errant vine and sliding helplessly on slick rock. I tumbled into a bramblebush, pushing Christian out of harm's way before I plunged headfirst into the misbegotten backwater of a summer-shrunk creek. I pulled myself out of the deep and stinking sludge, clawed my way up the granite, and reached for my crying son, his blanket caught precariously in brambles. But my foot lodged in a fold of robe, and then I fell without stopping, slamming backward against the great unforgiving rock.

The distant thrumming of the hooves still shuddered through me as the stone caught my head on the way down.

I woke in near darkness, my head throbbing as if it had been used as a blacksmith's anvil. There were voices around me, a deep baritone and a pair of tenors in some uncertain argument.

With bitter mud and the iron tang of blood in my mouth, I cautiously lifted my head, the pain coming in a fresh wave. I swallowed hard. It seemed I had bitten myself when I fell, my teeth knocking together, nearly severing my tongue. There was a swelling in my mouth and a broken something: it felt like one of my teeth.

My heart leaped up into my throat. Where was my child?

Three men stood above me in the dusk. The oldest short and small, skin burned nut-brown by sun. The second, taller and redheaded, standing close at hand, staring, picking nervously at a bit of mud in a bedraggled soldier's sash. Heavy muscles for a young face: a deserter from some army, by the looks of it. And then the third: tall, with the noble face of a god, a smoothly handsome visage under an unruly sheaf of golden hair.

I'd later learn their names: Geoff was the short brown one; Liam, the nervous redheaded one; and Salvius, the strong leader with the golden hair.

I wrinkled my nose at the smell. Even their leader stank. The stench of the men was richly pungent, redolent of hard labor and old food.

These three were no knights errant. The redhead's sash was the only sign of rank or station. They otherwise wore the tattered shifts of peasants. The tallest—the golden-haired one—was the cleanest and most comely. A line of neat knots tied his cloak closed. The others let their open tunics hang to their waists.

Goats bleated around them in the bracken, udders pendulous, eyes running brown with rheum. As I watched, a strand of nettles disappeared in one masticating jaw.

I wiped my mouth and tried to speak. I choked on my swollen tongue, blood still draining in my mouth, and no sound came out. I tried to move and staggered as I stood.

The nervous redhead spoke. "He looks for the little one."

I made to speak again as they watched me stumble forward.

"Yes, the babe," said Salvius patiently. "He wants to know where the infant is."

By "he," they meant me.

"I dunno," said small Geoff suspiciously. "What did he do with the mother?"

Redheaded Liam lifted Christian from the ground to show him to me. My babe was, as ever, perfectly serene, his blue eyes staring wide and unafraid, his little face bemused, uninjured but for a small scratch from a thorn. He seemed happy and unconcerned.

A purple-dyed cloth was wrapped tight around him, a handmade weave. I had never seen that pattern or that piece of cloth before in my life. And he was chewing on a new twist of rag, dribbling white out of the corner of his mouth. It seemed that someone had given him a rag dipped in milk.

When I saw small Christian eating without me, my body itself was jealous for his touch. My body longed for him. Truly it did, for I was swollen, my breasts aching with his absence.

But the men grimaced at me. They thought I'd stolen this sweet young thing.

"Where's the mother?" said Geoff. "You bloody monk, what you done with her?"

I saw myself through Geoff's narrowed eyes. I was slathered in mud and filth, my eyes staring whitely out of the black muck, the stench of blood on me. I looked the very picture of Satan, risen from the depths of the earth, an evil creature giving sacrifice to my dark god.

I gestured at myself, struggling to speak through my broken teeth, my swollen tongue.

"Who wrapped the babe? Who fed him?" asked the redheaded one suspiciously.

I had thought it was these men who had cared for little Christian. But who had done it, if not them?

Behind the men, I caught a glimpse of some shape moving away from us in the forest. It was a woman: somehow I sensed that. A furtive one who moved without the need to prove her strength, a specter in the leaves trailing a faint scent of lavender and mint. Gone now, a shadow in the woods.

Christian looked at my muddy face, and he began to wail. Geoff handed me the baby. He wrinkled his nose in disgust and repeated himself. "Where's the mother, eh? You got a tongue in your head—is she buried in the pit?"

The blond Salvius spoke calmly. "Tell us true. Are you the child's father?"

I was on the verge of sliding that ratty monk's frock down off one shoulder, so that I could still Christian's hungry cries. At the moment when all would have known I was a woman, I managed to hear the last word: "father." They believed my disguise, they thought I was a man. I was helped by the mud all over my face and body.

So I threw the baby up onto my shoulder. I jogged Christian up and down, holding him close and tight. He was quiet now, and so was I.

"Who are you?" they said to me.

"Me… Mear… Mear…" my mouth stuttered, an idiot sound, trying to say Miriam with my cut tongue. Only later did I realize that if I had succeeded in saying my name, I would have been exposed as a woman just as quickly as if I'd shown my breast. But at the time, I could not speak, not clearly.

The men eyed each other nervously.

"Harebrained fool, he is," said Liam. "Mad as the wind."

Inspiration came to me then, as suddenly and clearly as a finger of lightning. I brought my arm up from my side and drew my fingers carefully down my throat, as if I'd been cut deep there. I grimaced and shook my head as if in weariness of constant explanation.

The men stared. My heart sank, but I made the cutting motion once more, trusting that God would not grant me the seed of such a hope without allowing it to take root and grow.

Young Liam rubbed the reddish stubble on his chin. Then he grinned, revealing the cracked teeth that populated his jaw, like lost and yellowed pawns. "Bugger it, 'e is a mute."

"What's that?" Brown-skinned Geoff cracked the knuckles on one clenched fist, looking me over carefully.

"Mute," explained Salvius. "It happens. My cousin like this can't talk to save his life. Couldna ever get a buggerin' word outta him."

"I dunno." Geoff pulled anxiously at a wayward goat.

"He could still be dangerous," said Liam. "Could still be mad."

"Well now," said Salvius. "Let's say he can't talk, but that doesn't mean he's mad. An' he's not lookin' down into the mud, so maybe there isn't a mother at the bottom of that damn'd pit."

I shook my head emphatically, pointed at my own chest, and at my child.

Salvius saw my reaction and shook his blond hair. Then he glanced down into the morass. "Don't look like we'll ever know what happened, not unless this mute monk can draw us a bloody picture." He came closer to me, wrinkling his nose at the reeking mud.

"Look, you," Salvius said to me. "I know you can listen at least. You'll be alright now, hear? Just tell me true, the babe—is the child your own?"

I nodded carefully, my head still throbbing with pain. I tried to speak again, my throat straining.

"Mear, ear—whate'er your name be," said Salvius forcefully, as if commanding the others. "I'll take care of you."

The blacksmith had made up his mind.

Salvius laid a gentle hand on my shoulder, his fingers broad and bluntly tipped, a warming strength coming through his blacksmith's grip. I grew to know this man's ways well in the years after. The charming blacksmith, strong and powerful. My friend and patron in the village.

"Don't you worry, we've got you safe now." He gave me a broad smile.

Yet the others were unsure. The darkly scowling Geoff backed away, making the sign of blessing broadly, crossing the air over my head thrice, to ward off devils. "What if this Mear is one of those who bring the plague?"

"The black death?" I can still recall Liam's wide-eyed stare: so young, so suspicious. Open-mouthed, stubble-faced Liam, before that dark-red beard grew in.

Geoff made the sign of the cross again. Even now, he is quick to cast blame. "Those blasted goats found this false monk. An' you know that billy goats can see every devil!"

Liam laughed aloud. But Salvius knew Geoff wasn't making a joke. "I said I would protect this one." There was a threat in his deep baritone voice. "Would you put my word to the test?"

"A witch thing," muttered Geoff. "He is a devil, an' a witch."

Salvius moved toward me, and I flinched back.

Somewhere came the gusting scent of mint and lavender again, and then a distant whiff of smoke. Burning in the air. *Was the other woman in the forest here still, tracking us?*

But the man with the bright hair, handsome Salvius, winked at me, a sly and subtle movement only I could see. I wasn't scared anymore. He won me over.

"God's wounds, if he has a demon, I can beat it out of him." He cracked his knuckles. "If he doesn't have a demon, then we will have a new man in the village. Let's take 'im back with us."

"But the child—" began Geoff, tremulous fear still in his voice. "He could be a devil too!"

Salvius spit on the browned and muddied grass at my feet. "The child isn't a devil—not yet at least. I can use another man, to work my bellows in the smithy, an' I choose this one here. He owes us one harvest at least, for savin' his life, an' that of his child."

The tide had turned.

That stuttering stillborn attempt to say my name were the last words I said out loud in public for many years. I locked my speech in an iron chest—buried deep in frost. It was the one gift the Abbess had proclaimed God's own gift to me—and I hid it for ten years, as the fool buries his gold in the earth.

And now I have known these men for a decade now. Geoff has mellowed with time, although he is suspicious by nature: only Liam's jokes can turn him from finding fault. Liam himself has begun to feel the weight of time, pushing down on his bright spirit and endless jokes. The knowledge that he will never be anything but a poor woodsman hurts now.

Only Salvius has not changed much. He remains a masterful man, sired and named by an errant priest, and our men still listen to whatever he says. I have seen him use his power to influence men to their better natures and to serve the greater good. And in that moment when my life hung on a knife blade, Salvius found a way for me to live. He could claim he needed another man to run his bellows, and none would challenge him.

I have earned my bread for years now at that smithy. And for all these years, I have always remembered his grace and that great debt I owe to him: Salvius was the one to save me. Salvius kept me alive that day, and ever.

CHAPTER 8

DISTANT HOOFBEATS POUND away over the snow, reverberating in my flesh. The top of my snowy grave shifts and cracks open. Light and air flood in.

I can breathe. Then another piece is pulled away. My head is free: only my waist and legs are now encased in this jagged crypt.

Tom paws at the snow with his great bare hands, digging as a dog hunting for a stoat. Liam carefully pushes apart frozen snow with the blunt end of an axe. Benedict lifts chunks of ice out of the hole.

My breath rattles in and out in ragged gasps.

"He lives!" grunts Liam.

"It's a miracle!" says Tom as I turn my head to look at them. "I think my son brought 'im back from the dead to be with us."

Liam and Benedict ignore Tom's talk of ghostly saviors. Liam sits back on his haunches, gazing upon my anxious face with a wry satisfaction. "Well, that's only two still missing then. Think the bandits took them?"

"Nah," says Benedict. "They looked for gold an' rich booty. We had neither. They never even found our cart—leastwise, not when Cole led them off into the woods. Sav'd us, he did."

Not for the first time, I wish I could speak. These men never heard the bandits talking. They do not know that the thief and the slave dealers knew Hob, or that gold had been exchanged. And they don't know that Hob has been taken by them.

A shiver runs down my bones: no one knows except me.

I look from side to side. *What did Liam say about Cole?*

Tom pauses in his labors. He must have seen my wide eyes. "Don't fret yerself—you're alive, but we lost two of our company."

"Hob and Cole, both gone," says Benedict. He stands and limps to the side. His leg has a gash in it.

"Those men took 'em!" Tom declares, and I wish I could tell him how close he is to the mark. "Indentur'd servants are worth their weight in gold, I tell you."

Carefully, Benedict scrapes ice from my chest with the flat end of the axe. I keep the flinch from off my face, although a dull ache runs through my tender breast.

"If you're a highwayman," says Benedict, holding his leg, "you can't be sellin' lads on the open market. Only way you can sell 'em is to a lord—you should know that."

No, I think. *None of us knew that. Why would you know that?*

"An' that Cole," continues Bene. "He has a foul look an' a scarred face. He wouldn't be worth much—"

"Geoff is lookin' for the missing ones in the woods," says Liam.

Benedict grimaces, the pain in his leg showing in his face. "I dunno if he'll find a trace of 'em. If they're dead, the snow will cover 'em fast."

Then we hear Geoff's hoarse shout. "Help—help the lad!"

Benedict starts limping as fast as he can down the hill of snow. Liam tries to lift me out of the hole—although I resist his awkward help. I pull myself up onto my feet, the blood throbbing in my temples, my head aching. I can stand on my own though, and to my surprise, none of my bones are broken. I can see the entire extent of the avalanche now. The spots where Tom and Geoff lay before were brutally erased by that white tide.

As I limp down the icy hillside, the wind gusts me forward, a stinging residue of grainy snow in its teeth. The protection of the overhang is gone. The wind floods straight down off the King's Highway now.

I was the one who brought the attack upon us. I started the fire, telling every man for miles that we were here in this hollow. My fire was how they found us.

Yet my thoughts are stilled by a sign I see: on other side of the hill, there is a very faint path out of the woods, a solitary set of hoofmarks. I look around, but no one else in our company seems to notice these marks.

I peer closely at the tracks: a single horse with a crack in the near hind hoof.

The tracks are deep but melted at the surface. So someone came in the hours of darkness and did not come back after dawn. Our hiding place, such as it was, worked to fool at least that solitary man. *But who came out of the woods? Who followed us along the village track?*

When we find Cole, he is shivering at the bottom of a ravine, his flesh blue with cold, still holding the stolen sword. Geoff tells us he discovered Cole by the sound of the lad's chattering teeth. All morning, Cole had scampered ahead of the bandits, and kept them chasing him through the woods, until he slipped down an icy crevasse into a half-frozen stream.

By that time, our cart was entirely covered in snow, and the rest of the men had hidden in the woods, so there was no camp to plunder. After some searching, the horsemen seemed to give up and rode away.

Cole was fortunate, for when Geoff found him, he was nearly helpless, his legs trapped by ice. By the time we pull him out of the water, he is frozen half to death.

We cover the shivering lad with all of our furs, and Tom wraps him in his great arms, warming the boy with his bulk. Cole is alive. And that is a miracle in itself.

Yet no one except me saw the men take Hob. So half the morning, they waste in calling for him. At first the calls are strident and angry, and then desperate, and finally empty of hope.

"Hob!"

"Hob, mate, come back!"

"Hob, help us!"

"Hob!"

In the search for Hob, the men find standing stones at the edge of the King's Road. They are engraved with Roman letters and numbers, but there are no arrows to point the way.

Hob would know which way to go. But he is gone.

The hoofprints of the bandits have been covered by blown snow, and even if we knew which way they went, it is far from certain we would want to follow them.

Hours later, Benedict has given up on Hob. "Pack it up," he says in a flat and distant voice. "We need to move on."

Liam and Geoff stare at him in shock. Bene continues. "We should take Hob's things as well. Mayhap we will find him on the road, mayhap he has gone ahead." The last was said in a querulous tone, as if Bene did not expect to be believed.

"Oh God, Hob," said Geoff, his voice cracking with desperation. "What are we to do?"

"Go on," said Bene. "We will continue. We will seek justice, as he wanted us to do. At the monastery ahead."

"I tell you, we should turn back now," says Geoff. "There ain't no sense in going on."

"No," says Benedict. "I can't go down that hillside again with this wound in my leg."

"An' we seek justice," bellows Tom. "Go to the monastery! We must get the protection of a lord for our troubles, show the bodies to the Abbot. And then we can—"

"We can't go back," says Liam. "We know now there are bandits close-by, and despite what Hob said, I think someone is in the woods. We could make a run for the monastery. It would be a straight shot at least."

"But if we're going to go on, which way?" says Geoff. "I can't read these stones, can you?"

"No. And I can't run," Bene says, pointing down at the blood on his leg.

Geoff speaks in a bitter tone. "You and your injured leg, Benedict. That is what is holding us back from safety."

"True," agrees Liam. "I say we leave you here for the bandits, and go for the monastery on our own."

Benedict limps forward. A hard disappointment crosses his face, and anger blanches his features. "You're one to speak, Liam, with your feckin' crime still unaccounted for, and who's to know you won't do it again. Now you're just a feckin' hand-to-mouth woodsman. You're nothing!"

"Why don't you know which bloody way to go then? You brought us here!" says Geoff. But Benedict isn't finished yet.

"You may be grown, but you speak as a child. Sure, you two bastards go on the open road. And who's going to miss you if you don't come back? I'm the one who has to get back to the village. The folk there need me. Real lords and ladies need me. Goddammit—Lord Peter of Lincoln relies upon my work—who but your stinking dead son needs you, Geoff?"

"That's enough out of your bloody mouth," says Geoff, and he reaches for a branch to strike Benedict with.

Hob, Hob, Hob is gone. It chants through my head, a hopeless rhyme. Our leader is gone, and we are fighting on the road with bandits around us.

I turn away from the men as they struggle in desperation, and I look at the stones. On one, LONDINIUM is carved, plain to see. No one else can read, but I know the Roman letters.

I point. That way. South. Toward London.

No one notices, so I grip Tom's arm hard, twist him towards the stones. He sees my hand pointing and stares.

"Mear knows which way to go for the monastery," Tom says in surprise. The fight halts, the men breathing heavily, steam rising from their mouths.

"How the feck does he know?" Liam squints with suspicion.

Benedict shrugs. "Does it matter? Let's go on then."

"We don't need to keep going!" says Geoff again. "Turn back and we can—"

"Shut yer mouth," says Tom, and he pushes the cart so hard it starts rolling down the long hill of the King's Highway, and Geoff must run to catch up.

We are on the King's road now, and our passage is the more dangerous. For we have no blessing or sanction from our Lord, Sir Peter, to be abroad upon the open road. This makes us vagabonds; any man may kill or injure us without consequence.

We are outside the law.

Ahead is a great breadth of countryside stretching out, forests and farmland. Hillocks and haystacks rise up, isles in a smoking brume.

After the snow of the night before, the day is washed clean: all is silver and bright with ice, and a light wind moves us forward. Here and there snow has blown aside, revealing the line of the great white stone road that slices through the hills. It is an unswerving line marked by the Romans, carved straight out of this untrammeled landscape.

By the hour of Sext, Cole has warmed his bones. The men try to put both of us on the cart, but I push back: I am fine. Cole still shivers uncontrollably with cold though, so I make him sit high on the crossbar. Up there, he is swathed in blanket and he sights ahead for rocks and dips in the way ahead. When Benedict stumbles and bangs his leg once again, Cole is the one who calls to the rest of us for a halt. And when I seem tired—as I often am on this long track of winter thorns—Cole is the one who encourages me: "Aye, Mear, keep goin'—don't give up now! Keep pushin'—you're doin' fine."

"Oh aye," replies Tom. "You're one to talk. You're sure pushin' us along!"

"Ayuh, how's the view from up there?" laughs Liam. "Cole—think you can hold a jousting pole up there? Fight off them bandits for us with one hand?"

Cole chuckles, grateful for their jokes. We listen to him with every roll of the cart's heavy wheels on the snow. As we labor hard, his voice is like flowing sweet water, soothing our passage.

The long day passes slowly. With his keen eyes and high vantage point, Cole is the first to spot the glint of sun on that great black roof, a speck of shining mica in the white wilderness. "It's the monastery!" he calls.

There is a palpable sigh of relief. The monastery will mean free food and lodging.

"Bread," says Geoff simply. "All's I need from that monastery is a loaf of fresh bread."

"Venison," Benedict exclaims, his heavy brow wrinkling. Monks have the right to kill the King's deer.

"Ol' Mear, he's told me many a time of the glories of that self-same monastery," Liam jokes. "Ayuh, Mear tells tales all the day long!"

The men laugh at mute Mear, and even my face cracks in a rare smile. Something in me, an unreasoning hope, thinks I will hear of Edward at that monastery.

But I know for truth that if we do not move faster on this road, we will not reach the place before Vespers, when the gates are locked. And it comes to me that we have not buried these dead, as the law demands. So what will the monastery make of our burden of bodies? *Will they take us for penitents or heretics? How will I mark Christian's life?*

I glance back at the open road. A faint whirling in the air appears, and from this distance it seems as small as a dust devil. But this is no summer day—that is no dust. It is a puff of snow kicked into the air by motion far away along the road.

The same troupe of bandits may have found us again. It is the sign of distant horses.

Desperately, I gauge the time remaining to us. The ones who follow us are three hills back—so we have a bit of time—but what will we do when they arrive?

The sun is higher in the sky, but we are not yet at the crest of the long hill when someone's stomach growls.

"Ah, I hear that," says Liam. He slows and wipes a sweating brow before he peers up at the light of the sun. "Noon—time t' eat."

The cart slides to a halt. Geoff pulls the coal box and the tinder out. The men speak of food and fire. Tom takes his empty wineskins down and packs them full of snow so we will have water to drink later. And then we gather wood.

Hob would have prevented this halt, but he is not here to advise caution. And by the time I realize what they intend it is almost too late. I stand, and let out a sudden howl of fear. The laughter stops.

"Mear, what's wrong?" says Cole. I point at the far-off dust demon. Benedict shades his brow and squints. His eyes are not as keen as mine, and he is not as decisive as Hob.

"Ah, I see them," Benedict mutters finally, his mouth pursing in concern.

The riders move out of sight behind a curve in the road. From behind the hill, we can see a great puff of gritty snow being thrown into the air by the horses that bring our pursuers closer. Someone is riding hard, or there are many riders.

"Well, what next?" says Liam.

Hob's absence is like a tooth missing—everyone feels the wound, but no one knows how to fill the gap. The men are still numb and purposeless at the loss of their leader. They still expect someone else to tell them what to do.

I glance from side to side. The road is bordered by gorse bushes and rough-hewn logs: there is a gap in the logs ahead where a cattle track wends its way back to a snow-filled wallow.

I make a plan, pointing at the gorse bushes, urging them on.

Benedict hesitates, and then the distant clamor of horse hooves fills the air, a terrifying punctuation. The sound is closer than expected, another trick of the winter air.

I gesture furiously.

"We need to get off the road," Benedict says in slow realization. "That's our only chance." He claps his hands together, finally taking action.

"Alright," he says. "Get off the road! Gerroff the road!"

The gorse and bracken will conceal us from any quick-passing stranger, but perhaps not from the searching eyes of a thief. It is, at best, a stopgap, a makeshift battlement.

But the men echo Benedict's shout. "Gerroff the road!"

Cole is off the cart in a wink, wrapped in his layers of blanket. The cart is trundled quickly off the track and into the wallow, nearly spilling our load as we bury it deep in the snowbank. I keep urging us farther down: we must hide well.

I am surprised to discover that Liam knows how to hide in the wilderness. Years ago, he must have been a fugitive, for he is quick to take a branch and brush away our cart tracks.

Moments later, when I look at the road, there is no sign of the cart, as if it had floated away in the fresh snow.

Even so, they may find us here. But though they whisper furtively, the men don't seem to realize that we can hide our possessions better. Even if they find us, they may let us go if we have nothing on us to take.

Again, I must fill the gap created by Hob's loss. Quickly, I take everything that was hidden in the cart and I gesture to the men to give me what treasures we have. I take a small sack of gold out of Benedict's coat, as he tries to fight me off and then glares at me in silent astonishment. Then I clamber down the hillside to find a new place of concealment.

My feet ache with cold, but I must go as far as possible. The heavy cloaks, the furs, the gold pouch, the food. All of these I bear in silence, holding our life in my hands.

When I slide over the last boulder at the foot of the bank, I find a heavy stick gouging at my thigh. I am struck by its yellowed whiteness. Bone.

I've landed in an open grave. A place of bones and stripped bodies. A few rags left, but all cloaks gone. Mere months ago it happened, for there are still hanks of hair. But no cross, no priest, no burial. This curve of the road brought someone desperate here, who did not balk at killing.

I push our cloaks and belongings under the bones and stuff snow around the verge. A fat crow flutters near at hand, watching for fresh kill.

I climb out of the pit, away from our hiding place. If they find me, I do not want them to find everything we own.

My breath is a ragged razor in my mouth as I reach a flat place near the top of the hill, and sweat sheets into my eyes.

From behind the bushes, I see the same sallow man with the missing arm. He rides ahead looking from side to side, scouting the road. He reins in his steed as he comes across a fur dropped at the side of the road, a clear signal that someone passed this way not long before. Inwardly, I curse our carelessness.

The man stretches down from his horse and picks it up. Then he smells it and feels how warm it is.

My skin crawls as the man's gaze sweeps through the bracken, across the gorse bushes, in the direction of my hidden face. I tremble, hoping he cannot see us.

But the other riders thunder closer. Just before they reach him, the one-armed man kicks his heels against his horse's flanks, and waves his men on. All of them gallop past as we hold our breath in the shadows.

Then the iron cage jounces past on misshapen wheels, and everyone can see the form of Hob inside. He's huddled miserably against one bar, holding on against the constant shaking, and blood trickles down his scalp.

For a long time afterward, we are frozen there in the bushes, the rest of the men realizing, finally, what has happened to Hob.

The road is empty of sound and sight, a white expanse, the snow slowly drifting across it. We wait a long time, but the bandits do not reappear.

Finally, I notice Cole's teeth chattering, like quick and nervous laughter. That sound spurs me to action, and I scramble back down the hillside to retrieve our heavy clothes, the gold, and the food.

Now we must pull the cart back onto the open road. It is not an easy task, even with Tom's great shoulders behind the mass of it.

We have half the cart out of the bushes when a new sound comes. We turn to look, but it is too late.

A single horse clatters around the distant corner of the trail, out of the copse of ash and rowan trees it comes, the boughs breaking asunder, the load it bears driving it forward like a rabid hound. My throat chokes with urgent pain, a moan breaks out of my lips.

Hurriedly, I seize the notched sword and swing its heavy weight high in the air, holding it like a brand.

The tall man riding hard and alone is within reach of the sword now. His face flashes toward us.

I can see a head of wheat-colored hair, a strong jaw, and a strong mouth that smiles with each thump of the horse's hooves on the road. The sides of his steed are flecked with white lather.

A foam of sweat is dripping from her, steaming on the cold snow. It is an old smithy horse, a mare, not bred for this kind of pace. My heart hammers.

I know the horse. We all know the rider.

CHAPTER 9

A HANDSOME HEAD OF hair that gleams golden in the light, a spiky and uneven beard, a noble way of turning his head, a brave curve on his full and handsome lips—it is Salvius.

I stand there, frozen in surprised joy.

His breath gasps out in ragged blats of steam. Then he wrenches on the wooden bit and bridle.

His old piebald mare trembles and jerks back and forth, swerving only at the last moment. I can't imagine when she was last out of our village.

"Halt," Salvius says to his wayward steed. "You beast, halt!"

When the horse finally stops its frantic motion, Salvius looks down at us, his eyes as penetrating as ever, his hair and beard shot through with slivers of ice.

"Ah, I've found you," he says, and I let the heavy sword drop to the ground. My limbs are suddenly weary with relief. *We are saved*, I think. *Saved by strong Salvius who can direct us, and lead us.*

He swings his long legs off the horse and looks ahead at the empty road, then down through the gorse bushes into the cow wallow, where the cart rests with our dead sons.

Salvius takes hold of a wineskin that hangs off Tom's pack, and swallows quick gulps of melted snow. He grimaces at the chill water and wipes one hand across his beard. Then he glances at the men cowering down the hillside.

"Alright, you lot can get out of there now—those bastards won't bother you no more. Full of bluff an' bluster, nothin' more. But—"

"They took Hob," says Liam. "They took him. Put him in a cage like a beast."

"Those bandits took him?" Salvius's face goes white for a moment in consternation. "What did they want with him?"

"They hunt men," says Geoff. "They hunted Cole too." Our story comes out in a flood. But when Liam tells of Cole's heroism, Salvius points at the lad.

"Him?" Salvius laughs. "That lad? I've tried to make him brave, but no luck. He's scared o' demons and haunts—and yet *he* drew them off you?"

Cole looks abashed.

"Good on you, lad, good on you!" Salvius slaps him on the back.

Then Salvius lifts his cloak and shows us what he wears as a blouse. It's a white tunic with the lion rampant and the faded red bars of Sir Peter of Lincoln. It is the Lord's property, and any who wear this sign would be safe from molestation on the King's Highway.

"You fools," says Salvius, but in a kindly voice. "You left with no writ, no garment, no sign of a Lord's blessing. I went to your wife, Bene—"

Benedict starts forward, glowering.

Salvius holds up his hand. "I went to Sophia—an' she checked the weaving shed. She found for me this old tunic, rejected by the Court—"

"Aye, it went wrong," says Benedict. "I miswove that three summers ago. The pattern in the back is awry, and the Lord did not want it."

"But from the front, none would know of its flaw." Salvius proudly slaps the red lion on his chest. "So I took it as my own. It's already been challenged once, some brash soldier on the road. I showed the lion to him, an' passed the test."

"I brought it for you, to preserve your lives," Salvius says. "This will safeguard our passage through the vale of tears."

The men eagerly reach out to touch their salvation. I can see the tunic is old and spotted, threads coming out. But it is a noble standard, the sign that may save us. Always, he thinks of the good of the whole.

The men gather around Salvius as if he were a standard that will rally our courage. He listens to Tom and Benedict tell our story—how I saved them from the snow overhang, how I urged them off the road when I saw the slavers, the bandits, in the distance.

"Well, at least you had the village idjit along to save your pox-ridden arses," Salvius laughs.

Benedict is telling the tale now, and when the moment comes that we find Cole freezing in the woods, Salvius stalks over and approaches the lad.

"Oh, nephew, I am so glad to see you alive then. I was thinking for two whole days that you were one of those who had burned."

He gives Cole a rough clinch, an embrace that speaks of tough times they both have shared.

Then I think of Nell, and of the warmth Salvius showed her. She trusted him. When he told us all that she was dead, I saw him cry like a babe. What embraces did he give Nell before her death?

Can he help me find the truth, in this maze of lies?

Salvius shakes his golden head again, as if to dismiss my unspoken questions. "With Hob gone, who leads you?" he asks.

The men glance at one another. I have led them this morn, but no one would point to me.

There is a nickering noise in my ear. The mare is asking for help. No one else is taking care of the enervated horse, and I know that she may be worth more than treasure to us on the road ahead. So I scrape foam off the old mare's hide with a bone comb from the saddlebags. Then I wrap her heaving sides in a blanket. I squeeze a wet cloth in her mouth to moisten her tongue and rub her legs to get rid of the sweat before it can freeze. Her legs still tremble with the day's long exertion, but I think if she can walk now, the hard run will not cramp or cripple her.

Liam helps me now, walking the mare in long circles, cooling her slowly so that she will not founder in her own freezing breath.

Salvius helps pull the cart back onto the track, tells Tom where to tie the rope anew, how to balance the load, and how fast we can move this day. I feel a weight lift off our shoulders as I watch him work. Salvius was the one who befriended Nell, he is the one who rescues me with wood or fire or with food when I need it. With his help, we will confront those murderers who took our children from us.

But Geoff is having none of it. "Look what happen'd to Hob. He's a dead man, he is, and I'm not dying alongside my boy out here. My other children need me."

"Goddammit, Geoff—we can avenge our sons!" shouts Bene. "If we follow—"

"Follow those ripe bastards?" says Geoff. "With their swords an' horses?"

"I hear my son—he calls to me!" calls Tom suddenly, and his voice is strange, unearthly. His shatterpated gabble sends a chill up my spine. "It's 'is blood, he cries out to me!"

"It's alright, Tom," says Salvius.

But Tom puts his hands in the air in a great gripping motion, as if he grapples with an enemy we cannot see. Then he glares around at all of us.

"A dream come to me in the night!" Tom points at the road ahead, his face quivering. "A vision of my son being tortured by a Jew with the fiery darts of the devil 'isself!"

My French father had words for such talk. *Avoir le diable au corps. Non compos mentis.* Yet I shiver, for I had a vision too, one of fire and doom and death. And I woke to something worse than imagination. My son is never coming home.

Liam spits on the ground. "Take that for yer visions an' schemes. I'll go home with Geoff. And I'll be takin' my son with me." He strides to the cart and seizes a protruding foot in his hand.

Benedict points at him, a barking, pained laugh in his mouth. "See, there you go—you'll repeat your crime, eh?" I wish I knew more of what Liam did, of what Benedict fears.

Then Tom cries out, "We follow that villain! I can scent that Jew now, I tell you. An angel guides us on this track, on the path of the murderers!"

"Aye, those men are the ones we will accuse," says Salvius. He crosses himself fervently.

Liam laughs, a cackling mirth. "An' that's enough for you? Mad Tom's damn'd vision? A villain who Tom can smell? What is Tom here, a feckin' bloodhound? How's that going to help us 'gainst arm'd bandits?"

Tom's keening cry cuts through the din. "Find them Jews, track them down!"

Liam hauls back on his son's foot, and the bodies shifts in the cart. "An' what are we going to do when we catch them, eh?"

Salvius grips Liam's shoulder hard. "We'll make them pay," he says. "We'll force 'em to pay for our losses. You and I, Liam—all of us—we've known each other a long time. You can trust me—they can't take from us without payment."

Liam shrugs off Salvius's hand. "Gold?" His voice rises in agony. "Feckin' gold? How much gold is enough for my son's life?"

"Kill 'em all!" bellows Tom. He shoves wildly at the cart.

"Ah'm going to bury my boy," says Liam. "Right here, on the hillside, where he can see the country. I don't care what you do, or why you're here, but Ah'm here to bury my son."

Salvius comes close to Liam, speaking loudly as the wind rises around us, blowing snow in our faces. "I'm here 'cause you're stupid enough to be on the road with your history—with your life debt hanging over your head! So I must feckin' watch you, Liam, an' take care of you."

Liam shrinks back ashamed, as Salvius shakes fresh snowflakes off his hair. "I'm here to take care of fools."

"Right he is," says Benedict stridently.

Salvius's voice has the ring of authority. "Quiet, Bene." Salvius looks from side to side, his gaze taking in Liam and Geoff, Cole, and me. "You all hear now, our only chance on this road is to be together—an' you agreed to leave the village, didja not?"

Liam nods sullenly, rubbing a mark on his arm. "But I don't see how—"

"Goddammit!" Salvius's voice is loud with anger. "I swore to the village that we would track down that villain who did this to us all. And that we would seek justice, come heaven or hell. So we're keepin' all the bodies in the cart, you hear? You want your son, you go with us. You don't want him, you can go home. Go on now."

Salvius points down the distant empty road, back toward the village. No one moves. After a long moment, he turns and points the other direction, up the road after the bandits. "That's your vision of blood an' terror, Tom. Those are the fiends who killed our lads—I followed those bandits, and I will fight 'em! We will free Hob, and we will get our vengeance!"

The men gape at him. *He was following the bandits? He means to fight them?*

Salvius looks at us, like some great lord surveying his serfs. The wind comes again. We all squint as skeins of snow are lifted off the ground, flung against us like sleet. Finally, the wind dies down.

"Goddammit, quit mucking about," Salvius growls. He tousles Geoff's hair and strikes Liam lightly on the back, a false heartiness in his blows. He points at the cart. "Git on the trail—put your backs into it—git this damn thing back on the road, my friend."

Liam moves forward sullenly. Gently, he pushes his son's foot back in among the rest and wipes his face clean of tears.

Salvius points ahead. "To the monastery," he says. "That is where we will plead our case. We must accuse those bandits there, seek God's justice against those bastards."

Cole glances at me, but I do not let my face betray my thoughts.

Even if those bandits were the ones who made the wrong-way tracks into the village in the night, I know they didn't set the flames. Yet those men knew Hob, so perhaps they knew Benedict too. Some conspiracy wraps around us like a spider's web.

By the time we lift the cart out of the gorse bushes and cow-gouged hollow, the sun has fallen low in the sky, and the White Road has been stomped and ground into a matted brown mire by our efforts. We have lost many hours here.

Even Salvius breathes heavily as we finish our labors, and finally the iron wheels are turned toward the south again.

It is the middle of the afternoon. And I know the clarity of the winter air deceives us—we have many furlongs to go before we sleep in the Cluny monastery.

Yet all of us have visions of shelter and warmth, and hot food. So we race the sunlight, down the long hill, hoping to reach the gates of the monastery before nightfall.

We are helped by the pulling of Salvius's smithy horse, which is hitched haphazardly to the whippletree. The mare has a weight and a grit to her, and on the hills she helps the heavy load move faster. Yet on the open stretches, the truth of her weariness comes out. She staggers from side to side, as if in mockery of our own exhausted plight.

Salvius strides back and forth on his long legs, urging us to greater effort like a master of arms, his blond hair disheveled by sweat and streaks of frozen mud. He works beside his mare, holding her back and pushing her forward by turns, as need drives us. His voice is deep and powerful—the sound of it inspires and renews.

Then one wheel sticks in a deep rut, and as Benedict is pushing, Salvius comes up and tells him to wait for the count. "Hold then," he says. "We'll all push together."

In that instant, Benedict tilts his head back and lets go of the cart. His cuffed hat falls to the snow. His balding pate is dappled by sunburn and long labor, and he stares at Salvius, breathing heavily. He does not seem to notice his hat is gone.

"Damn'd priest's son." A warning rasp of anger is in his tone. "Is that how it is with you then?"

"What's that?" says Salvius. He does not pause in his circuit of the cart, preparing the wheels to turn under his guidance.

Benedict raises his voice. "You have the nerve—telling all of us what to do, and you never lift a feckin' finger!"

I wince. As any man can see, Salvius is working as hard as any of us. He may be fresher to the work, but he is not lacking in exercise.

Salvius stares at Benedict a moment, and then he grins broadly, as if he's heard the best part of a long tale. His politic good cheer has always struck me as the work of a master, appearing like a sunbeam in a thundercloud.

"God bless ye," he shouts heartily. "Tell me how 'tis then, Bene! A pox on me too, eh?"

"Aye—a feckin' bloody pox on you," mutters Benedict.

"A pox, eh?" Salvius leans close and murmurs to him.

Benedict's knuckles tighten and go white. He hisses under his breath at Salvius. "I know while I was gone you tried to have Sophia. I know you want her, but you cannot steal her from—"

Then Salvius whispers words I cannot hear. Benedict's face flushes, and he glances from side to side like a trapped beast. He sees me looking, and I move past as if I did not notice.

The men are pulling hard, and I seem to be the only one who notices this moment of fear in Benedict. In my own mind, I urge Salvius on. I hope that with his authority, he will be the one to question Benedict closely, to find the truth. I want him to uncover the villain—to unveil whatever plot envelops us in darkness and confusion.

Salvius steps back, rubbing away a mud mark on his face. Benedict still seems shaken. Then Salvius reaches out, holds a hand on Benedict's shoulder. "Damn'd women always have us by the bollocks, no? A pox on all of them!" He claps Benedict on the back in hearty acclaim.

Benedict's worried face changes and relaxes. "Let's get to the monastery ahead," he says. "Strike a blow on this stuck wheel, wouldja?"

Salvius puts his shoulder down and holds the wheel. Benedict pauses and looks at Salvius uncertainly. But then he heaves the wheel out, and the axle emerges from the rut. The cart rolls again.

✠

We walk for hours along the top of a ridge, where the curve of the road is swept bare by wind. Now, as we descend from the hills, we enter a deep dale. The surrounding bowl of hills shelters the valley, and the sunlight rarely shines here in the winter months.

Months of snow have fallen and frozen, fallen and frozen, in this vale of shadow. The road is a river of ice, slick and unforgiving, a harsh sweep of white iron, cold enough to freeze any uncovered flesh to its surface.

The cart slides from side to side, the horse's hooves giving way as she shambles forward. We slow to a crawl as the monastery lights glimmer ahead in the falling dusk.

We struggle up that last stretch of open road as if swimming through an ice-choked river. Still far ahead, it seems to me, there is a square opening—a gap of light where we can see a fire, steaming pots, a long pathway. A great house, it appears, in this uncertain light—a mansion of many rooms.

We must make it to the monastery before dark, for outside the walls, we could be caught at any moment by the men who took Hob.

We can see others camped outside, perhaps the permanent camp of outliers that accretes to the lee side of the great walls of castles and abbeys alike. The mimers, jongleurs, and landless, lordless folk—all who ply a trade outside the sacred ground. The fog around the monastery is lit by their small rude fires.

We see men at the gates now too, moving the great doors from their resting spots, setting the night watch.

Benedict cups his hands around his mouth and calls "Allo!" to those closing the great gate. Cole joins him in shouting. Salvius briskly slaps his steed. The piebald horse trots unsteadily faster for a moment, as do we all.

The doors swing ponderously. The slamming thud of sound comes moments later, and then the monastery is closed.

We are but distant shadows in the gloam.

CHAPTER 10

In an exhausted half-dream, I unhitch the smithy mare. She has known me long from our smithy work and she trusts me. I do the work I have done so often in the village: I wipe her down and hobble her so she won't leave our camp. Then I give her water and I kick at the snow until I uncover some parched bits of grass for her to graze.

When I return to the fire pit, Salvius gives me a grateful look, but he does not speak to me, as there is something tight and anxious in the air. Salvius pulls Cole to his side, and the boy's face falls, an angry sneer evident in his narrowed eyes.

I had not been listening to the men while I worked with Salvius's horse. Now I rouse myself and hear angry voices, and then Salvius giving effuse apology.

"I know right well he was your hero today, an' for that deserves your praise. But I'm also right sorry that Cole took these things from you—a thief unmasked, I say. An' here to you, your lot as was taken, Benedict."

Salvius hands Benedict a pair of knitting needles, made of wood and varnished in nut oil. They are the ones Benedict sometimes uses around the fire.

"An' here is yours too, my friend." Salvius holds out to Liam a broad dull arrowhead. It is a thing precious to Liam, from his past. I can well imagine he has not missed it yet, and it would be easy to thieve.

Then Salvius gives to Tom a small clasp-knife, one made with his clever hands.

All these things Salvius says he found in Cole's pack—things taken from us the first night, while we slept. It seems all the time he has traveled with us, Cole has thieved.

My heart sinks. *Ah, Cole, poor Cole, a thief. Why?* I clench at the ring on the chain around my neck. It is the only precious thing I have, but it was well hidden. And perhaps Christian's old boots. Those are precious too. Cole took nothing of mine on this road from Duns.

Yet still I am suspicious. For Cole carries a fresh burn, hidden from all of us, a burn my keen eyes have seen gleaming red and angry on his neck. It tells that he was there the night my boy died, and he knows who else was there. He was about to tell me somewhat of that night. And he will, God willing—he will tell me the truth. But now he has proven himself a liar and a cheat. A thief. *So how am I to believe any words he tells me? How am I to trust?*

Salvius seems to share my indignation. His face is grim and sad, his bright eyes dark, his jaw clenched. He is often humiliated by this lad's misdeeds, for he is the lad's uncle in name if not in truth.

The men also cast dark looks Cole's way, and one or two kick at him as they go back to their bedrolls, pushing their possessions deep into their cloaks or packs.

The meat of a fresh-killed coney sizzles on the open flames alongside winter turnips. But I can find little strength to eat; all the marrow has gone out of my bones. The only one here who seemed to know the truth, who wanted to help me, a liar and a thief.

Benedict waits a moment by the empty fire pit. I cannot hear what he is saying to Salvius, but I can see supplication in the look upon his face.

As Salvius listens to Bene, a certain conceit comes over him. Always, he has carried something of nobility about him, and that false blessing we bear—the torn and tattered tunic—seems to give Salvius pride of place in our troupe. I, for one, am glad that it is Salvius who bears this tunic. Those from outside our village often mistake him for a noble when he walks about at the fair. It is clear that we once again have a leader.

Salvius directs the guard for the night, the shifts all will hold. The small, weaker ones—Geoff and I—are given short shifts. Geoff is at Matins, and I am after him, in the early morning, at the hour of Lauds.

I sit with the rest by the warmth of the fire, but my thoughts are drawn to Cole, who was our hero and is now our outcast. I turn to look at him skulking under the cart.

The wheel of the cart behind that forlorn lad reminds me of that great wheel that Fortune turns. One day, a king rides out to battle, his forces following in splendid array. The next, that king lies in a ditch, cheek by jowl with peasant folk.

The wheel of Fortune turns one way and another, taking us to the heights or to the depths. That is the great wheel on which we all turn, tied to destinies that move up or down at the whim of God above.

Stars flicker above, points of bright ice in a dark river. I pull a heavy sheepskin around my legs and stretch my feet toward the fire. Despite the cold, Liam plays his flute, the sound whistling through the night. Soon my eyes are heavy, my head nodding.

I open my eyes at the deep melodious baritone of Salvius's voice telling a tale. Liam's flute is silent now. I have heard Salvius tell many tales on market days; he is known for his memory of wandering minstrels and mummers who visit us at Whitsunday and through Midsummer. Salvius is a mockingbird: he can give a fair charade of the rhythmic tones of any wandering bard or any noble of the Royal Court.

In this darkness, his eyes catch the light like a cat in the night.

"Oh Christ, our God, how marvelous your name!" Salvius raises his hands like a priest, declaiming in scholarly tones, blessing the remnants of our mean little meal, in a priest's words. "By the mouth of our children, you give us your great bounty, so that we may declare your great worthiness, just as our children do today..."

I glance at the profane cart. If our children in their laughing life declared God's worthiness, what do their tortured bodies declare now?

But Salvius continues. "I tell thee now of a holy saint of youth, of Hugh of Lincoln..."

Young Hugh of Lincoln. That old drinking story of the pure little lad taught by his mam to pray the priest's way, in Latin. And the hocum-pocum that he parroted so well—that old *Hoc est enim corpus meum*—it was enough of an excuse for some jealous lad to push him in a well.

A sentimental story, and a bloody one.

"God willing, just as young Hugh of Lincoln did his mam proud, so all our boys will."

It is maddening to me to suspect what Salvius knows of Bene and of Hob, and yet not to know for certain. I have to fit the pieces together in the dark. *What was Benedict's plan with the lads? Where was he taking them? What signs of the murderer has Salvius seen, and how will we know when we find him?*

Now Salvius tells a story about another secret. For it goes without saying that when young Hugh's swollen body was found, no bully admitted the deed; instead, those hapless Jews were blamed for killing this widow's son. Every drunken sot knows the sordid tales of the Jewish rite of sacrifice, the blood bond the evil ones among them pledge each year by killing Christian children. At every drunken party, somebody drags out this story and lay again young Hugh's death at the Jew's feet.

I sigh. Christian would inquire of the truth of this tale. He would plague the teller with questions.

Benedict interrupts the story now, but not with questions, with accusations. Bene tries to draw Salvius into argument again.

"Sal, you need to know that Geoff here, son of a buggering fool that he is—"

"Nah," shouts Geoff. "You were the one who let them go from—"

"You're the villain!" shouts Tom.

The accusations fly back and forth across the fire pit. But Salvius does not enter the fray. He listens, and finally he stands, holding out his wide blacksmith hands in peace.

"The villain is not here. But in front of the Abbot here, we will ask for justice." All stop to listen to Salvius's loud voice. "We will seize on those bandits who killed our boys! We will keep our watch strong this night, so those villains do not come on us unaware."

"Where did those bastards with the cart take Hob?" asks Liam. "Did they go into the monastery?"

"No," says Benedict. "They would not dare go to the Abbot—we have a grievance, they do not. If they went in there, they would be accused. They cannot steal a man."

"But if they served a Lord of the realm," ventures Salvius, "if they carried a Royal crest, then all their acts would be judged lawful."

"Feck that!" cries Tom. "Lawful, my bloody arse! They took Hob, they tried to take Cole, they—"

"Aye!" agrees Benedict. "But we must hope they went beyond the monastery. We must hope they carry no Lord's blessing."

Liam speaks up now, his voice hoarse and fearful. "And we must think how to approach the Abbot, so that we are not accused ourselves."

There is a sudden silence. All here have known the authorities to make judgments that are found later to be wrong.

Salvius nods. "We must tell our story in a way that ensures our safety."

Tom mutters something low, and then he speaks aloud. He is not drunk this time, and his words are crystal clear. "Aye, my mother did not tell her story the right way. She was not guilty, but she died, you know. She died innocent."

I do not know Tom's story, and I want to hear more, but Salvius ignores Tom.

"We will find a way to talk to the Abbot, appeal to authority," replies Salvius. "Perhaps at the monastery, perhaps even take our grievance to the Throne—" He holds up a great strong hand, forestalling Tom's interruption. "And we will tell them true how poor villagers such as ourselves are beset on all sides by villains who steal our children."

Liam claps in acclaim. "Hear, hear!"

"Yes," says Salvius. "Those bastards who took Hob would even steal and sell our children as servants and serfs."

Bene looks up with sudden attention, as Salvius continues. "These many villains steal riches from our long labor. They steal always from our fields and our livelihoods."

Liam grinds his teeth. "True it is, true. That is why I did my crime, that is why—"

I lean forward, trying to hear what Liam did.

But then Salvius speaks in the powerful voice of a commanding general, the rich tones of a lord rolling off his tongue: "We will fight! And this last blow—our children burned—it is a final blow that cannot be borne! Those bandits and murderers always work for some lord—and too long the lords have oppressed us. The shackles of those lords are the last of the long grievances I would take to the Crown! I will cast my plea before the King, and beg his judgment of these villains! We are oppressed on all sides, but we are not beaten. We are afflicted, but we do not despair!"

The men are breathless with his boldness, but I have long seen the connection between these many wounds. Like me, Salvius thinks beyond the moment, beyond the present grief. He makes a piece of all the pains we suffer, and this last, most grievous blow.

It is close to treason, this accusation he will launch, yet this is the reason Salvius came to us on the road. He came to command us, to give us hope and purpose.

"We will fight," he says. "We will fight, even against kings and nobles, I tell you!"

A log falls in the fire. The sparks rise in bloom. The men are silent in their thoughts.

"The story," says Geoff at last. "Tell the rest of the story of Li'l Hugh."

"Aye," says Salvius hoarsely. He wipes his eyes and clears his throat. He drinks. Finally, the deep baritone tones roll off his tongue again.

"As you all know, Li'l Hugh sang even in death. Even when his soul was gone from his body, he still sang praises to the Virgin. His mouth opened, his dead throat singing..."

Only a few years after his body was found, and already they are saying that this Hugh's death was a miracle, that his body sang like a martyr's after death. Someday, perhaps they will tell that our children sang to us along this hellish winter road, joyous at our sacrifice, hymns sounding from their frozen throats.

I feel dizzy and chilled in my soul. My son is dead, there will not be any singing. Nevermore.

"But there are those who do not love the sacred songs," says Salvius. "Those who would take small ones, God's own children, an' sell them to the Jews for sacrifice. Those are the ones who are curs'd forever!"

The men shout in acclaim. Salvius's eyes flicker across them, across Tom and Benedict together. "Yes, curs'd, I say. For God knows the truth in the hearts, in those who sell their souls, who reap a harvest from those small voices of innocence!"

Salvius takes another swallow of water, and he grimaces at the icy cold, as if he feels the same chill that is in my bones.

"See, the town I speak of had let those Jews remain—they had kept the Jewry for their foul usury and villainous money. To sell the bones and drink the blood."

I roll myself tight in my blanket and listen close as I shiver in the chill.

"The Jews, my friends, they are Satan's hornet nest... In this town I speak of, there was a Jew woman, a temptress, and in this village, all the Jews lived along one street..."

In fact, this was once true of Duns village. I have heard there were three Jews who lived there once upon a time.

But there is something in Salvius's tale that seems to answer a question. Some thread in a pattern I am trying to work out.

I glance at Benedict's grim weathered face. *What does he think of this story, since his wife, Sophia, has Jewish blood?* There is no expression that I can read as he takes his hat off and rubs his round bald head. His face is a cipher in the dim light.

"Through that street of Jews, men might ride or wander at will, for that street was free and open at either end," Salvius says with a wink. Then I catch a vicious chuckle from Tom at the double meaning: there is a slur here on Sophia. How easily these men find fault with their wives and sisters. Holy Virgin or cursed whore. There are no other pictures they can paint, it seems.

Yet there is a design in their words I would do well to understand. A pattern made of fire, and death, and some hidden hatred. A story still being woven in Tom's vision of his son, Geoff's suspicion,

Liam's old crime, Benedict's many lies, and Cole's thefts. Sophia the Jew who hungers for devotion: Salvius now slandering her. *Why? This tells me what?*

I have missed the connection, and so the picture does not fit together yet. I cannot see through the world's twisting, darksome mirror.

I weary of Salvius's tale. I stand and stalk back toward my tent hovel in the snow, but I can still hear Salvius's sonorous tones, his voice resounding across our small campsite, as he recites the words memorized each spring when the priest visits our village.

"Oh cursed folk of Herod—them damn'd Jews! Murder will out! Martyrdom shines bright as rubies—sing together now, prove to heaven that your child will come to the Virgin's holy lap!"

From my bedroll, I can see Salvius standing now, dragging the tired men up with him. "Let us sing to heaven!"

Tom leans over and kicks poor sleeping Cole awake. Salvius tells Tom to stop, but then, when wakes, Salvius calls to him. "Sing my lad, sing for yer sins—and perhaps Mary in heaven will forgive your many lies."

Cole's voice is quavering at first, rusty with fear of punishment and thick with sleep. Slowly, the rest of them join as well, their voices grinding out the old tune, their faces glimmering with tears in the firelight.

> Alma Redemptoris Mater, quae pervia caeli
> Porta manes, et stella maris, succurre cadenti . . .

I hunger to see the pattern, to fit the threads of truth together, to see through the lies. *Help me, Alma Virgin Mother, to know the truth.*

In the dark night, I close my eyes and I swear I can hear Edward's youthful tenor joining with the voices of the men beside the fire, his voice ringing in my ears.

Alma Redemptoris Mater, quae pervia caeli
Porta manes, et stella maris, succurre cadenti...

In my reverie, I imagine myself with Edward, and at our side, Christian, our child. As my mind opens to the shades of night, I see Edward waiting on the open road ahead, bearing the bright livery of his house, holding a white horse for his lady. For me, his love. And he is singing too:

Loving Mother of a Savior, hear thou thy people's cry...

Star of the deep and portal of the sky!
Mother of Him who Thee made from nothing made.
Sinking we strive and call to thee for aid...

CHAPTER II

I WAKE TO A muttering in the frigid darkness. A man leans over the cart, speaking in a voice almost too low to hear. It is Tom, in a hoarse and furtive tone.

"Son," he whispers to the corpses. "I know who done this to you... It's the same crime what was done before... It's him who lit the fires..." And then Tom's voice sinks, and although I strain to hear, I cannot make out the next words.

He speaks more plainly after a moment, his voice rising in a whispered promise. "I swear to you on my mother's grave, you will be aveng'd. This time, I'll make that witch pay for your death. By Christ's blood—"

The crackle of frost falling from Liam's blanket rings sharp as he rolls over next to the fire. Tom goes silent, his oath unfinished; he stalks away to piss in a snowbank, as if that were his intention all along.

No one else stirs in this glacial hour. My cloak is frozen stiff around my nose and mouth. I lie with my eyes open in the pitch darkness. I cannot sleep now.

Tom was sober, and he speaks of a witch. Does he know something true, despite his blathering? And did he mean a man? Liam perhaps, repeating a past crime? *Or did Tom mean a woman?*

At that thought, a bowstring quivers in my breast, a twinge of fear that I will be discovered and accused as a witch, like Nell. I bury that fear, as I have so often before. For there are others who could be accused as witches. Men and women. Many of them.

And perhaps Benedict thought of this too when his house burned. I now think he came on this journey to save Sophia from accusation, as a Jew and murderess.

But now here we are, at a monastery. Benedict and Salvius are planning carefully, to tell the Abbot the story of our grief. They will demand justice, recompense, and perhaps even burial in hallowed ground.

Their story will not include Tom's witch. They will tell a different story. All of us have stories that we don't want to tell.

Hob had a scheme with our lads, but he was discovered—he made some bargain that turned on him.

Benedict made a plan with Hob, the plan went awry, and he's lied about it. But could he really have burned the house, with his own son in it? Even to conceal a villainous crime, why would he do such a thing? And I think Benedict accuses Geoff of buggering the boys, to keep Geoff quiet.

Tom cries out in pain, but he makes an oath to his dead son. That is not the act of a murderer.

Now my house of suppositions falls apart, like the straw it is made of. For Salvius knows something of Benedict's plan, and Tom knows a portion of the truth as well, but neither dares to tell. Tom has lost a son, and if Benedict killed him, Tom would be the first to call him villain. But he does not.

Cole is here out of sorrow for his friends. He is the only one of his age to survive, and he failed to stop their deaths, and he means to atone for that.

I turn in my bedroll. Near at hand is Cole's sleeping face. His eyes are shut, and his breath comes in tiny gasps. In this half-light of early dawn, his cheeks are flushed with deep sleep. Yet I would wake Cole, to try to get the truth out of him, except for the fact that someone might overhear him speaking to me.

I remember Cole and Christian as small lads, playing in the woods beside the stream. And Nell watched them for me. I remember her soft voice in the forest gloam, singing to me. For she was the one I'd sensed following me in the woods. She had tracked me, and fed my little Christian when I went sick or lame. I remember her quick eyes, her soft strength. *How much did she suffer before she died?*

My friend Nell. Gone these many days now. And she too never told me her story, her secrets.

I had settled in the village, bellows-blower for the smithy, woodcutter for his insatiable fires, jack-of-all-unsavory-trades. I had learned the rhythm of the village, and the villagers had grown used to my presence. They had lost some men to the plague over the last two years, and so Salvius's need for me was clear. Others appreciated my eagerness for work as well. I did scutwork, built sheds, slaughtered chickens, and cut wood and I was paid in food or barter.

Somehow, I kept my son alive while I did all these things day and night. He still wanted to breast-feed, but I could only give him that sustenance when we were deep in the woods.

Once, months after my arrival, I was hidden in an alder copse when I sensed her again, that watcher in the woods. I could hear the muted whisper of her footsteps sliding softly on rotten leaves and old mulch, smell the scent of lavender and mint. I wondered if she was holding a bow on me, an arrow nocked and ready.

I lifted Christian from his sleeping place and crept deeper into the woods until I found a darker, more hidden place—an old cedar, its pungent branches circled like a fallen nest. I needed to nurse my son.

From that spot, I finally caught sight of her: a slight and careful figure, tiptoeing around the fairie rings and fallen logs, plucking carefully the purple loosestrife, the wild rose and thyme. She was the only other soul I'd ever seen so far afield, for this was where wolves and wild boar roamed. Only those of us with great need traveled here; in fact, I had thought that only I came so far, so deep. She was a woman my age, but small as a stripling lass, her hair thin and bright as flyaway straw. I watched her for a long hour and thought I had escaped unobserved.

As the early spring day flattened into dusk, I made my way back, a load of heavy wood upon my back, Christian sleeping in my arms. A little wind rushed through the elms, a chiffchaff called, the scent of rain was on the air.

Not yet in the village, not on the commons, I saw a little light in a wattled house built in a dark hollow. A dog barked, short and sharp, and the woman appeared.

No arrow on a bowstring. No secret spy.

She tripped gaily down the path from her abode. Then she spied my worried face and, with quiet solemnity, nodded toward the house.

Inside, I found that the evening joined us, for there was something unusual there—holes in the walls covered with thin oilcloth. The dusky twilight outside suffused the space, and dust motes drifted in the warm light. She gave me a cup of broth to drink.

"I saw you nurse your babe," she said simply. "You're a woman, but no one else in t' village knows it."

I stared at her and wondered if I yet had the power of speech. My tongue was still swollen after all this time, for I'd cut it straight to the root when I'd fallen on that stone. Now it swelled anew in my mouth, filling the space with fear.

"No need to talk, lass." She smiled. "No need to fear."

We took our supper there in charmed silence. Christian woke, and then—with no secrets—I nursed once more.

"Do you need an herb to stop the milk for good?"

Numbly, I nodded. She reached up to the ceiling beams, where herbs hung drying. She pulled down dried sage and sorrel. Then she gave me these to boil in water. By that time, I had placed her: she was Nell, the one who would prepared tinctures and brew, for all the villagers.

She wrapped more herbs in larger leaves. "Soak your breast in vinegar and caraway. Come here any time you need to give 'im suck."

She leaned close and kissed my forehead, a tiny spot of dampness on my brow. "My lips are sealed, upon my grave." She laughed, a light and tuneful sound.

After that day, often on our way from the woods to the village common, Christian and I stopped at Nell's little place. We would greet her dog, and pass the time in silence as Nell shelled peas or tended to her herbs, or fed her brewing cauldron with hops and fresh barley.

The herbs she gave me helped me wean, and soon the lad took his milk from a rag dipped in a bowl of goat's milk. There was swelling and some pain, but my dugs went dry in time.

✠

Spring grew into summer, and the rhythm of my life now included Nell. I learned that her secret thyme and mint beds were deep in the woods, out by the chuckling stream that disappeared underground.

She gathered plants she needed every day, and she was as a child who gathers flowers in May, setting them in bundles, choosing with caprice, singing to them, naming each plant and leaf with fondness. She danced in the sunlight and the shade. Even watching her a moment, my spirits lifted.

Once, though, I came to her croft on a dark day, and she was curled in the straw on the floor, refusing to open her eyes. "They're gone," she murmured over and over again. "All gone, all gone forever."

I sat and waited, while Christian nursed.

Nell whispered low. "Ah, my babies, all gone. Ah me."

She repeated those words like a rosary, like a spell that would hold her safe. And she said one more thing that day. "I promis'd meself that I'd live as if my family never drew breath a'tall. I'd never dwell on their deaths."

It seemed to me then that she strove for happiness as a bird beats its wings against the darkness, just to stay aloft.

When I came back next day, there was a smile on her face, a skip in her step, and nary a word of pain. We never spoke of the dark day again.

All through that year, the days were dappled light and grand. Nell whispered and giggled in my ear, like a small child.

"Come," she said, on a sudden. "Let us dance!" And she whirled me around like a fairy in the woods, laughing, giggling, carefree.

Breathless, she flung herself to the ground and plucked a daisy. "'E loves me, 'e loves me not, 'e loves me..."

She looked up at me then and blushed. "'E has always been kind to me," she explained. "And a handsome one, 'e is!"

She put down the flower. "Y'know," she said seriously, "he comes by my croft, he does, and buys herbs and beer from me. As if I'm a merchant just like any other, and he stays and talks betimes."

I gave her a quizzical look. *Who?*

"Ah've got a sweetheart," she said. "Ah'll show you who he is." She cleared a spot on the forest floor and then drew a picture, stroking the outline of a firm jaw. She used blue petals for his eyes. Then she found straight stalks of dried grain for his yellow hair.

"You know who 'tis?" she whispered to me. I nodded. Handsome Salvius, my employer and patron.

"Truth to tell," she said. "I think about being with him—for it's hard alone."

It must have been hard indeed. A man has the blessing of God to rule. But a woman without a master has no right to rule over wealth, or beast, or land. Thus, Nell had no legal right to sell or barter with a man.

"Sal wants me now, y'know, but I won't take him into my bed—I told him no the other day. Ah've told him so. I won't do that anymore, not any more of my days." Nell's eyes grew wistful then.

Why did she refuse him her body? Did she not allow a man to come into her bed because of her life before? I never knew. Although she told him no, I wonder if she was lonely in her cruck house and her bed of straw.

"I live as a man, alone and free, y'know," Nell always said. "I'm not bound to any other. And that is how I'll die, I guess."

I would not live in our village as a woman. At first, I planned to stay only until Christian was old enough to travel. Then, as one year turned into five and five into ten, I told myself I would stay until Christian was old enough to claim his birthright. But in truth, I think I stayed because of my friend Nell and the companionship we shared.

The rough darkness of my memory comes over me, a wave that chills me.

Does Salvius miss her now, as I do? I may never know.

I scrabble out from under the cart, turning my bedroll and finding a warm place near the guttering coals of the fire, where Salvius snores. Here, I seek comfort in that deep and roaring sound, like breakers on a distant shore.

Yet I remain cold as the grave, for I know how Nell died.

BOOK II

CHAPTER 12

I WAKE AGAIN AT Lauds, as night blurs into dawn. It is my hour to watch for bandits. I roll over and beat my hands against my sides so that I can feel them again. Then furtively, I check the bindings on my bosom, as is my habit every morning.

But as I sit and lift my arms, my elbow collides firmly with Liam's sleeping face.

He gives a grunt of pain. "Ah—God! What the bloody hell?" he blubbers. His nose is red and leaking, a smashed fruit. Dazed, he reaches up and brings back a wet slurry of blood in his palm.

Hurriedly, I reach for fresh snow and press it into a compress. I try at first to place it on his nose, but he shakes me off. Through sleep-sodden eyes, Liam gives me a bleary grin. I am lucky that always he is quick to forgive.

I grimace in apology, and mime the moment again with my elbow, explaining without words the cause of his pain. Finally, he takes the handful of wet snow and applies it. His fingers leak red and pink for a time, and then the bleeding stops. Liam gives me a mocking snarl and then drifts back to sleep, his breathing jagged.

I leave off the binding of my garments. Instead, I bend my chilly fingers. They are unwieldy as I fumble with the scorched cold sticks in the firepit until I find glowing gleeds buried beneath layers of old ash. The cold catches in my lungs as I blow on the banked coals.

When the thin, wavering smoke finally rises from the fire pit, it becomes a line of gray against the translucent blue of the horizon. Dawn has crept up on us.

I can see, too, that some brave soul inside the monastery is laboring in the same thankless way: a smudge of smoke rises from what I think are the refectory and the kitchens. And I can hear the morning choir preparing for the Lauds Mass. The distant tune is muted on this winter morning, as if it echoes through miles of cold blue water.

Far above, the sky is dark and gray as old ice. The men begin to stir in their bedrolls. Our fire flares bright on a pocket of forgotten pitch, as we wait on the doorstep of the monastery.

When the sounds of early morning prayer cease, four novice monks—garbed in Cluniac white—roll open the great iron gates.

I feel half-alive—I am an uncertain thing on dead limbs tottering forward through the gates with my companions. My soul is parched and weary within me.

Benedict and Salvius talk quietly, still making their plan of how to ask succor of the Abbot, how to speak to our loss, our grief, their accusation of the heinous Jews. It is dangerous ground they tread, but if they tell the story aright, there will be justice in the end.

For now, we find spaces to rest.

The monks give each of us a half-size solitary cell. Mine has a small and unsoiled bedroll, a cracked chamber pot in the corner, and a crucifix on the wall. To my eyes, it is a spacious place. After we leave our things behind, we are taken to the refectory, where we are fed a break-fast of boiled oats with raisins and cracked wheat berries, rich treasures in this deep midwinter. Our group clusters together at one large table, sipping at warm mulled wine sweetened with honey.

Then we wander in different directions. Salvius will go to talk to the Abbot's men, while Benedict goes off to see the church—he says he wants to offer prayers for his son. But as we scatter across the monastery grounds, I am curious to see that Tom seems to be following Benedict. I remember his oath in the night, and I wonder what he wants with Bene.

So as I make my way out of the refectory, I keep close watch on Tom. If he knows anything, this may be the place the truth comes out.

I know this place and its rhythms. Although it is not the abbey I was raised in, it is familiar enough that I can find my way circumspectly through its corridors and byways, and hide here as well as anyone.

When Benedict and Tom come to the great hall of the church, I take a deep breath, for I had forgotten how palatial is that vast dome—like a hollow meadow found in the midst of a grove of ancient trees. The pillars reach up toward heaven into murky depths where great beams are dimly glimpsed and the tiny patterings of a sparrow or a bat echo in the campaniles.

It is as if time has not passed here at all, over the intervening years. The old stones under my feet, the open breadth of the sanctuary, the overrich scent of incense, the great lines of white candles flickering in a winter draught, they are the same. Benedict's footfalls resound on the flagstones of this great cruciform hall.

I hide myself in an alcove before a statue of Mary Magdalene when I hear quick footsteps in the narthex, the heavy stride of Tom. In the cathedral nave, Benedict halts, seeing Tom. I shrink to the shadow behind the statue as Tom seizes Benedict hard.

"What did you do to them? Did you . . ." The rest is indecipherable.

"I only meant to. . ." begins Benedict. "I wanted. . . the gold. Yes, I did."

Tom pushes Benedict against one of the great arching pillars. "But will you swear that you didn't..." His voice goes quiet and then rises again. "Even if I tell the others about how you got your..."

Frustration boils in me, for I am too far away to hear half of what they say: the voices drift in and out in insidious whispers.

"I did not do it. I do not know who did." Benedict's voice quavers, shakes. "Tom, I would not set such a flame. I may be usurious... greedy for her, but..." His voice is a pleading murmur. "Goddam, Tom, for the love of all that is holy—"

I hear another sound then, a strangled moan. I push my head beyond the statue to see. Tom chokes Benedict against the wall—he shakes the man and then flings him aside, a bull catching a dog on its bent horns.

Benedict sags against the wall gasping, his hand rubbing anxiously at his throat.

Now I see why Tom let go of him, why they now bow their heads and stand back. A line of chanting monks processes out of the sanctuary. Tom and Benedict both subside against the wall.

This is my chance to get closer, without them seeing. I am wearing an old gray shift, so I hide myself in the long line of monks. But as I move into their line, there is a face I recognize.

His name comes to me, drawn out of the deep well of the past. Moten, with the small potbelly, the quick mouth, the ferret-like face, and bright and cheery eyes. Brother Moten.

I put my head down quickly, folding my arms like the rest of the monks, willing him not to see my face, not yet. I was last here in this monastery ten years ago, but even after all this time, I remember that Brother Moten is from Yorkshire, trapped here with his country accent, amidst all these cultured Frenchmen. His pinched and narrow face has a bright-eyed and natural Yorkshire expression, like a stoat in the wild.

Those many years ago, I sought him out for advice and shared my confidences with him. He was, perhaps, my friend. Still, he knows my past, and if I say something to him now, my secret could be uncovered.

A shiver of fear runs up my neck, but I when I glance up, Brother Moten is gone, out of sight around the corner of the narthex. Tom and Benedict are nearby now, but as I am moving forward, Tom turns and slinks out of the cathedral. I wait at the back to see what will happen.

Benedict makes his way forward and lights a candle and says a prayer. Then he leaves, but this time I do not follow him.

I cannot tie the pattern together in my mind: I cannot grasp the threads of Tom's deceit, Benedict's scheme, what Geoff suspects, what Cole knows. My mind spins like a whirligig, scattering thoughts adrift.

I can only think of Christian. I can only see his face. His eyes. My loss.

Ahead are the cathedral altars, glimmering gold, seeming to float upward in shafts of light that fall from the open windows, and beyond them the *paradise* of the colonnade, that space between the altar of Christ and the earthly wall. In some greater paradise, does Christian wait beyond the altar? Does he wait for me?

It is Candlemas season, the Purification of the Virgin Mary. I remember well this week—the novices garbed in white, the endless prayers for Mary, the ranks of glowing candles.

I come to the outer altar rail, beyond which I may not pass. Standing racks of burning candles gutter and drip, their sandalwood scent so sweet it is near to rotten.

And now my knees automatically bend, my fingers take hold of an unlit candle, and I dip it forward into the trembling flame. The dark shadow of my arm and the bare white stick of the candle flicker along the nave, across the stained glass, over the altars, and down. And down, and down.

The candle drops out of my hand, cracking apart on the harsh flagstones, and then I am falling too, my knees landing hard on the floor, my arms outstretched. I sink, catching myself on my palms only at the last, as sobs break out of me.

I miss my son. Oh, I miss him so.

I cry, shriek, scream, weep with what sounds like an awful hilarity—great racking sobs, paroxysms of grief that tear out of me unbidden with every gasping breath.

I am stretched in a weeping pietà across the altar rail, inarticulate, when I feel a hand on my shoulder.

I turn.

It is Brother Moten, the monk who knows my face from those many years ago.

I cannot hold myself still as the sobs take me again. I bury my head in Brother Mot's rough monk's habit, my tears soaking through the thin garment. He seems alarmed at first, but then he settles under the wave of my grief. I grip him so tight that I know my fingers will leave bruises in his flesh.

I gulp out misery on his shoulder, a bald grief, an everlasting throb of pain.

When Brother Moten pulls back, I wipe my face with the back of my hand, and pull away the straggling auburn hanks of hair that obscure my sight.

When I glance up at his face, he is looking down. The front of my cloak has fallen open, which would be no great loss except that on this morning, in the midst of the injury I gave to Liam and my own numbed state of mind, I left my bosom unbound. The swelling of my breast can be clearly seen.

And in this man's eyes, I see something worrisome, an appraisal of my femininity in his face. For ten years, my body has not been weighed by a man's gaze like this, and I am unprepared for it. I have not missed it, not at all.

Yet it is clear that regardless of how ugly my face might appear, or how weatherworn from the road, he sees me as I really am. He sees me as a woman.

CHAPTER 13

I REACH UP QUICKLY to close the cloak and conceal my bosom. I smear away the tears and dirt from my face.

"Miriam?" he says. He seems amazed to see my face after all these years.

"Tell me what is wrong," Brother Moten says gently. "What causes you such grief, my sister?"

This Cluniac monk does not remember an old peasant in a man's garb, but a talkative and youthful auburn-haired girl, holding always a tiny child. And I am suddenly fearful of him. For here we are surrounded by educated men, those who read through the puzzles in texts—what if they read the truth in me? I am a fly back in the web now.

"Miriam? Speak to me," says Moten.

Then it comes to me, perhaps I am the spider: perhaps I can use this man's worry and concern to unveil the truth. This Moten trusted me, years ago.

In a fierce moment of hope, I think that Brother Moten will help me unravel the mystery of what happened to Christian and the other boys. The men of the monastery are ecclesiasticals, followers of logic, intercessors for divine truth. When our mystery is presented, the deaths revealed, they will hold a trial, following that thread of truth down any dark hole, wherever it leads. They will ask questions of Cole, Liam, and Benedict. They will find who is true, who is false.

I clear my throat and whisper hoarsely, "I am… disguised, my old friend… I am unable to tell you all the truth now… My voice is not strong." Truth be told, the whisper does hurt my throat; these are the first words that have come out of me since Christian died.

Moten leans close to hear. My words come out as a wisp of sound. "Someone has murdered our children, and the people of our village come to find the truth."

"Ah yes," says Brother Moten. "I had heard we had visitors from a village to the south. But I never expected to find you among them. We must tell the Abbot of this crime and—"

I hold up my hand to stop him from speaking, and he stares at my still-tearstained face. "Brother Moten," I murmur. "You must keep my confidence. To them… to all of them… I am… mute."

"Mute?" says Moten, a puzzled look crossing his face.

"Yes," I whisper. "Swear it. You will not tell another I can speak."

He nods solemnly. "I swear it."

And then he seems to catch himself uncertain and surprised. "But you will really act as mute? You will not speak to others? Not at all?"

I shake my head emphatically. I wipe a finger up and down on my throat—the sign of muteness, as if I have no tongue.

"Ah, you tell them that your tongue was cut out? That is what the villagers think?"

I nod slowly, considering the answer anew. Always it gives me pause, for those who lose their tongues by punishment are traitors and liars all.

Moten stares at my face. "Where is your child now? What happened?"

Where do I start? How can I provoke him to ask questions of the others? Should I tell him of the men who followed us and took Hob? Or should I tell Moten that the person who lit the fire may be traveling with us, as one of our company? Should I warn him of Benedict and his schemes to profit from our boys? Do I tell him that Liam is a fugitive?

I choose to say nothing more. Instead, I simply take his hand. We walk out of the entry apse and into the nave, passing burnished metal and wood screens that divide nine chapels. The open windows are covered with great tapestries made of glass, so that frigid air cannot pass into the hall. Despite this glass and the warm flues that pass under the calefactory during services, it is cold now. Our breath passes out in steamy gusts, clouds lit red and green by the stained light.

Outside the nave, we walk past the scriptorium, the refectory, the sacristy and vestry, until we reach the house of novices. There we pause for a moment, and Moten starts to lead me into the poorhouse, where my party have our cells for the night. He must think I seek my lodgings.

But I pull him to our cart, which rests haphazard against the wall of the monastery. I take the edge of the road-worn sackcloth, fling it back, and show him my son.

Brothers of Cluny emerge from the refectory as Moten calls out, his voice shot through with horror. My companions run toward us too from the lodging house, drawn by Brother Moten's uproar, his weeping and his outrage loud for all to hear.

I had thought to continue our quiet conversation, to show Brother Moten the evidence and speak to him of what I knew. I would point at Cole's scar, and I would tell him of Benedict. In my own mind, he would soberly nod and then he would do what I would ask him to do.

Brother Moten would be the inquisitor, and Tom would break on the rack of his lashing questions, and Liam too. In the end, Benedict and his accomplices—whoever they were—would answer for the truth.

But Brother Moten does not do these careful, thoughtful things; he is woven of a different cloth. Instead of pondering and inquiring, he is dismayed and distraught by the sight of so many dead. He calls out, hailing all far and wide to come and view this tragedy. And when many of the Cluniac brothers and my fellow travelers gather around, our attempts at telling the story go awry.

Liam tries to explain. "We take them to the Jews—"

"Not to the Jews!" says Salvius. "We take them to the Abbot and the King."

"Yet you have left them unburied, unblessed, unsanctified?" asks Moten, breathing heavily, his voice hoarse from shouting.

"An' how else are we to claim justice for the crime?" replies Salvius. "Their souls will not sleep in peace. They will not rest until justice is done against that Jew."

Moten stares at him, his bright eyes blinking rapidly. "A Jew did this, then?"

Benedict rushes forward, quick as a dog answering a hunter's call.

"Who else woulda done such a thing?" Bene says. "We woke in that hellish dawn to find our boys burned to death, and who else but a Jew would set such a fire? Who else but a witch and a Jew to set a fire?"

"A sacrifice, dontcha know?" adds Tom uncertainly. "A sacrifice to them Jews' pagan gods—"

A look of confusion spreads across Moten's face. "Jews with pagan gods? That has little sense to it. Leaving such children unburied is wrong beyond—"

I burn with frustration. I had thought to bring the truth here, but now there are just raised voices and uproar.

Tom steps in front of me, his heavy arms pushing me back. "Whatcha been tellin' 'im, eh, Mear?" Tom barks at me. "You been fillin' his ears with lies, is that it?"

"You feckin' idjit," says Liam. "How can mute Mear talk to a bloody monk?"

Benedict throws up his hands. "Well, what the hell is the monk doin' here then, disturbin' our boys, tell me that? What the hell was Mear doing, showing him our grief?"

Liam takes hold of my shoulder and turns me back. "He meant nothin' by it—didja, Mear?"

Brother Moten stares at me. "Mear? He? Who?" I curse his slow mind as his eyes widen at the behavior of those around me who so blithely treat me as a man.

Salvius slides in from the side, unctuous and ingratiating. "Ayuh, don't let ol' Mear, my smithy helper, bother you none. He's an ol' mute. We can take care of our own. Why dontcha just leave these boys alone—we bring them to demand justice, I tell you."

Brother Moten sighs and shakes his head. "So, you did not bring them here for burial?"

Salvius shrugs. "Only if the Abbot will honor our demands. If not, then we go to the King. We must do what we can for these innocents." Salvius pauses, at a loss for words.

I look at Benedict. Some unspoken truth is in his face, covertly revealed in his sunken haunted eyes, his bald and mottled head, his trembling hands. Geoff glares at him in clear accusation.

But Benedict deflects Geoff's stare, speaking quietly, as if out of grief alone: "We will avenge them—these innocents are our own flesh, and they did not deserve such a death."

Salvius leaps in then, adding melodramatic flourish. "Such murder cannot be done without recourse to God's justice, without the King himself honoring them!"

Moten glances at me uncertainly, as if to prompt words I do not speak. His face fills with regret, and he glances upward at the crowd of angry men before he looks at me again.

"Then I have done wrong perhaps," he says quietly, "to tell of your grief, your pain."

An older monk with a long face steps forward and places his hand on Moten's shoulder. He speaks with the voice of authority. *"Non, vous n'avez rien fait de mal, Saint Frère Moten.* Wrongheaded, ignorant country men."

"Saint Frère, they are not all ignorant, I would guess," he says. His questioning eyes slide toward me. "They knew enough to—"

"*Non,* this offense against God cannot be borne. I will send for the Abbot," says the older monk.

Moten looks up at Salvius, at the surrounding stern faces. "My friends, you must know that what you have done here is an offense against the rule of Cluny, and of Saint Benedict, and above all, against the grace of our Savior, Jesus Christ."

"What the hell d'ye mean by that?" Tom says. "We take care of our own boys."

Moten takes a deep breath and then another, as if he cannot catch his wind. He looks around at the collection of grim and horror-stricken faces. He points farther back in the crowd, and my heart sinks. I see the large swarthy man and one-armed man who seized Hob, who whipped our friend into a cage.

"Those men," Moten says, "who serve Lord Bellecort of Orange, they have already made an accusation. The Abbot sent out monks at dawn to search the countryside, but we looked for a group of lads on the move, not dead ones in a cart."

Moten turns his distraught eyes to me then. "You are already accused."

The long-faced monk speaks loudly. "Yes, indeed they are!" I look at his habit—it is bound with a complicated knot of gold and silver thread—and then my gaze is drawn up to his face at his next words.

"They have not buried their dead—so these men are not only thieves, stealing from Lord Bellecort, but also they must be heathens."

"No, we do not know enough to say that yet," says Moten judiciously.

"*Saint Frère Moten*," says the long-faced monk. "You must admit that there are those in the countryside who still follow the Old Gods."

"Aye," says a large monk with a dark beard. "The heathens sacrifice children in the darkness of winter—they spill blood to bring light anew." He strokes his beard. "I have studied these evil practices."

Someone I cannot see agrees with him from the crowd. "True—some have even cooked their children into diabolical wafers, for to worship the Beast."

"*Le massacre de Infantes*," says the long-faced leader. "Slaughter of the Innocents."

"Look at this," calls out the swarthy man—the one who took Hob. He has found his own notched sword in the cart. "They have my sword. They stole a noble sword, from one sworn to serve the Lord of Bellecort!" He crosses himself piously.

Moten's cry was like a small stone gathering a landslide. The accusations pile on top of us. Moten tries to speak again, to undo the damage, but it is too late. The monk with the long face speaks over Moten then, the weight of authority in his voice. He speaks precisely in English but with a Gallic accent. "By the grace vested in me as Headmaster of the Magdalene School, I declare these lost souls under the protection of the Priory of Saint Mary Magdalene, and I—"

"That is not necessary," says Moten emphatically. "Not until we hear their story."

"We must give them sanctuary," says the long-faced Headmaster. "We are bound to it."

"We are not guilty of theft or murder," says Liam. "Forgive us, we seek no sanctuary."

"And if you evil men sought it, I would not give succor to such as you." The Headmaster does not look at Liam or Benedict. Instead, he covers the bodies in the cart with a piece of sackcloth. "These poor dead boys, I have given them sanctuary. These bodies are given to our hallowed ground. We care for them in God's grace. We will bury these poor dead lambs.

"And you then, vile thieves and murderers, are seized for punishment."

CHAPTER 14

THE HANDS THAT seize us are gloved in hard chain-mail. We are dragged across the courtyard to the chapel.

The Headmaster brusquely points at Liam. "Him—seize the redhead first for penance. I heard him say, 'Forgive us,' so perhaps he will be the first to give a true confession."

"But, Your Lordship, I beg for mercy—" Liam speaks only these words before the guards strike him with heavy blows. I wince as they beat him back and forth like a bantam bird.

My limbs turn weak and watery, for I know I am next, and this will hurt.

At the end of this penance, a novice in white douses Liam with icy water and barks out words: "Herewith water for the baptism of your soul. Confess your sins."

Liam gives a halting reply as he blinks and shivers. A guard kicks his legs, and Liam goes down to his knees. "But what am I confessing?" begs Liam.

The Headmaster stands forth now, and speaks a proclamation. "Now, at the request of these men—" He motions towards the swarthy man and the one-armed man, who stand gloating. "These men, in Lord Bellecort's service, they have requested summary judgment, for these rough peasants have stolen children who were rightly the property of Lord Bellecort. And so we will find confession before punishment."

The priest now begins that long Latin chant of Confession that I know so well. Liam receives a wafer and is beaten once more before being dragged from the room by a guard. As he reaches the door, Liam glances blearily toward me, water and blood dripping off his face.

Will I ever see him alive again?

Then the blows come thick and hard on my flesh. I cower and cover my head.

"*Dómine, non som dignas,*" chants the Confessor. But my mind works always, despite my pain. I can hear that this country monk misspeaks the Latin phrase. It is *sum dignus* he means to say. "*Ut intres sub tectum meum: sed tantum dic verbo, et sanabitur anima mea.*"

Lord God, I am not worthy that Thou shouldst enter under my roof; but only say the word, and my soul shall be healed.

I have not confessed in nearly a decade. Every spring at the traveling fair, I see the priest and receive the wafer, silent as ever. But here I will be forced to open my mouth. *What tongue does God speak? Latin? Would God speak my father's tongue or my mother's tongue?*

The men of my village would think it a miracle to hear my voice. Years ago, I sealed my mouth to protect my son. So what now do I protect? Can I protect my life—or their lives—by using my tongue?

They are waiting for me to speak. A guard approaches, holding a hazel-wood staff high for a heavy blow, to force words from my mouth.

Out of the corner of my eye, I see Moten in the crowd. He pushes through the gathered monks, elbowing through the crowd, and approaches the edge of the confessional table.

"Forgive me, Brother Herbert," he says. "She... He... he... This one here... is a mute. Cannot speak. Has no tongue. I wish you to know this before..."

"Ah," the Confessor relaxes his grim face. "We will consider his sins confessed then, by intercession of the Lord God."

Someone shoves a thick, unwieldy wafer into my mouth. I choke on the sawdust taste as the priest continues his chant. Then comes a draught of sour wine. And in my hacking cough, I almost miss the Confessor's next words: *"Accipe, frater, Viaticum Córporis Dómini nostri Jesu Christi, qui te custódiat ab hoste maligno, et perdúcat in vitam aetérnam. Amen."*

> Receive, brother, the Viaticum of the Body of our Lord Jesus Christ; and may He keep you from the malignant foe, and bring you to life everlasting. Amen.

Viaticum is the last sacrament you receive before the end comes, food for the *via*—the way—into death and beyond.

My flesh is suddenly wet with a cold and clinging sweat. Viaticum. Last rites are being read to us. The punishment is death.

Implacable, the priest continues. He yawns and crosses himself. "*In nomine Patris et Filii et Spiritus Sancti. Amen.*"

Last rites. Confession. Water and fire to cleanse our flesh to the bone. There is no time to think, no time to find what to do.

They take me out in the cold air. Logs are soaking in cauldrons simmering with pitch. Each log will be placed in a heap beside green stakes as strong and tall as a young tree.

I quake in my very soul at the sight of the wood. For I have heard the screams and I have seen a man burning, his viscera exposed to the flame. Yet he lived and cried out as he burned.

The guards take me past the waiting wood. They take me across the courtyard and fling me into an old stone barn. An iron gate clangs shut.

And there is Liam, alive and whole.

My friend is warming his bruised hands by a fire lit in a blackened pit in the middle of the barn floor. This is the holding gaol for the monastery: a building so old it must have been built by Romans, a fortress of a stable. Each of the narrow horse stalls has bars across the front to hold a prisoner inside.

But until all of the prisoners have arrived, the bars are flung open, the stalls empty. For now, we can huddle by the fire in the center of the floor.

We have been judged guilty, all in a heartbeat—accused by the men who took Hob, men who are sworn to Lord Bellecort's service. And now the monks have convicted us of stealing the boys—our own sons—who had been sold to the Lord as his property. *Damn Hob for selling our children's souls for silver.*

We might argue against the accusations of theft, but we have done much worse in the monastery's eyes. All good Christians bury their dead. But according to these monks, because we dragged dead children across the land, we ourselves are worthy of death.

Outside, I can hear the simmering tar, the thunk of the wood being dipped in pitch. The sound chills me to the bone.

Liam looks at me. "What do you think happen'd?" he says finally. "I think I know."

I squint at him. *Solving this mystery won't help us now.*

He raises a hand, waving off my skeptical look. "Don't misunderstand. I been thinking on this a long while. It's taken me all our journey to find a way through the thickets of lies."

I just stare. *Doesn't he know we are about to die?*

"You wonder why Bene never raises a hand to Tom?" Liam says. "Benedict is wealthy now because he stole from the dead when the plague came.

"Remember that Tom vouched for him when he was accus'd. And you can see how Tom is paid back. He keeps his wick wet, that one does."

I shake my head. *I don't understand.*

"You know," insists Liam, "how Tom climbs in Bene's wife's window every chance he gets. Bene pays him back by turning a blind eye on Tom's amours with sweet Sophia."

I did not know. *How did I never know of Tom and Sophia?* Am I blind as well as mute?

Liam still speaks. "An' what's sad is Benedict thinks he'll hold onto his wife more closely if he has more gold—that gold will keep Sophia close to him. But she don't care about the gold."

I shake my head. I wish Salvius were here—he I can communicate with, without me saying a word. He would know the answers to this puzzle.

Yet despite my distrust of him, Liam is right about Sophia: she has never cared about being rich. She needs some other treasures to fill her, for she has a howling wilderness of desire within. Her everlasting hunger is never filled by her husband, and I do not know if it could ever be filled by anyone.

Liam shakes his head sadly. "She just wants his love. An' Benedict, he don't care. He just thinks he owns her, like a man owns a cow. So she lies with Tom. I dunno why she needs to."

Although Tom is big and strong, he is not the one I would have chosen either. Yet Sophia has always longed for someone who will look at her and know her. She yearns for that, like a flower yearns for the sun. Perhaps Tom gives her what she needs. *But what does Sophia's need have to do with my son?*

I give Liam a quizzical look.

"That's why we were asking about the boys. Since she sees other men. So if Benedict heard of a new lover and—"

The sound of wood splashing in the pitch outside seizes my attention. The truth of this day comes to me afresh. None of this matters now. I wave my hands. I try to tell him of those last rites we were read: *We are about to die.*

"No, you can't think Geoff did it," says Liam, misunderstanding my hand gestures, my sudden urgency. "Geoff could have done it, but the truth is Geoff was—"

And on that thought, the great iron door swings open. Edges of ice fall from the door and shatter on the floor as the guards fling Tom in to join us. Then the door clangs shut again.

Tom has been dumped face-first onto the stone floor. He lifts his face to us, a strange hunger in his eyes.

"I heard ye," says Tom. "Geoff, eh? I'm going to kill Geoff before this night is out. He lit those fires and he killed our lads, that son of a buggerin' fool."

Liam sighs. "Geoff is innocent. Why do you unbury his da, that ripe bastard?"

They are speaking of Geoff's cruel and lascivious father, who was said to take him in the night as some lads take a sheep. I imagine that old sinner unburied in truth now, his face gray and haggard as a corpse, leering at us in the firelight.

Tom's face flushes with anger. "Like father, like son. Geoff did this sin, buggered 'em—"

"All those years ago, no one believed Geoff when he told what happen'd—why do you believe it now?"

"There was one who believed him," says Tom. "My own mam did."

"Aye, so she did. And she took young Geoff's side."

Tom's voice is unsteady with rage. "An' the men of the village—they killed her for her trouble, an' now—"

"An' now you'll do it to him, eh?"

Tom glowers. "Well, why was my ma killed, and not that ruttin' old goat? Geoff connived so that his own da lived, an' she died—that's what I say."

"Tom," says Liam. "Bene has you tied to his leash, and he—"

"I'm not anyone's dog!"

The latch on the door of the barn rattles open, and without further warning, Geoff is shoved into the room.

"You," bellows Tom as he rushes toward him. "You kill'd 'em."

Liam puts out a foot, and Tom goes flying to the stones again.

"Damn you, Liam." Tom pushes himself off the floor.

Geoff steps warily around Tom. "What's wrong with 'im?"

"You killed 'em," grunts Tom. "You buggered your son an'—"

"Damn your foul tongue!" Geoff lunges at him. "I never—"

"Geoff didn't kill 'em," Liam says. He seizes a blazing branch from the fire and thrusts it between them. "I saw him that night. He was on the other side of the village, Tom."

"But why did it happen then?" shouts Tom. "Why'd she die? Why'd they all die?"

The past puts the bit in Tom's mouth and rides him like a demon. His face is thick with rage. "They drowned her as a witch! She weren't no witch like Geoff's mam! That bitch!"

Geoff tries to get to Tom again. "Bloody bast—"

"Dammit, Tom." Liam swings the stick like a burning sword, keeping the men apart. "Geoff wasn't even there."

In this light, holding his flaming brand, Liam looks like an angel of death. A heavy clang echoes through the room as the bolt is shot back once more and the iron door bangs open. Cole and Salvius stumble in together, snow swirling around their feet.

Tom points up, at the sky beyond the roof. "I had a vision, I tell you. A vision of a witch in the woods. She worked with Geoff to light this fire. I saw her in the night, coming to the—"

"Ripe shite!" shouts Geoff. "There ain't no witch, no vision—someone really killed 'em."

Salvius stares at us. He is wise. I can see in his face Salvius knows the fate that's been decided for us.

He spits into the fire. "Still, you lot argue over this? It's all over now, dontcha know that now? We're going to die in the morning."

Geoff gestures furiously. "Justice! I want justice! Our dead lads are why we're here."

Outside, I can hear the monks rolling barrels into the central court. They will fill each barrel with stones. The weighted barrels will keep the stakes upright, as the men tied to them roast.

Liam points at Cole. "He was going to go with Benedict that night. Weren't you, Cole?"

Salvius sits down wearily on the floor and sighs aloud. "Who cares of your damn'd justice? It doesn't matter now."

"It does matter," says Liam. "Tell us what you know, Cole, what you saw."

Cole leaps to his feet. "I know what happened! I wanted to go with them."

I lean forward. But then Salvius hauls Cole down and backhands him across the mouth. "Shut your blather. None of your lies anymore. Let these fools argue—you stay out of it."

Cole, cowed, crouches down beside the fire to nurse his bleeding lip.

Tom hesitates. "Truth be told, it weren't Bene's fault. He was just trying to help us all. It was a terrible harvest, you all remember. And if we got nothing, we would all die."

Liam and Geoff nod as one. They are the poorest, their families were the worst hit by the bad harvest, by the starving time. When we left the village, their bony children looked like tattered skin held up by bony sticks.

Tom continues. "We were desperate – our children needed food. There was but one thing to do and that was—"

A thundering crash signals the arrival of Benedict; he is shoved through the iron door by a guard's blow on his back.

Geoff seizes the blazing stick from Liam and thrusts it forward, holding Benedict hostage.

"Goddam you, Bene," Geoff shouts. "What did you do to my boy?"

Tom stands and holds out his arms, protecting Benedict. "He didn't do it," Tom says stolidly. "Bene, tell them."

Bene squints at us in the firelight. He has been beaten long and hard; his head is bruised, his eyes almost swollen shut.

"I'll tell you," says Bene in a low and strangled tone. He pushes past Tom and sits down by the guttering fire, the light flickering across his battered face. "I'll tell you lot the truth."

"I gather'd all our lads together to take them to Lincoln town," he says slowly. "An' I told the lads to keep it a secret. I told them I would take them to Lincoln for work." His voice cracks. "I tol' them we'd be back in a fortnight, fed well and rich as kings. That's why they went with me—they believed me. But that weren't the truth."

Geoff huffs in disbelief. "Pay for their dead bodies? What kind of—"

"No, I didn't burn them. I didn't light any fires."

"Ripe shite," says Salvius. "If not you, then who?"

"I didn't do it," Benedict chokes out the words. "Truth is, Hob said Lord Bellecort would pay me to bring the lads to him for servants. Serfs. Indentur'd for life. I'd be rich."

Liam releases an agonized moan. "You bastard—you were going to sell our boys?"

Geoff points his burning brand at Benedict. "I'll feckin' kill you."

Liam throws a hard fist out, and Benedict takes the blow to his shoulder stoically.

"Why?" asks Salvius. "Why would you do such a crime, why would—"

"I had to do it. I had no choice. I needed gold."

Liam gives a bitter chuckle. "You don't need gold. Not really. You bloody plague-ridden bastard. We should cut you apart."

Bene looks up at us. He doesn't seem to care of any threat. His eyes glimmer with tears. They fill his eyes, spill down those weathered cheeks. "Truth is I wanted her," he whispers. "I wanted her all to myself. And only gold would keep her with me always."

"What of your own boy?" says Liam. "Would you sell him too?"

"I took my own lad with us, but he wasn't to stay. He was comin' back with me from the town. My son was not for sale."

"You bloody selfish arse!" says Geoff.

Benedict raises his voice in protest. "But they have been eating—every day! Can you imagine that kinda luxury for those lads? And they'd be alright: sure, they would have been in service in Lincoln town. But think of it—every day, a meal to eat. They wouldn't struggle no more, dammit, caint you see that?"

"That's enough, Bene," says Tom. "You don't have to say any more."

Geoff rounds on Tom. "You shite! Why would you cover for him? Why?"

"My wee ones would have died this winter," said Tom miserably. "We have no food. The stores in the mill went moldy in the fall. There was naught to keep us alive. Bene told me sellin' my oldest would let the others live."

From outside the door comes the sound of a guard sliding back the hatch. "You lot, shut yer mouths up. Make your confessions, an' that's all."

There is a long silence. I hear the men breathing—panting like broken beasts. I consider what Tom has said. *What parent has never seen their child close to death in the wintertime? Every year, another babe dies.*

Almost every mother I know has wet the ground with tears on at least one small grave: some do not even name their offspring until three years have passed.

Tom speaks again. "So Bene said he'd give him food and a life in the city. It would be a good life, an' he could—"

Cole pipes up. "I wanted to go, I tell you. But I didn't know 'bout Hob selling the lads. It were secret work, Hob said, for all the strong lads. An' money too."

Geoff drops his stick in the fire and starts to sob. "No, no." He rocks back and forth. "He wasn't killed for your vanity. Your damn'd feckin' gold. Not for this."

"I tell you, he wasn't," says Benedict. "I didn't kill any of them! I don't know who lit the fire—any of those fires—maybe it was one of you!"

"Like hell," says Salvius. "You'd dare accuse us of this?"

"You're a bastard," snarls Liam. "I don't believe you. Not a word."

"Listen to me," shouts Benedict. "The boys were suppos'd to meet me at Compline. When I got back at Nocturns hour, my house was already aflame, the boys tied up inside. I did not tie that damn'd knot. I don't know who did it. I didn't burn them, I just gather'd them. I didn't do it!"

From just outside the iron door comes another shout from the guard. "You shut yer bloody yaps! Do you want a beating?"

There is again a moment of quiet. I look in Benedict's streaming eyes, his pale frightened face, and I believe him about lighting the fires we saw in the village. He is as much in the dark as I am. Someone here in this room did that night's deed though, someone tied that knot.

"Bloody feckin' fool you are," cries Geoff. "You an' Hob killed them."

Benedict raises his voice in protest. "I'm ashamed for what I planned to do, but the truth is I never took 'em from the village—an' I never burned 'em! I wouldn't hurt a soul, not me!"

"*We* will be hurt," says Salvius. "We'll die because of what you did."

The bolt slides back again. "Ah'm warning you lot, this is yer last chance!"

But Benedict can't resist protesting his innocence again. "I'm not guilty of anything! I never took them to Lord Bellecort, I never sold them! I never gave those boys up for the gold I'm owed! Someone else killed them—I tell you true!"

"Damn you, an' your lovely gold." Liam swings his fists in furious blows.

A maelstrom of wrath fills the stone barn as Liam shouts in fury and attacks Benedict and Tom. Tom bellows out in pain and Benedict is thrown over, but Salvius steps in front of Liam, protecting them. Geoff seizes the burning branch anew, and suddenly Salvius's ragged tunic is alight, the last symbol of Sir Peter of Lincoln going up in flame.

A shriek. A yowl of rage. Guards rush into the room. A bucket of snow splashes across Salvius and hisses on the fire pit. The light goes dark and a choking steam fills the air. Men-at-arms seize each of us and thrust us into the small stinking stalls, slamming bars across our animal rage.

Geoff still cries loudly. His voice echoes for a long time in the howling black night, a child's primal scream. *"Justice! Goddam it to hell, I want justice!"*

In the morning, there will be a time of judgment and confession before the Abbot. Then each of us will be tied to a stake. They will light the wood around each makeshift Golgotha, and that will be the end.

CHAPTER 15

The Abbot of the Cluniac order of Saint Mary Magdalene bears a magnificent leonine head, his hair silver, his jaw firm and commanding. Monks file into the hall behind us, each of them hanging his heavy outer robe on a hook by the great wooden doors. They enter the hall in plain white and plain black habits, genuflecting before the Abbot as they take their places on the floor to watch this trial. Gathered here is every living soul from within the walls of the monastery, a crowd of faces alternately lit by beams of light or sunk in deep shadow.

When he clears his throat, all eyes turn toward his throne. "*Les oeuvres de charité chrétienne...*"

After all these years, the French from my father is still quite clear, and I translate in my head as the Abbot speaks: "You know as well as I do what are the works of charity: to feed the poor, to give drink to the thirsty, to clothe the naked, to harbor the harborless, to visit the sick, to ransom the captive, and to bury the dead."

Yet to common villagers, the French is strange and alien. My companions do not speak the Gallic tongue, and they stand ignorantly staring at the opulence of this chamber, the glittering stained glass, the flashing gold of candelabra and throne.

Years ago, the brothers of Cluny came to this country, under invitation of the King, to plant a fertile field of faith here far from

France. Yet many of these men of the Holy Orders have never learned the English tongue. In the Church and Court, French is so commonly used, it is the language of those who lead and order the lives of those who rest at the bottom of Fortune's vast and hoary wheel. We peasants are left behind, our speech and customs marking us out as lesser in every way.

"*Enterrez les morts*..." the Abbot continues in French. "Bury the dead. This is the rule of charity. We will punish those murderers who go against Heaven's decree!" He raises his hand. "*Au nom du Père, du Fils, et du Saint-Esprit*..."

I look around and see not a single look of compassion. To these monks, we are vagabond, outlaw, and subject to every law of Heaven and of earth. Shackles hold all the men except me, for my limbs were too thin to be held tight by chains—my hands slipped right through the manacles. Instead, a guard holds the manacles on my arms.

On the other side of the Abbot, the men who assaulted us as bandits stand proudly, as if their association with the Lord Bellecort makes them the King's own advocates. The swarthy man now wears the Lord's tunic, a self-satisfied sneer on his face. He looks at us with haughty eyes—as if he would own us himself.

I grit my teeth. In this hall these men do, in fact, have the right to accuse us, to seek our deaths.

Yet despite the imminent threat, we quarrel. Geoff hisses his rage at Benedict, while Tom is still trying to convince Liam of his vision of some witch in the woods. There is a sudden uproar as Geoff shoves Bene.

The Abbot pauses at the commotion and then continues in English:

"For those novices of the common English and for those"—he glares at Geoff, who now battles his own guard—"untutored and uncouth peasants, I now give instruction as to my ruling. Thomas Aquinas instructed us that the dead must be buried. And those who kill in pagan sacrifice must suffer death to burn away their terrible sins. *Au service de Dieu*, and in accordance with words of the sainted Aquinas—"

Thank Holy God, Salvius raises his voice in protest. He shakes his blond head, as if shaking off a nagging horsefly. He leaves behind the tussling Geoff and Benedict. He steps forth defiantly in his chains. But even though he raises his voice loud, Salvius has lost some of his stately bearing. The torn and burned vestment from Sir Peter now appears unseemly in this opulent chamber. The clanking chains interrupt him. And his melodious voice by itself cannot carry the day.

"Now I dunno o' this Thomas Accunes you speak of—but whatever this Thomas said, I know it be our right to treat our own get as we see fit, from the moment of their birth, to every day beyond. Ah an' my kin claim that right—"

"*L'un d'entre vous ose interrompre?* You wish to debate?" The Abbot stares at Salvius as if he mouths a foreign tongue.

Although Salvius speaks with authority, he can only pretend to Gallic elegance—for he speaks the English tongue, the language of those who but rarely know the pleasures of a goose-feather bed or a jewel-encrusted throne.

The Abbot leans forward, speaking vehemently. "So tell me, oh lordly peasant, *pourquoi*? Why have you subjected these bodies to such a plight? You will tell the truth to God, and die."

Salvius, emboldened, speaks louder. "I come to you for the sake of all who have suffer'd wrong, those who forever seek justice. We have seen a witch before in the woods an' we wish to tell you—"

"*Quel emmerdement*," the Abbot hisses. Then he speaks in English to Salvius. "You wish to debate, yet you have no ecclesiastical standing. You and your peasant companions have bare command of your native tongue, such as it is! *Foutez le camp*."

I am shocked by the Abbot's rudeness, and then my thought is lost as I am jostled aside by Tom's guard as Tom shoves himself forward, catching Liam by the ear. "I tell you true," Tom whispers loudly. "There is a witch who did this—I seen a vision of her!"

"Shut your yap, Tom," says Liam. "Benedict did it—I'll tell them all of his perfidy. He and his wife killed them—"

Geoff pushes Tom. "Aye, we'll tell the Abbot the truth! You and Bene did—"

A guard strikes Geoff with his mailed open hand. The clash of armored rings raises a welt across his face. Liam shoves the guard.

The Abbot reaches out and pushes Salvius's scorched tunic with the heavy gold-shod tip of the staff. "*Assez de ces paysans vagabonds!*"

Salvius staggers backward into the crowd. We have lost our champion.

Who will rescue us now?

The swarthy man gives a slow clap of his hands, mocking our attempt. As the crowd grows restless, Tom and Geoff struggle and shout on the floor.

The Abbot shakes his head in disgust. "*Saints Frères*— Holy Brothers, I am sorry for such a sight. Seeing as none of the *premier état*—the first estate—will defend these vagabonds, I now pronounce sentence, punishing these miscreants with—"

"Your Grace, I will speak for them," says a loud voice with a twang of York in it. We all crane our necks to see, and a murmur of surprise moves over the crowd of monks. With surprise, I see that Brother Moten is stepping forward.

He speaks no French, but he is clearly a Cluniac brother. Moten raises his voice in clear challenge. "As a Brother of Cluny, I beg Your Grace for a debate. I would speak with you in the common tongue—may it please Your Grace."

The swarthy man strides forward now. "Your Grace, there is no need for any debate. We ask only for what is right, given their most grievous harm to our Lord Bellecort's property. We ask only for God's right punishment."

But the Abbot holds up a regal hand. "I will hear this. On what grounds would you debate, young monk?"

Moten genuflects. "Have pity on me, a child of Christ. I would debate theology of the flesh with you, my Lord. I believe your reading of the most rever'd Thomas Aquinas is mistaken."

The Abbot stands and moves closer to the crowd. The lights of Epiphany glow around him, the tiny flames flickering in reflection on his gold vestments as he stares to see who challenges him.

"Brother Moten," the Abbot finally says. He speaks with resignation, as if this was only to be expected of Moten.

"Yes, Your Grace." Moten bows his head and sketches a quick cross across his mouth, demonstrating his fealty. "In my most humble reading of the sainted Augustine, it does not touch the immortal soul whether a body is buried or not. To condemn peasants to death"—he fumbles and finishes—"you are wrong in this, Your Grace!"

The voice of Brother Moten is a reedy thing, and he speaks the country tongue – a coarse speech from the rough Pennine fells and the open moors. He does not have the elegant turns of phrase or the deep baritone of the Abbot. Yet like a stone dropped in a pool, the words he speaks ripple into every corner. The murmur begins again.

The Abbot holds up a hand thick with golden rings. Slowly, silence falls except where Tom and Geoff wrestle. A guard pummels them with a staff, but still they are not separated.

The Abbot huffs at the rude interruption.

"I will debate," he says at last, facing the assembled crowd. "It is necessary for every monk and novice to understand that burial does indeed profit the dead. I am correct in this." Then the Abbot lifts his hand, as if writing in the air. "For Damascene, in his *De qui in fide dormierunt*, writes, 'Burn fragrant oil at his tomb; for things of the funeral nature are pleasing to God and you will receive a reward from God for devotion to the body after death.'"

There is a sudden cry from Tom as Geoff's thumb gouges his eye. My guard releases his iron grip on my arm and moves to pull Geoff from his clutch on Tom.

Moten speaks loudly over the interruption, his voice strident. "Your Grace, the citation is irrelevant. Damascene is said to cite the pagan Athanasius in this regard. And in citing a pagan's counsel, he does not take into account our hope of resurrection in our Lord Jesus Christ! He is also thus mistaken. Surely, we must see our way to mercy in this case."

The Abbot sits back in his throne. He seems uneasy and uncertain after Moten's correction. "Whether the citation is pagan or not is immaterial, Moten. You must acknowledge that the act of charity toward the dead is given... uh... as Saint Thomas observes in the *Summa Theologica*, I believe..."

Moten's mind seems to move a little faster, and words trip nimbly off his tongue. "Your Grace, you are mistaken. Saint Thomas wrote of this matter in the *Prima Secundae Partis*."

The Abbot blinks. "Just so," he admits.

Moten gives a quick riposte. "But in truth, Your Grace, Saint Augustine corrects Aquinas in the second part of *De cura pro mortuis*, when he writes 'Whatever service is done to the body is no aid to salvation, but an office of humanity.'"

Moten's face is flushed with excitement, his lip trembling with the ardor of his thoughts. This may be only a sport to him, and yet our lives hang on his every word.

Now Benedict is embroiled in the fisticuffs on the floor. The manacles binding his hands are wrapped around Geoff's throat. There is a hacking urgency in Geoff's attempts to escape. Liam punches Benedict, over and over. My guard has lost any sign of interest in me as he pulls apart the combatants.

Moten raises his voice over the grunts and shouts.

"Acts of mercy may profit the dead. But if we read Gregory of Nyssa, we will know that those who are buried with grievous sin may have their souls actually harmed by interment in sacred ground."

The Abbot's gaze is now steady and intense as he declaims from his throne, "I tell you clearly, Christian charity demands burial. There is no *raison* for these bodies to be left unburied! We can only assume—"

This time, Moten holds up his hand, silencing the Abbot. "Your Grace, I must tell you, there *is* in fact such reason in this case. You must show mercy and grant—"

The swarthy man bellows in protest and points at us. "These men, Your Grace, these men took Lord Bellecort's property. We have already seized the worst of them, a man named Hob. And that miscreant has confessed, I tell you, he has confessed to this most grievous crime. These men burned up five souls in sacrifice—these men steal from the nobility, from God's own blessed Lord!"

Moten stutters, but recovers quickly. "Yes, perhaps such a confession is true. But what if these children came from noble parentage? What if these children were destined for interment in a royal manner? Would we not then—"

The swarthy man sneers at him. "What manner of nobility do you see here?" He gestures at the wrestling, grunting peasants. "The king of swine, perhaps?"

The Abbot nods.

"Nay, Your Grace, I would offer proof," says Moten plainly. "Many years ago, a woman was sought by the Earl of Hereford."

"A witch?" asks the Abbot sternly.

"Nay, Your Grace. This woman sought refuge here. She fled with a royal treasure, and I have information that I can share with you—privately—showing that the murder of these boys may have been caused by the King's enemies, to hurt the woman, and to hurt the King's relations."

My heart leaps and then sinks again. Just as Moten revealed the bodies to all, what if he now reveals my story? Even if he manages to save us from the fire, he would do so by betraying me, by offering me as a sacrificial lamb on this altar. *Moten means to tell my secrets. Moten will betray me.*

I edge through the crowd. My guard is still yanking on Benedict and punching Geoff. No one has seen me go.

"If this is a matter of nobility—of an offense against the King," says the Abbot slowly, "then I would do well to refer such earthly matters to the King himself, to the Star Chamber. It is not the Church's concern. If this is true..."

I push backward through the mass of rough black habits. The crowd of monks thins out. Abruptly I feel the rear wall behind me. Guards in chain mail and Cluny sable wait by the doors.

There is a shout from the front.

"Separate the miscreants!" bellows the Abbot in frustration. "We cannot conduct holy debate with these uncouth peasants battling here. Separate them, so all are accounted for. Make them listen as we debate their fate!"

Guards hurry forward, leaving the doors unguarded. I must be quick. Soon they will miss me.

Around me hang the monks' heavy outer robes and cloaks, all gathered together on hooks. Gently, I slip the manacles off my arms and lay them on the floor, hidden under cloaks. I reach out trembling fingers and find a worn black robe and cloak. I step into it and slip the hood over my head. Now I am invisible in the sea of Cluniac habits.

I keep my eyes on the floor as I approach a small door. Then as I touch the door, it occurs to me to wonder whose identity I have taken.

Which monk am I?

I glance down at my waist and find a badge, just like the one I bore years ago. According to the brooch, I am a revered and senior monk. I am no longer Mear. I am Stephen, named for the martyr.

"There is one missing," comes a shout from the front of the hall. "Where is that last peasant in chains?"

I push through the door and stumble into the bright and snowy light.

CHAPTER 16

QUICKLY, I TURN the corner of the abbot's hall, past the cloister hall. No one follows me yet. I need to know what Moten knows of me, and what he suspects. If his practices are still the same as in years past, there is one place I can find all his secrets, one repository for the stories he collects like a magpie. My feet quickly take me there.

The sign of scrolls upon the door marks it as the same building as my old refuge at Canterbury. The scriptorium.

As the heavy wooden door closes behind me, I pause. If the men-at-arms pursue me here, I will have little chance of escape: there is only one door. I have barely pondered this fact, when a man approaches. He has the quick and certain step of an Armarius —a librarian or holder of the text.

"My good man, you cannot wait in the doorway." His tone is haughty, his eyes crinkled with suspicion. "Be about your business. If you have a message, give it to me quickly. I have work to do." His office is revered here, and even the most senior monks must listen to him. Yet there are some in any monastery who have taken a vow of silence, and I can pretend the same.

In fact, his arrogance inspires me. Simon Sudbury himself once gave me permission to read, to learn Latin and to study my mother's tongue. And I have heard tell that Simon is revered now, the Sudbury Rule, they are calling his orders.

Yes, I, *a woman,* esteemed by Simon Sudbury. I can feel my cheeks burning with sudden resolve, and I feel suddenly as young and unafraid as the Miriam of old.

Quickly, I step forward, taking a handful of sand from the basin on the lectern. It is used to blot the drips of ink, and with sufficient rubbing, sand will sunder ink from vellum too. I scatter the golden dust across a bench. There, with the tip of my finger, I sketch two words in Latin. *Ego lego.*

Then I write also in French. *Je peux lire.* The Armarius leans forward to read my finger-script with its clear letters: *I can read.*

When the Armarius stands up again, I can read in his eyes that he is taken aback by the words. French is from the Court. Latin is of the Church. Some can speak the lines that I have written here. Few can read such words. Fewer still can write them.

"Ah, yes, yes, of course you can." He bows and backs away carefully, leaving me alone at the table. "You are a scholar, as any could see... My apologies... I will leave you then, to the books."

He retreats from me and goes to his lectern. The hall of books is largely empty, for all were called to the abbot's hall. I stalk from lectern to empty lectern.

I will search through all that Moten holds dear, and I will find out my true danger.

Outside, I can hear men calling to each other. "Over here," they shout. "He went this way."

But what escaping prisoner would seek refuge among the books? I may yet be safe here.

I glance swiftly down at the leaves open on the tables, looking for Moten's carrel with his records, his manuscript. As always, the monks in the scriptorium work to inscribe the secrets of the ancients. Each lectern holds an ancient book and a new. The ink wells are covered, the quills sharpened to nibs, and the books wait here with half-complete lines of drying ink.

Long years ago, I did the same. I searched through every book for the knowledge I needed. I read every language I could find, memorizing citation. I rejoiced in my hard-won privilege, for so few of my sex have the power of letters. I delved deep into the ancient scripts, even learning Greek and the oft-neglected Jewish tongue of Hebrew. I hoped to use my knowledge to fulfill my mother's last wish, but I have not been able to do so, not yet.

I look down at the paper to see a fragment of cosmology: now I read it hungrily, my ability to read undimmed behind a wall of mute, mad years.

> Nine spheres there are that rotate across the great firmament of the heavens. As Pythagoras wrote, each sphere holds the stars like glowing jewels on their surface, whirling ever in their orbits. At the center of those vast moving orbs of quintessence rests the unmoved rock of this earth, our Eden and sometime Hell...

The ancients understood all things, from the mysteries of our frail flesh to the languages spoken by animals and by angels. Here are all the remnants of their knowledge we hold. The voices of the past echoing into our diminished age.

The shouting outside comes closer. Perhaps the guards have found my footsteps in the snow. I come to the corner where Moten's carrel stood. It is gone. The spot is empty.

My errand here was fruitless.

I shiver: the burning pyre still awaits me in the courtyard. I may go to my grave knowing nothing else about what Moten knows, or how he knows it.

I must find a way out of this monastery as quickly as I can, even if it means leaving behind my son, and abandoning my promise to my mother.

Then the door bursts open and a man-at-arms steps in, sheathing his short sword. I turn the corner quickly, ducking behind the fireplace that keeps the books free from damp and cold.

"Armarius," calls the man by the door. "Have you seen a strange prisoner? A man with marks on his face from beating? The footsteps led us here."

"Why do you bother me? Whom do you seek?" says the Armarius. His arrogance and ignorant questions will buy me time.

As I edge into the corner, here is a carrel that suffers under a weight of disordered manuscripts. I would recognize Moten's workplace anywhere.

Torn folio leaves and parchment pages are stuffed into the shelves. Old ink stains cover the wood. Over the years he has accumulated many bits of vellum—the discarded remains of making books. I find his own manuscript on the lowest shelf: he was always stitching pieces together, writing his own thoughts on these pages in a florid hand. I see that he has continued to add his writing in this thing he calls his own *Chronicle*, his history.

In this history, he writes the small things of his own life. He had just begun this strange and furtive practice when I met him, scrounging manuscript leftovers wherever he might find them. Each page of vellum contains an entry marked with the day, the month and the year. This is the secret record I sought.

Swiftly, I turn the pages. The years flick back like magic. And then my eye is caught by my own name: *Miriam,* it says here.

15 Augusto, 1365

Sister Miriam came to the Monastery this month with her child, Christian. She is an erstwhile sister of Canterbury,

> and she tells me all her tale. Of her lover Edward, and how he swore to her that he would use the name of her house, Houmout, on his own crest. The Earl of Hereford has instructed men to seize her. She is distraught but brave in her hope of love. She shows me the proof with which Edward promised her his love. For he gave her—

If I tore this page out, would I then be safe? What possessed me those years ago, to tell Moten all my tale? Perhaps I could not help myself. I was so young then. I thought Edward's love was real, and then I was told it was not, that he had never loved me. I fought my fear out loud, seizing on Moten, the closest person I could find, a friend. I shared with him my heart's desire, my deepest hopes. I spilled all I had.

I wish I had more time to read it, to understand what Moten knows, and does not. Does he intend to betray me?

The Armarius raises his voice. "The Abbot has declared those who work here are not to be disturbed, I say. There is no cause to invade our sanctuary of holy scrip. Scholars are at work!"

I sit down at the carrel and hunch over, as if I labor long. I gaze down at the lectern, reading every line fervently. I lean closer to the manuscript, intent on my work.

"Brother," says the guard patiently. "We seek a prisoner, and the Abbot bids you..."

That is when I see two monks in a quiet corner, beside the fireplace. They are old and grey. One has a tonsure that has spread all over his head—he is nearly as bald as Benedict. Such venerables as these have seen endless debates, and this day they have chosen not to watch another debate, no matter what the stakes shall be. Instead, they are playing a game that can last for days at a time.

The guard is walking closer to Moten's carrel. I decide to leave, but against taking the manuscript with me, for fear I may have to run in the snow.

I step away from the carrel slowly, and edge close to the fireside, where I can watch the monks play. Perhaps this guard will think me part of their game.

It is a game of the Court called *échecs*, which Edward taught me to play.

The pieces, carved bits of bone and wood, are small shapes of folk like you and me. Sometimes we played with curiously shaped stones, as Edward said the Moors play. But in the game I know there is a king who is beset and his most powerful captain of arms, called the *fierce*. Two *fools* of the Court, whose power is deceptive, and two *chevaliers*—knights proud on their steeds. The game is cornered by a *margrave* tower with battlements at each corner. And in front of the characters of power—taking the brunt of punishment, as in life—are all the common folk, the motley pawns. Sometimes dice is thrown for their lives, sometimes not. Today, the monks play with no dice at all, using wits alone to find their luck upon the board.

In a game like this, Edward and I always played in quadrants, one of us with red pieces, one with black. These monks do the same: one blood, one death. One monk moves his powerful *fierce* forward.

In France, they sometimes call this piece *dame*, which means "the Lord's Queen," and often Edward jested, saying that I would be his *fierce*. I jested too then, but now the joke tastes bitter in my mouth. Why should I not be his queen, with all rights and honor proper to the mother of his son?

A sudden intuition wakes in me—I must go to Edward. When Edward finds out the truth about his son, he will want me near. And all will be well when I find Edward. *All will be well.* He needs me, and I need him if I am to live in this world, bereft of my son.

But I cannot leave now—I am in danger. I try to concentrate on the game. The other monk takes a piece and puts it down. He does not seem to know what to do next. I lift my hand and point at the little pawn. Then I point at the back of the board.

"Ah," he says. "Thank you, friend." He moves the pawn, and with a stroke of his hand, transforms it into a *fierce* direct: commoners can ride Fortune's Wheel too.

And so it might have been for me. I was the assistant to the Abbess when he found me, of high stature in the Church, and none thought it strange to see me there at Court. To move from Canterbury Abbey to being consort of that Lord would have been unusual, but not impossible. The Earl of Hereford resented me. But always, Edward swore his love, giving me token after token in his name.

The guard approaches. My heart trebles in its beat. He sees me bent over the board, hood hanging across my face, intent upon this game.

"You are—?" he barks at us.

The first monk grumbles and holds up the brooch at his waist. I do the same, offhandedly, not deigning to look at the guard, even though the hood falls far over my bruises.

"What's this all about then?" the other monk grumbles. "Why do you invade the scriptorium? What gives you such right, eh?" But in the end, he tells the guard his name, and the guard stalks away to the door.

I breathe once more, slowly, with caution. As I wait for the guards to leave, the fire warm against my back, I wonder if I could hide here forever.

What if I went to the nunnery, as one who took a vow of silence? What if I became a woman again? What if I entered Orders once more? It would be as if I never left my old home in Canterbury Abbey.

A log falls in the fire, a shower of sparks. I sweep them away with my booted foot and watch the embers die into black streaks on the floor. Once a fire, now a bit of ash and dust. *A river entered into once,* wrote that philosopher, *cannot ever be entered into again, for it will not be the same river again. That river is gone, is lost forever.*

Outside then the shouts come again. “Not here. Not at the middens. What of the scriptorium?”

“I checked. No one in there but a few graybeards playin’ at a board.”

“You’re a sodden git. Cain’t do anythin’ right. I’ll check it again.”

Heavy boots stop on the steps outside the scriptorium to stomp off snow and ice.

“I tell you, the prisoner stole a cloak—Stephen’s. Look for Stephen’s cloak.”

I move quickly now between the lecterns toward the door. As the guards enter, I let the hood drop low. I seize on a manuscript on a shelf near at hand and hold it near to my face, as if I cannot be stopped from my studies, even in the midst of perambulation.

I sweep through the door of the scriptorium, imperious in my black robe, manuscript held tight. The guards stand aside in respect as I pass, and then they enter in to search again for that poor prisoner.

Narrow is my escape.

CHAPTER 17

IN THE DEEP *places of the earth I will hide myself.* That ancient holy king, David, he sought such refuge when pursued. Under the sanctuary are the catacombs, where the dead wait for resurrection. The living do not venture there.

If I can hide until Vespers hour, then the search will cease for the service of prayer, and that will be my time to flee the monastery.

The catacombs are illuminated only by dim shafts of light from the sanctuary. The walls are etched with flowers of frost, but at least I am out of the wind. It is warm in one corner here, from the flue that runs under the calefactory. I curl up against the grated opening where the heat eddies. Dark bays line the hall in front of me, a vast rabbit warren, each hole filled to the brim with the scent of the past.

I still clench the manuscript from the scriptorium tight in my hand. I look down at it. A prayer book. When I crack it open, my hand lands on a page with "The Burial of the Dead."

> . . . for none of us liveth to himself alone, and no man dieth to himself . . .

And at those words, I remember Edward.

We read those lines in a graveyard. I stood there beside Edward as we buried his companion-in-arms, one injured at Poitiers, but who lingered for two long years, wavering between life and death, before succumbing in the end. I was the one to show Edward the correct passage for his funeral and final blessing.

It was books that brought me into Edward's orbit, always the books. I was of the novitiate when I first began to show an aptitude for language and for ancient texts. There were no others of my class in the scriptorium when I first went there, and perhaps this should have been a sign to me.

I did not realize for nearly a year that even those of the noble class merely recited by rote the Latin, the Greek, and the ancient Hebrew, their eyes dark of comprehension. Even that great heiress Theresa of Avignon, who journeyed as a postulate for the months of her father's foreign conquest, was largely ignorant. In fact, Theresa quickly grew jealous of my quick way with the scrolls and the pen, and sought to have me removed. It was only Simon of Sudbury, the armarius and librarian who intervened to grant me access to those texts that became my lifeblood, those ancient voices that still haunt my dreams. No one knew that I searched always for more of what my mother taught me. No one knew that I carried her words in my head, and that I hoped to find her last secret repeated here, buried in the ancient books. Always, my head was bent over a text, eyes squinting, as I tilted vellum pages toward the candlelight, the better to translate the faded script.

It was in such a hunched pose that Edward of Woodstock first found me. To this day, I do not know what errand brought him to the scriptorium, but I do know that within minutes of his arrival, he had found some excuse to approach my desk. He spoke, but I did not listen. I looked up and found his wide eyes, deep enough to fall into. I saw his pursed and upturned lips, that edge of arrogance in them, and I held his gaze.

I was fearless. I did not look away, I did not rise from my desk. In fact, I did not even glance down at the crest of white feathers on his breast and note the unattainable height of his station. Instead, I stared into those deep-blue eyes that sparkled with the ceaseless ghost of a smile. Something stirred in me, unbidden.

I had not heard what words he spoke. But it did not matter. I simply waved him off with one hand as I returned to the codex, dismissing him as some peculiar noble who would not understand my answer even if I gave it. I dismissed the thrumming in my breast as well, little thinking that I would feel it again, and ever stronger in the weeks to come.

My duty at Canterbury Abbey took me only once into the catacombs. Close-at-hand were the sepulchers of the dead, piled in ancient ranks. And that was where he took me, in that holy sanctum. Edward's eyes were closed, his lust overpowering him. After that first time he took me as consort, I was tied to him. And I think he knew that, for a certain arrogance took hold of him, as if I was conquered territory, a victory won.

That incipient haughtiness was distasteful to me, and even more than that, I hated the yearning of my flesh for his, so I rejected him. I refused his every entreaty, and pretended that my heart had no need of him.

Yet eventually my own hunger for him took us back to the deep sepulcher, the only safe and secret place in that vast abbey for a noble and a nun. Time after time we returned there—and above our heads was the great edifice of the cathedral, the dead beneath our backs. At times, we could hear the monks in cloister singing the antiphony, and it was as if they sang our ecstasies to heaven.

I close my eyes now, and there is his scent. Leather and old smoke, Jerusalem sandalwood oil. I draw in breath through my nose, so close I can taste him. Ocean salt and deep woods, cut by a fragrance sharp as cypress, the musky perfume of battlefield armor.

Edward, with his aquiline nose and his arrogant strength. His bright curling mass of hair and his rough beard. I find myself trembling, my feeling for him still fresh after all these years.

What was I thinking, in bedding Edward?

It is a curious thing that what we cannot have draws us, lures us onward—the urge of a child. But in our marrow we are all children. It is a stain in the blood passed down from that first child who could not have what she wanted: Eve. And in that tale is the caution and the curse, for she took it.

Just as Edward took me. For because I first rejected him, he came back, again and again and again. He seemed always in the scriptorium. Studying ancient warfare—Thermopylae and the Peloponnesian War—so he said, but now I have my doubts. In a matter of weeks, he managed to wean me from my lectern and my inkhorn.

There were long walks in the springtide evening air as I made my way to Vespers, and warm mulled wine brought to me at Lauds.

My fearlessness was what drew him, what ensnared him, for I did not mind his advances or fear his overtures. I would say I did not understand them, but that would not be true. Given that, if I'd had any sense, I would have fled. I knew all too well his intention.

But I played with him, as a cat bedevils a vole or shrew. In truth, it was a play with great stakes. Just as Everyman played games with Satan and discovered only later that the contest turned on his own life, on his eternal salvation. I tormented Edward, and was tormented myself by my own fearless longing. I did not fear the Church, I did not fear him. In all ways, I was heedless of consequences.

And that was how we began in the catacombs, our bodies bent together, my eyes, my mouth, my body gorging on that forbidden fruit. Oh, how I ate with abandon, how I relished it! I took, I ate, and knew not I had been given the apple of my death.

In after moments, Edward told me always that his heart would remain with me. Yet when I asked for a token of his love, he gave his gentle, cruel-edged smile. He said as proof, he would beg his father that he not be buried not with his fathers, but in the crypt of Canterbury, where we took our pleasure. What morbid romance youth gives to death.

Edward touched the bare stone floor of the catacombs, and then brought his hand up to cup my trembling, eager flesh.

"Here," he would say. "I would be buried here, forever, with you."

"Proof," I would whisper. "I require proofs of your love. A token, I plead, a favor."

And he gave that to me too. It was more than any commoner could ask, and yet I was resentful. Perhaps that was the start of all my troubles. Perhaps that, in the end, was my mistake.

I open my eyes now in this labyrinth tomb. The light is fading, the shafts from above failing as the day dies. There is a painting on the wall above my head: Saint Michael with his scales, weighing the souls of the dead. I cross my breast, although there is no faith left in me.

✠

Dust falls from the roof of the catacombs, small flecks of plaster pigment dropping from Saint Michael's blessed garment. I hear a thumping irregular rhythm. At first, I do not recognize the heavy tramp of mailed boots on stone.

They are here.

I run for the back stairs that lead through the choir loft, but as I ascend the laddered steps, I see a pair of feet blocking my passage. They are already posting guards, so quickly I scurry back to my place under the painting of Saint Michael.

"Sit you down there," comes an order up in the sanctuary. I can hear the sound of several men being cast roughly to the floor. "Here's your last blessing then." And the priest starts muttering in Latin.

The men sit just above my warm grate, and I can see their actions through the slots in the grate. Someone loosens the thick welded chain that holds their manacles tight to one another. The line of iron links drops to the floor. The heavy clang echoes through the catacombs.

Yet even without the chains holding them to each other, the men do not move, they do not run for their lives. Instead, they rest on the floor, talking amongst themselves, as the priest drones on.

"Damn'd thieves," grunts a high voice I recognize as Geoff. "Those bandits want us to suffer for their wretched dealings."

"He sold our sons—this ripe bastard here," says Liam. There is the sound of a blow and then an agonized choking sound, accompanied by the thunk of Liam's manacles against Benedict's flesh. "Ow!" grunts Benedict.

"You there," says the harsh voice of a guard. "Drop him, leave 'im be. You'll soon have enough to keep you busy."

A man falls to the floor. I can see his bald head through the grate. It is Benedict, and he still proclaims his innocence, a hoarse whisper into the darkness. "I tell you, I didn't kill them—I had naught to do wi—"

"Shut yer yap," hisses Geoff. "Just leave off all that shite."

The chanting voice of the priest begins in the distant background. I am sure the Abbot is giving them extreme unction before the fires are lit and the men are burned.

My bowels turn to water, but even now, the men above me do not seem to recognize their peril.

"Sir, sir, I have a question," Salvius calls. I can hear Salvius and a guard mutter together, but I cannot hear their words until Salvius walks over my grate again.

"Look, you lot, once they find that other prisoner, then we're on our way."

On our way to doom, I guess. It will all be over when they find me. I skulk back into a far corner.

"Those feckin' bandits," laughs Salvius. "They cut their own throat, what with their talk of nobility an' their lord's honor, and all that shite. The monks would have burned us, if they hadn't spoken up."

"Who were they gonna burn?" asks Cole shakily.

"You fool, they would burn us all," says Salvius dryly. "Thank God that bloody damn'd monk beat him at his own game, and thus we live on another day."

We live on for another day.

Liam laughs wryly. "Truth be told, the old Abbot is sending that monk away until all forget the Abbot had his arse drubb'd by a monk from Yorkshire, dontcha think?"

The Abbot is sending Moten away?

The sound of tramping steps comes louder now, echoing in the catacombs. Guards coming down the back stairs.

I rouse myself from the calefactory grate. My legs feel dead from my time on the floor, and I hobble to the front. Gently, I swing the door open. The rusted hinges groan, and the door thuds as it hits the wall.

A shout. They've heard me. I shamble awkwardly, sparking pin-pricks flooding my legs as the blood returns. Then I stumble over a stone casket.

"Heya!" comes a shout and a thrown torch. I dash across an open pit, my shadow hitting the light. A crossbow bolt shatters the stone just above my head.

I scurry like a rodent through the hidden hallways in the dark as their torches come closer and closer. I slide around a corner and collide head-on with a man in chain mail. The collision bowls me to the ground.

"You! I held you tight, but you left my sweet company." The guard standing over me is the same one who held me in the abbot's hall. "I should throw you in the fire—!"

His heavy hand seizes me, shaking me as a dog shakes vermin in his jaws.

"You!" he barks. "You're gonna be the first to burn." The memory of Edward's sandalwood scent is long gone, I can smell only my sweat—reeking with the raw tang of fear—and the powerful oxlike odor that comes off of the guard.

Outside, I am sure there is a crowd, every face leering demonically, greedy for blood. The ravenous mob is already tending the fire, heating the pitch, preparing the spit on which my body will turn and crisp ever so slowly, and die.

"Gonna burn you!" he shouts as he pushes me toward the stairs.

My friends were wrong about their reprieve. The door to the sanctuary opens under the guard's hand. My skin goes cold and wet with dread.

CHAPTER 18

A RAUCOUS CLAMOR FILLS the air outside the sanctuary as crows flock high on the roof of the monastery. At the sound of the bells, a black-feathered murder of them springs up into the open wind. The bells are chiming the hour of None, the ninth hour.

"Gonna burn you!" The guard pushes me out of the doorway, down the heavy stone steps, into the daylit afternoon. Stakes and piles of pitch-soaked wood still wait for us across the courtyard.

Wasn't it enough that my son died, my only hope extinguished like a wandering spark, snuffed out so soon? Do they need to crush me too?

"Leave 'im be," Moten's voice brays out. He always knew my hideaways. He must have been the one who led them to find me in this secret place. *He betrayed me.*

Moten takes tight hold of my arm. "Go on, go on!" he shouts at the guards in chain mail, and they put their crossbows down and move away.

I can see monks working at our cart. They lift bags and sacks, putting them in the old village cart. *What are they doing here?*

But Moten pulls me back into the sanctuary and glances from side to side, his narrow jaw tight. "I don't know what you done to these boys, or why," he whispers. "The Abbot thinks now this is a matter of temporal honor, of kingly judgment, not for God to judge the truth of it. But you still have the power of speech—why do you not use it?"

I do not respond, and he stares at me. "I will find out the truth, so help me Heaven," he says.

Cold fingers of dread walk underneath my arms and across my back, the hair rising on my neck. I drag in a slow, rasping breath.

"They haven't come to kill you yet, my dear," Moten whispers. "We go to the King. But this journey ain't for the tender ones. The Abbot commanded me to be master of all your fates. Truth be told, I'm a prisoner as much as you now. Just remember, I know all your secrets."

✠

Moten lets go of my arm. His words resound, repeating in my head, reverberating like the tolling bells.

I urge myself forward, out of the church, legs quivering, head faint and hollow with fear. I stagger down the steps, but no guards catch me. No one stops me. The monks are carefully tying a swath of new oiled canvas over the top of the cart.

We came here with rotten old barn straw, corroded sackcloth, and naked frost-flecked flesh. To my surprise, I see each of our thin boys entwined in a white burial shroud, a luxury unseen in our town of Duns for many years. And the white-swathed bodies rest now on fresh-turned straw.

I recognize my boy by his tousled hair. Christian still rests silent among the dead. A crow lifts its wings and flies close over the bodies in the cart, as if to mark them.

"You almost made it," Liam says to me. He flaps his arms in mockery of the crow. "Now if you'd just been able to grow wings and fly away, you would've escaped!"

I stare at him. None of us have been burned yet.

Salvius responds to my quizzical expression. "The Abbot suspended our sentence for a time."

"That ripe monk tol' him what for." Tom jerks a thumb at Moten walking down the steps. "The Abbot was near convinc'd to let us go as innocents."

Geoff leans in, his voice bitter. "An' then those feckin' bandits who took Hob, they spoke up—protested that it was a matter of lordly honor. That we'd offended their Lord."

"Bloody shite," mutters Liam.

Salvius pushes Geoff. "So we're going to the King—a matter of noble honor," says Salvius.

Benedict gives a braying laugh. "Ye should have seen the look on the bandits' faces—like a hawk when the mouse runs into its hole."

"Aye." Benedict's face goes dark. "An' then when the Abbot says they have to bring forth Hob to go with us, the bastards have to tell him that Hob has died already, under questioning."

I shake my head. No answers from Hob then. We will never know the truth of his actions. Salvius crosses himself. "Bless Hob," mutters Benedict. "Bless—"

"Feck Hob," Geoff blurts out. "May his soul rot in hell."

Benedict gives Geoff a shove, enough to knock him down on the stone steps. The guards stride over, and Geoff gets up shakily from the ground.

"We're going to the King for justice," says Liam after a moment. "Can you imagine my son and I—going to the King?"

"As a bloody prisoner," says Salvius dryly. "You aren't going as a petitioner. You're going as a prisoner."

"I'm going," says Liam stubbornly. "I'm going with my son."

"Bloody prisoners," says Salvius again. "Sent to the Royal Court and some Starry Chamber they got there for summary judgment. The Abbot was all in a lather to get us on the road to London, he said the judges wouldn't be around much longer, I guess."

Moten approaches. The men are wary, but they keep talking. He is slowly turning into one of us, caught as he is now in our journey.

"We've got over a fortnight until we reach London," says Benedict to Salvius. "Should be long enough."

Moten shakes his head. "Might not be enough time. The Court leaves for Cornwall on February tenth, Shrovetide week."

"What's in Cornwall?" says Salvius.

"The New Year—and this year, the New Year begins on March twenty-fifth. The Court always sits in session in Cornwall for the New Year."

Benedict shrugs. "So what does the New Year matter to us?"

"If you can't be tried by Shrovetide, you'll wait until the Court can put you on trial in the Star Chamber again. You will just rot in London Tower for the next many months."

Geoff shudders and blanches. Even in our remote environs, we know that men die in the Tower. Cold, starvation, and torture take the poor unfortunates, who are then eaten by rats.

Quickly, I count the days on my fingers. It is the end of the week of Candlemas here at the abbey, the second week of the month of January. If we are to survive this dark season, we must make London by Shrovetide, in February. If the Court dissolves—and with it the Chamber's powers of justice—by February 10, then our troupe has but eighteen days to move across the land. And this in bitter winter.

Moten turns and stalks away to see about the horses.

Tom scowls at Moten's back. "Why is that mouthy bastard the one given charge of us? Why didn't the Abbot listen to Salvius?" He makes a rude gesture.

"Could be a pardon awaits us in the King's Star Chamber," says Benedict. "We can make our case 'gainst them Jews."

"Shut your feckin' mouth," says Geoff. "It's your own fault they died." He will not let the quarrel rest.

Liam gives me a weary grin and holds out my cloak and bedroll. "We must leave the monastery today—the Abbot says we must be gone 'fore the sun is gone from the sky."

By sundown. According to the Cluniac Rule of Order, mortal remains cannot remain in the open air for longer than the span of one day. The Abbot has conformed to that rule by ordering us with our dead out of the gates before daylight fails.

The Abbot has given our troupe two strong new cart-horses to pull the burden, while Salvius's old mare is tied behind the cart. Three guards go with us as well, they place their helms and crossbows and extra armor in the cart, alongside our frozen boys.

The men treat me no differently, but wasn't Moten telling my story to the Abbot and the crowd? *Are my secrets exposed? What do the men know of me now?*

There is one secret I have never told, one puzzle no one will ever unlock. Despite that, the rest of my mysteries are enough to murder me.

But then the great gates of the monastery creak open, and the two strong new horses the Abbot has loaned to Moten breathe out billows of steam. We move.

✠

On the other side of the monastery from where we camped the first night, mud spreads in trailing fingers and veins. There are paths here, tracks wending their way between half-thatched hovels and ill-pitched tents.

Here, beyond the wall on the lee side, out of the wind, there are others like us who travel abroad without bond or license from a lord, and outcast monks, those who fell from the rule. This camp encompasses all as are not permitted within the grounds of the Priory of Saint Mary Magdalene, including thieves who bear the marks of punishment—a missing limb, a gouged-out eye—and jongleurs, mimers, wandering players, and the like.

Our cart of the dead halts alongside a cart with a burden nearly equally strange: a mass of large wooden faces. I can see masks and the wings of an angel next to the claws of a dragon—the Beast of the Apocalypse. It is a cart that holds the stuff of players. They practice that shameful craft—*artem illam ignominiosam*—pageantry and playacting, which has no license from a lord, which is forbidden by the Holy Church.

Around an open fire is the group of players, a lad of straw hair, a maid of indeterminate age and sour face, a large man squatting by the flames, and a slight and sallow one whose head bears the mark of an outgrown tonsure.

They practice in the frosty mud, hoping perhaps to have their play permitted inside the monastery.

"*Thou worm!*" declaims the one who wears a great crowned head that sparkles with small shards of glass. "*Thy wiles so sick—Thy false fables, they are so thick!*" When he shakes his head, the bits of glass glimmer, as if his skin is scaled in light. He is God Almighty.

The others in my group are already unpacking our cart, but I do not lift a finger to help. I am transfixed by the players. Deus speaks again:

> Adam, because the apple thou didst eat
> Go naked, hungry and barefoot.
> Eat herbs and grass and root.
> As a wretch in the world you must wend.

The Devil rises then. He speaks, and God responds. We have little enough to unpack, and soon the guards watch too, passing around a flask of cider. Soon, the players finish their act and collapse by the fire, wearied by their labors.

Moten retrieves sausages and turnips from the baggage and sets Benedict to cooking. We are astonished at this feast, and we must share such luxurious fare—Salvius adds wood to the players' fire and widens the circle.

"'Ere then," says Tom to the players. "Ah've got a story to tell too! It's the story of our boys who lie here dead, the story of their victory." I have heard Tom's tales many market days. He can give a fair mockery of the wandering minstrels and mummers who visit us at Whitsunday and through Midsummer.

Tom guzzles from the guard's leather flask. Then he stands and raises his voice so it sounds over the sizzling sausages, the sparking fire. "The house burned up with blackest smoke. They fought with bloody knives in hand! They battled—"

Geoff snorts. "How'd they fight, I'll have you tell us? They died in a feck'ng house fire! Innocent of blood they were—none of this here war and knives and shite."

Tom glowers at Geoff. "Shut your mouth, you buggerin' fool."

Benedict gives a scornful laugh.

Tom strikes a knight's pose. "Our boys wove the heraldry flags, the saddles and the battle raiment! They were a-sewin' for Sir Peter and his pilgrimage. It was two hours 'til daylight, in hopeful spirit and with holy heart, they hoped to make their victory."

The guard who seized me takes the flask from Tom. The guard has told me his name now—Roben Broussart—and he smiles as he passes the flask to me. Strong cider, distilled over the smoldering fires of August, the taste of rotting apples bitter on my lips.

"A good story!" says Roben. "The story of Englishmen!"

Tom belches heartily and wipes his mouth. "Our boys did not know the house would burn with blackest smoke. While they slept, the treachery of murder in their beds!"

Geoff laughs bitterly. "They weren't even sleeping, you bloody idjit! They tried to get out—the door was lock'd on 'em."

Tom hiccups drunkenly and raises his voice. "When them firebrands whistled wetly, their blood ran in holy sacrifice. For every thread they wove, blessed by their innocent blood, an altar fire burned so bright that God's great temple in heaven could see the sight!"

Liam mutters in my ear. "Ripe shite! Is this what he really believes?"

"Now do your duty, knights so young and proud!" Tom stands, swaying over the fire, the syllables slurring off his lips in a sordid stream. "Fight the French! Up spring the spears, twenty feet tall, and out come swords all sharp an' silver bright!"

"Aye, as at Crécy, where we beat them damn'd French!" shouts Roben.

I remember Crécy. I heard of it from Edward's own lips. He was sixteen and afraid, surrounded by grizzled veterans twice his age and four times his experience. On his first day in the field, a French lance went through his squire's helm. He watched the man's brains and blood seep out until his death.

But Edward's father had given him that Moorish armor black as ebony, telling him it would make him fearsome to others. And in some way, even on that first day, it did so. It is a strange thing, but in time the black he wore to mask his fear became his outer attitude. On the grounds of Crécy, garbed in black, he won his spurs at the age of sixteen. And so from those days forward, Edward wore always some token of that battle: a black sigil, and the three white feathers he took from the French. I always imagined the fresh-faced lad with deep-blue eyes going fearful and knock-kneed as the lances thundered toward him across that bloody meadow.

As Christian grew older, his face became ever more like Edward's. I imagine my son replete with honor in the lists, his own blue eyes glimmering like frost within a lionhearted helm.

✠

Tom seizes the flask again, takes another long swig. Then he swings a hand up flat, as if he thrusts a sword, and holds it. "The black they wove bright as a raven, and the lion's claws thereon, the red sparklin' like red-fired rubies, the yellow glittering like the sun—"

Liam chuckles dryly, a mocking laugh. "What happened to our boys, Tom? Your story's got naught to do with 'em now. Why're you talking 'bout the Frenchies?"

"Our boys sew'd the noble heraldry into hauberk and breastplate," slurs Tom.

Geoff snorts. "Pig droppings. Big fat feckin' pig droppings! I want to know—"

"Pig droppings, my arse!" Tom bellows. He staggers drunkenly, glaring at Geoff, at all of us. "You tell your own story then, Geoff, you swine!"

"Our boys lie there dead"—Geoff points, and his firm carpenter's hand does not tremble—"an' I for one, want justice for their deaths!" He leans forward, taking us all into his confidence.

"Truth be told, I'm still followin' those who done this deed."

"You've gone crack'd," says Liam. "The bandits—those who served the Lord Bellecort—they burned up our lads."

"Nah," says Tom. "That witch is here, the villain who did this to us all."

"What villain?" says Salvius sharply.

"It was a spell, I tell you," shouts Tom. "A spell to cover up our eyes. All the time that witch was in league with Hob—an' she found a way to have us accused, to take us to our doom."

"I thought so!" says Geoff. "The witch who worked her magic on Hob."

"What of that woman the monk described to the Abbot?" says Salvius.

"You"—Tom points at Moten—"You talked of her. A woman in hiding? A witch, eh? A female witch!"

"For once we agree," says Geoff. "A witch did this. And she's here with us, tonight."

Moten clears his throat. "That woman I spoke of... The truth is..."

His eyes slide toward me. I sit stolid, my heart pounding.

Moten opens his mouth again.

CHAPTER 19

THE FIRE BLAZES, sparks rioting above the earth, rising into the night. In the reflected blaze, the masks of the players packed in their cart glimmer behind us, false faces shifting in the light.

"She's real enough," says Moten. "I know where she is now."

I look away from him, and Moten's mouth closes hard. He furrows his brow.

Benedict leans forward. "Why did you say that witch was at the monastery years ago?"

"Well... I..." Moten stutters. "I did tell the Abbot of the rumor of a woman who stole a treasure. And that woman had cause to flee." He pauses.

"C'mon then," blurts Geoff. He points at Moten. "What is the truth of that story you told to the Abbot 'bout a noblewoman?"

Moten works his mouth, but no sound comes out.

"Speak!" says Salvius impatiently. "You made our boy's deaths a matter of noble pride, did you not? Any man with a tunic has a right to argue before the King. So you told the Abbot of some woman of the Court who fled with a royal treasure. Is it the same woman—the witch we spoke of?"

Moten splutters. "Well... I... uh... I too heard rumor of that woman years ago." Then he pauses again. My heart is beating so hard I am sure the men can see its fast rhythm. "She came here, to this monastery. There was a message after she left here, a messenger from the Crown."

"Aye, I remember," grunts Tom. "Nine, ten years ago, there was that messenger came out to all the villages from the Crown, offered a reward."

Roben the guard leans forward. "A reward for what?"

"For some rich woman who had stolen a treasure of the Crown," explains Benedict. "So we kept our eyes open for fancy carriages, for a nice horse, someone flaunting their ill-gotten gains. But no one like that ever showed up in our village."

"I tell you the truth, I think she made it to our woods," says Geoff. "She's follow'd us here—that witch kill'd our boys, an' I'll have her death for my boy's life. I seen her near our village."

I blink in surprise.

Salvius gives a mocking smile. "Aye, did you see her in one of Tom's drunken visions?"

"A vision came to you too?" asks Tom.

"Nah," Geoff snarls. "I seen her deep in the woods, dancin' once with the other witch—you remember her, dontcha, Sal?"

Salvius flinches, and in that moment, I know he loved Nell.

"I tell you, I saw this strange woman with her, a woman I'd never seen before. They were laughing loud an' singin' their songs, deep in the woods. They were far away, cross the valley from me, but there they were, celebratin' something. Maybe the death of a child they'd killed!"

"A will-o'-the-wisp. A spirit woman," whispers Tom. "Witches!"

Roben guffaws. "What witches are these?"

Tom is laughing too. He stops when Geoff points at him.

"You know who the one witch was."

"Nell," Tom says.

"Ayuh." Geoff nods. "The one who was found out in her craft."

Liam is quick to speak. "I dunno if she was killed for witchwork or not, but—"

"You knew that Nell." Geoff points at Salvius. "You were her friend, eh?"

Salvius gazes back at him. He clears his throat and then his eyes go steely and calm. "I went to her for a tincture for mine own boy here—for Cole—when he suffered from the palsy. That is all."

The log hisses and spits a tongue of flame. There are sparks in the air. The tiny lights wink out, but I can see a faint afterimage floating down. Steam and ash.

Salvius saves himself. But if they can point at me as a scapegoat, then all will be lost. I will never know who killed my son.

"Goddammit, I'm tellin' you the truth!" says Geoff. "There was another woman with that Nell. They were dancing an' singing in the woods, deep in the woods, where only woodcutters go. I were there looking for cedar for a carving for the Lord Peter. He wanted a cedar carving for his Yule feast with the gentry. So I were deep in the woods. That's when I seen her."

My blood runs cold at the memory. Geoff did see us in truth. I remember when we put flowers in our hair, and Nell coaxed me to dance with her. For the first time in years, I felt like a girl again. Obviously, someone else thought so too.

"Why didn't you say something?" says Roben.

"What? That I seen two women dancin' like li'l children? It's only now—all these years later—that I know there was a dark secret in them woods."

"Is she part of a plot with that woman of the Court? Or is she the same woman?"

"I dunno."

But Roben seems to understand. "An' when that one witch died—"

"Nell," says Liam.

"Ayuh," Geoff glances at him. "When she died, the other one was never found. I tell you, there is a secret woman in the woods. A wight, and she had an evil plan. An' when I saw the hoofprint of the horse with the cracked hoof, I knew she was ahead of us on this road. She led the bandits to us—she sent her evil thoughts out to them, cursed them to kill us all."

"That's shite!" says Cole suddenly. "There ain't no witch out there—no woman who wishes us ill. The truth is—"

I am suddenly afraid that my son Christian told Cole the truth about me. Then Salvius catches Cole in his great arms. "Cole, lad," he says softly. "Hush. It ain't no good to talk of that Nell. Shuttum."

I am grateful to Salvius, but something turns in me, hearing Salvius mutter these low words. Nell must have meant much to him, and I wish he'd tell more of her story.

Cole murmurs, but he subsides. I think the matter is dead, and I breathe a sigh of relief.

Unexpectedly, Liam revives it.

"I hunted that woman once," he says.

"Who?" says Geoff. "Nell?"

"Nay, that woman of the Court you spoke of. You know my crime."

Geoff nods. He gestures at the men gathered around the fire. "You would tell them your secret now?"

Liam shakes his head in resignation. "Ah'm in chains already. What more can they do to me? They'll all know soon enough. I'm a deserter, my friends. I left the King's service."

Roben the guard leans forward, his eyes wide. "You served the King?"

"Aye," says Liam. "See, I was an archer of the King, you know, and I was assigned to hunt her. That grand lady who had stolen a great treasure from the Crown."

Roben's mouth gapes in surprise. "You were an archer?"

"God's truth," says Liam, holding a hand over his heart. "I swore allegiance! Archer for years in the King's army, and then they sent me to spy out this fugitive."

My head whirls. This is the first I've heard of Liam's past as an archer and a spy for the King. *This was Liam's long-hidden crime? Desertion from the ranks?*

I knew Liam had arrived in the village only a few months before I came there. But I had almost forgotten he was wearing the ragged remnants of an archer's sash when I first met him.

Does he still serve the King as a spy?

Roben takes another guard by the arm. "Get out the beer—beer all around for the longbow archer in our midst!"

Beer is poured in tankards as Liam continues. "An' I thought I'd be an archer for the rest of me life. But you all know what happened to me in our village."

"Aye. You met the prettiest lass this side of the Thames." Tom holds his beer up in a toast to Kate's beauty.

"Right, Kate snared me with her wiles. An' so I stayed put in the village of Duns. So we have two boys together." Liam takes a gulp of bitter brew.

His face goes dark as he glances toward the cart. "Only one now."

But Roben has warmed to the subject. "Tell of the King's quest! You were a spy hunting out a fugitive, eh? What was your mission then?"

"They didn't tell us much a'tall. She'd been seen moving north, but she'd gone to ground. Last seen, she went on the road that took me to the village. An' that's where my hunt ended."

"I deserted my ranks, I stayed behind. I never did find that witch, or whoever she was." Liam shrugs. "An' so I betrayed my oath, and I am a fugitive from the King's ranks, even now, after all these years."

Roben laughs. "I suppose you could still look for her, eh? Did they offer gold?"

"Aye, she was wanted by the Crown. Great deal of gold offered for her! They made out she was on the run, but I don't know how someone like her could hide. Anyone would 'ave seen a soft thief from the Court from miles away. On her fine horse an' all."

"Sure that's true," says Benedict. "An' them women at Court are weak an' small in frame."

I glance at Geoff and Liam. I am taller than both of them. Once I was small, but bearing a child and the work at the smithy and the mill has changed my shape. I am no slight slip of a girl any longer. My arms are now large and strong.

"Yeah, I like 'em weak like that," slurs Tom.

"You're a fool," says Geoff.

"An' you're a bastard!" Tom swings wildly at him. Geoff knocks his legs out from under him, and soon they roll on the ground.

Liam speaks over the brawling men. "They told us her long tresses were bright as the sun. That's how we'd know her."

I finger my unkempt hair. Once my long mane was burned gold by the sun in the summer, and bright as copper in the wintertide. Now my shorn locks have begun to show some silver and dull lead. It is shorn ragged and short. I give a wry grin: I am in no danger from this disclosure of Liam's.

"She carried a treasure," says Liam. "But what it was, no one was told."

I glance at the cart with its horrible burden. I could hardly take my eyes off my child, sleeping or waking, the thread of my life woven into his. My only true treasure.

"So did she bear silver and gold?" says Geoff. "Would we get to keep it?"

Within my cloak, I can feel that rounded edge of the necklace and the ring, cold against my breast. My last bit of true silver still hides there, gripped tight by the bosom binding. My last heirloom, safe.

Moten raises his voice. "I can tell you more than I told the Abbot," he says loudly. He glances at me. "I can tell who she is and—"

Geoff rolls dangerously close to the fire, his fingers pulling tight on Tom's hair. Tom yelps and curses. I decide to join this melee. I stand and jog Moten's elbow, spilling beer all down his cassock.

"What're you doing?" Moten splutters. "You just—"

And that's when I lift my fist and strike Moten in the face—as hard as I can hit.

Benedict gasps. "What did that monk do to Mear?"

Cole cheers blindly for a fight.

"Mear must not have liked all that talk of witches," says Liam, backing away.

"Mear—Jesus Christ—don't strike the monk, you bloody fool," says Salvius.

Moten raises his arms and pushes me back, but I brush away his soft scholar's hands so I can strike him again. I pummel him in the eyes, blinding him while I trip his legs and push him down into the mud. Roben the guard stands then and staggers over to help Moten, but before he reaches me I punch again, sinking blows into the monk's belly. Moten's eyes go wide and fearful. The whites show all around as the guards pull me off.

God help me, I want him to be afraid of me. He will not tell my story. He will never tell my secrets. I want him cowed and silent.

A blast of frigid air sends a flurry gusting madly around, bits of ice dance on the wind. Flecks of frost pepper my hair, a plague of ashen insects.

The guards seize me and throw me on my bedroll. I am beset on all sides, behind and before. I have no Christian, no Nell, no Salvius, no Moten. I am utterly alone. The world has turned its face against me.

Frozen rain hisses into the failing fire. The night is full of sleet and snow. It swirls into our eyes as the last light flares and goes dark.

CHAPTER 20

IN THE MORNING, the sky is dark and gravid with snow. We depart early on the White Road. The monastery fades away behind us, like a smudge on an oilcloth window, until it winks from sight.

"We could be in London within the fortnight," Moten declares. "A map I copied shows that one may quickly travel on the White Road between Peterborough and London, given fast steeds, mild weather, and good luck."

No one has the temerity to point out to Moten that our steeds are slow cart horses, the sky stinks of snow, and our luck runs counter to the dice. A journey of this distance could take many weeks. And as I count them, we have only seventeen days left to make London.

We travel now with a raggle-taggle of fellow pilgrims, who band together on the open road for the common welfare. Our fellow travelers include the players with their motley cart and others of a loftier sphere. The party of armed men who bear heraldic tunics and hold noble weapons also join us. The noble they ride with is a Lady clothed in red and gold—I'd seen her in the abbot's hall, wearing the gray veil of mourning over her bright livery.

At midday we take our luncheon, and the Lady lifts her veil to eat.

Her face shines with clean oil, and underneath that sheen she has written a curving line on each eyebrow with a twist of charred hemp. Each cheek glows pink and rouged with pretended warmth. I remember how Theresa of Avignon would plunge a needle into her thumb, extracting two thick drops of blood and rubbing one drop across each cheekbone, so that her face glowed with pretended warmth.

With a shock, I recognize the Lady's face.

I know her.

She began as an orphan at Canterbury, a novice like me. And then went to be a girl in the first Lady of Doncaster's service. Now, in her maturity, this girl has apparently replaced that august personage, becoming the Lady of Doncaster herself. Perhaps His Lordship found this young lady in waiting appealing to the eye, and perhaps for such pleasures as he took in his bedchamber. The Lord is the very person Her Ladyship now mourns.

Her sharp eyes glance my way. I quickly hide my head.

In the midst of her red and gold-clad troupe of soldiers, this lady stands with an attitude of authority and grace. Yet in my mind I see the slight and limping girl she once was. Fortune's wheel turns on chance, and with it every life.

I am now on the other end of Fortune's wheel, held as prisoner by the guards. Geoff and I must both walk in chains for the day, punished now for the blows we gave the night before, and they've found a way to chain me so the manacles stay on this time.

The rest of the men from Duns are nominally prisoners as well, but they go free among our wardens: there is no sense in constraining travelers on this dangerous road.

Moten walks near the Lady. He does not look at me, except to stare at me sideways when he thinks I do not see. He bears a blackened eye and a bruise across one cheek. He still does not understand.

Salvius has ingratiated himself with Moten, and he walks in a lordly style, under noble livery, alongside Moten of Cluny and this Lady of the Realm.

To the Lady and Salvius, Moten declaims the particulars of his debate with the Abbot, and then, as the Lady loses interest, he tells tales of a monk and maid wandering the monastery together, tales of their adventures. In truth, I recognize the maid he describes: every detail recalls the younger me. The portrait he paints is true to history, but I have nearly forgotten those escapades he describes. After all, I sojourned in his monastery for only a season, a slight summertide, before I heard rumors of men on the open road who pursued a woman of my likeness. I left unexpectedly one night.

And in the intervening years, I have moved on from a maid with a babe in arms to life as a father—and secret mother too. I raised a child, I became a man, and lived the life of a mute. During all that time, I was in the midmost stream of life, the rush of events in all their vicissitudes rushing and flowing, splashing and streaming around my child and me.

Moten has been becalmed all this time, eddying in his monastic cell. Nothing has changed for him in the still waters of the Priory of Saint Mary Magdalene. The memories of my short summer sojourn are fresh to his mind. For poor Brother Moten, it is as if I left the monastery the night before.

As I watch Moten glance worriedly back at me from time to time, I see him now in truth as a naïf. He would betray me only from ignorance and innocence. He is a child in a world of men.

Yet my heart does not bend further: I did what I could do to preserve my life. I have kept a hold on his tongue, and I do not regret my injury to him.

Late in the afternoon, we come upon a skeleton of smoked timbers, wattle cracked and fallen, staddle stones scorched and broken apart by fire. It calls to my mind the fire that killed our boys and the memory of Nell's burned croft.

The cow byre nearby is a yawning wreck as well. Stones have fallen from its walls—they rest black and uneven across the new-fallen snow. These stark remnants are not covered by snow, and so we can tell that the burning only just took place: someone ate and laughed and slept here. Now they are gone.

I remember Nell wandering in the deep woods with me, telling me the names of each bird that called. Fieldfares, pipits, larks and chaffinches. I can still hear a chaffinch's little falling song, echoing down these many months.

There is no chaffinch here, no birds at all. A solitary tree stretches its branched and crooked fingers over these recent ruins. On the lowest branch hangs a shred of a rope. That sight too starts a deep bell ringing in my breast, the rhythm that dictates all my years of fear. A sight with me every night, in all the moments of tormented sleep.

Nell the day after. The rope with that strange and twisted triple knot tied tight around her neck, her flesh bruised and battered. And the last sight I had of her, raw earth spattering down on her silent face in the hole I'd dug so very deep in the ground. This memory is what keeps my tongue so still.

The bit of wound hemp that hangs above this burned house upon the road could be harmless—the remnant of a child's woven swing—but my mind can see only Nell's body twisting slowly above that empty cauldron, beside that awful horror of a charred house.

I cover my eyes and turn away. None others are so affected on the road.

The Lady, for one, thinks this burned place to be a mere curiosity. With her serving man, she steps gingerly over the scorched threshold and charred straw. Then she turns and smiles at that overgrown apple tree. She little knows what horror she embraces in my mind as she steps close to the branch, grasps the shred of rope, and swings in her bright red livery.

She may be noble in her state and quick with wit besides. But half her gaiety is not assumed at all—it is her natural state. And in her gleeful face, I can still see the girl I remember—limping fast to join her playmates years before. I watch her move back and forth in the breeze, uncaring and unafraid.

All is not lost in the world. I find that I can breathe once more. I think of Edward, and I still hope.

My thoughts drift years away, walking hand in hand with Edward on some spring day when the hazel is in bloom and the scent of lilacs graces the air. And it is then that I hear a voice speak his name.

"... Edward at Crécy in forty-six, when my Lord rode with him. Indeed, Edward was given armor dark as damson." It is the Lady, her voice high and bright.

Moten and Salvius are both listening now. "His first battle," says Salvius. "But wasn't he just a lad then?"

"I can tell you, Edward wasn't alone in the venture." The Lady raises her voice in pride. "One of those who helped Edward lead his men at Crécy was my own Lord Doncaster—blessed be his memory. My Lord commanded the flank beside him."

I note that always Salvius has his eyes upon the short swords of her men, those elegant things in scabbards gilded in gold. In fact, late that afternoon, Salvius makes most bold. After much flattery, he asks to wear the livery of Doncaster, in fact declares that he would be honored to wear it, in memory of the Lady's fallen Lord. The Lady accepts the compliment with grace and gives him one of the bright red and gold tunics of her house.

Salvius replaces the old burned and misshapen tunic of Lord Peter's house with this bright new red one of Doncaster. He wears it with pride.

The Lady continues her talk of battles and of glory. She speaks now of the battle of Poitiers, where Edward's renown grew. She describes the arcing lines of men with lances, the striking heraldry of battle. She tells of how Edward used the same tactics he learned at Crécy, drawing the French forward with a feint of weakness, and then crushing them with a heavy blow. Her voice is bright and cheerful, the sound drifting back merrily to us who walk behind.

"Edward married upon his return from Poitiers," she says. "Joan, the fair maid of Kent, the lass he knew as a child."

I feel that I almost cannot breathe: Edward was married a mere year after he lost me at Canterbury. And if memory serves, Joan was flighty as a swift, moving from one man to another restlessly. She was married before, and more than once, I think. To some, bedding another is a sport, the game that lustful courtiers play. Always, Edward spoke of that practice with disdain. *How could my Edward marry her?*

The Lady babbles on. "Yes, to the fair maid of Kent. They lived at Aquitaine and Woodstock both. Now they had two children, one passed away, but the other—"

It is a marriage of convenience, designed to give him heirs, I decide. *He does not love Joan.*

"The other child lives, but is frail they say, a little lad and weak, even to this day. And always we meant to go to Woodstock, as we visited them awhile in Aquitaine. Then as I said, that wasting illness came upon Edward."

Edward is ill now? The priests say Antichrist comes soon, and we are visited with plagues—even our lords fall victim to such pestilence.

But I would be with him in his pain. I could go to him now and nurse him in his old age. As we make camp for the night, I cannot stop thinking of him. He is trapped in a loveless marriage, his child dead and gone.

I will go to Edward. I will comfort him in his grief and loss. *All will be well.*

✠

Upon the turning of the road beyond the burned cruck house, we come to a parting of the ways. One way is the White Road, and very old. It is the Roman way.

The other road tends east, away from this late sun. It is a newer way, and full of mud and ruts: the road to the county of Ely and to Norfolk.

The noble company prepares now to depart to the lands of Doncaster and with the Lady goes every other pilgrim. The players go with her as well as their motley cart of masks. Our small party under guard is left alone to travel the White Road to London.

The Lady bids farewell to Moten and Salvius. She gives both Moten and Salvius tunics and cloaks with the gold horse on a field of red, the noble token of her house. She seems to have mistaken Salvius for more than just a peasant, for she even tells him that he can wear her colors on the open road, which is a high honor. Salvius proves himself worthy of the honor, bending low to kiss her hand and thanking her most gracefully.

Moten, also grateful for the gift, offers to speak to others on her behalf. "When we arrive at Court, I will speak to Edward of Woodstock about your house of Doncaster."

The Lady shakes her head gently, with a little moue. "Edward of Woodstock is dead. Did I not tell you that? The Lord of Woodstock is gone to heaven's halls."

A heavy stone drops in me at her words, sinking with my heart into the depths. *Edward is dead.* My vision blurs as thick lead seems to fill my veins.

Above us, scudding clouds cover the sky. Each cloud seems weighty as lead, vast pillars permanent as stone. Yet moments later the greatest cloud has died, collapsed into a spreading mist. Time moves on, and with it all flesh.

"The best of the Plantagenets gone. First, Edward, and then his father too. Now there but remains a ten-year-old lad in that line. And John of Gaunt, of course, who watches ever that noble seat."

"Ah." Salvius is surprised too. "Sad to hear this news. The Lord was buried then, at his family estate?"

She laughs her trill once more, but it has a hollow sound. "You would not believe where that lord asked to be buried. Let me tell you..."

But I am no longer listening to her vacant prattle. I have spent the last years of my life building back up that possibility of love, that faint thread of hope. But now that hope is gone: I cannot find out the truth of my love with Edward. I never will know. The Earl of Hereford won.

The Lady turns her horse away, one last phrase drifting back to us. "Yes, Edward is dead—and with him all the chivalry in this kingdom. *Au revoir.*"

The clouds above are dark, as if their centers have rusted out, as if the sky itself will fall in upon me and consume me in a roiling whirlwind of pain.

But I can't go to Edward, because he is gone. I can't prove the truth of anything now. He is dead. Buried in the ground.

When I left Canterbury Abbey all those years ago in the dead of night, I grasped Edward's ring like a holy relic, holding it tight as if it alone could put the lie to what I had been told, as if that one small thing would keep me alive.

The memory of my life with Edward washes over me now, powerful and cold, chilling me anew, carrying me away.

CHAPTER 21

When Edward took me as his lover that first time, I was surprised, distraught even. Not unwilling perhaps, but unprepared for the pain and shock, as if a hot blade cut me. It was not as I expected, not caresses extended or kisses sweet. The act hurt, yet there was a strange pleasure mingled with the pain. And something unseen linked us then.

I was determined to leave Edward and his high conceits behind me. I would become a scholar and an Abbess in the years to come, and never again would I think of love or pleasures of the flesh. So I buried myself in books and ancient lore.

Yet Edward would not let me forget him. And he changed his mode of hunting me. Instead of being haughty in his bearing, he became a pilgrim to my shrine, traveling every morning to the scriptorium.

After that first sordid time in the catacombs, I had told him not to speak with me again, and so I was surprised when he proved his ardor only with tokens of his love. Irises and lilies he brought me in the spring, sunflowers in summer.

There was no arrogance left in him, no sense that I was lesser than he. He was a thirsty man in a desert, or so he seemed to me. And so, he won me over a second time. I began to find him pleasing to my eyes again, trying desperately to conceal my own need, wanting to be strong, not weak.

As fall arrived, he brought fresh ripe apples, and my heart softened at his yearning.

Just as that first lady fell at the taste of an apple, so perhaps did I. But whose heart would not melt at Edward's childish longing? By that time, he was not some condescending noble, but a child in need of any caress I would deign to give. Beneath his shell of power, he was so very weak. And so I spoke to him again, and we resumed our lovemaking and our talks in the catacombs.

Months later, as spring came once more, I found my bloody flux had ceased, and doubt came on me. *What would Edward think?*

And again, I was surprised. He was beside himself with joy.

I thought perhaps he would take me as a consort, in a house under his name. But Edward had loftier plans. Even though I had been born a commoner, I had grown in knowledge and authority. I was now assistant to the Abbess, and esteemed. Edward told me he would grant me lands, that he would give me a name beyond my station. And more than that. For without a word or prompt from me, he made plans to take me from the abbey and wed me outright.

All through the misty days of March, April, and May, I traveled with him, away from the abbey, to estates far and wide, until I knew all in his circles. Every lady greeted me as equal, and every knight gave allegiance to me.

Yet all during my travels with him, I had not lost my vows, and I returned every month to my cloister house for absolution.

Finally, we went to London, to visit at Court, and then I took a day to answer my mother's last request. I tried so desperately to fulfill the promise I had made. I told no one of her words, but even in secrecy, I could not find the people she spoke of. Now I know I should have tried again, I should have gone as far as my authority could take me when I was exalted. I failed to act then. I was distracted by Edward and all that he promised.

But I never forgot what I must do for her, what charge she gave me in the end.

☩

Once, Edward took me to the coast, to the very place I'd lived as a child, overgrown and abandoned for many years.

"This was my home," I said to Edward as I stared around at what remained of the old sheep-walls and broken-down crofts. I felt as if I walked in a dream, the pathways of my childhood full of vines and tall grass now.

"Yes," he said. "I found it after much searching. For you, and for you alone. A nameless place now."

"Once it had a name," I said. "When folk still lived in this place, it was called Houmout. My father, God rest his soul, he named this place."

"Courage," said Edward. "That means 'courage,' in the low tongue."

"Does it?" I murmured, thinking of my father. I do not tell Edward that last charge my mother gave me. Perhaps the name *Houmout* has somewhat to do with that secret, that promise I made. I do not know.

But Edward took my hand. "Yes," he said firmly. "So that would be your name too."

"What do you mean?"

"Where you are from—just as I am Edward of Woodstock, you are Miriam of Houmout."

"Yes," I said. My lips seemed numb from the welter of memory that surrounded me there. Memories of running on the tall grass near the ocean waves, laughing with my mother nearby. And later memories, of watching my family suffer and die.

On her deathbed, gasping and shivering with pain, my mother brought forth words no one else could hear, and she gave them to me as her last secret, making me promise to fulfill her dying wish.

For no one else was left here to take her name forward: none were left alive from this village.

"I am the only one remaining of this place," I told him. "I am the only one who will ever hold this name, evermore."

Edward grasped my hand firmly, and brought it to his lips. "Then we will keep the name alive, I will keep it alive. For I will be Edward Houmout. Houmout will be on my crest, I swear it! It is a fine name for a leader of men, a lord—and even a fine name for a king!"

I laughed and kicked a wave so that it splashed his heavy, solid boots.

"Ah, you play with me," I said. "You are Edward of Woodstock—such a name of a small village is not for such as you!" I shook my head at his romantic fantasy. "Come, Edward, don't be foolish! This is but a common village, and I am but a common girl, whom you would tease with—"

Without warning, Edward drew me closer, and then suddenly he was sinking to his knee in the washing wave. "You are no common lass to me. You are noble in your soul, better than any other that I've met these many years, and I would make you my Lady. I would be your servant, Miriam Houmout." Then, in his own mother's tongue, in that Germanic language he seemed always to revert to when strong emotion took him, he spoke again: "*Ich dien Houmout.*"

I gazed into his eyes, those eyes that so often were hard for me to read. Yet now, they were full of tears, his face open to me. He was a mystery, so strong and powerful in war and battle, so vulnerable and weak in matters of the heart. And now he placed his soul in my care.

He meant it, every word. I bent forward and sealed his lips with a kiss. I closed my eyes, and then a sudden wave rose up and caught us as we embraced on the beach, soaking us to the skin. I blushed and laughed and pulled away.

But still, he would not let go of my hand, as if he feared to lose me. He kept me close all that afternoon, gazing often on my face, on my swelling belly too. Now I wonder if he sensed the future, and all the perils that would lie across our path.

"Houmout," he said. "Houmout." He made a song of it that day, and crooned it to me in our bower.

Still, I was stunned by his love, by his need for me. How was it that by rejecting him, I had made his ardor stronger? How was it that by showing my own mettle and my pride, he found himself humbled by me?

"When?" he demanded. "When shall I be able to fetch the priest, and be with you always?"

I laughed again. He was so serious, so emphatic in his demands. I knew that he was to leave the next day from the harbor to campaign in France. How could he think to be wed and then depart to war? His desire still seemed as a dream to me, one from which I would wake and find that all was shadows and dust. But when I gazed on him, his face was set. This dream was his, and he would make it real to me, and to the world.

"How long are you on campaign?"

"One fortnight," he said briskly. "And then I shall return, and have you beside me at Court. Always with me. Always. Houmout."

I could not help it—I laughed again, a shiver of delight, of hope and joy. His dream could be real. It could be mine as well.

"When you return to stay awhile," I said firmly, "then you shall have me—and your child. Come back, I beg you, before the child comes. Else he will be a bastard."

"Our child will be no bastard—he will be my son, in name, and all else." He held my hand again, so hard it nearly hurt. "This I tell you true, Miriam Houmout."

"One fortnight," I said. "The child is due in three months' time. If you return as planned, we can still be wed in time."

Edward put his arm across his chest to swear upon his heart. He raised his voice in proclamation. "Upon my knightly honor, I swear fealty to you and I promise that I will—"

"Enough!" I said. "Enough of your florid talk! Just come back, I beg you, come back and wed me, and we will be together then. No more words or swearing—just return."

He dropped his arm and stared at me a moment. And then he smiled and laughed at my exasperation. Another wave crept up to soak me, and he seized me, lifting me into his arms with one swift move.

"My love," he said to my face. "I shall return to be with you, my love."

I never spoke with him again. Two months later, my progress grew quite near. The Abbess commanded me to flush the child from my womb. But I would not do it.

Then the Earl of Hereford tried to intervene, having heard of the child from Edward on campaign. Always, the Earl schemed and poisoned. He worked with devious purpose and hidden hands.

But from the Earl's efforts, at least I knew that Edward thought of me, far away in France. That in itself, gave me hope. And I would not be swayed by others' words.

Finally, one day in June, I saw a thunder of riders on the road to the abbey. The snows and rains had gone, so a dust cloud rose around them as they came.

They rumbled out of the dust, garbed in the colors of Edward's house. A troupe of armored men, a herald going before. And in the midst of that crowd was Edward's tousled head, a panoply above. They were far away from my upper window, and so in my sight were as small as dolls upon the open road. But I was certain it was Edward, come at last for me, his love.

I watched from the window as they came to a sudden skirling halt. The center figure dismounted. Then I saw the Earl of Hereford beside Edward, and all the armored men who rode with these two great figures. As they came to the front gate, they waited, bowing low before the cross and gate.

The Abbess, a small figure far away in her white habit, came out to greet them and give them welcome to the abbey hall. The men entered in, and I waited to hear the call that would bid me from my cell to the central hall, where I would be reunited with Edward once again.

I brushed and combed my auburn hair. I rubbed that aromatic unguent of lavender across my skin, and put on my best tunic before I donned the red and royal habit only worn on feast days and on Easter dawn. Edward had come for me, just as he said he would.

I was clothed as a bride, and as the psalmist writes, I trembled like a virgin for her bridegroom, my soul overflowing with joy. I took the rich and golden signet ring that Edward had deigned to grant me—the token of his house—and I hung it on a slim silver chain. It was too large for my hand, but it was the highest sign of my honor in his eyes, and so I wore it around my neck.

I looked down at myself after I was garbed. By this time, I was great with child. The change had added new layers of luxury and weight to my long hair and to my body too. My face was thick and full as well, rounded and glowing in the evening light. I ran a finger across the smooth skin of my belly. Edward would be amazed to see the changes wrought upon me by the child. He would take me in his arms and—

Then I heard a horse neigh in the yard. I looked out and saw the men emerge from the great hall. They were not staying the night at the abbey, they were not remaining behind. *Was Edward not with them after all? Did they bring some news, some tidings of his doom?*

Then that tall and regal figure I knew so well came out from the hall. Edward was indeed here, he had removed his helm, and his waves of bright hair shone in the evening light. It was him, my love. But even from my distant vantage point, I could see that his face looked dark, his posture in a stoop.

Something was wrong.

Then he and all his men mounted their steeds and rode away.

The Abbess called me in after the dust had settled in the yard. Her face was grave. "He does not love you. He does not want to see you ever again," she said. "Edward of Woodstock is gone away from this place, never to return."

"Miriam, my great assistant," she said to me. "Miriam, you have my pity."

My face was numb, as one struck by a heavy blow. She took my hand.

"Now will you not listen?" the Abbess said. "The child is not for such as you—"

"No!" I stood without her leave. "No," I shouted, "I will not listen to you! I will have him. The child is my own."

"Then you leave me no choice," said the Abbess. "I will tell the Earl of Hereford. I must tell him what you intend to do, what you so selfishly…"

I stopped listening then. God only knows if she told that vengeful man. I know that weeks later, the Earl's men pursued me and almost took me down. But for many days, they left me alone. After I left the Abbess, I went to my cloister cell and barricaded myself inside. The other novices brought me food, and such water as I needed for the birth. But none broke in, no one took me from my room. Only after the child was born did I let a novice in to help me with the afterbirth.

Two days later, a guard I trusted came to me. He told me that there was a rumor in the abbey—that perhaps the Abbess had lied to me. Hope woke alive again in my breast. So I commandeered a carriage and horses, using the abbey's name to hold them on the Road, and I traveled north, away from the Earl of Hereford's lands and kin. But the Earl was forewarned by the Abbess, and his men soon pursued. The guard was slain by arrows, and the horses too. I fled the carriage with Christian before I could be caught.

For a day and a night I fled by myself, but I knew if I stayed afoot with a tiny child, we would be not long for the world. And so, cutting across the country, I came to the monastery and found a few months of peace.

To this day, I do not know the truth of it. For years I convinced myself that the guard had been right, the Abbess wrong. For ten long years, as I watched my Christian grow, I told myself and every ghost I could summon that her words were lies, and that Edward truly loved me still. I was sure that when Christian was old enough to travel safely on the road—ten—then I could take him to his father, and all would be well. *All would be well.*

This is the hope that had kept me breathing every day, the longing that made my heart still beat, despite every deprivation and disaster that befell. I convinced myself that Edward was my own, and that we would be together somehow, someday.

I touch the light, thin chain around my neck. The token rests there still, an empty vessel with no master now. It has no power to take me home to that imagined Houmout.

He is gone. The light has been put out. My soul breaks on this rack.

CHAPTER 22

WINTER CROWS TAKE wing. A cold wind blows, whipping skeins of snow into the ravine where our heavy-laden cart tips unevenly from side to side. It drives sleet against our skin, and turns our words around upon the air. My vision blurs, and after three days of walking into the whiteness, I am half snow-blind.

In my weakness, I tell myself a story I need to hear.

I see my son.

Christian walks ahead of me, his back straight, stride firm and unhurried in the drifted snow, pulling the cart back to true. He walks with me—he will keep me going.

While I slept, he must have escaped the flames. The others died, but he did not. He has been hiding in the monastery, waiting for me to come to him.

My legs ache, my heart aches. So if I do not live a little lie, if I do not let myself feel that Christian is leading me on, then I will surely die.

But Christian is leading me away from that black pit of despond. I follow him through the snow and the shadowed trees. My son walks ahead of me, sure-footed as a soldier on the road.

I imagine making camp that night with my son at my side. There could be a reason I did not see him on the trail until now.

While I slept, he escaped. The others died, but he did not.

I feel my heart lighten at the news, my breath become less ragged, even the semblance of a spring enter my limping steps.

I am sure he likes the crows above us, their cawing mirth. The endless circle they perform is like a dance. I wonder why they follow us, what they seek on this cold day, what they want of us. But I know that Christian is enjoying them, as he takes pleasure in all creatures of the woods.

Christian holds a hand steady on the cart as he walks. My heart stills its frantic cadence at the sight of that strong back, the breath surging in and out of that young, lithe body. I think suddenly, unreasoningly, that Christian can help me find the key to this mystery of his death.

Why was it burned? Did you tell someone our secrets? Who locked the house? Who lit the fire?

The questions are a ball of golden thread that will save me in this maze of pain. I hold the end, and roll the questions ahead of me, following Christian's footsteps in the snow. I am weary—oh so weary—but if Christian can walk this path, so can I.

For God's wounds, why, Christian? Why did you not tell me of Bene's plan?

Benedict spoke the truth in the gaol—I read that verity in his eyes. He did gather the boys together, lying to them of work in Lincoln town, planning to sell them into servitude. And was his plan so wrong? In some lights, it would have saved us all.

All in our village knew that the meager stores in the mill went to rot last fall, a leak turning our remaining grain to sour mush. I can hunt in the woods, and I know where I would seek my sustenance. Others are not so lucky. If I were Tom, with no hope of food for this long winter, I perhaps would not begrudge those terms—trading one child's life for the lives of his other children.

I think again of Benedict's plan. I might have chosen that bargain—my son and I together—but only if it were freely given to us as a choice, not out of deceit. Only if we were told of Christian's fate, and his chances in the town.

For children slip so quickly through our fingers.

At three winters, Christian almost died the first time. He was a little slight thing, yellow hair tousled by the wind and by his endless running in the woods. Then came the black time, when our land was seized with the malady that took human souls from earth like a man would smash flies swarming on fresh meat.

I watched the flesh melt from Christian's tiny bones, until he became the very image of death himself. I watched him gasp out a last breath, again, and again and again. It was a great torture watching his glassy eyes, his cracked lips, for signs of hope. In the end, he rose from his bed, begging for water and for food, the swelling gone from his neck, the burning fire within him extinguished.

I rejoiced and then I realized that there were only four other living children in the village. A score had passed that week. I was lucky. I had my boy.

Yet it is more a curse than a blessing, to live when almost all you know and love are taken from you, and you remain a silent island, standing alone and alive amidst the horror. My mother felt that keenly. She told me I must find others of her kin, others who would fulfill her last request with me. She would not be alone, even in death.

But now Christian will help me. Christian lived.

Then the lad who walks ahead of me turns on a sudden. And like a drop of ink blotted from a page, my vision of him evaporates.

No blue eyes here. This boy's gaze is iron black. A wan face frozen in a perpetual sneer, as if he smells corruption or has tasted a bitter draught.

This is not my son.

Christian does not walk ahead of me as the frigid air leaches through my cloak and into my soul. He has gone away for good.

It is only Cole.

I have lost the thread of Ariadne that drew me forward. And now we have only fourteen days left before we will be prisoners. Wild cawing laughter echoes across the road.

Yet there is a slim hope in my breast. I still have the proofs of who Christian was—of who he was meant to be. Christian was Edward's heir, and I his consort. If I can prove to the Court who I am, I can claim Christian's birthright. I can claim it all, in the name of my son.

✠

The snow whispers down all around. The white flakes fall on my skin, tiny stars melting into me.

A black feather drifts down to fall at my feet, dark against the glimmering snow. I pick up the feather and weave it into the collar of my frayed cloak. It is an omen, but what kind, I do not yet know.

Late in the day, Salvius spies a flash of something in Cole's hand.

"Give it here, lad," he growls. Salvius produces a short sword purloined from the Lady's company. Here is proof again of Cole's knavery: a fine small sword, scabbard and all, wreathed in silver and in gilt.

"Come here, lad," says Salvius. He draws the sword, a glittering dangerous thing. Cole makes as if to run away, but at the last moment his master catches his foot, and the boy goes down.

"So the punishment for thievery, you know as well as I," says Salvius. He holds the sword aloft, the edge catching the firelight. Is he really going to cut the lad?

"But I just—" Cole begins to speak.

Salvius strikes him with open hand across the teeth. Then the flat of the sword lands hard upon his bum, again and again. But I know Salvius must beat him, for the penalty by the King is maiming or death, and by this punishment Salvius may still save Cole.

After the beating is done, Cole's dark eyes glance my way. There is no one else watching him. His face twists in an uncertain question.

I lift one hand and pull my black feather from the cloth. I bend it with my fingers. I wave it back and forth against the falling snow. A child's game.

Cole waits a moment. Then he lifts his hand. He moves his fingers too, cautiously. But with that one small motion, Cole's mouth opens wide, graced by an honest thing I have not seen on his face in years. A smile.

My heart goes out to this beaten boy. I cannot help myself. I have lost Christian. I know that now. But my heart still calls out, to Cole. And he knows what really happened that night in the fire. He will tell me, and I will claim the truth.

Hope once again flutters her strange, bedraggled wings, a lark singing unannounced within my breast.

The drifts are deep in the vale where we have stopped. To protect from the thick snow, I make my camp under the cart itself. Cole and I will curl together against the frost, pulling heavy oilcloth down from the top of the cart to shelter us.

When I come out to the fire from making our camp, I see Liam stretching in the snow. He moves his arms back and forth, windmilling like a boy and laughing out loud. I turn back toward the cart to fetch my boots when something strikes me in the back.

It is an ill-formed ball of snow, and it falls apart even as I turn to see Liam's sly grin.

"Whatcha gonna do 'bout it, you feckin' Frenchie?"

Then I am flinging snowballs back at that rascal myself. Cole joins my side in the battle, his arms swinging wildly, his shout frantic with glee.

Geoff lets loose with a cannonball made of snow, and soon everyone joins in the game. Even the guards stagger about like demented children, ducking in and out of trees, flinging hunks of snow at their assailants, laughing like hooligans.

"Coney!" Tom points at a heather bush.

The game stops on a sudden. There is the flash of a furry tail, the hint of ears standing up in the bush. All of us are hungry for fresh meat.

The rabbit breaks cover, jetting toward the edge of the circle, where we are weakest. I cannot move quickly in this deep snow. So the coney threads the needle hole directly between Cole and me.

"Quick, quick! Get it, Mear!"

"Mear can't catch 'im—"

"He's too slow. Coney's pickin' up speed. Oh 'e's got a chance now."

I fall my full long length as the rabbit passes. Against my hand I catch the pumping of a rapid pulse, and then between one heartbeat and the next, the little life whisks through my fingers.

When I stand, I am splattered white as one of the haunts on the hallowed night before the Feast of All Saints. Christian always told such lurid, gory tales at the Feast. A thin grin comes across my face at the memory of my boy giddy with delicious fear.

Cole is chagrined. He only stood there as the coney dashed past. Silently, I edge forward and touch Liam's arm. I point with my chin.

"Over there," mutters Liam. "Mear can hear 'im in the woods. He has a hunter's ear."

Liam is too generous, but it is true that I have some skill with game. This is how I earn my keep in winter. I edge forward.

"Wait, hold 'ere," says Liam to the others. "Mear's gonna flush it out."

But Cole stumbles forward unthinking. The coney flashes past again. We separate and chase a skittering thing going deeper into the woods.

Liam gives Cole a push. "Go with ol' Mear— he's a lucky one."

Of course, all my luck is nothing more than a skill for silence. I go into the woods and wait perfectly still for long hours. The sky turns, the dusk comes, the small animals emerge. And I am but a stone, a silent log to them.

Then I take them.

The hunt has moved to another copse, but I motion Cole closer. The coney has gone to ground, and luck favors the patient.

Yet as we enter into the trees, a shout goes up on the other side of the copse. Someone has spotted it. It must have gone through. I breathe out a long disappointed sigh.

My limbs are still trembling from the turmoil of the hunt. As we leave our little copse of trees, Cole turns back.

"Wait a moment," he says. "Look there!"

It is the brown fur of a rabbit, crouched under dead leaves and filtering snow. Cole leaps and seizes it at the neck. But there is no movement from the coney.

"Cold," he says. "It's already cold."

Cole lifts it by the limp ears, the fur frosted to the hardened ground. It has been here for some time—a few hours, a day or more? We hear the sudden high scream of the other rabbit dying. It is choked off on a sudden, when its neck is broken.

Cole yanks the frozen rabbit off the ice and looks at me, an uncertain urge in his eyes.

"Well," he says emphatically. "I've got mine."

I shrug. I can motion to Liam later that the meat might not be good. He will listen to the doubts I give with my hands.

Yet when we emerge from the woods, young Cole lifts the rabbit high in the air, claiming it for himself. "I did this. Ol' Mear had naught to do with it."

I was about to demur, to shake my head in disgust at the rabbit. But now if I motion to Liam or to Benedict, it will look as if I am diminishing the boy, instead of just the meat.

"I've got mine!" shouts Cole.

"Two coneys!"

I look back at the copse where we found it. Already, the hollow where the dead rabbit rested is sifting full with snow.

Why not? What harm can this do?

Moten makes a stew for all of us to share.

BOOK III

CHAPTER 23

CHRIST WAS CONDEMNED to death in the morning—the hour of Terce—and at this same hour, I condemn myself to the cold. I cannot sleep. Cole has been groaning beside me, and the men made loud sounds half the night. Now I cannot sleep. Cole asks for water, but when I give him drink, up it comes again. I do not know what troubles him.

When I come out of the tent, I know.

I know what troubles all of them.

Our campsite is soiled with sordid spatterings. Every bit of the stew from the night before has been masticated, rendered brown and noxious by bile, and then spewed across the landscape. This explains the commotion I heard in the night.

When Brother Moten cooked our evening meal, he added too much salt. The taste was acrid and metallic—it choked in my throat. As I took one tentative mouthful, there was a faint tingle in my nose, an odor that hinted of decay and age.

After that first bite, I ate no more. I made my dinner of dried mutton and leftover hard bread. The others were not so prescient.

Disgorged bits of rotten rabbit now litter the white snow. The crows peck at the half-digested bits of meat.

I step cautiously through the haphazard camp, evading the residue of that putrid feast. The men moan in their beds as I pass, begging for some relief from that demon that torments their bellies.

"Water," Liam cries. "Ah, God, my damn'd gut!"

All three of our guards are moribund with clenching pain. Geoff and Tom are delirious, yet Benedict and Liam seem to be coming out from the other side of the malady. Young Cole is the worst off, his fever rising like a fire. He hacks and coughs, feeble attempts to vomit still roiling his empty belly.

My gorge rises and I turn my head away from the worst of it. It is then that I see the wisping remnant of the bonfire. We need wood.

I venture up the hillside into the woods.

Suddenly, there is a cracking splash. My foot has fallen through the thin, deceptive glaze into the depths of a muddy slough, colder in its unfrozen sludge than any ice. Underneath the trees, the ground is crazed and fractured, the mud running deep and dangerous under my heels. Carefully, I step into my old footprints, gathering what branches I can from fallen trees as I back away from the mire.

I squint against the daylight.

The whipping storm of the night before has gone, and the world bleeds bright. The glare of sun gives everything an afterimage—out on the edges, there are black spots everywhere. Some of the spots on the horizon are darker than the rest. I blink away tears, and those spots resolve into a moving, glimmering shape.

A glint of armor—perhaps it is a knight who will help us on this sordid morning.

But something in my memory tilts. A steep escarpment is on either side of the road. We are trapped here. Edward told me of such tight defiles, deep in France. A place where his army would camp above, and wait for enemies to come. It is like that game, *échecs*, where the pawns lay a snare, and then the *chevaliers* would attack.

An *ambush*, he called it, distraction with an open feint. I glance at the steep rocks and imagine ranked rows of charging knights or bandits.

They will not care who is a prisoner, who is a guard. They will kill all of us.

"Water," croaks Roben the guard, in the distance. "For the love o' Mary an' Sweet Jesus, water."

But even as I nurse the afflicted back in camp, the thought of an ambush does not leave my mind. I try to hide the two good horses the Abbot gave us, hobbling them in the trees on the other side of camp. I leave Salvius's mare behind. Then I strip the load off the cart, every basket and bag of food and supplies—everything given us by the monastery—and stuff it all under the cart itself, concealed by the heavy oilcloth that hangs down. Now it is sheltered there with Cole, who is fast asleep.

I look up at the slope again. The black spots have become three men riding, but it does not appear they have seen our camp yet. Two in bright armor, the third perhaps a squire. Noblemen, or at least men-at-arms. I squint to see clearly in the bright dawn.

There is something strange here. No banner of heraldry is carried by the squire, no lance for knight errantry alongside one of the horses. Neither of the two armored men wears a sign or symbol of any noble house. One cannot know where their allegiance lies, and this seems intentional.

My heart quakes, and I move quickly through the campsite. I go to Moten first. I snap my fingers, and his eyes flutter open.

"Ah, Mear," he mutters. "What have you read of Pythagoras?" He is delirious.

I move to Roben the guard, whose short sword lies beside his bedroll. He does not stir at first, and so I clap my hands loud. His eyes open, and he stares blankly. "Oh God, what is it?" he moans.

I use my hands to mime a man riding a horse. His brow wrinkles in confusion.

Frustration sweeps over me. Then it comes clear—something I did to entertain my boy. I nicker like a horse, neighing into his face.

"A rider?" With effort, he pushes himself up off his bedroll. "Jesus, Mary, Joseph, where?" When he stands, he is sweating and pale, but he reaches for his sword. "I dunno if I can do much, Mear. What kinda shape are my men in?"

I rush to the other two and clap my hands to rouse them. Both stand at Roben's command, but they sway, uncertain on their feet.

Roben barks at them and points at the distant hillside. Their horses are strong and fast—close enough to hear now. They thunder across the snow. Then they go out of sight in a hollow, and the sound stops.

We wait with bated breath, huddled close around the fire. The heavy swords the guards hold drop slowly to the snow. They lean on each other, feverish with nausea.

Something stirs in the hollow. Two figures emerge, helms closed, bright metal glimmering on every limb. The warhorses are stamping and steaming in the frost, held by the squire while the armored men fight on foot.

The bandits we met before were vagabonds hired as mercenaries by a lord, to seize poor folk for him. But this group of highwaymen are no amateurs. These men are skilled and practiced soldiers—champions for lords and kings, paid gold to fight and win. And when they cannot be paid, such men rob travelers on the road.

With their helms already closed, we cannot see their faces. One holds a crossbow cocked and ready. The other draws a longsword, the blade gliding from his scabbard with a ringing metal echo.

Roben tries as best he can to stand tall. He lifts his hand high in the sign of peace and holds aloft a crucifix. I hope that a sign of Holy Orders might give these knights pause.

"Ho there, we are holy travelers on the road," says Roben. "What is your house and lord, my friend?"

The man with the crossbow stops moving for a moment, and the guard next to Roben seems to take heart from this. He raises a hand as well.

The other guard's voice is thin and hoarse. "My friends, we are of the House of Saint Mary Magdalene—holy brothers of the Order of Cluny."

I watch closely. The armored man with the crossbow pauses in his tracks to raise the sight to our level. He aims.

"Aaah," I cry, throwing myself to the ground just as the bolt comes whistling hard through the air.

There is a meaty thwack. The guard next to Roben lets out a gurgling moan. The leather fletches of the crossbow bolt stand out from his tunic, the bolt planted deep in his chest.

Roben has raised his sword. His breath heaves quickly in and out of his mouth. He is afraid, but he is ready to attack. I stagger to my feet again and see him glance at the other guard, who still stands, burbling out a slew of blood and pain. Then the guard falls forward, driving the bolt deeper as he dies.

The champions move forward rapidly, relentless in their heavy stride.

I motion desperately to Roben and Liam. *Back. Back behind the cart.*

The first champion has cranked his crossbow back. Another bolt comes whizzing through the air. This one misses Roben by inches.

He turns and follows me as the armored men advance on the remaining guard, who wavers in the snow, holding tight to his short sword. The champion with the longsword steps forward and swings hard. The guard parries the blow with a ringing clash. Then another swing, and another, each one parried in a desperate swing that sends a blow reverberating up the guard's bony arms.

The guard's short sword is hopelessly outmatched by the girth and length of the long silver blade wielded by the champion. Finally comes a blow that knocks the sword from his hand. The champion chops at him then, as one would chop wood, and I turn my head from the gore.

"Ah," the champion sighs at the end. Then he lifts his helm and reveals a thick black beard. Out comes a steamy breath. He seems satisfied with this day's work.

The bandits do no more killing. We are weak and sickly: hardly worthy of a blow before we collapse. Our men are pummeled to the ground with the flat side of the sword or an extra cudgel.

Liam is not on the ground—he hides with Roben and me behind the cart, where Sal's old mare neighs in fear. I point at the hollow, where their warhorses paw the ground.

"I see what Mear means. We circle 'em," says Roben quietly. "Attack the squire. Take the horses—they can't escape."

"Is that wise?" whispers Liam. His face is still pale with illness.

"It's the only chance we got."

So we creep like mice behind the drifts of snow, making our secret way all around the camp. The champions quickly search our things. They find what warm clothes remain, but little else. I hid it all too well.

"Dammit, why'd we ride hard? You see any church treasures? Any gold to take?"

The bearded one frowns, a heavy crease on his brow. "They're all sick as dogs. Sick in the winter, dead 'fore spring. Hell, dead afore the morrow!"

The other one laughs, a sharp bark. "Lookit this damn'd camp, full of rotten puke. Good timing for us—otherwise they may 'ave fought."

The bearded man guffaws. "Nah, they didn't 'ave a snowflake's chance in hell. Idjits like these deserve t' die."

"But there's someone 'ere hiding out, knew we was comin'. They up an' hid the food."

"The cart," says the bearded one. "Look in the cart."

The two dismounted men turn away from the helpless, feverish men around our sodden campfire. They scrape snow off the open-faced cart.

After a moment, the other man lets out a cry of surprise. "Lookit this, some of 'em died already—they got burnt up."

My mouth goes dry with dread. Benedict moans with pain, and one of the men snaps a riding whip nervously.

"Look underneath!" says the bearded man. "There's a hiding place under the cart, sod it all—it must be there!"

"They'll get the food," whispers Liam. "Shouldn't we—"

"We fight them head-on, we're dead," replies Roben. So we wait.

I raise myself on my elbows to see across the ice as the champions strip the heavy oilcloth from around the wheels of the cart.

Cole is there. But he is awake, already on his hands and knees. Defiantly, he makes to stand. He holds a makeshift cudgel, and in his other hand, my long knife is gripped tight in a white knuckled fist.

The armored men are on either side of him in a heartbeat. There is a moment during which he spars back and forth, his cudgel against the flats of their swords, but he is racked by great shivers of cold, his skin running with sweat and uncertainty.

Cole raises his head, and he sneers at them, an arrogant contempt washing over that young face. "Devil take you!" he shouts. Cole curses them, blasphemous obscenity spattering out at every blow.

Then they beat him with their mailed hands. The knife clatters down, and his legs give way. Cole stops speaking, stops groaning. There is a numb silence. The champions pause before they pick up the provisions given us by the monks. They carry them toward the hollow, where their steeds wait for them. They leave Cole with a few well-aimed kicks from their metal boots. Cole grunts and moans, the snow spattered red now with his blood.

"Now, now, now," whispers Roben. Into the hollow we go, ahead of them, Roben swinging his sword wildly, I holding a heavy wooden cudgel.

The one who holds the horses seems small, and his mouth bears some reddened wound. Roben's blow strikes true, and the squire sinks to the ground.

I stare down at him as he fights for breath. This is no squire, but a child. The lad's mouth gapes unnaturally. He is a harelip, cursed from birth. An angel's knife in the womb cleaved him apart, nose to tongue. He is a child slave who held horses for those men.

He is as guilty as we are, in the end.

"I'll get the horses," gasps Roben. "Catch them—catch them quick!"

I bend down to the lad and try to still his pain. But his face goes slack and in a moment, he is gone.

The men-at-arms have seen us now. They drop the bags and sacks. They push their helms down with one hand. They draw their longswords and lift their bows.

One of the horses rears high as Liam tries to seize the reins. It is a great destrier of a steed, who knows this is not his master's hand. The warhorse knocks Liam to the ground.

Roben proves his mettle then. The men-at-arms stride into the hollow, implacable, unstoppable. Even as his hand shakes, Roben raises his sword high. He moves forward toward the armored men, turns his blade in their faces, a whirling wing of steel.

But Roben never stands a chance. It is like a pair of strong children catching a broken-winged butterfly. He moves, he sways, but always he is off-balance—he can never touch them. They turn from side to side, dancing around him. They pluck his sword and slap him with their blades, sending him helpless back against the hillside.

The bearded man mounts his great charger and tries to ride us down. I dodge and drag Roben out of harm's way. The champion slashes at me with his knotted quirt, that whip cutting a sharp line from my temple down to my shoulder.

Roben staggers again, and I catch at his arm.

I pull him up the slope and into the trees as the champion turns and rides us down again. He must want to finish Roben. We skirt the mud: I pull Roben with me around the edge of the ice.

But when the warhorse drives forward, it sinks immediately in deep quagmire. And by the time the bearded man hauls his steed out of the muck, we are on the other side of the trees and out of sight.

The champions take their ill-gotten gains and ride for the horizon, leaving their slave behind to bleed and die.

But we've made it. We've escaped.

Roben is leaning ever more heavily on me, and I struggle to push him upright. Then I look down.

Roben's legs are soaked dark with blood. His tunic is slit apart from one side to the other. They did more than slap him with their blades. His belly is pierced—he is bleeding to death.

He grimaces apologetically, his eyes wet with pain. "Aye, Mear, you've helped me as long as you can. Sweet Jesus, just tell me, am I the thief on your right or your left?"

I lay him down on the snowy ground as softly as I can. He gasps and breathes urgent words in my ear: "Be sure to save it! The Abbot told me. Brother Moten knows..."

What does Brother Moten know? I want to ask. *What is 'it' that I am to save?*

"Whatever happens, make sure to get it to London, to the Throne. He needs to take it to—"

The guard's mouth trembles. A rattle comes out of his throat. His eyes glaze over and go dark.

CHAPTER 24

WINTER CROUCHES OVER us, sipping away at our souls, as a devil's cat steals a newborn child's breath. The gray circle of the sun is low in the sky. It is already past None and approaching Vespers.

Roben expires now in my arms. The guards are all dead. My vision blurs. My skull throbs with pain. The quirt that hit me in the side of the head opened a deep cut at my temple, and blood is running down my neck.

The living men, nauseous and beaten, curl cold as lost animals in the snow. Our fire has gone out. Even Benedict the strong is shivering like a frightened child, his bare pate whitened by frost.

But I will not give up. I pack a handful of snow against my neck and get the fire lit again. I gather firewood until my limbs tremble and the heap is higher than the cart. Soon there is snowmelt bubbling in the pot, and a great log steams out heat.

The men gather around, nursing their wounds. They take up their bedrolls and huddle in a mass close to the fire. With the warm blankets and sheepskins I hid, most of the men are saved from the cold.

Cole is the worst off. The air chokes in his blood-clogged mouth. The bruises are thick as flies on the flesh of his face and neck. His eyes roll white into his head, and his lips are purplish, limbs cold to the touch. Still, only in one spot do I feel the grating of bone against bone. He was lucky to get away with a single broken rib.

I pack him tight with blankets and furs under the cart, where the wind cannot reach, and I nestle close to keep him warm. Roben's words are in my head—I cannot forget them.

What did he mean? What do we need to take to London, besides ourselves? And what does Moten know?

Cole's face has swollen almost beyond recognition. His slight chest quakes as I rub away the caked filth and dried blood. In this light, that long-seamed fire scar he wears seems to fade away. And his closed eyelids are soft as an infant's.

I used to watch Christian sleep like this, my breath twinned to his, the hours whisking by. One long autumn evening, as Christian's eyes were fluttering closed, he mumbled aloud, and I leaned closer to hear.

"Why dontcha ever talk in the daylight, Papa?"

"*Hush.* Hush now," I whispered, that cracked timbre the only voice he ever heard from me. "I just don't."

He reached up a little hand, soft with baby flesh on top, already growing a rough edge of callus underneath from hours of harvest labor. Christian stroked my cheek.

"It's alright, Papa, you don't have t' talk, if you don't wanna."

My heart went out to him then. I trusted him. My lips brushed his cheek. I would tell him that last mystery my mother told me, the one tie we carried in the blood, binding us forever.

"I have a secret, li'l one."

"What's your secret, Papa?"

"Promise not to tell?" I whispered. "It's just for you. No one else can know."

His eyes opened wide. "Is it magic? If I tell the secret, will you turn into a frog?"

At his words, I realized he was not old enough to hear, to keep it silent forever, as I had done, to save my life and limb. I should not share my mother's last words, not yet. Instead, I told him my real name.

"Here is my secret," I murmured, close to his ear. "My name in truth is Miriam. I am your mother Miriam of the village of Houmout. You can't ever tell my true name, my true sex, not in the daylight."

"Oh, Mear-iam," he sighed. "I'll always be with you."

I had not heard my own true name on a single tongue in five years. I hugged him, my eyes full of tears.

When I pulled away, his breathing was already deep and regular. He was asleep. I did not even know if he had fully understood my words. But Christian never said my name, not out loud.

Under this cart with its terrible burden, I look down at the living lad splayed out in sleep. This boy does not have the smooth skin and the mild blue eyes of my son, yet once he was someone's treasure too.

As Cole stirs, his brow folds in a worried way, wrinkling as an infant gathers effort to cry. But there is no cry from Cole. Instead, his brow lowers even further as a vague resentment floods through his features. Memories shadow his face as he swims toward wakefulness, tiny lines etched by envy and by rage painting harsh strokes around his mouth and his eyes. His plump lip twitches in an unconscious sneer even before he yawns.

Now that livid line of seamed fire on his throat seems to define him, as it never did in slumber.

Cole groans, his breath smoking, and settles on the quilt that covers us. Our steam has frozen through the night to every surface. The sackcloth that hangs down around us is covered in white.

Cole speaks then, his voice blurred by pain. "I can't see my mam's face now. Sometime she come to me in dreams, but when I wake I can't 'member her face."

He pauses. He tries to breathe. "I… I… I wasn't more than weaned when the fever took her. Mine father too… I…"

But although Cole's tongue catches on his words, I do not crease my lips in contempt or concern. Gently, I take in a slow, deep breath. Cole blinks and watches me. And when he breathes again, the words flow out.

"Tell you truth, my mam nor my da had any brothers or sisters, so I dunno how Salvius know'd 'bout the demon in my blood. He ain't blood of mine.... but he sav'd me when my kin were gone. He... he..." Cole coughs, his brow tight with suffering.

I nod, in sudden sympathy. I wish Salvius—Nell's longtime friend—could have saved her as well. I wish she'd taken him into her house, into her bed. If so, she might have lived.

Hush, I think. *Go to sleep now, boy.*

But still Cole mutters on, feverish and feeble. "I thought they were mine own. But they wasn't my friends, not at all. I... I... an' the demon came an' took them all..."

I want desperately for him to be at peace, for his torture to cease. Cole breathes out again, his breath curling in white wisps. "The demon what took 'em... the demon who kill'd 'em all..."

I am transported back to Houmout. I was a small child when I left that echoing village of the dead. A fortnight after they all died, I was found and taken in by the nuns of Canterbury Abbey. I became what I am—what I used to be—purely because they took me in. I have said many words that bound me to a life in cloister, a life of books and prayer. Yet none of the vows I took were stronger than that last oath to my mother.

Perhaps Cole became what he is because of who took him in.

How much we are shaped by our saviors.

I crawl out to the fire to warm a rag in boiling water. Then I gently wipe away the blood that still seeps from Cole's many wounds, his skin peppered with blows. For hours, I drip warm water into the corner of his dry mouth. But even the tender care I give may not be enough to save this broken lad.

Guilt weighs on me. It is my fault Cole suffers. By hiding the provisions under the cart, where he lay, I made him take the blows. I can assuage my guilt by one action: I will never do anything to hurt him, ever again.

It is a promise larger than I know I can fulfill, with my sinful heart, my weak-kneed soul, my long deception—but I can at least strive for something, and this will be it.

If he survives tonight, I charge myself to protect him, to do no future harm to Cole. If we survive this black night, we will only have twelve days to seek the justice of the Star Chamber. It is not enough time: my thoughts run frightened around in my head like a mouse in a trap.

Cole writhes and turns in my arms. He babbles out loud, fever-talk bubbling out. "I didna do the fire, I didna... I wanted to save them all, I wanted to get them out, and I wanted to burn with them, but he... I wasn't brave enough to burn... The demon made me... The demon..."

It's alright, I want to whisper. *It's a nightmare, I know you did not.*

And Cole seems to hear my thoughts. His voice becomes softer and more articulate, a whisper of sound, a low mutter.

"I watch'd them burn," he mumbles, so low I can hardly make it out. "Burnin', burnin' in the night... They was tryin' to get out, an' it shoulda been me... I wanted to burn with them, I just wanted..."

All through the winter night, I nurse Cole's wounds, applying what poultices I can from the packets I find at the bottom of Moten's bag of cooking herbs. There is nothing left to purify his wounds, but I wash out what I can and wrap the open cuts in cloth and grease.

After Matins hour, the boy wakes, moaning and crying out, his fever burning hot. He tries to sit up, and gently I urge him back under the blankets. He stares at me, his black eyes shining like lit coals.

"I... I... I'll tell you the truth, Mear," he says. "I'll tell you what happened. You want to know the truth, don't you?"

I nod, my heart in my throat.

"I seen them burn the house, I tell you. I watch'd 'em when I was hidden in the woods. Two men burned up the boys. One of them is the one who killed that brewer an' herbal woman—that Nell— too."

A bell clangs in my breast. *Cole knows who killed Nell?* I can feel the pulse thrum in me as I bend close to hear his whisper.

I caution myself. I hope he does not lie. The words are real, but what Cole remembers could be but hysteria, the false memories that come out of the deep-roiled waters of his fever. But he does not speak of Nell again.

"After the boys were gather'd together in the house—I was suppos'd to be there with them, but I was late. I... I... I didn't make it inside, an' then it was too late after that other demon lit a fire. The big one came quick an' tied the door shut. He was an evil man—he had a demon in him, I swear to you. The one who lit the fire ran away then. He ran away in fear."

He stares up over our heads. The wood of the cart is dark as pitch, each line of grain painted in subtle strokes of frost, like a message only he can read.

"I... I ran to the house from the woods... I ran to try to help. But the fire burnt me. You've seen the scar—ah've seen you looking." His finger traces the long red line that curls like a snake down his neck.

"So I tried to untie the door, but it was too late. The house was goin' up in flame."

My eyes well up with unbidden tears, cutting runnels across the frost on my cheeks. Cole glances at my wet face, but he does not cease to speak.

"I tell you true, they're here—the ones who done it—they travel with us on this road. It ain't no witch, it ain't no Jew. The two who done it are here in our midst. He tied the knot, he tied them in, and that other one lit the fire. I watched them. An' those men are here with us. Now."

Then he coughs again and winces with pain. I rub his brow, and his eyes flicker closed.

Cole gibbers and moans, delirious, long into the night. But I remember every one of his words. In the flicker of the firelight, I stare at his sunken eyelids, those twitching febrile lips, and that vivid scar that fades in slumber. Cole sleeps, a feverish babe in my arms.

He will live. I will know the truth.

CHAPTER 25

DAWN IS A breath of frigid air as someone pulls aside the sackcloth. I open my eyes from a dream of Nell. *I know who killed you*, I tell her. But it is only a dream, the face I seem to recognize evaporates as I wake.

Night is fading from the sky, and a last faint star etches a bright line. It falls off the edge of the ethered darkness, a light winking out.

"An omen," Geoff mutters. "What soul dies this day?"

Then he gestures broadly at the roaring blaze.

"I fed the fire. Don't know where you got all this wood, it's a rum'un."

I grin. This is Geoff's thanks for my labors.

"We've got naught to eat," says Tom. "No food except for oats—we'll hav'ta eat horse food. But we're warm. The furs were safe under the boys. An' you saved our horses too—hid them in the trees.You know how to hide an' how to fight. I thank 'e, Mear."

Liam is more boisterous. "How's about some coney tonight?" he shouts aloud.

All who are awake groan and laugh.

After the chuckles die down, Moten speaks. "Well, I'll still take you to London," the monk says. "We've got only a dozen days until

Shrovetide, but we'll try our best to make it. Even though I'm your prisoner now, it seems, I will help you on the way."

I take a cup of boiled oats and turn and look at the snow-covered camp. Our three horses are nosing through the snow for old grass. The landscape glimmers, white as a field of diamonds under the sun. The bodies of the guards are already covered in deep drifts. The morning breeze furrows across the frozen white waves, catching a spray of snow from every smooth hard crest.

Salvius stands. "Anyone hear a sign o' life from the boy? How long has he been gone?"

A dull shock settles onto me. Despite all my labors, Cole is gone. Far away, I can hear the chittering sob of a squirrel in the forest. The sound moves in and out of hearing, a distant, fearful cry. Moten looks at me. "Mear," he says. "You were up in the night with the lad. When did Cole there quit breathing?"

I turn toward the cart and crawl back underneath. In the wan light of day, Cole's skin is not just battered and bruised. It is gray and yellowed as a corpse.

Cole does not stir when I touch his chest, and I cannot feel a pulse at his neck, but he is still warm to the touch. I wish I had a mirror to test his breath, to see whether death has truly taken him.

I try to listen for a heartbeat through all the cloaks and furs, but I despair.

I will never know who killed her. I will never know who burned our lads.

When I open my eyes, I am surprised to discover that I've been asleep. The sun is higher in the sky, and there is a pitched discussion outside. There is a respectful tone unfamiliar to me in the words by the fire.

"He's a tough ol' bugger, is Mear," says Tom.

"Ayuh, Mear kept goin' when the rest of us went down," Liam agrees. "Kept up all through the night too—nursin' Cole, keepin' us all alive."

The sound of voices abruptly halts as I stir and come out of the tent.

The snow has been cleared off the cart. Everything is packed, except the furs and cloaks on Cole and me. The bodies atop are covered tight in sackcloth, the wheels dug clear of the frost. The Abbey's horses are hitched to the front again, and Sal's old mare tied behind. The cart is ready for the open road.

I pull on my leather-laced boots and walk a few paces up the hillside, looking ahead.

"Alright, even Mear's given up," Benedict says." There is no sense in stretchin' this out."

The men strip Cole's body. They peel back the solidly packed furs, take the heavy cloak from off his body. The boy's white flesh is battered and bare on the raw snow. I would listen to his heart now, if I still had hope.

But Cole never flinches.

I turn away. I cannot see Cole dead. Tears stream down my cheeks, but no one sees. My movement to them is a sign of strength.

"Braver than I. He's movin' on. That's what you have to do."

"We've got only twelve days until Shrove, eh?"

"True, but look on Mear—he knows we can make it. There he goes, scouting the road ahead already."

The White Road is empty, the words dry and poisonous as ash. If ever I felt that I could speak again, I disavow that urge now.

The star fell. All our work is meaningless, a scatter of bones and dust.

The only thing that takes me to London now is that charge my mother gave me: I will fulfill her plea, or I will die trying. And in so doing, perhaps I will redeem my son as well.

I keep my face turned as I wipe away tears with the rough and frozen scarf. The water freezes to my cheeks. The sob stings my nose and tingles in my chest, rising as empty steam. Slowly, I come back to hearing the men.

"Got to keep the body then?"

"'Course we gotta keep Cole—he's one of our own."

"Put 'im on the cart with the others."

I cannot watch as they lift Cole's nearly naked body onto the cart with the rest of the boys. I remember his words in the night. *I wanted to burn with them.*

Maybe this is where this lost lad wanted to be all along, his long loose white-skinned flesh resting alongside the blackened bodies of his friends.

When Christian was born ten winters ago, a single star glimmered in the darkness as the tide of my labor rose and fell. Upon his death, I would like to think it dwindled and winked out. In every star is writ the hour and way of death for every man, from Achilles to Caesar to the Holy Roman Emperor to the small and unmarked life of Cole from Duns town.

When we gain the shoulder of the White Road, there is a sudden gasp.

I glance around to see who made the sound. I see Geoff's impassive eyes, Tom's stolid face, Liam's hollowed but quiescent eyes, and Moten's strained face. Benedict comes around the corner of the cart to look at me. I stare back at him and shake my head.

The choking gasp comes again, and our eyes shift wildly upward. Someone is moving on the cart.

It is Cole. He lives.

✠

The boy chokes for breath and moans, his eyes wide and staring. In the glacial air, Cole shivers, violently alive, as we move to lift him, hold him, rescue him. Quickly, we wrap him in woolen blankets, in fur-lined cloaks, and in every warm wrap we own.

"Goddam, he's got a spark of life!" gasps Tom.

Moten's long face is pale with shock. "Mayhap the cold brought him back. 'E was fading, and the cold woke him."

"We couldna hear him breathing," says Benedict as he wraps another blanket around the boy.

As we repack the bundles we tore open to find a furs and cloaks for Cole, each man sees some excuse to touch Cole, to pat him on the arm or shoulder, to tuck another bit of fur under his feet. Cole is weak and wavering, but awake.

"What happened after the fight?" he asks. "Why are we stopped here on the road?"

"Ach, lad, we'd thought we'd lost another," murmurs Geoff. He pulls his heavy pack up onto his shoulders once more, bright tears standing in his eyes.

"Another?"

"Ayuh," he mutters, wiping his face of tears. "Another fallin' star, dontcha know?"

All that day, we surround the wooden box of the cart, each holding a hand on it, like children around a treasure. Cole is like Orpheus singing to us, come back to tell us all that death is not so fearsome, that we too may survive to breath another day.

We have no guards left around us, no chains that hold us. But we have no food and few supplies remain. The road ahead is stark. Salvius calls a halt.

"Let's bury our lads here," he says. "Our lot has done the best we could, we fought hard to find a way. But we've reached an' end, my friends. To go forward may kill us all. Even if we reach London, we may not get the justice we seek. We cannot make the Star Chamber now."

"Aye," says Benedict, dry-eyed and thoughtful. "Back at home, my other lads may be starvin' too—they need their menfolk home in these cold winter nights."

"An' your Sophia too," begins Tom with a wink. "She might need you at night, or another may take her an'—"

Benedict strikes without another thought, backhanding Tom across the face hard.

"Oh ho," says Tom, and he cracks his knuckles for a fight.

"No." Salvius steps between them. "Not now."

"Look," says Geoff. "We must go on, I tell you. I want the King to find the truth, to know who did this deed." He gives a baleful look at the gathered men. "The Star Chamber will discern the truth. Don't you care to know the truth?"

There is a dark muttering in the group.

"You can go on to London on your own, you bloody bastard," growls Tom.

Geoff steps back toward the cart, toward his son. "You won't bury him here!"

Would they leave us behind?

No matter, I decide. I must go to London. I cannot abandon this only chance. All my intent now is to fulfill my mother's charge, to release my mother's soul, to give her what she asked when she died. I will not give up now, not after we have come so far. I will fulfill my oath. And if we push hard, we may make it in time. We may yet get justice in the end.

So I turn and seize on the monk. I shove Moten forward. I pummel him. He glances at my face tremulously, and he sees that I want him to speak in favor of the journey.

Hesitantly, he tries. "Gentle folk, the road ahead is long, but we should strive..."

I push him harder. His words grow stronger as I push him in the back. "We should go on," he says abruptly, glancing back at me. "The Abbot will have you killed if you return on the road to the monastery. I tell you, he will take that as evidence of your guilt."

"So we go on only to save our lives?" says Benedict, shaking his head.

"The King's own Court will find the truth of this," says Liam. "You've got to believe."

"Damn cowards," mutters Geoff. "Don't care of justice a'tall, do you?"

Salvius sighs. “Alright,” he says. “We go on, but only until we can find safety. Maybe there.”

He leads us by pointing at the distant hill. Far ahead is the tiny shape of a building. I squint into the snow-blinding daylight.

A manor house.

CHAPTER 26

On most nights under the winter moon when we have made our camp, around us echo faint sounds of that other hidden world—the one of meadow and forest in the night. The melody of whip-poor-will, the cry of hunting owl, the scurrying rush of vole and chasing fox.

This night, the land is empty. The silence is deep in stark and open heath. The woods carry no sound. Our horses survive on wisps of straw we pull from the cart.

The oats were used up on the first day. We cooked it long, we ate it rough, and now we have nothing. It is as if some great razor scraped the life from this sheet of white-edged vellum, leaving only blank.

We starve.

First is a ripping agony of hunger in our gut, a faintness and a shadow in the eyes. Then there is emptiness entire. Now our bellies seem to float away, flat and empty as a bag.

A weariness is on me, one I cannot shake. I go to sleep weary and wake up weary. Rest does not bring me strength.

The next day brings snow. The black trees all around are edged each one in flakes, a pale white line on every limb. Jagged serrations of ice cover the road, hard as iron. When we move out of the ravine on the straight again, we can see that the manor house has grown slightly closer. The two small guardhouses of the manor stand between the road and the valley of a river.

If only we could reach the manor house, we might be safe. But it is too far away, a mirage on that distant hill.

I pull aside the soles that are strapped to my feet. Underneath, my feet are streaked with cuts and dark abrasions. Thorns, branches, and sharp ice have graved their signs on me, a medley of runes written in some strange tongue. I stare down, bemused by the sight, for I have felt no pain.

The leather is wrinkled, wet, and useless against the ice. My feet are numb of feeling, and my head light as air.

I am sorry, Mother. I cannot find a way to make my oath complete. I cannot find those you sent me to find. I cannot say the words you gave me.

I can feel myself going, rising with the sun in the sky, as if my soul pulls away from my body into some realm of light. The world fades to white as I fall to the snow.

A strange deep voice calls out. "Allo, *allo*." I open my eyes.

Standing around us are a group of men wearing soiled livery, and coats of fur beside. The furs are moth-eaten and unkempt, but still the clothes are rich beneath. They must be men from the manor house. The two men hold tiny mice in wool-wrapped finger-gloves.

Fear rises in me. I can see Cole shrinking behind the cart, struggling to pull out a cudgel, ready to fight back.

I can see the tall man is gaunt with hunger, his hawk-like nose reddened by the winter cold. He grips a ratty hedgehog corpse by the tail, and a sheaf of tiny papery bulbs like onions—both together but a single mouthful for a small child.

Benedict steps forward boldly. "Are you here to plunder us? We have naught—"

Cole slinks out from the cart, a weapon in his hand at last.

The gaunt man ignores Benedict's question. He ignores Cole's fearful threat. The man looks down and lifts my foot from the ground. He peers closely at my flesh.

"Mortmal," he says shortly. He sniffs and drops my foot, as if he is not surprised. "Your friend will die of poison in the blood."

"Yes, 'tis true," says Benedict. "But we are still strong, and we have horses. We can fight back."

Geoff stands tall now, a sword he took from a dead guard in his hand.

A short man next to the gaunt tall one stares at Geoff. He seems to be weighing something. "What do you have for us to take? You would kill a horse and let us dine with you?"

"No," says Benedict, his jaw tight and trembling.

Moten holds up a piece of folded vellum: the Abbot's missive in his shaking hand. "We are permitted on this road. We have a letter of passage, a license for the road, from mine own Abbot. The Church has given us God's writ of passage, to go to London, an' we will—"

"Do you see a bloody church here?" The gaunt man gestures angrily at the empty hillside. "Does it look to you as if God gave a tinker's damn 'bout this blasted, burned land?"

There is a sudden silence.

"Do you have food?" says Liam.

The gaunt man's gaze seems to go right through him. He does not answer the question. "You have nothing," he says. "An' we have nothin' to give. We will not hinder you here. Go on your journey, an' be damn'd." He motions to the short one and to the five others behind him in the road.

"Wait," calls Liam. "If you are not here to plunder us, help us—I beg of you!"

Yet just as the men from the manor put a foot on the path toward the hill, the gaunt man turns back. "You have something in that cart, for you all guard it like gold. What is in the cart?"

Moten pulls back the canvas and shows the white-wrapped bodies to him. The gaunt man takes note of this piteous thing, that we carry our dead children with us on the road.

He nods, he thinks, he rubs his hawkish nose, he looks again at the short man, as if in silent consultation. "And how long ago was it that your boys passed from this life? Are they not rotted on the road? How long since they lay unburied?"

Benedict speaks loud now, desperate. "They have lain frozen since the day of the fire, over a week now. God willing, the frost will remain until we have our day in Court."

"Ah," comes the reply. The gaunt man touches his mouth, and his tone changes. "You have my pity, and my charity. You are welcome in the manor hall this night. Come, be welcome."

But the man's face belies him. He hides something, I think.

Benedict looks at him, a wary worry in his eyes. I am with Bene. I do not trust this man, with his short talk and no answers.

"An' who are you to say so?" says Moten. "Why should we come with you?"

"I am the lord of this dead land," the gaunt man says. He turns, as regal as he can in his disheveled fur, and proceeds up the hill. We can hear his words as we follow. "I am the Lord Paul Anders. You are welcome to what little firewood and warmth we have to share in my manor hall."

I note he does not mention food, not even the forlorn hedgehog he holds in his hand. And I wonder now what that Lord knows that we do not. *What does he hide?*

BOOK IV

CHAPTER 27

THE MANOR HALL is grand and dark inside. Thick columns are carved with figures ancient and fantastic. Iron braziers hang on every side. The short man stirs the embers inside the fire pit beyond the great hall's hearth. A fire is kindled with the new wood brought in. It crackles merrily, spitting smoke and sparks.

Draughts of smoke curl through the stabbing shafts of light that come in from the west, through the mullioned windows. Then the draught catches, and the fire blazes hot, warmth spreading out across one end of the great hall.

All along the walls are great columns with stone carvings that have been worn down by time—carvings of men and birds and animals. Inside this grand space are bundles of straw, where all the company sleeps. Beyond the straw stand the remains of wooden tables that are being hacked up into logs and fed into the hearth. One large table remains on the floor. A place to dine, if we had anything to eat.

Floorboards groan beneath the men who shuffle and stamp like dray horses in the inner darkness of the manor house. The air inside is damp, for our expelled breaths gather on the beams above and drip steadily, condensation oozing down as from the ceiling of a cave. The manor Hall reeks with the stench of an underground bunker: burning tree sap and old sweat, flatulence and the bitter tang of spilled beer and singed fur.

We are all huddled together around the hearth. Here, in a great cauldron above the fire, the men of the manor are making a thin stew with the carcasses of mice and hedgehogs.

I hobble down the hall, searching for a place where I can pass water. At one end of the great hall is the fire and the hearth. At the other end are three doors. I find a garderobe behind the door on the right. In the garderobe is a seat and a long hole through which night soil can be dropped to the stinking midden pit below. Through a narrow window in the room, I can see men from the manor settling the horses and the cart in a byre built into the hillside.

I can also see that a drawbridge below is tied to the two guard-houses by ropes as thick as my arm. It can be lifted in times of war or peril. Far, far below is the frozen river, with its heavy floes of ice unmoving now, waiting for a thaw. After I am done in the garderobe, I check the other doors, curious what lies behind them.

The first door I check—on the left—is dark and locked, the door wedged tightly closed with bits of stone and wood. This door gives off the sweetly rotten stink that plants a seed of fear.

I have known that stench from an early age. When I was a small child, living within sight of the great sea, my father stank of it for five days before he passed in agony and *delirium tremens*, aghast and full of fear. When my mother in her sickbed smelled of it too, I was afraid to go near, even when she begged for water, when she whispered to me. A fortnight later, the sisters of Canterbury found me, all alone among the dead.

I am still afraid of the smell of plague. It visits me at night in my dreams. The fell wind of it is with me in the mornings, a memory of terror when I wake.

I leave the locked door quickly.

But the large middle door is not locked. In fact, it stands a little ajar behind an carved archway. This is the iron-belted door where they took the wood earlier, and I can see a sliver of flame inside the room. Perhaps behind this large door is a bedchamber for the Lord and Lady of the House.

I limp back to the fireside. My skin is slowly thawing. My feet are white with the bite of frost, the edges and the toes tinged with the heavy purple of grapes pressed for summer wine. Yet after the sparks of pain die out in the rest of my skin, strangely, there is no pain in my toes.

Our men are gathered to help Moten, who has a plan for the healing of my foot—Geoff, Salvius, Benedict, and Liam too. But all my distrust has blossomed anew. I fear them now. *One of them killed Nell.*

I trust Brother Moten, though. And Moten insists that we wash my toes—it is something he read once, in Hippocrates. So even though I shrink back from the ice-cold drench, the variegated spatter of clotted dirt and old sweat is washed away, and I am surprised to see skin so white and pink.

But the spot on my toe remains dark with rot. And there is now a thread of blackness, a tiny thread, reaching up my toe toward the arch of my foot. It has not reached beyond my toe yet, but it carries the poison they spoke of on the road. *Mortmal.*

Moten leans close to me as he gently washes the grime from my flesh. "Mear," he whispers. His voice is so low I can hardly hear it. "Mear, I never told the Abbot about you. I would not betray you, even though I doubted you an' your intent. When I spoke of a noblewoman to the assembl'd monks, I told them the legend of that Saint Theodora, who was saved by a monk. I implied that there was more here than we knew in heav'n an' earth. An' now for these many miles we have traveled, I think you are a saint unknown."

I start. I turn to look at him. He glances up, but no one is watching us as he dries my skin.

"See, to escape the monastery, I argued the Rule of Cluny—half of which the Abbot had forgotten. I was the scholar tasked with the Rule, an' I know it better than most. If there was no cause to bury the bodies—as I proved in my ecclestiastic points—and the men who claimed to serve Lord Bellecort stated that your crime was against the nobility, then your offense was an earthly one, and demanded the King's justice, not God's. In the end, the Abbot acceded to my point. That is why you lived, an' why I was sent upon the road with you."

I listen, bemused. The Abbot was convinced by words to let us go, with no proof of any kind?

"I tell you this now," Moten whispers, "because I do not know if you will live after we cut your flesh, an' I wanted you to know I do not think you a witch or a demon. You are forgiven of your sins." He gives the sign of the cross.

Then Moten leans nearer still. "There is one last thing. I have this boon the Abbot granted me, a treasure of the monastery, and I must take it to the Court—"

Thunk! An axe sinks into the wood near my head. "Are you ready then?" says Geoff.

The carpenter pulls the axe out of the wood and begins to hone that blade on a sharpening stone.

"Sharp," says Moten. He stands tall now, away from me. "Make it sharp as can be."

"Ayuh," mutters Geoff. "But flesh is softer than wood, dontcha know?"

The hiss of the sharpening blade is terrifying close. I have no moment to think on Moten's secret, to connect it to what Roben spoke of at the end. For now my breath comes fast in my throat, so fast it seems to burn.

Liam watches me. Out comes his flute, and he plays a quick and subtle jig that draws the men of the manor toward him. He aims to distract me. He raises his voice in jollity. "Aye—I've got a tale 'bout a carpenter."

Geoff waves his hand and ceases his stropping of the blade.

"An' my carpenter had a rovin' and a lecherous eye," says Liam. Geoff winces.

"An eye for woman flesh and fair!" laughs Liam. "See, he had an eye for those with pretty legs, dontcha know? And he found a lass he loved more than 'is life. Her name was Alison—a fair a name it was. Eighteen winters she had, and like a wild lark she was. So he held her in a narrow cage, that sweet and luscious girl, Alison."

Now the men know the tune that Liam will play, and their faces brighten with anticipation.

As I hear Liam's words, I see only Nell: like a wild lark, sweet with pretty legs, and fair and strong. *Who would break such a bird?*

"Ay, Mear, I see you listen to me! Hear this. Alison's apron was white as mornin' milk, and her body graceful as a li'l stoat"—someone howls and whistles loud—"but she also had that eye o' lechery an' lust!"

Tom licks his lips. "Ah, such a wench is fun t' be with!"

Liam laughs. "Aye. So happy a darling—a bright shining face—and 'er song as loud and lively as any swallow in a barn. Oh, she put the game afoot, laughin' like a lark!"

One of the men of the manor leans forward now. "What was it like to kiss such a lass?" There is a longing in his voice. This is more than lechery—those gathered here yearn for the touch of a woman tender and soft. I see in their faces an aching hunger for a woman's grace, all her winsome ways.

Liam hears this note, and echoes it back. "Ah, yes, fair Alison's mouth was sweet as honeyed drinks—or as a hoard of apples long in the cellar. She was a primrose, a little pig's eye. But sad to say, she landed with this ripe old carpenter!" Liam grins and points his flute at Geoff. Our carpenter holds up his axe and bows to the assembled men.

The men hoot by the fire.

Salvius ties a heavy thread around my toe, and makes it firm.

"Ay, we're nearly ready now," says Moten, close-at-hand, but he speaks to Benedict. "Put the knife hot in the fire, until it glows." I look down to see Benedict sliding a blade into the coals. *What's the knife for?*

"One day comes the student Nicholas, when the carpenter was away," Liam says. "He was subtle and sly. He got lovely Alison by speaking so fair—"

"Bite down on that"—Benedict puts a bit of leather in my mouth—"when the pain comes."

But I am looking as far away as I can. I am listening to Liam's story, every sound. I am engrossed in the story of Alison, of what we do for love.

Nell, Nell, Nell, I think. *Who killed you?* What would Nell have done with such pleas, such begging for mercy? Would she have taken him in? Would she have allowed some lover in her croft?

Geoff raises the axe.

Salvius comes behind me. He takes hold of my arms and grips them tight. Liam raises his voice louder. "That Nicholas spoke so beautifully, pressed her with such clever words, that at the last, Alison granted his wish and—"

There is a sudden crushing blow. I hear the crunch of bone. A throb of agony reverberates, like a finger of lightning, up my foot and into my thigh. My head goes faint as my leg erupts in pain.

In the far distance, it seems, the men by the fire are laughing. Liam goes on. "Our Nicholas and our sweet Alison lay down together. And there was revel and melody then!"

Benedict lifts the knife from the fire. It is glowing red. My lips tremble, and I silently say the Paternoster as the blade comes closer, radiant with light in the gloom.

With a sudden piercing hiss, Moten puts the red-hot knife to my flesh. The pain wells up through my leg, pushing on my lungs until I can't breathe. A moan comes out of my mouth, and all turns to black.

CHAPTER 28

SLEEP AS A babe, dead to the world. In my dream, I am a lost child again, cuddled with the rest of the orphans into that great nest of straw in the open hall of Canterbury Abbey. The warmth of sleeping bodies drew me in—I curled deeper into the straw. My belly full of warm gruel, embraced by other children, hearing their breathing light and sweet in the night, I felt myself in heaven.

But when I slept that first night in Canterbury, I found myself in hell once more. Throughout my childhood, my nightmare was always the same.

I saw the face of my mother in her final week. The red petals burst out all over, the bloody roses covered her skin. She gave me those words to memorize, she made me learn them as she gasped, she urgently whispered to me her last secrets, the ones I can never share with any soul.

Yet I was horrified by the spots of blood all over her skin. And then the black pustules at her neck seemed to throb. And I could smell it strong—the scent of plague, that sweetly rotten stink.

The vision filled my senses, and I screamed, opening my eyes to an angel, dressed in gray and white.

"Child, you're grindin' yer teeth," said the sister. She was plain in words but very kind. "You woke the others."

I stared at her, wide-eyed and shivering in the night.

"Ah, child." She took me in her arms and rocked me back and forth, her scent yeasty and warm, like rising bread. "Here, drink a bit o' barley wine. Perhaps your dream will settle. Ah, orphan child. Ah..."

✠

The night is so black that it seems fogged with little bits of soot. I float in and out of sleep, in an ocean of pain as my mind wanders once again to Nell.

I had always thought that strangers killed Nell, in a drunken rage. But Cole says someone in our village killed her. This I had never known. *Poor Nell.*

The broad-shouldered sheepherders had come to town, and I had always thought they were at fault. Heavy swarthy arms they had, coarse talk and rough manners from labor in Lincoln city far away. They were hired by Benedict that autumn, for in the spring we had a heavy crop of lambs and it was time to make them ready for market. Some needed to be culled, some sheared, and most to be taken for sale in other towns.

Each morning, those heavy rough men staggered out of Benedict's empty hold, took over the pasture, and worked across the herd. By midday they were thirsty, and by afternoon thickheaded with strong ale. In evening, their raucous voices sounded in the woods as they drank every drop to be found in our small town.

Some from the village joined them every night, for everywhere they went was a great and raucous revelry. I wish now I could remember who went with them, for that might tell me the truth of what Cole murmured in the night.

It was on one such evening, when the harvest moon hung low in the sky, that Nell's brew was ready for the season. Her cauldron cold now, the heady scent of barley wine was pungent in the open air. She hung the symbol of her wares—the old broom—from her byre, out upon the tree for all to see.

Salvius reported later that he told the sheepherders about the sweetness of Nell's brew, but he did not know they would go to her croft so late. They were already deep in their cups, he said, and he thought they were done for the night.

But they did go. They went late and stayed late.

I did not know this when I woke at dawn to bring the day's wood to each little home. Most every house I came to had a fresh flagon of barley wine beside the door. Nell had been generous giving out her brew, I thought.

But deep in the woods, there was a wisp of untoward smoke, and I wondered at the sight. Then I saw a man lying on the village path, dead-drunk asleep. He was one of the sheepherders from Lincoln, and he bore a burn across his face. He woke, and for a moment, I thought he looked ashamed.

That night, I found out more. Hob took me by the arm, loudly asking me if I've had the taste of this year's barley wine. I shook my head in answer. *No.*

Hob laughed aloud, a hollow sound, and took me to the edge of the village and into the woods. All the men of the village seemed to be out that night, faces flushed with drink, talking loudly as if to cover the sound of silence in the forest all around.

Casks from each house were filled with Nell's fresh barley wine. Her brewing cauldron was upended now on the forest floor.

But then Hob took me deeper into the wood, and when we arrived at her small cruck house, it was barely standing, timbers scorched by flame. And high above the scene, Nell hung from a rope upon a tree, flies buzzing around her gaping mouth.

The shock came over me like ink rushing into water, filling my soul with black horror. A shiver ran from arm to arm and I found myself weak as death. I shook with fear, but then I pinched my flesh harshly, so that I would not faint. And I forced myself to look up again, to follow Hob's pointing finger.

Nell's harmless body twisted in that evening's cold cruel breeze. There was a thick strange knot above her head, one I, the daughter of a fisherman, had never seen before. What a curious knot it was: I marking the tying of it carefully, tracing every movement of the line. A triple knot, tied fast across a half hitch.

✠

The story was bandied about that night, and I listened close, through my shock and fear. The sheepherders went to Nell's house after she had gone to bed. They woke her and demanded that she pour them barley wine. But when told the price, they decided the price was too high. For they did not pay—they tipped her cauldron over.

I was sure those strangers did this to her, a woman alone, knowing there would be no call for justice.

Tom had not the courage for murder, but I remember him putting a flagon warm in my hand. "Aye, Mear, 'tis from that tub of the old bitch."

"Strange one, that," another voice slurred out. "A woman who tried to till the land, make her masters an' her betters pay for drink."

Who was there that night? Can I remember now any sign that would point to the villain?

"She lived as a man, y'know," said one of our villagers. I can almost remember who it was.

"Aye, dere's truth in that. Lived as a man by herself! What if she were a witch?" added some sodden sheepherder.

Though the men seemed ashamed of her death, some quickly found a way to justify it.

One of the swarthy sheepherders stepped into the gap, his cup sloshing against my hand. "Here's to that ol' witch."

"Ayuh, what if she were? Then whoever kill'd her did the Good Lord's work this day in hangin' her high. Rid the world of a devil spawn."

The talk flickered back and forth from mouth to mouth. They were jackdaws fighting over a bit of flesh, ripping this grisly matter back and forth until nothing of sense was left.

But I did not want to hang upon a tree. I did not want my child bereft. I did not want what little we had taken in a madcap drunken riot.

So I forced my mouth into a vacant grin and pounded my fellows on the back in mock hilarity as they laughed and they joked: "She lived as a man, y'know."

They could not understand how she could live without a man as her master. A man has standing to address a lord. A man can even go to Court. But a woman cannot—God has not given her such right. And such that break the rule will be broken upon it.

Somehow, in the end, I found a way to spill Nell's sweet barley wine upon the ground. I clapped Tom and Hob furiously on the back. Eventually, when someone heaved, I took my leave.

✠

In my dreams, I see Nell's clever face—her mouth the same, her laughter bright and gay. But always her eyes are glazed and dead. And I see that strange knot that held her tight. It twines and interweaves, and I cannot undo the line, no matter how I twist and turn, so desperately.

I know now it was the same knot tied on the door of Benedict's house, the same knot that killed my child.

CHAPTER 29

DEEP IN DREAM, I drift back through the years, to the day of Christian's birth in my abbey cell, where I was barricaded and alone. My moans made plain my secret to all around: I was with child, in the abbey. And soon, I would give birth. But none could come to my room, for I had blocked the door.

I can still hear the sounds of my loud birthing moans, the cramping pains, the slow and agonizing outward push, the joy. The babe opens his eyes, and they are Christian's eyes, strong and bright, golden and lustrous as a rising sun.

My foot throbs, a great wrench of pain reverberating up my leg, and I swim awake from my fog of sleep. I can feel the places on my arms where Salvius held me so tight: I must have bruises now.

I open my eyes. Morning is come again. I am in the manor hall at daylight, lying curled on the straw. And I am no longer young. I am nearly thirty years of age—old by any reckoning—and I lie bereft and hungry, in a dark Manor hall.

The dust of dreams lies crusted in my eyes. I wipe it away and push myself up on my elbows.

Tom hunches nearly double at the long rough-hewn table, supping thin soup to break his fast. He scoops it with a wooden spoon from a blackened trough, scarred from a thousand fires and the abuses of a thousand spoons. When he is done, he wipes his mouth on the sleeve of his cloak.

I must get to the chamber pot quickly, but I stumble as I rise. And then Geoff hands me a stick—he has carved it for me, stripping bark away and keeping one slight branch outstretched for my hand. It is a cane to hold me up. And when I look down, I see that someone has changed the wrapping on my foot.

But despite these kindnesses, I find myself distrustful. My dream of Nell's death is too fresh. And I believe in my heart that someone here with me now, someone I know, killed Nell.

The pain is there in my remaining toes—a nasty, fiery ache the minute my foot touches the ground. But I can move, though halting and lame.

I use the crutch and limp to the garderobe. Through the slit window, I can see the moon outside now. She bulges, as if with child, nearly full. With the sight of the room, I remember that this is my time of the month. I sigh with irritation. Always, I must steal what rags I can and stuff them hard against me, to conceal that bloody flux. But with the lack of food and long travel, there has been no flow.

Christian's birth still runs through my head—a strange residue of dream that has stayed with me, some fog of long sleep that infests my mind. During my rise from the straw, during my limping walk, and with every throb of pain, I can hear a series of slight and high-pitched moans, the panting sound of birth.

But when I leave the garderobe, the sound remains. My head is clear, my eyes wiped of sand, my belly rumbles. I am awake. And yet I hear the sound of birth, echoing faintly down that small dark hall that smells of plague.

And I realize: there is a girl inside that middle room who births this day.

No one seems to pay her mind though, and I am hungry. So I hobble to the trough, where I find a cup of water thinly laced with meat. There floats here a tiny rib, a sliver of rat bone and gristle left behind. That is all we have left.

The rest have already eaten what they can. They are gathered now around the hearth. All are silent, listening.

There is an edge of fear in that moaning from the far end of the hall. It turns into a high keening and then subsides.

As I turn back, I see the Lord's eyes watching all. His fingers stroke his hawkish nose before he clenches his hands together and apart. It seems the girl who is birthing makes him worry.

"Tell us a story again," says one of the men of the manor, pointing at Liam.

I'm certain he wants a story to drown out the sound of fear and pain. No men will enter to be with her; only women can be in that room now.

"Ah, I dunno." Liam licks his lips nervously, tugs on his beard.

Salvius stands up. "Alright, I'll do it! You remember Alison—"

"Who would not?" says Cole. "What a lass, to kiss and hold and love at night—"

Benedict snorts out loud. "When have you ever lov'd any lass?"

Cole looks shamefaced and falls silent. But the restless men look to Salvius.

"Well," Salvius says. "Fair Alison, she had more than one lover. She were first married to that ol' carpenter."

Salvius points at Geoff, who groans and claps his hand on his heart.

"But this other chap—Absolon—he was in love with lithe li'l Alison too! An' he was a monk, a clerk like Moten here."

Moten sighs. "Don't involve me in your blasphemous tale. I'm no Absolon!"

Salvius points and laughs. "Why, there he is. He speaks!"

Moten glares, but as the rest laugh at his expression, he laughs too.

"Now Absolon sang at Alison in the street, all for love woebegone. She never pays mind, until one night when Absolon knocks at her window—like this." Salvius raps a fist on a piece of wood at the hearth. "He knocks at the bedroom window, which is low to the ground, and he sings a song to her."

Salvius sneaks behind Cole and takes him by the neck. "Sing a song, young Absolon!" says Salvius.

Cole looks like a puppet—grinning and gawping in the air, as Salvius moves him around. Cole sings out some words, laughing. "Ah, my love, I long for you! Please, at least, give me a kiss. My mouth is hungry for you. Awake my love, and speak to me."

"More, more!" shout the men.

Over the sound of jollity, I can hear the moaning rhythm in the middle room, calling to me, speaking above the sound of the laughing crowd. *Is she the only woman in this house? Who is she? Why is she locked away?*

Salvius is speaking once more. "Alison said, 'Get away from that window, you jack fool, I love another, so get on your way, or I will throw a stone! Let me sleep in peace!'"

The men hoot and holler.

Salvius gives a hangdog look. "Poor Absolon," he says.

And Cole stands up again. "Ah," he cries in the voice of the lover. "That true love was ever so ill-used. Please to kiss me—for the love of Jesus! An' fer me!"

I glance down the hall. The woman is keening in pain.

Nell died alone, even with men all around, laughing perhaps in riotous mirth. When I cut her down, that complicated knot behind her head held her firm. *Did she have to watch them laugh even as she died?*

Nell died alone. I may die alone. This girl need not be alone.

"Now, that girl Alison, she was clever as a crow," Salvius jokes at the fireside. "So here is what she says: 'If I kiss you, will you go away?'"

I remember the Abbess, remonstrating for long hours, begging for me to lose the burden I carried. She cited the Book of Numbers, telling me that only the select should carry a child, that God would select the few. And those *not* of the select—like young and common Miriam—should necessarily take the draught from priest or abbess.

The Abbess spoke so softly in that warm, rich room of books and light. She stood above me, reason in her voice, malice in her heart: "You are to consider your part. Your part alone. There is no other at fault—he will never acknowledge this child. You must rid yourself of this burden."

But I did not drink that acrid tea the Abbess had prepared. I would not kill the child in me. And at the end, I locked myself in my cloister cell, so that I would be alone in my birthing.

I was old enough to know what to do—or so I thought. By then, I had helped two other girls birth their babes, and I knew of the swelling tide of pain and pushing that overwhelms, the way one must move into the rhythm. It is an ocean dance that carries you away, and if you are to survive the mounting tide, you do not resist—you let it spill over you, in tearing pain and final pleasure. I knew enough, and still, I was terrified alone.

"Sing to me, my fair bird, my sweet cinnamon," Cole yelps loudly. "I have such a love-longing I am burning up. I love you such that I refuse to eat, from love's pains!"

The men roar with laughter.

I rise from my place near the hearth. I hold onto the wall, pulling myself along with my crutch, and limp along toward the further end of the hall. Some of the manor men are going back outside to work, and I time my journey down the hall with theirs. Yet one man sees me. Out of the corner of one eye, I can see the hawk-nosed Lord moving with me, down the center of the hall.

I approach the iron-belted door in the archway, but the Lord comes even with my limping progress.

The girl's cries are louder—I am close to her door now—she is panting in and out. I fear for her. I raise my hand and I knock hard.

The Lord stares at me quizzically. "She'll 'ave to suffer alone. Only a woman can help her in her labor, and we have none o' those."

But the door opens, even as he speaks. Backlit by flames, the woman's large shadow, swollen with child, falls across the hall. She leans on the doorjamb and takes a deep and pulsing breath.

I vacillate a moment, and think of turning back. Her childbirth is not my concern. But I think of Nell, helping me keep my secret. I seem to hear Nell's voice, whispering to me. *Help her, help me.* And then the woman gasps again, her face heavy with fear and with distress. I cannot wait any longer.

I take the hood from off my head, and look into her eyes.

"Well," she says to the Lord, impatient. "What're you lookin' at? Can't she come in?"

"No, me dear," the Lord says. "The rule of women is that only a woman—"

The girl laughs loud then, her mirth stopping suddenly with a gasp as a labor pang cuts across her breath. She moves toward me, she looks into my face, and then she takes hold of my collar and pulls it wide, peering down my shirt to where my bosom is bound tight. Every face in the manor house watches us now.

"Are you all blind an' deaf an' dumb?" she says. "Do you mistake your dogs for pigs as well? Any woman could tell this was a sister in her very face."

She laughs again, shaking her dark mane of hair, mocking them all. "All of you thought this one here was a man?"

Every man stares back at her, looking nonplussed.

"Jesus and Mary!" The girl holds up a hand and bends herself until the newest pain passes. "Let her in! God knows I need her help!" she gasps.

I did not expect this, but now it is done. I take a step forward, yet before I go in, I glance back to the gathered men. Benedict's face is white. Liam takes a step forward from the hearth, his mouth open broader than his beard. It is as if I have grown a tail and a pair of horns.

The Lord says nothing. He bows his head and parts the way. I step into the archway and enter the doorway with the girl. I open the iron-belted door.

It comes over me then, like a cold wave that covers me in saltwater. I am breathless.

I am a woman again.

CHAPTER 30

The room is round as a turrent and full of light. The roof curves up to an arch. The fire has a screen, and through narrow metal holes carved in cunning shapes, comes a rosy glow. Rushlights burn on each wall, beside tapestries that cover closed and shuttered windows. It reminds me of Nell's neat croft—the arch she added to the door, the glowing oilcloth across the holes in her walls. Nell's house was like a tiny hall of a lady or lord, a woodland nobility.

A loose-knit linen cloth hangs as a curtain around a great couch filled with straw, for lords and ladies to sleep. Blankets and furs lie strewn about. The hanging linen cloth shines white in the light, as thin as a cobweb, floating as a cloud.

The girl's face looks up at me. A drift of curling raven-black hair, lips red as any apple, and wide, deep eyes of gray. When I swing the door closed behind me, I can see her face more plainly. Her forehead is spotted with sweat, and her eyes narrowed with pain.

A moment later, her pang fades away, and she opens her mouth again.

"Who are you?" she says, panting again, even as she speaks. I glance behind my back, I am far down the hall and safe behind that iron-belted door.

I open my mouth. “M- Mear,” I murmur. I try to say more, but my tongue feels thick and unwieldy, heavy with anxiety. I cannot get another word out. Finally, I draw my finger across my throat.

“Ah,” she replies, and her face shifts from tight to loose again. “Mear? You’ve done this thing before?”

I nod with confidence. I give a reassuring smile.

“Ah,” she breathes. “Good God, I need you then.” Her face creases with an incipient pang of fear. “Please help me.” She reaches out, her fingers clenching tight on my hand. And so we enter that path together.

First, I make a way for her to walk. And holding my hand, she begins to pace round and round. My limp and her pregnant rolling walk together make a strange pair.

But my presence seems to calm her, and as she walks, the waves of pain come less strong in her face. Instead, she speaks to me before and after, as if to tell herself that she is no longer alone.

“Cramps, y’know—it clenches, squeezes the breath outta me.”

I nod again. I give a gentle shushing sound.

But she cannot help babbling. It seems she has been locked away here, nearly alone, except for those who bring her wood or water every day. Now, even in the midst of her labor, she needs to know I hear.

“See, Lady of the House got the plague. They locked her in, to save us all, says the Lord. An’ even before she come down with the illness, I lay with the Lord. But when she died, he stopped lovin’ me. I know not why. An’ then the famine come, and about that time, I get with child.”

She pauses and pushes back a strand of curling hair that had fallen across her face. It is rare I am so close to a woman. I have almost forgotten what it is like to have hair long to my waist, what care I used to take to rub sage or mint into my curling chestnut locks, and how the talk of women differs from that of men.

A surge takes her, and a tiny pleat appears in the middle of her brow. I smooth it with my thumb, caressing her brow. I breathe in and out, slow and steady, to show her how.

But as soon as the cramp has passed, she paces with me and talks once more. "He didn't cast me out, for if I could have a livin' son, then I'd be worth somethin' to him again, you see?"

I don't see. But I cannot tell her that.

"All others 'ave died, dontcha see? My boy would be the only livin' child. The Lord's only son. When 'e is born, if I call out, they'll all come then. That lot will have to come."

The surge comes again, and her eyes crease closed. She concentrates and remembers to breath.

When her eyes open, the words come again. "But we're in danger here. 'Cause the folk of the land come here for food, and now we're out. An' them lot don't forgive—they want what's comin' to them. But now we're sav'd, he says, 'cause you come here, all of you."

I wrinkle my brow. *What is she talking about?*

Her eyes squeeze shut in pain—the pang is heavy this time. She halts and pants on me, holding my hand with a grip of iron. "Ah, ah," she cries. "I can't keep on!"

I take her head gently and turn her face so she is facing me. Her eyes squint open, she holds my gaze, and slowly, the surge fades away. The wave has passed again, this time.

She shakes her head and bends down, leaning on the bench, taking the weight off her legs. She opens her mouth to speak, and I put my hand over her lips.

"Nah," she grunts. "No, it can't wait." There's something she must say. She struggles to raise her eyes.

"You bear the dead," she says. "Your own kinfolk, dead."

I nod and frown.

"That's our food," she gasps. "The dead are lawful to eat—*in extremis*—says the Lord. For many months now, that is all we eat."

I blanch. But I do not believe her.

She must sense what I think, for she pulls aside a tapestry that hangs over a window and shows me what is below. The round room hangs above the cliff, so that we can see the river and the open valley for miles. She points to the byre on the hillside below. "Look there."

I can see directly into our cart in the byre now. The men of the manor who worked outside are laboring there. The oilcloth has been pulled off, the linen discarded. They use great flensing blades to slice something apart.

My mind flinches. *I must be seeing things.* I rub my eyes.

"No," she pants. She pushes a long bone into my hand. "You've got to take this . . . tell them . . . get your boys away."

I look down at the yellowed length in my hand. The marks of teeth are clear and round. No animal chewed this bone: Only a man.

I gasp. *What she says is true.* I should leave, find a way to the hall, get the men out of here. My eyes shift to the iron-belted door.

Then she shifts her legs and gasps again, nearly falling down with the pang of labor. Her body is shrunken, her breasts withered—all is thin except her rounded belly. She will not be able to birth without my help. I lean closer to her, hold her tight, but she is still speaking to me, explaining.

"He says the holy priest does it too. *Eat this flesh, drink this blood*—that it is Christ come to save us with a new communion. But I canna do it," she adds. "I canna eat this flesh."

I shake my head emphatically.

"Water," she says, reaching out. "I need a drink."

I find a flagon and give her sup.

"Ah." She wets her mouth, her lips, her face. "You need to unnerstand—it's not our choice. Ev'ry new moon, the peasant folk come to the manor house. They need more, ev'ry time, 'cause the land is empty—it died. And now there's but you and me against death's tide."

A wave seizes her once more. I've let go of her hand, and she is left all alone to take it as she may. I put my hands on her shoulder, but her eyes are closed. She wails loud and long, the keening sound I heard before begins again. Tears roll down her face.

"It hurts," she moans. "It hurts. But I've made up my mind. I'll throw him away, at the end."

Her eyes open, tears swimming in pools of gray. "Even if he lives, we are all dead. I'll kill him, save him from a worser fate. I'll pay that great high feckin' Lord Paul Anders back fer his words of hate. I'm not gonna call out when the child is born. I'm gonna let him die."

"Ah," I cry out loud. "No, you must—"

She does not listen to me. "Why bring him into this world of pain a'tall?" she moans. "Why let him live a'tall?"

I do not know how to answer. In my mind, I can see only Christian's face. His eyes at birth. At two, walking awkward on the dust, his legs naked, his face smiling and alive. At three, and five, and eight. And then last spring, at lambing time, when he took an ewe in hand and brought a live lamb out. Smiling in the firelight, crying in the dark. Even now that he is gone, I treasure what I had.

Every moment with your child is precious, no matter how long they live, no matter the number of their days. I try to tell her this.

"I dunno," she whispers back. "What if..."

I seize her shoulders as hard as I can. I pull her to my breast, so she will look into my face.

All the years of my life are scribed across the thin and wavering parchment of my skin. There are crow's nests of lines around my eyes from squinting under candlelight on long winter evenings of study at the abbey, and a faint twitch in my round apple cheeks that I swear I never had until I birthed a child. There are all the small injuries incurred as Christian came of age, the flat place on my pate where old Cecil's cow kicked me when I rescued him, and the fall we took together in the woods—that left a scar. All of these are treasures. None of them I'd trade away.

My lips are trembling and fulsome, my eyes glistening, full of water. *You must let the child live. Take what's given you—let him live, come good or bad. We know little what shall betide us, what fate awaits.*

Then abruptly I am aware of my appearance, a pitiful old thing with disheveled hair, tears covering my cheeks in a sheen of rheumy memories.

Yet she does not look away. She seems to understand. She grunts. She nods. "Alright, alright, I'll help him live, upon my life." Then her face clenches as a pang overtakes her.

After that, for many hours, the pangs come close together, one on top of another. She does not speak again while the sun wanes in the sky and night comes. All that long evening, she breathes in and out quickly, as if before the plunge. Finally, it is too much.

"Ah, God," she shrieks. "Jesus and Mary, I can't! I can't do this. I can't. Ah!"

I stroke her back in a long, firm caress. *Let it push through you. Don't hold back.*

"Ah!" She strains again, the cords standing out in her neck. "Ah, is he here? Is he?"

I bend down, I look between her legs, but there's nothing. I reach in and feel—there is a swelling roundness, but no head. Then her legs tremble and tense again.

She grunts with effort. "Ah, ah, is he comin' through? Is he? Is he?"

I hold up my hand, I measure for her. About a finger wide.

She tries again, a greater effort. Then she collapses her head against the bench. "Ah, there's nothin' happening when I try, when I push. Why? Why's there nothin'?"

I hold up my hand. "The waters," I whisper. "A moment."

"You'll burst the waters?" she says. "That'll help then?"

I reach up and score my fingernail across the bulging sac. Water pours out on the floor, and then the head is there, touching my fingers. She tenses once more, she pushes hard, and then the top of the baby's head is firm against my hand.

She shrieks. "Ah, it hurts, it burns. Ah, God!"

I hold my hand up flat to stop her from pushing. *Wait now, wait now, not yet.*

I feel the rounded head is in my hand. I bid her wait, although it hurts. She must wait, else her flesh will tear. Then, at last, I let her push again.

There is a long hour while she thrusts him forth.

Finally, the babe is in my hands. It is a boy, his hands like little starfish, his hair is fine as silk, his eyes open and black, his cord alive with blood. But the babe does not move there, in my arms. He is perfect in every aspect.

But stillborn.

The girl cuddles the babe close. She does not want to let her perfect child go. My heart throbs with hers, every beat. I hold the boy too. He is wet and warm from the womb, yet there is no breath in him, no beat of the heart.

Even while I watch her, while I cry, I look anxiously at the door. I must tell the others that they mean to take our children from us. It may already be too late.

The girl looks at me, her face still stretched and pained from the labor, a rare and tired beauty in her wide pupils, her eyes turned into wide gray pools. "You're going now, aintcha?"

I nod my head. I come close. I murmur gently to her, a sound to give her peace. *Whatever happens now, he was yours.*

"I can't take care of him. God done it already." Then an awareness comes into her eyes. "The peasant folk come soon. I know it in my heart. They'll devour him. But his body is mine, they canna have him." Her words echo my own heart's song, my own fear.

"They can't have him. 'E is mine, always and ever—'e is mine to do with as I will."

She lays him gently down. Then she goes to one of the closed and shuttered windows of the round room and opens it wide. This morning, in the hour before dawn, the world is covered in a bank of fog: the cliffside and the distant hills are islands in this mist.

The wind comes gusting in, seven small snowflakes melt upon the babe's warm skin. Below, a flowing river of mist fills the basin with a gray light, a color that echoes in the young mother's eyes. She holds her child close, she wraps him in that linen netting from above her bed. I whisper some words.

Oh Alma Redemptoris…

And then the girl lets him go, out the long cold window. In this utter silence before the dawn, I can hear him fall a long way, the linen catching the wind and guttering loud. When he enters the gray vapor below, there is no sound. It's as if he has drifted out from the cliff on silent wings and floated away into the misty dawn.

The girl closes the shutter and the window and pulls the tapestry to cover it again. Then she wraps the afterbirth in a small cloak, tight, as if it is a babe. She holds it close and then looks up, as if she has a mind to do another thing entire. Her eyes are full of tears, but her jaw is tight with resolve.

I stand a moment, empty-handed and bereft. But she comes close to me and holds my hands. "If I can't save him, I will save you." Her eyes are strong, and her voice does not quaver. "I will wait one turn of the candle on the wick. Then I'll call them loud—get them all in here, so you will not be seen as you go. Go then. Go now, be quick."

She means to give us nearly an hour by the sun—one bell, one turn of time.

CHAPTER 31

MY HANDS ARE streaked and stippled as with strange and bloody tears. As I crack the door open, I can hear footsteps in the hall. It is the gaunt lord and his shorter liege.

The deep lines in the shorter man's face catch the hearth's dim glow. He is as still as a stone statue.

The Lord folds his long arms tight across his chest in the cold dark. He looks afraid. "How long 'til the people of the land come again an' demand food?"

"Two nights—full moon, then the peasant folk come. Next day after that. We should do it tomorrow."

"Did the rats get to them in the byre yet?" says the Lord quietly.

"Nah," replies the other. "A leg nibbled. I kill'd the rat. Added 'im to the pot fer dinner."

The Lord stands and gazes out the mullioned window at the three-quarters moon. "The rest still frozen?"

"Ya, that lot are good as a winter pig hung in the smokehouse," the short man says to the Lord. "We can 'ave a feast. Let me show you what I found." And the two of them pull on their cloaks, open the door, and leave the manor hall.

I am trembling with fear. But quickly I limp down the hall to our slumbering men. Liam's face is near to me. He sighs the long slow breath of sleep. I can see a little better now in a quiet gloom. It is the blue hour before the dawn.

But then I start with surprise. For Liam's eyes are slit open in the dark. His snoring breath is a lie. He brings a finger up to his lips in careful silence.

I slide the gnawed bone out from my tunic, revealing it to him.

"Aye, they said they would take our lads apart," he whispers. "I heard them in the night speak of eating the dead. Now here's the proof."

He sits up and chews a fingernail nervously. "What do we do, Mear?"

I point outside emphatically. *We go. Now.*

He nods, his face strained tight by terror.

Quickly, we go to each of the men in our company. I cover their mouths with my hand, shaking them mutely one by one from their beds. They glance at my face, at my wide fearful eyes, my trembling mouth.

I watch the byre through a small arrow slit in the wall. The Lord and his liege are still busy. They do not come toward the hall yet. And the rest of the men of the manor snore.

Quietly, soundlessly, we pack our bedrolls and our clothes. Our men get their boots or wraps on their feet lift their cloaks and furs off the rotten straw on the floor, and wrap them for the road.

Brother Moten is the only one not convinced that we should go. In fact, he wishes to discuss it in whispers now, at the most untimely hour! Then, after he has been convinced, Moten cannot find some tattered manuscript he brought. He wastes precious time searching. Then he finds his precious book, and we are ready to depart.

Just then comes a cry from the further room—the girl's voice, raised in a lie for our salvation. "A living son—His Grace Paul Anders has a living son!"

I can hear a waver in her voice, that edge of fear I know so well. She lies for us, to save us now. But what will she suffer for her words?

The men of the manor startle in their beds, and there is a scurrying in the hall as all rush toward the room at the other end. But the Lord has not come yet. So Benedict steps to the outer door and opens it wide. He echoes the girl's call, so it can be heard outside.

Then the Lord comes plunging in from the byre, throwing his snowy boots to the floor. He does not look around—he and his liege go directly down the hall. We wait until they are out of sight.

Now we escape.

I limp to the door, and then I spy the Manor Lord's left-behind boots. I reach down and slip this rich leather on my feet.

I take the Lord's fur-lined cloak as well, a rich and heavy one. If we are to be thieves in the night, then let us take all that we can find.

Outside at the cart, our boys' bodies have been hewed by an axe or sword, most every muscle severed. The cutting done to them was the work that one does to smokehouse animals: rough, uncouth, and deep to the quick.

The men's faces are mottled with rage and shock. Tom starts to exclaim out loud—pointing at the boys' butchered bodies—but he is quickly hushed by Salvius.

Quickly, we roll the cart out of the byre and down the hill, toward the frozen river and the bridge. We can only get at two of the horses—the other is far back in the byre—so we leave one behind. I ride on the high seat of the cart, with my hurt foot. The men move at a fast stride, almost a run.

The horses are startled by their early rise at dawn, but refreshed by three days of rest and a byre full of hay, they pull hard.

Salvius's old piebald mare and one of the Abbot's cart-horses are going at a steady clip by the time we come to the worn, rotten drawbridge. I am afraid as we trot quickly onto these old timbers, for there are creaks that tell us it is weak beneath our feet. There are shouts behind us now. Some from the manor house have run to the small guardhouse.

We drive the two horses faster, praying we'll make it across the river yet.

The men of the manor pull at the thick ropes, wrestling them apart.

And then the great ropes are untied. They whip in the air above us like vast serpents.

The bridge sways perilously from side to side. There is a deep creaking groan. The cart rolls backward, the horses slip, and the bridge is loose in open air. I lunge forward, reaching out toward Salvius's shoulder as he grabs for the cart. The bridge twists in death throes.

There is a moment in which we seem to float, then a sudden rending crash, a tearing thud as loud as a thunderclap.

Craaack! The bridge breaks entire off the other side of the cliff and falls to the frozen river below. Liam's head slams hard on the bridge as we go down. I am flung against the boys in the cart. The bodies are tied down, so they do not move, but the horses have no such constraint. The beasts are flung about, and they scream in fear, stabbing their hooves into the air. We are all nearly flattened by the landing on hard ice, and we fall about like rag dolls. *Craaack—craaack—craaack!* The rest of the bridge lands like a hammerblow, sending fractures out as far as I can see. The world we are on has broken apart: the river ice is shattered.

The men clamber quickly upon the cart, for icy water rises and falls around their feet. Salvius lifts Liam—with his injured head—up to the cart. Back and forth it washes as the floes push against each other.

The ice jumps under us then, in a great rush that throws the broken bridge and the cart along as swiftly as small leaves on a spring flood tide.

All of us must trust our souls to God, for we are trapped, caught on the spinning floes of ice, racing downriver in this frozen torrent.

Our only hope is to stay above the water that covers the floes in waves from time to time. Benedict and Salvius struggle down from the cart onto the ice. They take timbers from the bridge and prop our cart above the washing water, in a frantic attempt to help our floe stay above the general flood. They also wrap the horses' eyes in cloth, to keep them from rearing and running off our makeshift raft.

The men who work on the ice make me stay in the cart. It is my foot mostly, but though no one has said a word, I fear they put my womanhood apart now.

Finally, there is little left to do. We are at the mercy of this frozen tide. Late in the morning, as the sun shines through the fog, the cakes of ice move forward as like one great moving road. Benedict speaks above the rushing sound of water and crunching ice.

"What happen'd?"

Moten speaks up. "They were gonna devour our dead. These manor men feed the folk of the land with the blood of travelers."

"Ayuh," says Liam. His voice is slurred and slow from the blow on his head. "Mear and I heard them talk in the night. They aimed to eat our boys. They chopped them up."

"Those men deserve t' die," says Cole.

"Many do, lad, many do," Geoff replies wearily. "And many as die should live."

Benedict grimaces. "But what of this Mear—or this witch who called herself Mear before she transformed, eh?"

Tom stalks over to me, and without warning, he rips my tunic down the front. The cold air rushes in at my breast. He stares then, at my bosom.

"Mear is a woman," he declares. "I didna believe it. But it's true. A lie. A bewitchment."

Quickly, I pull the Lord's fur-lined cloak closed again, my humiliation rising red in my skin.

Salvius clears his throat and spits, "Goddammit, Mear—who are you, in truth? Is your name even Mear? What do you want with us?"

"I do not care what Mear is," Liam says. "Mear saved us by what was found out. I didna understand what I heard before Mear came back from the birth. Mear helped us."

"But how did Mear know?" says Benedict. "What manner of she-devil is this Mear?"

"I dunno," says Liam slowly, rubbing his hurt head. "Mear gave me this human bone here—which proved the evil."

Tom swears at me, his eyes narrowed with suspicion. "What manner of devil are you, to change from man to woman like that?"

"Mear came out with bloody hands," says Salvius darkly.

Men are never present at births, they do not know what happens there. *Of course I came out with blood on my hands, you fools.*

"No livin' soul can change like that," Benedict pants as he pushes another timber against the moving ice beneath. "What if Mear is a witch, or cursed by a witch?"

"Ayuh, all Mear did was lie to us," says Liam slowly, the words coming careful to his lips. "Mear is a woman, that much is true."

"Mear… he… she… whate'er Mear is," says Cole, "it ain't natural."

There is a deep resentment in his tone, the sullen irritation of one who has been deceived. The others look at me too, and I can see a great injury in their gaze.

"You took us away from them at the manor," says Salvius at last. "But at what cost?"

"I think this witch here gave them a fresh child to eat. You knew of this, with your witchy magic," says Tom. "You went to the woman's room, to find a way to feed them."

Perhaps now is the time to speak. Yet when I open my mouth, I feel a lock that seems to close around my throat. I open and gape, like a fish in the air.

Then Geoff joins in. "What if that child—that li'l one—was sacrificed fer our own sins, to set us free again? Ah've heard of such witch communions."

Moten tries to protest. "Witches don't act like the Christ. I don't think she—"

"Mear killed the babe!" shouts Tom. "A sacrifice!"

Benedict's face goes dark with rage. "What if Mear burned 'em all—and this whole journey is to serve her dark magic? Mear is a witch, I say—and the one who burned our boys!"

Liam blanches. It seems he will not believe such a thing, although he does not speak. A welter of blood leaks slowly from the wound on his scalp.

The rest of them lap it up all too greedily, like dogs licking up their own vomit, a tone of urgent relish in their mouths as they gulp that foul spew.

"We 'ave to float her!" Benedict shouts.

"You mean . . ." Tom's voice catches. "To prove if she's a witch."

"Ayuh." Bene points to a dark gap in the ice floes ahead. "There!"

"It's a test," Salvius says gravely. "To see if she's flesh and blood, or spirit."

My heart pounds. My tongue seems to fill my mouth. I am truly mute.

"Wait!" says Moten suddenly, his words frantic and rushed. "Truth to tell, it is a faulty test. Do not put her in the water. First, we should test the spirit and the soul in prayer, and then a priest should question her. You see, the soul must be shriven—must be cleansed—before any physical trial."

Moten means to defend me, but he speaks in convoluted ideas. No one here will listen to his proposal. His words are useless to me.

The sun sinks deeper as the cold takes hold of all the air, a spider spinning endlessly, wrapping our bones and viscera in frost and ice. The words of condemnation wrap tighter and tighter around me with the cold.

"There's no hope for it," says Tom hoarsely. "Ah'll do it." He takes ahold of my arm and begins to drag me forward. "If any should do it, ah should. Only way to save ourselves from a curse."

I stumble and try to stop, but my feet slide over the creaking ice.

"No! No!" I hear Moten shouting, but his voice seems distant and muted, far away.

Tom's eyes are filled with tears, and then he is weeping, even as he drags me onward to my doom.

"There's no hope for it," he cries again, and I remember with a chill Tom's own mother's death. "Mear is the reason fer all our ills. We 'ave to let her go if we are to live."

Tom jerks my arm forward, but not roughly. It is as if he moves on great puppet strings, unable to stop his own motion. It is the way of things, he seems to think, the way we must follow, and none can stop this turn of Fortune's wheel.

"Over here," says Tom, his voice breaking as he pushes me forward. "Into the river."

I tear at his fingers. I can see into the crack between the floes now. The deep water whips between the icy cakes like a black and streaming snake. I scrabble my feet helplessly.

The river roars, a ravenous dark mouth.

CHAPTER 32

MY THROAT GOES numb with fear—I cannot breathe. Tom pulls me past the wheels of the cart and I reach out frantically, gripping the wheels desperately, my fingernails sinking into the wood as the frigid river whips at my feet.

I slide swiftly toward the gap. My feet skid into the icy water. I scrabble for a hold, a rat in a rain barrel, about to drown.

Suddenly, someone grips my arm. I am pulled back from the brink.

It is Liam.

"What the hell you doin' this for?" he shouts. But he does not shout at me.

Liam's voice is hoarse, the cords in his neck standing out as he yanks me up off the little floe, as he pushes Tom back toward the cart.

Tom protests. "But we don't know if Mear—"

"I'm here, with these lads "—Liam slaps the cart with fury—"'cause I seek fer justice in their deaths, not 'cause I care who is a witch and who ain't. I just want my boy to be aveng'd!"

Salvius steps forward, his face flushed with anger. "And what if Mear brought their deaths?"

A sudden shout goes up from Geoff. "You feckin' idjit! Liam is right. Remember when Mear rescu'd us from the snow, and from the first bandits too? Mear saw them second bandits comin', an' sav'd us all when most of you were sick as dogs! Sav'd us all—you were there! Mear wouldn't 'ave done this thing."

"That's true," says Liam. He holds his hurt head in his hand. "Mear ain't a witch to be thrown under the ice."

"Our boys lie here dead"—Geoff points at Tom, and his firm carpenter's hand does not tremble, not a bit—"and all the time you and Benedict want to argue over whose cock was in whose cunt that night. An' I don't feckin' care—one of you did this, an' I want to know who!"

✠

No one else touches me again that night. My tunic is rent—my bosom unbound. I will sew it tight again when I can find thread. For now, I wrap the Lord's fur cloak from the manor tighter around me, but still I feel cold.

I am a wretched golem made of iced-over clay, every surface of me rough and numb. My face itself misshapen by my heavy beard of frost, with an old man's swollen fingers, calloused flesh, and long, rough, rimy bones.

I cannot sleep if I ponder the men's words and accusations long. Their fear is a torment, a fire in my breast. And in truth, I cannot sleep at all, not with this river endlessly surging around me. My foot throbs in the few spare hours of the night, pounding like a second heart. My leg feels puffy and swollen, my toes on fire. But when I look down, there is no change in the flesh at all. No fever, no infection, just the pain.

Cold tears as salty as ocean spray wet my face. I wipe my face with a handful of straw and look out on the floating ice. I groan and roll upon the straw packed into the cart. I remember my father's death.

The day before he died, my mother did something I still don't understand. She took me out in our little fishing boat, out on the open water of the sea—the thrum and hiss of surf upon the shore behind us, the rhythm never ceasing.

My mother waited until we were out of sight of land. She squinted against the bright sunlight, making sure we were alone. And then she taught me something: strange words in a foreign tongue, a lilting singsong cadence to it. My mother taught those words to me and urged me to memorize them.

"What I teach you now are holy words," she said. "This is Kaddish. Tomorrow we say Kaddish for your father. Promise that you will say Kaddish for me when I am gone."

Then she told me what it meant. "Miriam, my daughter, you are a chosen one of Israel. You are a Jew. You must find our people, to say it with them. I will tell you where they are hidden. Then you will say Kaddish and bring me peace."

My mother rowed us back, the waves lifting and catching us as I whispered the words in cadence. The boat slipped through the last breakers and came toward the beach, and my mother leaned close to me, kissed me on the forehead.

"Never forget who you truly are, but never tell a living soul."

At the hour of Sext the next day, when the gray circle of the sun is high in the sky, the river ice stops moving. There are rending creaks all afternoon as one piece of ice fights another for supremacy. But finally, little moves at all. We wait until nearly dusk, to see if the ice will break apart once more.

The river goes quiescent, and finally we unwrap the horses' eyes. Benedict and Salvius scout ahead, pushing a long pole against the ice, but nothing moves. The ice has solidified. It is like stone again.

Against the farther bank is a rough track that comes down to a ford, where one can cross the river when it falls low. This is the path that we make for now.

It is a perilous crossing, for we must surmount great humps and shoals of ice that stand in our course. Always, I fear that one piece of ice will give way, plunging us into the river. But nothing moves.

We do not know what the path is like on the other side, but we know if we go much longer without food or shelter we will die. Already, our faces shrink down to the skull, and our bones seem weak as water in our legs and arms.

All are weary beyond weariness. Salvius would like to camp right where we come to land and rid ourselves of this burden. He wants to bury our boys' cut and broken bodies in the river itself. But Geoff is adamant he will not rest until we reach the city. Geoff and Salvius almost come to blows. The rest of us sink into the snow, too exhausted to fight.

Finally, Moten takes charge, urging us on. All make a final effort and push the cart up the long hill. We struggle upward along the track, skeletons walking upon the road. Laboriously we move against the curve of the hill. It is Vespers now, and in the rays of sunset, our bodies against the snow seem black as the burned ones in the cart.

When we crest the rise, we are surprised to see melted snow upon a green hillside, white lace draped across a field, in the failing light. The sight of these spare tufts of verdant green strikes joy into my heart. In my father's tongue, *l'herbe*—the words good enough to eat. Ah, and the scent: a whisper of sweet thyme and faint dog roses. The thaw has come here already.

I can also see that the river has carried us out of the burned land. For on the other side of the crest, the White Road waits for us again. I can now see the hills of Peterborough ahead: I know it from the map at Canterbury of the Ermine Way. We have traveled many miles on the river. In fact, the river has saved us over a week of pain on the road. We have only six days left to reach London, but with luck, we may yet succeed.

The cart pauses in its incessant creak and rumble. And now I can hear other sounds. We are surrounded by whistles, calls, and woodland rustling. Birds. My ears are full of the faint rhythm of wood fowl settling down for the night.

I can see larks, swallows and waxwings. Bullfinches too, flashing their black and red plumage and white rumps as they fly away, chasing seeds that remain here, in these unburned woods.

Close-at-hand, a robin twitters on a low branch, and listens for another that answers from beyond the farmhouse.

For there is a farmhouse here as well. No smoke, no light, a broken roof, likely abandoned. But still, a croft not burned, not razed to the ground in ash and char. A sign of someone who lived once and prospered in this place.

The farmhouse has a great gap in one corner of the thatched roof, where swallows nest. But deep inside the hole of the broken croft, there is a hearth and grate. We heap the straw in the corner, and prepare our camp.

Benedict and Salvius set rope traps in a copse near to the old farmhouse. And before the sun fails from the sky, we've caught two stoats and a marten. Deep in the frozen garden I dig, and I find lost carrots and old turnips. We light a fire, and we are warm with food and hearth. We are saved. We will not starve this day.

The men have me eat last, after I have prepared most of the meal. Their greedy mouths finish off the stoat and the turnips, but in the end I have enough for my belly too.

The daylight ebbs into the snow. Above us the swallows rustle and nest. After the sun goes, there is nothing left here in this dark room but faces ruddy in the light of the flames.

As the smoke comes out of the chimney of this little fallen house, I can again see Nell upon the little forest way beside her croft, the stones patterned with petals and cedar boughs, scented with the lavender and mint she planted with her own hands.

When I curl up in the straw to go to sleep, it comes to me that they have not killed their new witch. But if they knew my other secret, they might abandon me, without a second thought. Even kind Liam.

I shiver with fear in the darkness. I read once of a woman who traveled a path this dark and cold. She went into the earth, a daughter of spring, and went from innocence and purity into the depths, to become the queen of suffering and desolation. That is perhaps what I have become. I sink down into the river of sleep. I take my place with her in Hades down below.

BOOK V

CHAPTER 33

I OPEN MY EYES and look out through the open hole in the roof. The swallows whisk back and forth in the light of dawn, they are like tiny black cracks in a bright-blue sky. I am alive: no one took my life in the night. I breathe in deep and inhale the raw scent of my fellow travelers, the musty smell of straw in this little croft, and the sharp stink of the horses outside, hobbled near at hand.

As I walk outside to pass water, I go near to the cart. And there, I notice something else, an odor strange and sour. It is a faint thing now, a rank aroma that speaks of thaw and rot. But if the frost does not return soon, I fear it will be worse every day.

I slip on the ice going into the woods. Benedict, Tom, and Liam are ahead of me, gathering wood, but none of them acknowledges my fall in any way. It is as if I am now nothing to them: nothing but a body that can clean and cook. In that, they do not act as if I cannot be seen. On me now devolves every dirty and laborious task.

Clouds are rolling in over the horizon. Already the azure sky is beset with gray tendrils of mist. I slip and fall again on the ice, but still no one speaks to me, as if all of our history has turned to ashes and dust.

For years, I had thought I could go to Edward, and all would be made well. I'd thought I could go as who I am now, yet claim the rights of all that I had been. I lived in a dream all this time. Weeks ago, when I knew that Christian was dead, I still believed— if we could make it to London, I felt that all would be well. But Edward is dead, my companions ignore me, and my hope of a better life withers on the vine.

I stumble deep into the woods. I want to find a place far away from anyone. *Ah, what grief I have brought upon myself!* I am a woman and a Jew, trapped here with those who hate me, with my dead son, for no reason and no purpose. Finally, I find a tree and the shelter of a pair of gorse bushes.

As I piss into the snow, I look up at the fast-graying sky. Mist is covering it now, like a weight of heavy fen surging in a great wave, filling the clear sky with gray fog.

I hear footsteps coming closer. I look through the gorse. Cole sees me as I peer above the bush, and his scarred face narrows with suspicion and disgust.

My heart sinks. I am surrounded by those who feel themselves betrayed, and who now can only show me hate. I have lost Liam, and Cole too now. I am weary of loss, deep in my bones. And I dread always being treated like I am nothing more than a liar and a burden.

Then, close-at-hand, I hear a little scratch upon a twig. A bird, near to my knees. It is a waxwing, one of those birds that wear that strange little crest upon their heads. A bird that comes in the winter. I saw them often when I was a child, but in recent years far fewer than before. They fly fast over the land and take all they can.

There are two of them here, in the bush beside the copse. One takes a hawthorn berry that it found and passes it to the other, carefully, in its beak. The other takes it gently and turns it 'round. But the second does not swallow, does not eat. Its wings quiver as if in pleasure, and then that one gives it back again. That little berry is passed back and forth as I watch—a present, offered to one, then the other, over and over.

With a chorus of trills, they leave the bush, swooping down to a hawthorn hedge, where other shriveled berries hang. I do not see who finally accepts the berry.

A gift, given freely. The birds and beasts have more kindness in them than the human heart.

A stream runs by me in the woods. I can hear it gurgling deep in the ground, an underground flood that runs beneath the ice.

I stand. I turn and walk away as if I do not see Cole at all. He passes close-by as if I am not here either. Both of us pretend.

I must learn to be as the bear in the cage with the stick that pokes it always, through the bars. The bear acts as if the stick is made of air, and takes no notice of it, even when it is sharpened and draws blood. I must do the same.

My shoulders are tensed and ready when Cole'sshoulder slams into mine. I am prepared to shake off his blow, unafraid of this abuse.

But then the ground moves uncertainly. Under my feet, the tiny bits of hardened snow crunch and shift like sand. My body jerks out of kilter, and I lean awkwardly away, my arms flailing in the air, struggling to hold me up as my injured foot takes the weight. My foot slides across the slick, hard snow until the gap where my toe was cut away wedges hard against a root. A shot of agonizing pain jolts up my leg.

I will my body upright, and then there is a skidding crunch as a bit of hoarfrost gives way. My head swings in a dizzying circle, and the trees fly past across the rushing gray of the sky. My legs go out from under, and I take a sickening tumble. My temple thuds against a ragged ball of ice, and something cold slices into my lip. I am facing back the way I'd come.

I reach up to my face. A patch of warm, sticky blood begins to spread out from my head.

I can hear crying, although I make no sound. I lift my head and stare.

Cole is on his knees. "I'm sorry, Mear,... I'm so sorry... I juest,... I juest meant to give a 'li'l shove,... and then you... you—" He puts his hands out and gives a helpless look, as if he had not been able to control what he has done.

His black eyes stream with tears—regret is written across his face.

I wipe my lip, a bright sheen of blood on my hand as I struggle to my knees.

"Look," he says, that helpless look still in his gaze. "I dunno why you lied to them... why you lied to me. But you were always kind to me... and I dunno why I did all this. I just... I just do it 'cause of devils in me. The demon pushed you, not meself."

I grimace and wipe my face again.

Cole struggles to explain. "That's what Salvius says at least... 'cause I don't hardly remember when I do summat that is wrong. I just do it in my sleep, an' then the whip comes later on. I dunno why I hurt you there... I dunno at all."

Finally, I am convinced by the look of utter loss on his face. He did not mean this: he is a child. I reach out, put my hand on his shoulder, and pull myself upright.

"Ah, you're bleedin'," he says. "I didn't mean it... I didn't mean to hurt you, Mear. I just... Should we get you back to the cart? Someone will have a rag, some salve fer your lip, an'—"

I put a quiet finger on his lip. I give an awkward smile. *I will be all right.*

I draw myself up further, to sit upon a log. Cole seems to watch my face for any lines of pain.

"I won't do it again to you. I... I... I..." Cole finally stops talking. He puts his hand together as if in silent prayer. Although my heart misgives me, I cannot help myself—I forgive him all his anger and his rage. He is still a child, my soul cries once again, and once I thought I would take him in as my own.

I nod in reply. I even smile a bit, to give him hope, although such an expression gives me pain.

Cole uses the sleeve of his coat to dab the blood on my lip, and he wipes at the scrape on my temple. I stand and sit once and again, testing my balance. I will be all right.

We sit together in the silence on the log. The clouds hang down as if drawn to the land. They cover it immensely, dimming all the light. From far away, a chaffinch gives its little dipping song, another answers close-at-hand. Then there is the call of a titmouse bird, *bing, bing, bing*. The air feels thick and almost warm against my skin.

"Tell the truth..." Cole speaks again, his deep black eyes blinking as he weighs something in his mind. After a moment, his voice drops to a whisper. "You don't talk a'tall, right? You don't say nuffin', do you?"

Even if I can speak again, I will keep what secret he shares, no matter what befalls me in latter days. Thus, I shake my head solemnly. *No*.

Cole's harsh, scarred face softens at my response, a momentary peace lightening the set of his heavy brow, the worry in his eyes. He has found a confessor.

"I lied," he whispers.

I can hear Cole breathing close to my ear, a rasp that still speaks of his broken rib upon the open road. It is a liquid breath that holds in it all the pain of a young man and all the yearning of a babe. He is hungry to tell me the truth.

CHAPTER 34

"I LIED," SAYS COLE again. His lips curve in a sibilant whisper. "When I tol' you of the night when the boys died, I lied when I said I watched from the woods. I wasn't in the woods a'tall."

Where were you then, Cole? I want to ask. But he does not answer that unspoken question. Instead, he speaks of Salvius.

"Sal always tells me I don't remember things aright—I take things, he says, and then I forget what I done, and I wake up with what I stole in my hands. An' then he beats me for not sayin' what I done. Not sayin' true.

"But it's never enough. 'Cause that demon in me always does it agin, the very next day. Salvius he says he tries to help, by beatin' the demon outta me. But it dasn't help," he says sadly. "An' no one likes me, for the evil that demon does."

It is convenient for Cole to blame some spirit for his evil actions. And I can well imagine that Salvius feels he must beat the boy for all the lies and theft he undertakes.

"See, I tried an' tried to be friends with your lad—with all them lads in the village. But none o' them would talk to me, none o' them would give me a word o' kindness. An' every time I find a lad who would want to be my friend, that demon takes his staff, or lamb, or coat. And that lad won't have naught to do with me, no more."

Cole rubs his fist across his eyes, his face smeared with tears and dirt and my blood.

"I get so cross, I try an' try—an' always I get to know a chap, an' then that demon hurts him in the night."

I wonder at this demon story—it is as if Cole doesn't believe it anymore himself. He looked so fearful at my injury, so truly sorry, that thinking of him as this "demon" strikes me odd.

Why does Cole not feel more guilt at his own fell deeds?

I stare upward, as if I will find some answers there. The clouds are dark as lead, they hang heavy and close overhead.

"Now, most nights when I get angry and in my mood," Cole says, "Salvius talks to me. Most nights after the beatin', I sleep on the straw in the corncrib, an' that calms me down. But not when I light the fires."

I gulp a deep breath in—*did Cole light the fire that night?* Cole looks at my face and tries to explain. "Sometime y'know, Salvius tries to tell me where the demon is, and helps me do what I can to fright the demon away, to burn him out. I would light my fire in an abandoned cruck, an old haystack. And when the fire starts, I figure Sal will keep me safe. He'll let me rage and burn something, but afterward my rage—it's gone from me. Salvius shelters me from the demon. So on that night, as long as 'e is with me, I don't mind what kind of madness is in me—he will protect me."

Cole breathes in a deep, shuddering sigh.

"But on that night, Salvius is different. He urges me on. I see on his face the same dark look he has when he beats me, and I must do what he says. And on that night he tells me that the demon is Bene's wife. And he tells me to burn that demon out with fire, an' I do it—I light it in a mad fury. But then, when my wrath goes down, I… I try to tell him who is in there, I try to call to them, to warn the village, but Salvius hits me so hard with the stone that when I wake up in the dark, I am all alone and the house is alight, with a rope tied tight 'round the door. I couldna do it… I couldna save them.

"It was me who lit the fire—not some other lad. It was me who was there at the door, an' it were Salvius who locked them in. In truth, it was the two of us who did it to them." He pauses, he breathes, he hesitates. "Or else this is all a lie of the demon in me. Mayhap I dasn't remember anything true that night."

I find that my lips are trembling, and my tongue. My flesh quavers all over. I want to run—I want to scream and hide away.

Salvius did this to our boys.

Salvius tried to burn Sophia because she would not lie with him. Even though she lay with other men, she would not lie with him. She was not an open harlot, and he could not see that.

How could he be so cruel?

And then that other voice of reason comes to me, a cold trickle of fear at my leap to judgment here.

There were at least three fires that were set in the village, and Salvius worked hard to fight them all. Cole is an outsider, brought here and raised from babe to manhood by a man who owes him nothing. He is a natural knave—his face even speaks of dissension, with his strange sneers and the ringworm scars.

And Cole began his tale thus: *I lied.* Who is to say he does not lie again? Cole is known for his lies, his thefts, his endless denials. Cole may be the one who did the burning. Or neither of them.

But if Cole lies about Salvius here, why? Salvius is our leader. He has saved me so many times, beginning with my arrival at the village all those many years ago. Even Nell trusted Salvius: she brought him into her croft. He was her friend.

In all my ruminations, I hardly hear the rest of what Cole says.

"'E says the demon puts me to sleep, and makes me do these things in my sleep. The demon rages, an' steals and lights them fires. 'E lies, and steals, and takes all 'e can, 'cause that demon knows that I'll get beat fer it—not him.

"But I dunno anymore." He shakes his head, querulous. "I dunno, 'cause I stay awake, sometime all night, to catch the demon at his fright. And once, I see Sal come in, and put the stolen bits in my arms. And I was awake, lying abed, when he say I took it. Y'know that sword Sal says I took from the Lady?"

I nod. I remember the sword Cole stole from Lady Doncaster.

"I didna do that, I know that most right. The sword was in my hand, but a moment afore, it wasn't there a'tall. I was awake, and I reach out to Salvius, and then I'm holdin' it. I didna take it from the Lady, I swear upon my grave."

I shake my head in disbelief. I saw it myself, flashing in his hand, before Salvius took it away and beat him with the flat. Is what he says possible though? What if Salvius gave it to him, moments before?

"But I know'd you would unnerstand, 'cause you're the one who kill'd the child at the manor. You're the one who allow'd them to eat a babe—and so if there's any demon in me, you might know him too."

My flesh crawls. Cole tells me this thing—which may be made of air, may be something he dreamed in the night—because he thinks that I, too, bear such demons in my breast.

"I owe Sal my life, though. Without him, I'd surely be consum'd by that demon—I'd be dead already. Like he tells me, his beatin' on me, it's the only thing what saved me. I'd do anything fer him, for he's the one rescu'd me, rais'd me, help'd me live. And for that, I owe him all I have."

What am I to do with this tale? Should I put a knife into Cole's ribs in the night? And what if I found a way to ask Salvius to tell the truth of this matter? What then? Born of a priest, and noble in his bearing, he is a man who leads, who cares for all of us, a master of both man and beast. And does not Cole envy the mastery and kindness of our leader, Salvius?

What is truth? What is lie?

I touch my hair, my lips, my mouth, my face. I check to see if I am awake, if all is real. I pull on a bit of hair, and it comes out in my hand. I can feel the sudden nip of pain. *I do not dream, but what I am to do?*

If Salvius knew that Cole had admitted to setting the fires and accused his guardian of playing a role, what then would Salvius do to the lad? Would he kill him?

I look down at my trembling arms, at my open hands, the dried blood streaked on them dark, the hairs on my fingers thin as spiderwebs.

In the bleak dawn, the clouds are heavy with snow. In this light, one cannot tell a white hair from a black.

CHAPTER 35

ROOKS HAVE CLUSTERED on either side of the long road. It is as if they line a grand parade route for our passage. Their black feathers are stark as soot against the White Road and the snow. They stab at the ground with their strange bare bills and unfeathered faces. The birds are like rough-edged black stones on a string around this stripped cold neck of road.

The old books tell us rooks bring the virtuous dead to heaven's gate, but I fear we have been too long on the road for Christian's soul to travel with them.

My bloody flux has finally come, and once more I curse my womanhood. Yet if I had not revealed myself, it would have been devilish hard to conceal the flux this time—it flows so fast and hard. And thus, my curse is muted: there is no need to conceal it anymore.

After a day of warm fire and food, we left the broken house and abandoned garden. We have less than a week before Shrove Tuesday, and we strive mightily to move faster.

Moten urges us toward Cambridge. He says we may find a graveyard there, where we can abandon our children in holy ground. For myself, I feel I must go on to London. I feel my mother calling in me, her charge new-woken in my breast.

When Cole and I came out of the woods together, Liam and Moten saw my bleeding head and lip, and took pity on me. They helped me to the fire, and now they treat me as one who lives in the world again.

Although Cole protested that I had forgiven him, Liam and Moten turned on him, and slowly the rest of the men come to agree with their anger. The men wanted me invisible but not injured, with no visible sign of my distress to trouble them. Salvius gave Cole a beating, but the lad smiled at me all the while, as if in serenity. Now he shows some tenderness toward me, and some small edge of guilt besides. He has unburdened himself. But he has given his burden to me.

Far ahead, a thin line of smoke rises into the gray sky: there is a village some way ahead. I wonder what the living will make of us, after all this time.

I am still wrapped in the rich and heavy cloak I stole from the manor. And I am grateful to ride upon the cart.

The air prickles at the skin, almost warm at times. Though the sky is close, no snow has come, and the rooks come close now because of what we can all smell. There is now a palpable stench from the wrapped canvas behind me, the dark stink of decay. We have no fragrant incense or herb to hide that odor, as one would upon a funeral day. If we could see this scent, it would be something dark and coiling behind us, a thick opaque thing smeared on the air itself.

I try to ignore the stench while I puzzle out the tale told by Cole.

When I lived in the village, I did not open my eyes. I did not see Cole's life. And if sometimes I saw Cole sadly walking in the woods or crying from a beating in the hedgerow near at hand, what did I care? It was not my lad.

Yet every day, I lived beside the lad. How could I not see that he struggled against some demon? How could I be unaware?

The fires were lit. With the last fire, the house was burned. The boys lie dead. Cole and his demon had a hand in it.

Yet my heart misgives me when I take this path. For I have looked long into Cole's eyes, and I saw no demon winking there.

Something in me sees only a confused and angry lad, one I held as a babe to my breast in the night.

Saint Paul said we wrestle not with spirits outside in the world, but with those most fell spirits who plunder the world from within our hearts. The good we do is hard to find, the evil always evident.

And like a untuned lute string that still gives a wrong sound, something in Salvius rings to me awry. Despite our long friendship, I have always felt there is a sour note in him, buried deep. *Yet how many of us can cast a stone?*

Cole himself is no perfect unformed babe, and I know that well. If there is no demon in him, there is perhaps another ghost that brings us harm, that feral animality in every human soul. To embrace Cole is to embrace the worst in each of us, perhaps.

And there is so much of good in Salvius. He saved me and Christian, he employed me, he brought me wood for my hut. He brought us the tunic to protect us on the open road. And I have often seen his wise intelligence: he fixed the sluice before the mill, he found a way to drain the field that was a marsh, he built a better bellows in the smithy. He is the one who speaks most clearly in the village council. He pulled the men's divided voices together when we first left our village, and he came to find us, to help us all.

He has earned our respect. And he earned the trust of Nell.

Ah, Nell, that you were here to speak to me once more, to reassure me in my worry and pain. To tell me the truth of Salvius!

The frost in front of us is riven with gray and black whorls, as if a great hand wrote the secrets of the world under the ice. If only we could read that script aright.

A steady rhythm sounds from the road ahead, a pounding clatter on the path. The rooks flutter into flight, rising in the distance slowly, the wave coursing along their ragged track.

Someone comes down the road upon a charger.

A great horse rounds the bend ahead. It is an immense, hulking destrier, and as I watch that stallion turn and canter down the path, it seems as gargantuan and dangerous as a child's tale of a dragon. Against the sight of this great mount tossing its head in the morning light, the two nags that pull our cart are little playthings.

The white horse snorts and blows out a gout of steam. A long tourney lance is tied along its flank, projecting behind and before. The rider goes on knight errantry.

The destrier itself is clothed in livery, a green lion rampant with clawed and angry feet. A shield lies over the saddlebow, and I see that crest again. A memory stirs in me: this is a livery I know from Court when Edward took me that once.

Above the horse waves a small herald flag, with the same sign upon it. The flag rattles in the wind of his passage, giving our horses fright. I take the reins and pull aside: we must make way. This is the King's track, and all of noble blood are given leave to pass.

The men are already moving off the road, their boots deep in mud and snow and ice. I steer the cart to the grass, striving to keep our load upright. We are scattered now, as the rooks were, all along the highway.

I am surprised to see the Knight slow as he passes Salvius in front. Many of that class would not, and mud would splash the rest of us from those pounding hooves. What is worse is that such a charger might strike a lad or man. A knight or noble might give a few pence for such a loss, thrown out behind, but a wergild of that like would never make up for such a loss of limb or life.

So we skitter nervously out of the way. And we do it quick.

The Knight sits at ease, wearing a sleeveless surcoat with green lion and charger, and a bright white tunic and furs underneath. He does not wear a helm—his armor, sword, and helm are tied upon the charger's rump. But a hood of fur hangs heavy on his head. He pushes it back as he passes, and we can see his heavy brow, pale turquoise eyes flashing underneath, and the curled bright waves of his hair that billow out behind. There are wrinkles around those pale eyes, as if he has looked long into distant lands, and a cruel edge to his mouth, a constancy of purpose in his jaw.

The Knight's gaze sweeps calmly over us. It is as if he is ticking off the odds, calculating cost. Then those turquoise eyes squint, and his nose wrinkles subtly at the bitter smell.

He touches the reins. He pauses. And in that pause is death.

CHAPTER 36

THE KNIGHT SLOWS his destrier alongside our cart. The horse does not stop entire. Instead, the Knight takes a short dagger from under his cloak and runs it beneath the edge of canvas on the cart. He lifts it and glances inside.

I can only imagine what he sees there: the linens around the bodies torn apart. Our boys carved as by a butcher's knife. The tortured burned faces, the reaching hands. A small vision of hell.

But the stallion does not stop moving, and almost it seems as if he will go on. We catch our breaths, and I take the reins again to move ahead. Above us, thick snowflakes gently dust the air.

A grating slide upon the track, a tearing sound of ice. I turn and look behind. The charger wheels on the road, a sudden and accelerated turn. The Knight cuts the canvas from the rear, holds his nose, and gazes fully on our dead sons.

Salvius touches his own horse's head, who snorts and paws the ground in fright.

The Knight still sits silent upon his steed. And after a long moment, he shifts in his brocaded saddle, puts a heavy booted foot into a stirrup, and settles his weight upon it. He pulls his sword in scabbard from the wrapped saddlebags, and he dismounts. The snowflakes swirl as he moves, like sand in an underwater stream.

The Knight stands heavy upon the ground. Then he advances.

That pale turquoise gaze, like a leaf caught under frost. I know the man now, by his strange blue-green eyes. And his green livery too. On the fields of France, he has seen much worse. I know this.

Edward told me of him, when we went to Court. He is called Phillip Gaumont, one who served as *chevalier*, who did the razing for Edward and his men. Gaumont has burned whole villages in an hour. He has slaughtered women and children, all for the sake of battle, in the name of God.

Death is no surprise to him. He has seen many rot before, but he does not like what he sees here in the cart. I know it by his narrowed gaze. I know it also by his sword.

There is a long and hissing *snick* as the thing comes out of its vast scabbard. It is terrifying to see, as the great sword shines and glimmers in the light. Silvery snow lands and melts right off. The Knight himself stares at the blade for a moment himself, as if in regret. Or perhaps in anticipation.

The Knight then looks at us arrayed haphazard upon the road, and he speaks.

"*Il s'agit d'une terre blessée, une terre dont le roi était malade, et est maintenant décédé. Je suis son messager, celui qu'il a choisi, celui qui apporte la mort.*"

Gaumont speaks with a florid precision in his French. I know what he says, but my companions do not: *This is a wounded land, a land whose king was sick, and now has died. I am his chosen messenger, who carries death in my hand.*

He speaks of Edward with regret. "*Mon compagnon et mon ami.* My boon companion and my friend. I aim to heal this land, by following Jesus in fishing for men who I must kill. I will do so here, upon my life today, *au service de Dieu.*"

The Knight stares at us with his strange and pale eyes. He blinks bits of snow off of his long lashes, which glimmer in the light. "*Ces garçons là*," he says. "*Qu'est-ce que vous leur avez fait?*"

These boys, I translate to myself. *What have you done to them?*

He sees we do not comprehend his speech. He goes to the lads, he touches each body with his sword, he points at them, he points at us. He is curious about the silver chain around Christian's neck. He lifts it with the tip of his sword. And then he speaks in French quite loudly, as if our ears are full of wax. "*Dites-moi la vérité, vous les paysans!*"

Tell me the truth, you peasants! He thinks we have murdered some noblemen for their treasure, and that now we will devour their noble flesh. He demands to know if it's true. "*C'est vrai?*"

Moten is flustered by the Knight. Some of the words he seems to recognize, but they come in a stream too fast for him to catch. He answers back.

"Ah, good sir," he says in English. "I would tell you true what you ask. But I cannot speak your tongue, and so if you will—"

"*Arrêtez*!" The Knight has little patience for Moten's stumbling attempts, and a dangerous concentration rises in his tone. "

My fear builds as I listen. *You are a false priest,* he says, *a monk who serves Satan, not the Christ. Did you do it? Did you try to eat them? You and the others here? Are you responsible for these murders, these atrocities?*

"*Oui ou Non?*" Then, in thick and awkward English, he repeats the final question: "Yea or nay?"

Time hangs on a razor edge. Snow comes heavily now, a scrim of white falling between us, muting all sound. My companions mutter, irritated and nervous. They do not understand a word, and this frightens me more, for this knight yearns for battle.

I turn back toward Moten and catch his eye. He licks his lips nervously, he seems to look at me for guidance. I shake my head. *Non*, I think. *Answer "Non."*

Moten will calm him, I tell myself. *Moten will find a way through, just as he did with the Abbot.*

"*Oui ou non*," the Knight repeats. His gaze narrows as he looks down at the carved-up lads, his words coming sharper. "Yea or nay?"

Moten holds my gaze. My eyes plead with him. Slowly I shake my head from side to side. *You must say "Non,"* I think desperately. *Answer him, but do not affirm this madness. Listen to me, Moten.*

Moten glances at me and licks his lips again—he seems to understand. I relax for a moment.

Then he glances into the pitiless eyes of the Knight, and he trusts his own way. He guesses wildly, and he guesses wrong.

"Yes, yes," Moten replies. "No doubt about it—yes, they are our children, but my dear sir, whatever you are about, I wish you would speak in English, so we may—"

The Knight lunges forward, and with a quick deft movement, thrusts the tip of that gleaming sword straight into Moten's chest. And as the monk stares down, the Knight pulls the sharp point out. There is a hissing gasp as air comes out of the bloody slit, and then Moten falls heavy to the ground.

And then as the snow falls down upon his face, his eyes stop moving, gone blank and glazed with frost.

A rook flaps by above, a screeching laudation in its call. Moten is dead.

The blood pours out, black and steaming on the ground.

CHAPTER 37

THE GREAT LINE of steel spins again in the air, making a bright and lethal circle against the winter frost. I can hear the whistle of its passing. This knight will kill us all. He comes closer with his questions, a fierce urgency in his voice.

"Avez-vous fait cela? Who else has done this? Have you tried to eat them? Did you murder these children and cut them up? Oui ou non!"

The heavy sword comes to a point of sudden calm. The Knight angles it and aims. His face is set: this man is certain he does the Lord God's good work. This time, his sword seeks out Liam's head, he of the trembling beard and blanched white face. The tip is at Liam's neck, held still, as the man speaks again. "Yea or nay."

I let go of the reins and stand so slowly, so very slowly, above my seat in the cart, that rich hood from the manor still around my ears. There is a chill in the air that came with the snow falling, a deep and weighty frost. A stab of pain runs from my foot and up my leg. Cole's face turns toward me as I rise. His mouth is open, a perfect O of surprise.

I can smell the iron of Moten's blood, and the scent of snow upon the air, and then cinnamon and sandalwood that roll from the Knight—strange to find these aromas here. The monk's blood pools beneath the cart and the fetid stench of our boys swirls like smoke around my feet.

They cannot understand what I try to tell them. They don't know what I know. So now I must speak.

I hear Moten's voice again in my head, on that fated and terrifying day when I came out of the catacombs into the churchyard. *You still have the power of speech—why do you not use it?*

My mouth opens, almost against my will. My tongue moves, a wild creature turning, pacing, back and forth in its long cage. My lips are wide, I breathe, and out comes one fateful, lonesome sound. A plea.

"*Christ, prends pitié de nous…*" I say, and my voice seems loud against the winter sky. My first words in ten years above a whisper or a cry. *I beg you mercy, in the name of Christ.*

I speak in my native tongue, that long-unvoiced French. "*Monsieur… s'il vous plaît arrêtez…*"

To my own ears, my voice is strange. It is much lower than that voice I bear inside, as if there were a great weight resting upon my chest, pushing out the words. The Gallic words that come out of my mouth sound to my own ear as unnatural as a talking crow. But speak I do, at last, and that quite fluently.

"Au nom du Père, du Fils, et du Saint-Esprit, retenez votre main. Nous emmenons nos enfants au trône du roi, pour obtenir justice en ces jours d'hiver. Nos gars ont été brûlés par la haine et la jalousie, loin d'ici. Certains disent que les Juifs nous ont trahi, ou les Maures."

Christ have mercy upon us, and still your hand, I beg. *We take our children to the King's high seat, for justice in this wintertime. Our lads were burned by hate and envy, far away. Some say that Jews betrayed us, or the Moors.*

The Knight raises his gaze to me, and he strives to interrupt, to clarify. But I hold up my hand, and to my great surprise, there is no tremble there. Snow falls steadily upon it.

"*Attendez!*" I say. *Wait. I know not the truth of these matters*, I say. *I strive with these, my faithful companions, for justice in this loss.*

"*Vous mentez!*" he says. *You lie!* His sword has not moved from Liam's throat. "*Vous me mentez!* You and your companions cut up these children for a feast!"

"*Non, pas nous,*" I respond. "We were betrayed upon the road. Some villains took them, to butcher them, upon a high and lonely hill, a place of hunger in extreme. We have but lately rescued them."

"*Mais ils sont encore ici.*" The Knight's gaze is impenetrable, his face wrinkles with concern. "Still they lie here dead! Why do you not honor them? Why do you treat them as beasts?"

"*Nous ne pouvons pas les enterrer,*" I struggle to explain. "We cannot bury them until we find justice upon this open way. One of those who lie here—the one you touched with your sword, the one who bears the chain—he is of grand and noble blood, and as such you may not touch him any longer with your sword. *Arrêtez votre main.*"

I tremble inside at my own bravado. I fear he will slice me limb from limb. "I bear him hither, I say, with the hope that he may be honored. *Dans ce temps de besoin et de chagrin.*"

The Knight glares up at me, his gaze striking as ice. It is only then that I realize why he has not cut me down already. I stand removed, upon the cart above the herd, much as a lady would ride. And by happenstance, I wear rich raiment, a hood and cloak tied in ermine fur, that grand and gaudy cloak stolen from the manor house in my hour of need. I do not appear to be a commoner, although I travel with a ragtag troupe of peasants.

"*Expliquez-vous de nouveau. Quelle est votre marque?*" says the Knight. He moves his sword away from Liam. The tip now points at me. "What lord do you then serve? And who are you then that travels on this road, to speak to me thus?"

"*Je suis une femme . . .*" And strangely, my voice drops to a whisper once more, as if I walk with that lost girl 'round her birthing bed again. "I am Miriam of Canterbury, good sir. A nun sworn to Holy Orders, and now a woman free of Holy Orders these many years past."

"*Vous n'avez pas de de titre de noblesse?*" he mutters back. "No title? Are you a commoner? For what reason should I allow you pass?"

I raise my voice again—my words ring out. I know this name will strike true in him, as an arrow to the heart. "Edward of Woodstock is the name I would wear upon my livery, for I was his consort. I bore his child. His heir lies there, as upon on a funeral pyre. *Il est mort.*"

I stumble, I hesitate, and then I elect to plunge ahead. "That one—my son—he is the late departed Lord's heir and kin. You, who I once knew as Phillip Gaumont, you would do well to protect him with your body and your words, defending his honor upon your life. *Je vous en prie, maintenant donnez-lui acte d'allégeance.*"

The Knight lowers the point of his sword. Thoughts churn upon his brow.

I had not known how tense my shoulders were. A great pain leaves them as I breathe out. With my sigh, the snow in the air is churned—it eddies all about. I stand and wait for the Knight's response.

The great charger snorts and shies to the side and the men around me scatter backwards. Their eyes are wide, they are fearful and confused by our foreign conversaion.

The the Knight turns to me and stares. His eyes are frost again, and lethal in this light. "*Quelle preuve avez-vous?*" he says clearly, biting off the words. "What proof do you have of this tale of Edward—what testifies that this lad indeed is of his blood and heritage? What may tell me that you do not lie, this day and always?"

I raise my hands to my throat. I throw back that dark hood around my head. The Knight starts back at my bare head with roughly cut and uncombed hair. But carefully, I unfasten my tunic, I lift the silver chain from around my neck, and I hold out the ring that Edward gave me. It dangles in the air, a strange and precious talisman, one that I have carried close to my heart these many years. "*J'ai été son amante et son amie.*"

I hesitate to give it to him. *What if this man takes my heirloom and declares it stolen? What if I am robbed?* He could kill us all between one heartbeat and the next.

The Knight holds out his hand. Then I drop the ring, the gold signet landing gently on his palm. "I was his consort," I repeat. "I bore the child of the Prince-in-Waiting."

The Knight examines the seal on the ring. Written on it is the royal crest, which few may hold upon their person or in their name, upon pain of death. My only token and my best, held all these years in secret.

When that knight's gaze is lifted to me once again, it seems profoundly changed. I still stand tall above him, as in Court. My voice now rings loud with a strange, brave confidence. "My son was the Prince's heir. He is royal in blood and name. *Il a du sang noble.*"

"And you seek justice for this crime," says the Knight, a note of wonder in his tone now. He has, at last, found a wrong that he can right.

He bends an armored knee, sinking right to the ground.

"My Lady *honorée*. Milady," he says, and lifts the ring between two fingers. It glimmers in the morning light.

"Milady," the Knight says again, and his language has shifted into those long loquacious tones of courtly French. "My Lady *honoré*, for the memory and oath I swore to my boon companion Edward, and in token of the esteem I bear his soul, I would offer thee the service of my own poor arm in his stead. If you must fight for honor or any man kill, that I would help thee, with a good will. I offer the sword of Sir Phillip Gaumont to your service."

My tongue cleaves to the roof of my mouth. I had not expected such a response. I had not known such a boon could be granted me, in these my old and graying years. A choking sob comes out of my throat, unbidden. Finally, I find my voice again.

"Earl," I manage to croak. "The Earl of Hereford, who had an eye upon the Throne? He—"

"*Mort.* The Earl is dead these many years." Sir Phillip Gaumont, looks up at me, and there is a mist and sadness in his eyes now. I think, in staring into his pale-green gaze, that this very knight could be the one who murdered that same earl. He could murder us the same.

"The Earl was found—" He looks away. "The Earl, my relation and my friend, was found to have betrayed my Lord Warwick and my Lord Edward. And yet he denied it. *Il est mort.*"

Then the Knight looks back at me. His gaze is clear once more. "I do my duty to the end, milady. Whatever may befall." He stands up from the cold harsh road. He lifts the ring to me and puts it in my hand. I put it back on the chain around my neck. I do not put it back under my tunic, for now the ring will lie upon my breast, forevermore displayed.

The Knight offers his hand in a gesture—he turns it in the air, as if he doffs his helm to me.

"*Voulez-vous aller avec moi?* Would you care to leave these peasants and these vagabonds, and go with me to Court, even now? I would rescue you from this place, upon my life."

It is then that caution comes back to me. *Why should I trust him?* Always, these champions play a game with lives, making alliances and betraying them on a turn of dice. What if this knight deceives me? What if he deceives us, to our deaths?

Unbidden, new words come onto my tongue, but they ring true in this moment. "I must stay with my child. I owe my Lord Edward that."

"Ah," says the Knight. Gaumont bows his head in thought. It seems I have answered in the right or else I have checkmated him. The Knight lifts his sword, and my heart plummets. Then he sheathes his sword with that awful hissing snick, and he looks up at the white flakes falling from the sky, as if seeing them for the first time.

"*Il neige,*" he says, surprise in his tone.

"It's snowing," I repeat. Inspiration dawns in me: there is a way to find the truth of the knight, and to prove his allegiance.

"It is cold this day," I say carefully to him. "And we would have shelter upon our way. Food and shelter as we take the child of the Prince to London. We seek the protection of the Star Chamber against our accusers. I seek my son's life to be redeemed."

The Knight gazes up at me. He seems resolute as he speaks in French. "Milady, I will go and find you such. I will ride to every village upon your track, and keep the way open for the Black Prince's heir and blood, to lie in state upon the way."

Gaumont looks at the gathered men, whose mouths hang open. The Knight purses his lips with effort, and then finds the English words: "I honor this Miriam—and the Prince, the one who comes of Edward à Woodstock. To honor him and thee, I ride."

"*Oui, monsieur*, I thank you," I reply. "I bid you Godspeed on your way, *au service de Dieu*."

"*Au service de Dieu*," Gaumont cries, relapsing to French once more. His voice rises stridently. "I will honor him—the heir of Edward the Black Prince. To honor him and thee, I go now. I will send word to Court ahead. I go now to raise the alarm throughout the land. Thus to the King's Court I will bring you, out of harm." He bows his head again.

I look down at the ground where Moten rests, his blood chilling in the open air. We cannot trust this Knight, not at the risk of our lives.

"*Je regrette votre perte*." he says in French. "I am sorry for your loss. I beg forgiveness, one and all, for my impetuous blade. Adieu."

The Knight mounts his charger, and turns and pounds away, back toward the village and London. We must take his route now, for ahead the Knight's great destrier forces a path for us through the drifts, and he will doubt us, he will chase us down if we do not follow.

That great fluttering snow, white and light and pure, falls down upon the heads of the living and the dead. *La neige tombe sur les têtes des vivants et des morts…*

CHAPTER 38

A SKEIN OF FRESH-FALLEN snow blows off the cart behind. It dusts me in an icy baptism. I am newborn in the eyes of my men. They stand thunderstruck, their faces astonished by the words that came out of my mouth. It seemed miraculous when I spoke—in French, at that—and then they were dumbfounded when the knight bowed to me.

But I do not answer their fumbling inquiries, their gaping torrent of questions. I cannot, I do not, trust myself to find the right words to explain my years of silence.

"Who spoke through Mear? Some demon?" mutters Tom. "What magic did she use to turn 'im away?"

"She's not a demon," says Liam. He is still pale and shaken. "She kept me alive."

"All I know is that she sav'd us," says Geoff. "That knight, he would kill us all, an' she used white magic t' save our lives."

"Will that knight come back an' kill again?" asks Benedict. "Tell us, Mear."

Finally, I tell them—now my tongue halting and uncertain again—that the knight protects us now, and that he has promised to go ahead, to clear a path. I do not tell them of my distrust. But when it becomes clear to them that I will not tell my tale to them now, they leave behind my miracle with dark looks and muttered imprecations.

The men turn then to the monk, who lies dead beside the cart. Already, the rooks caw over the fresh carrion.

So goes all knowledge, all truth, all light. All of poor Moten's knowledge is gone to the wind. I can see now that what I was taught at Canterbury Abbey to be true: we are but a tattered remnant, a small and bastard race who linger on the shoulders of that giant race, a memory that is always our better. We look backward always, scratching in the ruins, reclaiming scraps from their vast and long-abandoned table of knowledge. For we are a misshapen offspring, stunted in our ways and our minds, reaching blindly after the treasures of knowledge lost to time.

I look down on Moten's sad, dead face, his tonsure spread around his head—a spiked crown of death.

Moten thought that words carried all of the answers and would serve every end. But as I would have warned him, speech does not always unravel matters. Words can betray you, their labyrinthine threads tangled tight in knots, for we were cursed at that great tower of Babel, to speak always in riddles and never yet to comprehend.

One of his secrets goes with him to the grave. For what did Roben speak of? What is that thing Moten must take to London? We search Moten and his baggage, but find nothing of value, nothing that would speak to the King or the Court of the Land. Instead, there are only old tattered manuscripts, Moten's own and others. There are quills and vellum, sundry prayer beads, and two wooden crucifixes, but nothing made of gold, nothing of nobility.

The ground is dark and rich beneath the snow, softened by the recent thaw. A rivulet of water has cut away the earth, making a furrow deep in the frosted loam. This is where we dig a narrow grave for Brother Moten. We take one of his crucifixes, and Salvius ties it tight to a stick with a bit of rope. We plant that symbol of his Lord God above Moten's tonsured head.

Rough clods of dirt rain down upon poor Brother Moten's face and body and cassock long. I watch the grave fall in, standing there still. I hold in my hand Moten's oldest manuscript, made up of remnants and rags. The edges of the bits of vellum and parchment are ragged and irregular. He sewed this makeshift book of his own labor, out of what was left behind when the true manuscripts were made. It is the history he scribed throughout his life.

Two drops of Moten's blood have stained it, dropping on the leather cover dark. My fingers find a place to open the manuscript, and unbidden, I read.

> 17 December, 1366
>
> Now in this time of the Virgin and the Birth, I think
> always of Miriam who disappeared from my cold and lonely
> monastery. She was like a gentle wind on a cold sea, stirring
> up a wealth
> of feelings I never knew I had—now gone—

I slap the uneven pages closed quickly. I am reading Moten's own confidences: poured out on these pages are the secrets of his heart. This is no true history or chronicle of his monastery.

For his eyes alone, he wrote. I lift the book, I heft it in my hand. This manuscript should go into the grave with Moten. His secrets and his earthly life die with him. To another realm he now goes. And all his memories with him.

Then as I heave the book up into the air, a letter falls from the loose pages. It flutters down and falls at my feet. A heavy seal on it, red and weighty. Impressed in the sealing wax is the ring of the Abbot of Saint Mary Magdalene. Inscribed on the front of the letter are these words:

Greetings, Thanksgivings, Blessings
from Your Very Revered Father,
Abbot André de Bottoun of the Cluny House
of Saint Mary Magdalene.

To His Lordship John of Gaunt,
Regent in the Holy Name of Christ, by God's Grace,
Ruler and Holder of the Crown in the Name of the King,
Duke Most High of Britannica, Greater Gaul, and the
Empire.

It is the letter from Moten's own Abbot to the Regent of the Kingdom. At least that man had faith we would achieve our goal of going to the Court, even if we doubted ourselves during our long journey. Perhaps this letter commends poor Brother Moten to the care of Court for the duration of his stay. Perhaps it even speaks of this book he carries.

Perhaps this letter will give us safety. Perhaps it will provide passage through whatever lies ahead. It would be wise to keep such a missive, as a ward and caution against what may come. Who will speak for us, who will guide us through the twisted words of courtly questions, now that Moten is gone?

I hold this folded piece of parchment tight. And then I carefully place it back in the book, and I close those tattered pages. I will give the book to the recipient of the letter. He can take the book back to Moten's kin, the brothers of Cluny far away. It is not my decision, or the word of some armarius who will decide this small book's fate. I do not place it in the grave.

I stand and bless Moten now. I whisper a Paternoster over this lonely Cluniac brother.

Yet even as I bless him, as I speak, I see another friend lying in the ground. While the dark dirt rains down on his face, I remember another face cold and inert. I remember Nell.

I saw her hanging dead, hanging on the tree, with revelry breaking all around her feet. Hob would not let me cut her down that night, not with the sheep-herders and the other men so close at hand. He made me wait a day. And on the next morrow, that strange peculiar knot could not be undone. We had to use an axe to cut the rope, and then she fell.

Nell's body lay roughly on the raw earth, cold and stiff. The rope she'd woven with her own hands had parted in the end. Hob let me be alone with her then: I would bury her, unattended by any other.

I lifted her slight frame from the earth and carried her on my back deep into the woods. She was so light, so light in my arms.

I bathed her at the hidden stream in the woods, by moonlight, where the night scents of wild mint and lavender were strong. Under the cedar where once I had nursed, I hid her body under the forest-floor mulch, never to be found. I dropped earth upon her body, upon her face, as we cover Moten in rough clods even now.

For months, I have woken sobbing in the night, remembering that hidden forest grave. Always, in my dreams, my fingers trace that strange and torturous knot around her neck, wondering at its provenance and cursing the strength of its hold upon Nell's tender life.

When we come to the next village on the open road, we are surprised by cheers, by the trumpets and applause.

"The people's Prince, who fought in our name!" The crowds shout loud in Edward's memory, and at each little village, the people gather thickly around our cart. And at each small householding, I am greeted as a noblewoman, and my companions as if they are heroes returning from victory in some distant war.

The Knight who goes before us is as good as his word: he is clearing a way with his destrier, proclaiming our story to all he meets. He says always the same, and gives no further explanation, for his English is small, and few of these villagers have a word of French.

"The Black Prince's son comes in a cart—he is dead!" the Knight cries, like a ducal messenger. "Edward of Woodstock's heir has died. Honor him!"

Peasants hunger for distraction and a tale of heroism in the night, and the Knight who thunders before us has given them an excuse to leave their labors for the day. The snow keeps falling all through the long hours, but we are carried along as in the great current of a river, greeted by eager faces of commoners who holler their acclaim.

I am still in a daze, for now I find that much of my fear for these years was for naught. The Earl of Hereford is gone these many months, and no one strives now for Edward's throne, with machinations arcane and secrets long conspired.

The world has changed while I was gone. The Prince Regent's father, the King, is dead. And once they sought me out, to kill me—so that Edward's line would be pruned. Yet today Edward's youngest sits on the throne, and he is secure from all challenges, protected by a strong regent—John of Gaunt. And now that Edward's offspring is secure—and my own lad lies dead—none dare attack me, for fear of Edward's memory. How strange the world turns!

At the hour of Sext and luncheon, the villagers carry food to serve us, and raiment too. For all know now that we go to Court, and in their eyes we go as one of theirs—peasants who strive for justice in this land, our lads martyrs to the holy cause.

My troupe is also changed by the sight of those who greet us with acclaim. They have heard the name Edward of Woodstock, they have seen the people shout, but they do not know why we are being celebrated. I have told them the merest outline of my history, but they do not know who I am any longer—am I mute man or noble lady with lordly airs? Yet they are greeted everywhere by shouts and huzzahs from villagers on the White Road. They take the sweetmeats and the pork, they wear the raiment that is given in celebration, but they are still bemused, walking as if enchanted—this all is too close to dream.

Liam still seems astonished by the fact that words come out of my mouth. Cole is a different story. He glances at me with a dark, unnatural light in his eyes.

Salvius is the one who takes it all in, his eyes bright and hungry at the fame. At every stop, he stands quite tall upon the cart, his hair gleaming like any lord's. He tells a rich and glorious tale of his own crafting.

"These children was killed by Jews!" he cries. "By Moors and Jews who invaded our shores, long leagues hence from here. They burnt our village too, y'know. And our Miriam, she traveled for years in vow of silence, suff'ring long! But the Moors and Jews—they found Mear there, attack'd us in the night. We labor'd long, we fought them hard, but in the end they triumphed. All must now know our tale of woe, and we go to Court, for justice and for peace!"

I tremble, seeing all these faces raised in acclaim, the mouths open to shout out loud. For I know how quickly a crowd can turn from palms and parades to cruelty and torment on a cross.

BOOK VI

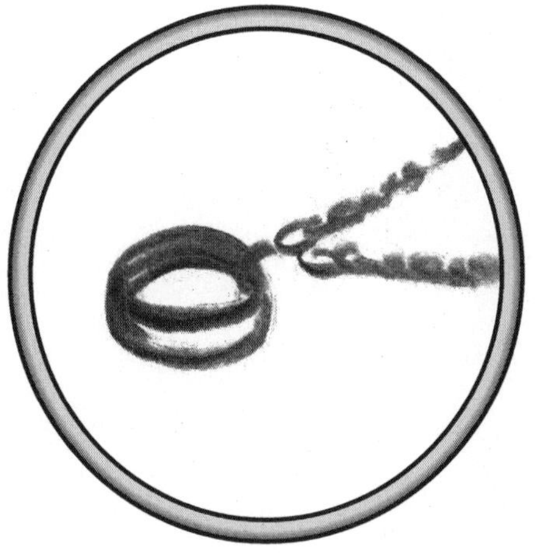

CHAPTER 39

WE HAVE A scant few days until Shrove Week, when the Star Chamber will disband, but with the knight's help we are moving as swift as the wind. Yet we are often stopped by villagers. Sometimes to give us food, sometimes to sing our tale back to us, in rhyme and merriment. And other times, simply so that mothers can hold their children up to touch our garments, peasant threadbare as they are.

Finally, we reach a clear stretch of hours undisturbed upon the open road. No crofts or villages here, and the Knight is out of sight ahead. We are on a downhill slope now—below us is the long line of an icebound river, and beyond that towers and towns.

I often feel as if another spirit were speaking through my lips on the morning when we met the Knight. For the fluent French that spilled out of my commanding mouth seems half-imagined. How could I, poor Mear of Duns, claim such a birthright, such authority?

Always, the men ask me many things: they want to know what tale took me to their village, those many years ago. What queen's offspring am I, and by what great conspiracy did I conceal my name? Did an enchantment lie on me those many years, other than my own? And by what ruse did I take Edward's ring?

Yet to these many questions—the true ones and the childish—I give few answers. For I am still unused to talk. There is a lock upon my throat, a heavy thing that bids me quiet. After those long years of silence, the possibility of speech still seems as removed as the heavenly sphere from our earthly one.

And I am wary of meeting Moten's fate. Even if I knew how to bring that freshet of words spilling out again, I know not how to tell my tale to the men I have long known. I lied to them from the moment we met, and how can I explain?

When the Knight returns to us this dawn and tells me plain that he now rides to Court, to prepare our way, I am struck dumb again. I cannot meet his icy gaze, for inside my cloak I shake in fear. He bears a bloodlust on his heart, taking men's lives as another one would swat a fly, and I don't know if his word is true.

What if he lies to us, and all he does is subterfuge?

In the end, I nod my head at the Knight's announcement that he goes to Court. I even find the wits to say, "*Oui.*" But I cannot hold the idea in me that we are come so close to reaching our destination. I am wracked with worry that all our hopes may not be realized. And I still don't know who killed my Christian.

The road ahead carries a veil of wavering snow that moves like rippling surf above its smooth surface. I squint into the cold air. Those are the towers of Cambridge town. We are come almost to the colleges and courtyards of those great halls of learning. I am a simple woman, and carry no great airs. I do not know what to say in the face of crowds and questions.

The men are gay when they see the town ahead. None among them have ever been to Cambridge. From here beside the river, the towers gleam and the rooftops of the chapels are white with snow.

"We will be upon the monks soon!" they cry. "Soon they will have a feast for us!"

And then as they shout, there comes a rending tear from beneath the cart. The horses lurch sideways, and the cart slides across the road and off into the verge.

The ties we'd put upon the lads hold them fast beneath the straw, but I am nearly lost and thrown wide of the cart. I hold my fingers tight against the bar, my nails digging into the frosted wood, until finally, it comes to a creaking and uncertain stop. The steeds are startled by the sudden halt, their eyes rolling white with fear.

A wheel has come off the cart.

Benedict and Salvius make a plan to walk across the open fields until they reach the town, a league away. There, they will find food for the luncheon meal, and a smithy where Salvius can work to repair our wheel. Tom and Geoff also wish to go. I think they seek more than acclaim and prayers—perhaps wine and revelry. And soon Liam, too, succumbs.

But I am weary. So I make excuses broad and vague. I do not know how to explain without a lie, so I motion to my foot. My injury is much healed now, but this they do not know. I will be the one to stay, to guard the cart.

Cole says he will remain behind as well.

Together, the men push the great hulk of the cart off the White Road until we reach the shelter of a great leaning willow tree. Underneath, we build a fire to keep warm.

As the men prepare to go, I observe a peculiar moment. Salvius turns and crooks his hand to Cole.

"You must take care that Mear is..." I overhear before they step away from camp.

I watch from under the bare branches of the willow as the Salvius and the other men fade into that vast field of white. The snow falls down, covering everything, and soon even their tracks are gone.

I look back at the fire, and see that Cole waits there, a heavy branch in his hand. The boy's face is wet with tears that spill across his cheeks, and his lip quivers heavily. He stares back at me across the flames, as if he sees me for the last time.

I give an uncertain smile. "What's wrong, Cole?"

"I trusted you," he mutters. "I trusted you to keep my secrets, and the secret that Salvius shared. You lied to me."

"You don't believe that," I say. "I did keep your secrets." But he does not seem to hear me, and a twinge of dread crawls across my neck, the tiny hairs standing on end with a sudden fear.

"You lied to me," he says again. Like a small child, he wipes his tears roughly away with his arm, so that his cheeks are smeared and wet. Cole stands and now comes closer, his arms trembling as he lifts that big branch in his grip. His nearness is unsettling.

"You said no words come outta your mouth. But all the while you could speak. You lied to me." Cole pushes his lips together in a forced way, tensing his jaw and shoulders together. "Goddam, now I gotta beat you. I gotta kill you. There's no hope for it."

He hurls the heavy branch at me, aiming for a furious blow. But I bend my head, I lift my legs, I push myself under that first and sudden clout. The branch swings close to my ear, whistling as it passes.

I struggle to keep the fire between us. We circle blindly, my heart pulsing, a quick and fearful thing.

"Cole, wait!" I cry. "I'll be your mam, I'll take care of you. Don't do this—"

"Ah, I'm sorry, Mear, I'm so sorry," he says, but this time he does not stop. The blows rain down, as I hold my arms up to protect my face. I turn my head, I roll, and then I see that someone is coming through the snow back toward us from the town.

A remote figure, a tiny head of wheat. It is Salvius. *Save me,* I think. *Save me now!* He approaches so slowly forward in the faint and covering frost.

Cole's eyes are wide with panic as I grip the branch and wrest it away from him. I shuffle to the side, limping away from the campsite as fast as I can go. I need to get to Salvius, he will save me.

I throw the branch at Cole's feet, and he stumbles and falls. But then he gets up again, following hard at my heels, like a wolf on the track of some wounded stag. And still he sobs and shivers, sounds most piteous coming out of him, as if he were a suffering tiny child.

I hobble forward, hamstrung by my hurt foot. He has the branch again, and each time he swings that deadly stick, I skip aside, I move faster than I think I can. His arms move as if he is a puppet on a string, unwilling to fight, but forced to do the bidding of his master. I almost believe some demon holds him, moves him with its malice.

I duck behind a tree, and then another. I lunge for the bushes. If I can hide from Cole long enough, I can find something to help me fight back. I stagger through a mass of gorse, and suddenly I am at the steep bank of the river. I can go no further.

Cole steps around the trees. His wild arms swing again, and this time he connects. The agony is immediate, a blinding pain in my shoulder. I cannot lift the arm on my right side. I throw my other arm up to protect my face.

Even as Cole cries and trembles, his arms keep on swinging that heavy branch at my head, my body and my legs. I howl and yank myself away.

This causes Cole to cry all the harder, and the look of terror upon his face to become stronger, even as his blows pound down more furiously. It is as if each cry I give causes him pain, but he has determined this is the only way to stop my tongue.

Cole's eyes are wide and white. He moves as if possessed, muttering always to himself, like there's some kind of spell or poison over his mind. "The demon," he mumbles. "I must wipe the demon out."

"Cole," I shriek. "You don't believe that—you don't believe the demon makes you do the bad. Cole—come back!"

But he drags me through the snow, grunting, sweating hard. "Dontcha see?" he groans in agony. His fists pummel me anew, pushing my protests away. "I owe Sal my life, and all I can do is pay him back. Sal is the one who sav'd me, and he tol' me I'm the only one to do this. And I gotta do what he tells me—he's my only friend. There's no hope for it, I gotta do it."

I can see Salvius approaching in the trees, but I no longer hope that he will help me. I am close to the river. I am caught by the trees.

The blows rain down, but I stare through the falling flakes at that faint figure. *Is there any other who walks with him? Any that could help me now?*

I thrust myself up from the snow as Cole strikes at me. I leap out between the trees, toward the river. I can see the frozen ice far below, but it is the only chance I have. And in that moment, Cole smites a final blow, his cudgel lancing down to land a violent thud.

The sound of a distant ocean covers me with surf, that tide that bears me back into the past, back to the place where I was born.

People come through the whiteness, through the bright light, but all of them are ghosts.

I see my mother's laughing eyes. Christian is here, too, his face wreathed in light.

Edward. Smiling beneath his serious brow, nodding at me with secret intent, even as he takes my arm and escorts me around the Court.

Moten. He turns and walks beside me on the road. His mouth opens silently, and he holds up his book. He wants me to read the words he has written there.

Nell. *Ah, Nell.* In my grief for you, I learned to be silent and to be hidden. Your death taught me all too well.

We are in the forest on the way to the deep stream beside the alder copse. There a plover calls in the deep woodsy stillness, and then a pair of martins dart across the overgrown path. Through the trees, I can see the thick and fast-moving line of flowing water, a steep bank beneath my feet, and the purple loosestrife and meadowsweet of spring.

Nell smiles at me, her face shifting in the light of the beech leaves and the vines. *Come*, she says. *I'll show you my bridge. Salvius gave me the rope.* She takes up a coil that lies near at hand and pulls it tight, anchoring it to a tree with a cloverleaf knot. Beneath my feet the rope rises, stretched taut to the other side. And then a smaller rope, making a slight uneven handhold above the first. When we hold the one, and stand upon the other, we rise inches above the flood. Together, we stand in midstream, looking up and down, the dappled light around us falling on shallows and deep pools alike, the water rushing always, without pause.

Come, says Nell. *Cross with me to the other side.*

And as she turns her throat, she bears that strangely knotted rope around her neck. She is dead.

I open my eyes, blinking off the new-fallen snow that already lies heavy and thick on my face. I hear the river beneath me, not that distant dappled stream.

I live, I move, I breathe. I will not cross yet.

CHAPTER 40

I AM BURIED IN snow. The flakes of falling snow no longer melt on me. I am too cold.

My flesh is festooned with spots of blood, and deep purple bruises that ache and throb. My head is a fiery mass of pain—it hurts to move an inch. I cannot see for the whiteness all around me.

This blanket of heavy snow must have kept me alive, freezing to my wounds and keeping my blood in my body. The cold caught the blood as it started to flow, and stopped it as a thick, congealing salve.

A wind blows nearby. The snow still falls, and the portentous silence is edged with the faint hiss of water running under ice.

I cannot see, but my left arm moves freely, pushing aside the drift, and into open air. My right arm is caught by something hard that jabs into my flesh. And my legs hang free and unencumbered, covered only by a scrim of slush.

Something is uncertain in the way I lie—there's a shift in my balance even when I move a finger or an eye. I turn my head, despite the pain, and squint. My vision in one eye clarifies, and I see the river waiting for me, far, far below. In its depths are endless floes of ice.

I am hanging upon the broken branches of a wizened gorse bush whose roots are frozen to the bank above the riverside, partway down the escarpment.

I am below the line of vision of someone at the bank. No one can see me here, and whoever pushed my body here meant to kill me.

Every time I move my legs to climb up the bank towards the hillside, I slide a little farther down, closer to the frigid river depths and the jagged ice. My stomach churns at the sight.

The sun is low in the sky. My poor ill-treated body must have hung here, unseen and unfallen, for many hours. Yet I have not descended from this unnatural perch. And if my wounds were open and severe, I would have died here, hung like some shrike's strange and gory sacrifice.

I use my free arm and fling my hand upward, pulling at what dirt and plants I can find, digging my way inch by inch up the hill. The gorse bush that saved me moves from shoulder to armpit to belly, and then to thigh. I am moving up the hill, ever so slowly.

And when the sun has pushed even lower in the sky, I reach finally the lip of that frozen riverbank. I heave myself up those last few steps and sit upon the verge. My limbs tremble, every inch of me seems numb and bruised. And when I stand, I find that I almost fall. My balance is not true. But somehow, in the long struggle up the bank, my head has cleared. There is still a throbbing pain, but my vision is no longer clouded.

And so I crawl. I crawl toward the line in that gray sky where a darker line rises. I crawl toward the smoke in our campsite, beyond a long rifted field of windblown snow.

I watch the men from behind a tall, knife-edged drift. They have returned from Cambridge. The cart is fixed. From where I wait, I cannot hear their voices, but I can see their deeds. They push each other back and forth, they shout loud, and seem near to blows. They seem quite fretful in their loss.

For their loss is evident: Liam holds my blanket and cries. Tom takes my cloak and points then at Cole, who is made to bow upon the ground. I am sure they shout, but sound does not carry this distance. From where I watch, the play they perform is a mummer's act, all motion and lightning, with no thunder to be heard.

The boy leaps. He makes for his escape. Then Cole is flung back and forth between them like a rag doll. He tries to get away once more, but someone always blocks his way. Salvius holds his short sword at the boy's throat. Then he flings a rope high over a willow tree branch. Now it hangs there, ready to become a noose around the boy's neck.

I get myself up on my elbows and drag my hips forward through another drift, my feet pushing me along as a serpent moves through sand. After I push through three more heaping towers of snow, I am close enough to hear their voices, hoarse and loud.

Salvius is speaking, in tones profound and sad. "The blood on his hands cries out 'gainst him and tells of his evil deeds. The lad ain't my son and never was. I done him a charity, and look how he repays that debt. With blood, with death!"

Salvius stares every man in the eye, but he does not look Cole in the face. I do not know the truth of things—of Cole and the demon, I am still unsure—but if they will hang him for my murder, I should at least sit in judgment.

I pull my poor legs under me. I stand and sway, but I do not fall. I stagger forward past the cart, and then turn the corner toward the fire.

As I come close, Liam is protesting the punishment. "What proof do we have? That's what I'd like to know. Mear is gone, that's true, but what proof do we have that Cole's killed her? There's bandits on these roads—there's more than meets the eye."

"I seen him," says Salvius. "I was the first back to camp, and I seen Cole come back from the riverside."

"And was Mear there?" Liam says. "I'd like to know—didja see her body dead upon the ice?"

I stand tall and close-at-hand behind them, careful not to fall in the slick hoarfrost.

Then I shout. "No," I call. "He did not, for I lay not upon the ice."

The men turn, their faces pale. They must fear they see a ghost, for I have risen from the dead. Like Lazarus, I come back.

"Fear not," I say, and laugh to hear those old and ancient words. "Fear not, I am of flesh and blood, not spirit of the air." And I point back upon the snow, where my tracks are plain to see, spotted with blood and muddy from the riverbank.

Cole stares at me. He may have had some hope before, some light in his eyes that Salvius would save him in the end. But now, his teeth sink into his lip until it turns white, and his eyes roll as he turns his head frantically from side to side.

"Wait," he cries. "I didna mean to—I just—wait!"

But Salvius holds the boy firm. I remember the bruises on Nell's arms, and with a shiver, I remember how hard and strong Salvius was as he held me on the table when my foot was cut.

Quickly, Salvius reaches for the rope, and with one hand he loops a knot, pulling it tight across the willow tree. Few would be able to construct such a curious knot. It is a knot I have seen only twice before: a triple knot, tied fast across a half hitch.

Salvius hung my friend Nell. And Salvius killed our lads.

CHAPTER 41

"MEAR!" SALVIUS SAYS, his voice high and bright, even as his hand makes to pull the gallows rope high. "How did you... Thank God you're alive!"

"You liv'd to tell your tale. Thank Holy God!" shouts Liam.

Salvius gives a grim smile. "We found this villain who did this crime—his hands all bloody!"

Geoff comes closer to me. "But wait—not all of us think Cole is to blame. You must speak—who did this to you?"

"Ayuh," says Salvius, pulling hard on the rope. "Tell us true of his wrong against you. I will punish Cole, once you speak."

He smiles wider as he speaks. I am sure he thinks he knows the answer I will give.

But Salvius is the murderer. He betrayed poor Nell, he betrayed our sons, and he has betrayed every bit of Cole's better nature, every day, with tales of demons and false thefts. Cole has no demon except the one who holds him now.

Cole's wild black eyes stare into mine, his gaze as strange and terrified as a beast caught in a trap, the whites showing all around.

I told him I would be his mam. And yet Cole listened not to me: He served the one who'd raised him, the one who told him he was kin. The one who holds that terrible knot above his head.

I feel my heart beat strong in me at the desperation in the boy's eyes. There is something thicker than blood that ties us together. Each of us makes it up ourselves, and it flows in word and deed.

I remember the words of the girl in the high, lone manor, speaking of her stillborn babe. *They can't have him. 'E is mine, always and ever—'e is mine to do with as I will.* Her eyes were strong, her voice did not quaver.

I think of Christian, my own beloved son. "I'll always be with you," he said to me.

And I forgive young Cole. *If I can't save my boy, I will save you.*

I stand tall, despite the bruises and injuries upon me.

And I lie.

"You are the one—it was you who did this to me, Salvius!" My words ring clear as any bell.

Salvius stumbles backward, so startled he almost drops his sword.

His mouth falls agape. "What is that you say?"

"Not Cole. It was you yourself, Salvius—it was you who did this to us all. You are the one who tried to kill me. You beat me long, and threw me to the river." I look around at the dark and frightened faces of the men.

I know now that Salvius's envy and lust brought doom upon our lads. Cole was but the tool held in his hand and turned whichever way he willed.

I raise my hand and point at the false uncle who beat Cole long, near every night, who forced him in every way against his better nature, who took what little innocence was left. This is the one who could not abide a woman who told him he could not have her as he willed. He killed Nell because she refused him, and then he tried to kill Sophia because she refused him as well. A cold thought comes to me. I remember that Salvius alone took Sophia back to the village on the morn of our departure. *Did poor Sophia come to harm on the way back to Duns? Will we ever see her again?*

Salvius is the one who does evil deeds. I shout it out.

"I swear upon my soul—Salvius is the one who struck me down. He tried to kill me, and he killed our lads! He tied the knot. He lit the fire!"

At this second declaration, Salvius is jolted out of his shock. "You're a liar an' a witch, ol' Mear!" He lunges forward with a grunt. "I'll have you now. How dare you—"

But even as his borrowed sword slices through the air, a larger blow glances across his blade. Geoff stands there, holding the axe from the cart. Salvius parries that blow, and then there is one from Liam to contend with—he has grabbed a branch of river yew. Geoff's blow strikes Salvius in the chest, doubling him over, but when Liam swings, Salvius thrusts back, shoving Liam so forcefully he is thrown hard to the snowy ground.

Salvius is a great furious figure on the other side of the fire, his expression stark and frantic, the gold Doncaster tunic on his chest flashing as he gasps for breath. He lifts the sword high, and then bends abruptly to the ground.

Salvius seizes the ends of the sticks and logs in the fire pit, and he throws them bodily toward us. The fire is suddenly flung up in the air, flaming brands live and dangerous. A sooty stick hits Cole in the face, and Tom is struck by a flaming branch.

Benedict yells. "He's getting away!"

He throws a stone at Salvius, who is dashing now to the hobbled horses on the other side of the cart. The rest of us seize stones as well, but Salvius has already sliced through the hobbles and jumped on his horse. Geoff darts to the road and waits there with the axe, his feet spread wide, looking for all the world like that angry angel at the gate of Eden.

With a shout of rage, Salvius turns his old mare and slaps it hard. The horse rears and nearly bucks him off. But then Salvius gallops back the other way, toward the river and the villages behind us. Tom runs with frantic urgency and manages to catch up. He grasps the reins and pulls the horse to the side before Salvius strikes him down.

Liam takes hold of Moten's bow and fires a volley of quick arrows. They whistle past my ears, dangerously near, but none of them hit Salvius or his horse.

Tom gets up again—he still gives chase, along with Geoff. Together they pursue as Salvius flogs his horse.

A moment later there is an unearthly sound from the woods, some primal scream. I hobble through the trees, to a place where the men stare across the surging river with its tossing ice floes. The snow is torn and ravaged in front of our feet.

Salvius must have attempted to halt his steed, but it was too late. They plunged over the side, and into the river, at almost the same spot where I was nearly killed. There is a great gouge in the escarpment here, a raw wound in the earth, the covering scrim of turf ripped, mayhap torn out by frantic hooves and by Salvius's sword or hands.

We gawk and look around at each other. Tom's arm wears a long red burn from the flaming brach, and Cole's face is marked by soot. Liam's head bleeds, and Benedict bears a heavy purplish burn and bruise upon his bald head—and I am amazed to be alive.

Far below, we can hear the tumbling crash of falling ice and snow, cracking and breaking on the floating river ice far below.

✠

Cole cries long upon my bosom. He is overcome by grief and fear. I hold the lad close and feel his sobs shake his body through and through. And he can't stop speaking, the words tumbling out, as if a fountain has been unleashed.

"Ah tried… ah tried to stop him. Ah'm sorry… Ah'm so sorry."

"Hush," I whisper. "Hush, it's not your fault."

"It started when I tried agin… to make a friend… of Matthew, Tom the miller's son. He were nice to me, and then another lad told him what the demon done to him—how all his things were broken up in the night. And then Matthew won't talk to me neither. They all go into Benedict's house, and I'm so cross and ragin' that I can't hardly speak. I follow the lads there, but there ain't nothin' I can do."

There is a yearning in his tone, and his eyes are wide as a little babe's. "You . . . you . . ." stutters Cole. "You can't make someone be your friend, can you?"

"And that's when I see Salvius outside the house. He is angry as a hornet. He takes me by my ear and says to me, 'What kind of thing are you doing here?' I tell him of my anger at the demon, and how I lost another friend. And instead of bein' nice to me this time, and tellin' me how he will help me, and beatin' me sound, he asks me what I'd do if I let the demon out.

"'Burn it away,' I say. And I am angry too, and I get wood to burn my demon out. I want an end to this cruel world I'm in. I want to burn the demon out."

Cole sobs in pain and regret. "And Salvius tol' me that the woman in the house—Benedict's Sophia, y'know—he tells me that she's the demon in this world. And if I burn that place with her in it, then the demon what tortures me will be gone."

Now I am sure that Sophia never made it home that day we left the village. Salvius had bent his mind to killing her, and she did not know her peril.

The lad plucks nervously at his coat, the tears spilling down. "That's what he says to me. And I'm so blind with madness and with rage that I don't stop to tell him that she's already gone away, on some cart that afternoon. I don't tell him that only the boys are inside the house, 'cause I rage at them. I wanted them t' die." He's still plucking at his coat.

I put my hand up to his coat and smooth his hand away. Then he goes on.

"I figure Sal will stop me, once I get too far."

"Hush," I say. "Hush."

"But when the fire starts, Sal dasn't stop it—not a'tall. Instead, he adds wood, piles it in front of the door. Then he ties a knot, so they can't get out! And when I try to pull it away, and use a branch to lift it from the gate, Sal pushes me. He hits me with a stone. He... hits me... I couldna move no more..."

All of his years growing to manhood in Duns, Cole was told he was a child only during daylit hours and a spawn of Satan at night, an evil spirit who must be beaten to within an inch of his life for his sins. Even when he and Christian played as little lads in the dust—young Cole believed this great lie. And when Salvius needed to travel away from Duns for a night, Cole would beat his own body, mortifying his flesh in the hopes of exorcising the demon that lived deep in his heart.

It was only in recent months that doubt had grown in Cole's breast. He found that Salvius bound him to speak to no one of his plight, and any that he approached as companions were injured when Cole was asleep. Cole thought his own corruption was again responsible for these slights, but even though he beat himself most terribly, something in him spoke against these wrongs. He wondered how he could both want kindness from someone and not know that he was hurting them. Salvius's duplicity was becoming clear: a child is easier to deceive than a young man.

But it was only when Cole watched Salvius refuse to let him rescue the boys from the burning house that the doubts he harbored burst through for a shattering moment of clarity. When he left the village with us, he hoped to leave Salvius behind. By fighting the Earl's bandits for us, he tried to prove he could be a different lad—a hero.

Then when Salvius found us on the road, the clouds closed in again.

For hours, I stroke his head and soothe him with a murmur and a lullaby. Cole lies on his side, arms curled to his chest. His brow is smooth now, unconcerned, cheeks flushed, a baby blushing in deep sleep.

Even as I hold him, I know that my heart's cry is not exactly true. This is no quiet babe in my arms. He is not even a small child anymore. This young one has been twisted to another's aims, and he will be truculent, cruel, and dangerous too, for he has lived long under a veil of deception and little knows the road that leads aright. A few kind words are a salve upon the surface—they cannot heal his deep wounds.

Yet from this wreck, I will recover what I can. I can repair what damage I can see, and in time draw out what good remains. In the time that is left to me in this world, I cannot save him entire, but I will try to give him peace in his life. It is all that I ask myself to do.

Now I do not hold the hand of any prince's son. My charge is not to take the heir of any throne forward to his inheritance. Cole is an heir to a different legacy—a legacy of wrong that must be made right. It is a kingship grand that all of us build, every day of our meager lives, and it is a castle made of sand. Every wrong righted seems to bring another misdeed tumbling down upon our heads.

But I for one will keep building such a kingdom.

Four nights before Shrove Tuesday outside of Cambridge town, we cut down that tall and leaning willow tree upon which Cole would have hung. Upon that crackling wood, we build a funeral pyre, and we burn all that Salvius left behind with us. We cannot find his body, but we burn everything else he had. Then we place the ashes alongside the boys he burned in lust, in envy, and in spite.

Later, when we tell the stories of our lads to the King, Cole might tell them his uncle was burned too, in that distant blaze in Duns. We are the ones who left the village all together: and we are the ones who will make the tale.

Around our cooking fire, late that night, I tell to my companions the true story of my years.

"I tell you now of Edward of Woodstock," I say, my long-closed throat now open. "Those many years ago, at Canterbury, I met the Black Prince when I was but a noviate nun…"

I tell them of the courtship of Edward at Canterbury Abbey where I was scholar and revered. I tell of growing great with child and how the Mother Abbess tormented me with fear. I tell of how I escaped when the Earl of Hereford tried to hunt me down, and how through happenstance I became a mute and man, hidden in Duns for all those years.

I tell of Salvius's perfidy—how he planned to trap and kill Sophia in his jealousy and rage. I tell of how I longed to see Edward again, and how heartbroken I was when I discovered he was dead.

And finally, I tell them how I bear the Prince's dead son hither to London town, with my long-suffering companions, my friends.

CHAPTER 42

LONDON TOWN IS a great and stinking warren. The smoke of many fires creeps around our ankles and our cart, and a stench rises from the open sewers in the lanes—a reek that rivals anything wafting from our cart. The narrow streets twist unevenly between leaning houses made of wood. Only one cart may fit between the walls, with people rushing all around. It is a stunted town, every stone blackened from fires. Like all the world we live in, this is a fallen place.

I have read that ancient London was a great city built by a race of wise giants, hale and hearty in mind and body. They crafted the great structures—the walls, aqueducts, and even the King's Highway we traveled, once the Roman road. We live in the cast-off cloak of it now. It is but a pale shadow of the world that once was.

Far above the teeming mass of the city rises the White Tower in its glory. Four battlements rise on each edge, like the *margrave* towers that hold the corners in that old game of pawns. For always, the kings think of war and defense. Thirteen towers there are that join to that outer wall: once Edward told me all of their names.

Three days we travel from Cambridge town, the crowds of people surging all around us every step. We are fed rich food along the way, and given lodgings for the night.

Always, villagers ask us for our tale. But since the night of Salvius's death, we no longer tell it. And so the villagers are unsatisfied as we drive on, a mystery through all the countryside.

I am still weak in body and bone from that beating given me by Cole, and so I ride upon the cart. Cole walks beside me, speaking to me constantly since the flood of words and feeling released in him, a torrent welling up. Often I quail, hearing of his treatment when none knew of what Salvius did to him—when we turned blind eyes, our village willingly complacent. I offer him what succor and healing powers I possess.

We pitch our camp one late, late night and wake at dawn on the Monday of Shrove Week to see London across the river, finally in our sight. At the hour of Prime, a flock of larks goes up in the sky, dancing in circles on the open air. Their song rises higher and higher as they loop up into the bright reaches of blue. The sight brings my tears afresh: the larks soaring, the White Tower gleaming in the spacious morning light.

The Knight, who goes before us as messenger and herald, rides with the sunrise, thundering back to our camp. His destrier is a sigil of gleaming silver and white against the dull gray snow-spattered hillside.

Sir Phillip Gaumont tells me that Court awaits us on the following dawn. The Star Chamber still is in session. We will be given a lodging within the Tower, but not a prison cell. Instead, I am told that there is a place of honor for all of u, which thought makes me strangely fearful with anticipation.

We wend our way through these narrow, twisting streets, making always for that Tower as our aim. Yet we do not meet with the countryside acclaim: few peasants ask to hear our song. For there are many folk about in a vast city such as this, and we are but one spectacle.

The curving, winding streets trace aimless paths through the great puzzle of wood and stone: it would be easy to get lost. But the Knight moves ahead of us, cutting through the crowds, crying loud and long, clearing a path, making our way plain.

At each step our men sink down a foot into the winter mire, and deep under the muck the cobblestones are hard under our horse's roughshod hooves. The road between these leaning houses, through all this stinking filth, seems too much at times. But I remember other roads, and harder ones at that.

As the knight passes by, commoners slow and stare. But the sound of the crowd has changed. The sounds have shifted from occasional acclamation into a more dangerous curiosity. I catch a murmur that speaks to me of the morbid interest that follows the executioner to his gallows. In the gaze of these city people, I am now fearful and uncertain.

My heart tells me that now we go now into the mouth of the beast.

At last, we turn a corner amidst great mansions made of stone, and there ahead is the bulwark, the Lion Gate. But we fear to pass, for at the side of the gate is a vast cage of iron that holds some creature ravening within. The great tawny length of it rises from the straw as our horse come close. Then the beast shakes its mane and roars a thunderous roar.

A lion rampant. I have seen such a thing at last.

Finally, the knight motions us forward. Trembling we go, into the courtyard, toward the White Tower.

Here in this great open square, all my fears come to a head. For the armored guards stand forth as one body, as if they have been awaiting our entrance. Our old cart-horse swerves and rears. The guards quickly take the reins.

The men around me shout and call. Yet on an instant, each of them is seized.

Two guards come for me where I sit on the crossbar of the cart. A guard with a black beard pulls out his sword and points at me.

"You there," he calls. "Are you the one call'd Miriam? The one they speak of, the one the knight says has the French words on her tongue?"

I do not answer right away. All around me, the men of Duns are being dragged away. Liam is shouting and raging. Cole is crying and distraught.

"Yes," I whisper, and hope rises in my heart again a moment. Perhaps I am the key to their freedom. I scrabble for the Abbot's letter to the Prince Regent. It is buried inside Moten's book, under the straw.

"I am Miriam," I state strong and loud. "Yes, I am called Miriam, I am the one who bears the body of the—"

"We know who you bear here," sneers the guard with the great black beard. "One from a noble house has told us already. And for that most foul murder of children in their beds, we now arrest you, Miriam the peasant of Duns, in the name of the Great High Regent, John of Gaunt. You'll be tried and executed on the morrow, God willing."

Manacles go on my wrists and ankles, heavy chains hold me tight, and I'm wrenched off the cart. I am unable to seize Moten's book and the Abbot's letter. Both are left behind. The cart is dragged into a dark corner of the courtyard, and I am hauled up a cold corridor into the heights of the Tower. A dark cell opens before me.

"You are a prisoner now," a guard shouts, "of the Tower and the King. May God have mercy on your soul!"

The heavy iron door crashes closed.

CHAPTER 43

I AM IN A raw hole cut between the great blocks of stone. I cannot sit or lie down. I cannot move. I am in a standing grave. Darkness seeps into it, like water in a pit.

After what seems an eternity, the heavy door of my cell is flung back. A candle in a graduated holder drips down on a table. This same candle was there as I passed through this room at Vespers hour. Only an hour has passed, by the burning of the wax.

A rough hand takes hold of me, dragging me into the room. All around us in the great stone walls are set other small cells, but nearly every door is open. The holes yawn vacantly, like gaps in a mouth of rotten teeth.

My eyes clear slowly. There is a faint fire guttering on the hearth at the other end of the room, a great ironbound door of wood, and thin slits that open to the outside, windows that show only the night's blackness. Closer to me are the instruments of pain: Spikes and curved iron manacles. The long bed of the rack, and the wheel that makes it longer with every ratcheting notch. Pincers and pokers, to be heated in the fire and applied to raw and trembling flesh. None of these great pains do they inflict on me.

Instead, the guard with the black beard retrieves a long wooden cudgel from a bench at the other end of the room, and then without warning, without a word, he strikes me to the ground. I make as if to stand again, and he hauls me upward rapidly, saying only "Stay on your feet—it will go better fer you if I don't hav'ta work so hard."

The beating begins at Compline and goes through Matins hour. The guards are silent and brutal. They tear the ring from around my neck and wrench every word of my claim out of me. And at every confession I make, they call me "liar."

I am numb and broken. My child's body is gone. My ring—that last talisman of love—has been stolen. And the story of my loss hasn't been told to the King; it has been beaten out of me by two uncaring louts. Under threat of pain, I have told them everything of my past. I have withheld only my mother's secret, which I will not tell, cannot tell.

As the great iron gate of my cell slams shut again, I hear the skittering sounds of insects and mice, and the distant shrieks of prisoners in other cells, but I do not fear the vermin or my guards. I fear the dark.

I can see nothing now in the utter darkness but the red lines that blossom out when I press my fists hard against my streaming eyes, striving to see something, anything at all. My chest closes tight, an unyielding clenching ache. I fear the darkness itself will suffocate me.

O Alma Redemptoris . . .

✠

When the door opens again, only the bearded guard is here, and the blows now land halfhearted and uneven. This guard knows I am broken. And even though he stands amidst all these instruments of death, I do not fear my own death. It can't be worse than the pain I've felt from the death of those I loved. Still, I cannot deny the bodily pain I feel. Even these weak blows open up the injuries given me by Cole.

I feel every one of the blows inflicted on Cole over the years—it is a song of pain that echoes in my flesh. After a time, my flesh seems to go numb. I wish I could ease his suffering now, for he has suffered enough torment in his young life. I would shelter him, if he were here,—I would shield him with my own body. *Where is Cole, though? Where are the others? And where is all that we left in the cart? And why were we seized? Why was I accused?*

The ironbound door at the other end of the room swings open and a new guard in livery enters. The fire flares with the wind in the door, and I catch a glimpse of wood piled high there, and a surfeit of soiled rags and torn parchment. On top of that mound is something that looks very much like Moten's old book, with the folded letter protruding from the edge.

The book and letter are on the tinder pile.

A desperate hope rises in me: if I can get the letter, someone will read it, and they will know that my story is true. I am no liar. We are no vagabonds on the road, killing and devouring flesh as we go. That letter will force the world to listen to me—it will give me voice once more.

I can prove to the world that Christian is the son I claim. It's a spark of life in the vast sea of death that washes all around us. I must strive, one last time, to redeem our lives.

O Alma Redemptoris, Alma Redemptoris . . .

In truth, I do not know what the Abbot wrote to the Prince Regent, but I hope that such a letter would declare us under the protection of His Grace. It will be my passage out of this hole, and the key that opens all the doors between this cellar and the high chamber of the King.

I shuffle forward, a little closer to the fire and the tinder heap.

"Where you think you're going?" barks the guard, and for good measure strikes me to the floor once more. I stagger upward to see the book still on the tinder pile by the door.

The guard who has come in has a homely pockmarked face. He takes a thin whip down from the wall and comes closer.

"Have you started the night watch then?"

The bearded guard strikes a great roundhouse blow, as if to prove his prowess to his friend.

"Ayuh, we'll go 'til Matins hour, and then break 'til Lauds."

I tremble at the words. But my feet are planted firm. Although I sway and quiver, I do not fall again.

"The others are already confessin' to a priest, got the executioner here already," grunts the guard. "But this one has to be prepared."

"Ah, well let me help you then," says the pockmarked guard.

"Now tell me," says the bearded one. "How is it with your Janey?" And then he strikes again.

"Not good," mutters the other one. "My Janey is not good a'tall."

The bearded guard deals a blow that doubles me over, even as he speaks to his companion. "When's the first one of this lot to die?"

"Noon," says the pockmarked guard with a grunt. "Hang him high at noon. Young one first–the one who looks like the devil's own child." The guard runs a finger down his face, from forehead to jaw.

Cole's scar. My heart has an urgent ache, a crack running through it at Cole's doom. After all this journey, after all he has endured, he's to die at the hands of the King's guards. The great wheel turns and crushes all below. But this time, I will stop it: I must free him.

I look up at the guard's uncaring faces. The candle flame flickers against the far wall. The instruments of torture glimmer in the light. The room has not changed—nothing has changed from my resolve.

"Why that sorry lad first?" asks the bearded guard.

The other one gives a dry barking laugh. "Has a mouth on him—they tire of the sound of his voice. They'll 'ave his head on a pike soon enough."

"Noon, eh? I'll have to watch. That's always good fer a laugh."

"Don't forget, the trial fer this one starts at the ninth hour. They might need this one there."

My mouth goes dry. There is an edge of light in the sky outside. It is near dawn by now, six hours until noon, and only three hours until my trial, if I read the sky aright. The trial will start without me, but I will be held for inquisition if the magistrates so elect, and I will be tormented so that I do not lie if called for testimony.

I have but the moments between now and Terce—the ninth hour of the day. In those few hours before my trial, I need to get the letter. I must save it from the fire.

The men resume their talk. Yet when they speak of me, it is as something removed and far away. They do not see me, even as they strike my body hard.

"I thought this one was supposed to be taken straight to the hanging gallows."

"Ayuh, goddam common folk. They kill'd those poor children—"

"That's a lie."

I am surprised to hear the second guard interrupt, a strident certainty in his voice. "I heard it diff'rent. These here are their own children—they had a madness of grief on them. They were rallying the common folk, to fight for justice."

"Ayuh, Crown can't have that," says the other guard. "Common folk doin' that."

The whip comes sharp across my legs and sends me flying. I careen from one guard to the other, like a skittled pin knocked from wall to wall in the bowling yard.

"Nah, Crown can't give 'em that," replies the bearded guard. "But if these poor folk are to be executed, why a trial fer this one?"

The pockmarked guard flicks back his whip and curls his lip in disgust. "Some noble gent turned up. Wanted to prosecute this lot for murder. From a dukedom, had evidence—that's what he says."

My mind whirls with questions. *Who has accused me? Is there any way to escape?*

"Goddam noble witness and all, it don't matter. This one ain't long for this world anyhow."

"Nah, but without the nobleman here, there wouldn't 'ave even been a trial. If you have an accuser of blood, then you have some right, an' you have a trial."

The bearded guard lifts his hand and hits me again. We move together in a strange and tortured dance. The steps cannot be halted, but I cannot keep the rhythm. Every now and then a blow strikes through my numb flesh, causing me to yelp sincerely at the shock of pain.

"Aaah!" I cry. "Aaah, mercy!"

But they do not ever seem to hear.

"Not a trial fer such as you and me, Gerit."

"Nah, 'tis true. Not fer us, Bern. Only if some nobleman wanted us tried and then executed."

The bearded guard, Bern, shakes his head sorrowfully. "Be better to go fast, if I had my druthers. It's an evil end, to be beaten to death." He says this even as he lifts his cudgel and strikes me another hearty blow.

"None o' this trial of my soul, and beatin' and wastin' my life in a cell," bearded Bern says. "Nah, hang me or chop my head like a noble."

"Ayuh," agrees the other guard, the one named Gerit. "Before I left fer the Tower, that's what my Janey says too. That's how she felt—like she's trapp'd in a prison by the plague. She'll be gone by Sunday, I fear."

Bern shivers and crosses himself, a warding sign against an evil end. But even in his fear, he finds it in him to make some gesture of sympathy toward his friend.

"Ah, I'm right sorry fer you, Gerit. My mam and da died of the plague—horrible way to die. I hope fer your sake, she goes quick."

Bern steps back, his chest heaving with fatigue, arms hanging loose and tired by his side. "'Tis dawn already. Do we break our fast?"

"Ayuh, put her back in the cell until after." Gerit sighs and shakes his head. His lip purses in a sad frown. But he does not seem to seeing me; he seems to be thinking of his Janey. "After breakfast, then we must start up again. Soft'n the ol' witch up fer her trial."

The first traces of daylight are staining the walls. The book and its hidden letter still wait for me by the fire.

The shapes of Gerit and Bern are outlined against the light—dark silhouettes in the approaching dawn. Their sweat-streaked features loom over me. These two men are young, but their faces are lined with long weariness, and with the effort of inflicting pain. This is when the lie comes to me.

I will use their weariness, their sadness, and their fright. I will use their fear to gain my freedom.

CHAPTER 44

MEMORY IS MY aid now. The sharp needle of bone would stab into Theresa of Avignon's plump little thumb, over and over again. Then young Theresa would squeeze her tortured thumb until the blood welled to the surface. Each drop she would smear across her cheek, with a bit of spit to blur and soften the rosiness she sought.

I do not want such blurring and softening, such an even pink glow. I want the bloody imprint to burst forth across my flesh, marking the plague unmistakable and stark.

I remember my mother's dreadful face as she spoke to me at the end. That terrible sign rising up out of her skin, as if it had been buried underneath all the while. The reddened wild eyes, and the panting from unforgiving thirst. This is what the guard named Bern saw in his mam and da. And these things I can re-create. First, I push the heels of my hands into my eye sockets until my eyes are hurting, red and leaking angry tears.

O Alma Redemptoris, Alma Redemptoris . . .

The swellings, the black pustules—I cannot find the wherewithal to create a forgery of these things. I do not care: the bloody petals are the key. If I am covered with such a crown of roses, then those who see me will know forthwith, and they will spread the word.

I have no needle. But my bloody flux still comes, even though it has lessened now after days on the open road. And when I pull aside the bunched and sordid rags between my legs, there is enough to wet the tip of my finger.

With a trembling hand and anxious heart, I dab at my neck and face, painting as carefully as any Roman master. This is my last chance.

✠

"I thirst," I cry. My ruse is ready, the marks of doom imprinted on my flesh.

"Ayuh, I hear ya." Bern's voice is muffled inside my cell. "Don't be in a hurry for your next beatin'—we'll have atcha in a bit."

I scream, "Ah God, I thirst!"

"God's wounds," says Gerit. "Throw that bucket of water on her. Lemme finish my breakfast 'fore we 'ave to beat on her again."

Water will ruin everything. I change my cry.

"Ah, I am in agony, I am dying." It comes to me then that I need someone who can read the letter, once I have it, a man others will believe. "I am too sick to stand—send me a priest, I beg you! I must confess."

"Now what is this? You say you're sick?" says Bern as he opens my cell a crack. I fall forward as the door swings wider, as if I am weak and helpless.

Red petals, bunched roses of blood, blossom up out of my chest and my arms, across my neck and face. My eyes are red and hollowed, streaming with tears, and drool strings out of my mouth.

"Aaah!" I cry. "What's wrong with me? The pain, the pain! I die!"

I collapse against the guard. The bloody spots are right against his face.

"The plague," Bern whispers, fervent terror waking in him. "The black death, here in the Tower."

He pushes me back frantically.

"The plague!" Bern finally cries aloud. "Goddam, she's burnin' up from the plague!"

He turns and bolts to the other end of the room. He pushes wildly at the door, and then finally pulls it forward with a frenetic urgency and darts out of the room.

The guard named Gerit stares at my unholy visage, the remains of his morning meal still on the table before him. Gerit is panting like a dog, his eyes wide, as he watches my stumbling progress across the room. I weep with pretended pain, but still Gerit is resolute.

"That Bern, he is a scared fool," he says tremulously. "I'm not. My Janey is nearly dead of plague, but I haven't caught a touch of it."

"I'm sick, ah God," I cry. "I'll die—send me a priest. Ah, ah, ah!" I stumble against the table and hold a hand to my throat, as if there's swelling there. The tinder pile is closer to me now.

Still the guard strives to keep from crying out.

"See these?" Gerit points at the pockmarks on his face, his hand starting to tremble as much as his voice. "I'm not afraid. I had the black demon when I was a lad, and I ain't got it ever since."

"This is death, I am death!" I cry and moan. "The pain, the pain in my gut—it's a demon devouring me!"

Gerit seizes a pike from the wall and thrusts it toward me.

"By God's damn'd Son, stay the feck away from me—you stay back from me, stay away!"

I stagger against the racking bench, still mocking the grip of plague. Then I make as if to retch on the floor.

"Ah, ah," I cry again. "If you won't help me, grant me a boon and send for a priest. I must confess."

Gerit keeps the pike pointed at me. "To confess your sins?"

"I have the right to confess, at the end of my life, do I not?" I retch again, and this time I fling out a handful of blood onto the floor, what remains of my flow held in a dirty rag in my hand. The letter on the tinder pile is almost in my reach now.

Gerit flinches and edges closer to the door. "Would you confess to this crime?"

"Ah!" I fall to my knees on the floor. "Ah, in Christ's holy name, a priest, I beg of you!"

Gerit turns and seizes the door. He slides it open a crack and glances back at me. His eyes are bloodshot, wide with fear. I hold myself still on the floor, hair hanging over my face. He gingerly leans away from me, into the crack of the door.

"Cap'n, the prisoner," he calls, "needs a priest! Wants t' confess!"

"What?" comes a shout. "Why's Bern run off, and what are you about in there?"

"The prisoner. Wants to confess," Gerit bellows back. "Cap'n, she thinks she's gonna die!"

"Aye—she will!" The voice in the hall is closer now, a deep baritone, thick with anger.

Gerit rubs a nervous hand across his pockmarked face. He opens the door wider. Thudding footsteps come nearer and nearer.

I am on my hands and knees, crawling, creeping carefully past the point of Gerit's pike and around the fire. *Be with me*, I pray to the Queen of Heaven or to any angel who will hear my plea. *Give my hands and my heart strength to deceive, and to seize the moment that will grant me justice. O, Alma...*

Then so quickly I can hardly breathe, I reach out and grab the tattered edges of Moten's old manuscript. I can feel the thick bend of folded vellum against my blooded fingertips. But the letter won't come out of the book: it is stuck.

The guard's eyes still face the hallway, his iron pike still pointing to the middle of the room. Ever so slowly, I open the book. And there is the letter, caught on a torn wing of parchment, stuck like a marker in the middle of the pages, the words inscribed on it in thick black ink:

Greetings, Thanksgivings, Blessings
from Your Very Revered Father,
Abbot André de Bottoun of the Cluny House
of Saint Mary Magdalene.

To His Lordship John of Gaunt,
Regent in the Holy Name of Christ, by God's Gra—

The door bangs open with a sudden thrust. A broad-shouldered man with a broken nose stands a head above the trembling Gerit. He wears the sash of an officer over his bloodstained livery. His eyes narrow at me, brows as thick and black as thorns.

"So what have we here?" he thunders. "Some poor sick prisoner making to steal what she can?"

"Cap'n… Cap'n… she was on her deathbed… and I just call'd 'cause…" Gerit stammers, gaping at me standing upright and silent as the grave.

The Captain pushes Gerit roughly to one side. The pike goes rattling to the floor.

"And what's this?" the Captain grunts, scratching a thumb across my cheek and neck. "You aren't sick a'tall, are you?"

My tongue cleaves to the roof of my mouth. I cannot seem to speak. I was so close.

He strides close to me, between one heartbeat and the next, and seizes the letter and Moten's book from my hand.

"What's this, then?" He holds the book of loosely joined parchment over the fire, the smoke curling around his clenched fist.

"No," I plead.

"And why not?" He grins, a certain pleasure at my concern glinting in his eye.

I see the short square shape of the letter protruding from the edge of the book. It is sliding slowly out.

"A letter," I blurt out. "A letter from an abbot. Don't burn that."

"This?" he says disdainfully, and pulls harshly at the folded piece of vellum. He turns it over in his fingers, his eyes widening at the red splotch of wax embossed with the kneeling figure of Mary Magdalene, her head crowned with the saint's spiked crown of light.

"Don't burn that!" he says loudly, mocking me. "Who are you to give me orders?"

His hand whips out, and there is a sudden pain on my face and I can taste fresh blood on my lips. The Captain moves too quickly for my poor eyes to see. Then he curls his hand again, as if he will throw the letter into the flames.

"No, no," I cry. "It is a letter to the Court!"

"Is it now?" He breathes heavily. "You know, many claim to be the King's own first cousin, afore their deaths. And they all do die, lemme tell you. Fer sure and certain."

"I can read," I say quietly.

He gives me a sharp look. "Can you now? Well, maybe you're not such a commoner as they say. Here then." He thrusts the letter into my hands.

I look up at him. Still, he holds the book over the flames, the smoke dancing up toward it. I lick my teeth nervously.

"It is a letter from His Grace," I read, my lips numb and trembling. "The Abbot of Saint Mary Magdalene, to John of Gaunt, Prince of—"

"I know John of Gaunt!" His eyes roll as he looks anxiously around the room. He lowers the book from the fire, holding it closer to his side. It is his turn to be nervous now.

But he cuffs me across the face so that I fall to the ground. "So it is a letter to the Prince Regent—to John of Gaunt. And why did you not bring this forward earlier?"

I gulp and choke. There is blood in my mouth now. "It was… It was by the fire, Your Honor."

This time, he kicks me. "Your Honor? Ha. I spoke not to you. I speak to the gentleman of the guard 'ere. Where the hell is Bern? And what have you to say for yourself?"

The pockmarked one starts and stutters. "It... it is as the prisoner says. It was by the fire... on the tinder pile. And the prisoner was in the cell."

The Captain leans close to him, his face murderous. "So you had to wait until the prisoner broke out of her cell, and seiz'd it before you would bring such a matter to my attention."

Gerit cannot hold the Captain's gaze. He looks down at the floor, streaked with my fresh blood, a fresh spattering over the old stains of other prisoners.

The Captain sighs, as if he will blow the guard off the face of the earth. The Captain's breath reeks of garlic—I can smell it from the floor.

"I will take this damn'd paper now to the magistrates, but you would do well to keep the prisoner in chains henceforth, so that her slight weight and weak arms would not overwhelm you once more, and take what is not her right."

Gerit's face snaps upright once more. "Yes, sir."

The Captain turns his attention to me. "You there, ol' bitch—what of this other matter?"

I shake my head in bewilderment.

He shakes Moten's book. "These papers—the thing that looks like Satan's own book o' spells."

"I do not want it to burn," I say.

"You do not want it to burn?" He repeats incredulously and thrusts it once more over the open flame. "Again, you look to order your betters!"

I speak quietly, pleading without hope. "It was my friend's book. It was a record of his life."

The Captain looks at me. "And no more a record of his life?"

"He is dead."

"Did you kill him?"

"No. He was killed by Sir Phillip Gaumont, upon the open road."

"So, verily." The Captain gazes at me, a strange envy in his face. "You have known Gaumont then. But you are not dead. Not yet. A curious thing. Did he vouch for you then?"

I stammer out an answer. "I... I... I thought he had."

"You thought he had."

"Yes."

"And what proof did he give you of that?"

"A knight's oath."

"A knight's oath! Oh!" He mocks me again, his voice high and surprised, as if it were the voice of a young girl. Then he slips back into his baritone.

"But you were betrayed, were you not?" He sighs. "Peasants," he says. "Gaumont likes his peasants, for they are simple minded. Simplehearted.

"But you bear a letter, and some old book, that you do not want me to burn. Very well." He sighs again. "I will take these old bits of rubbish to the Magistrate, and if all of your companions are not yet hung or quartered, then perhaps this letter might spare them some slow agony."

He turns toward the door. "Of course, you have not read it."

I shake my head mutely. *No.*

The Captain holds the motley collection of papers up in the air, and he shakes the letter in his other hand, as if it will reveal its secrets to him. "Of course not. So for all you know, the letter instructs us in their everlasting doom, and does not foretell their freedom, nor your own."

I tremble.

The Captain gazes on me, and something in his gaze softens. "Well, I will take all of it to them. You have only three nights until the magistrates depart. They have delayed their departure until the end of Shrove Week."

"Three nights," I repeat numbly.

"And if at the end of that time, they have not call'd upon you, we will be curs'd with having you here the rest of your days," says the Captain. "If you fool my guards again, I will have them cut out your witch's lying tongue, so that you will have no power over them. And I will burn your precious letter here, and your book."

The door bangs shut.

Leg-irons go around my ankles as Gerit nervously locks me in chains, fastening me into a larger cell with bolts in the floor. He splashes a bucket of water over me before the iron gate closes. The plague petals melt, the old blood dripping down, off the top of my skin.

This new cell is a chamber of echoes: I can hear every sound from outside the wall, from the execution yard. Every few hours there is another sobbing sufferer, another choking cry as some poor soul struggles in their hanging agony.

Each time, I ask myself who has died now. *Is it Cole's life that has been snuffed out? Liam? Some other unfortunate? Is there any hope that someone is reading Moten's letter?*

Three nights I am buried in the depths of the Tower. They throw me food through the grate, but that is the only human touch I know. All through those dark hours, the sounds I hear are the echoing thud of the axe, the skittering of mice, and the tiny rasp of insects making their way through the labyrinthine wall.

On the third morning, they call me forth from my tomb. I am resurrected, blinking and blind in the strong light of day. The Star Chamber has summoned me.

CHAPTER 45

THE CHIEF MAGISTRATE's face is weighted with burden. Deep lines mark his heavy jowls and drag his face down toward the earth. I have the impression he stays upright only by force of will.

His great houndish eyes stare into me as I am led through the crowd, stumbling and enchained. I am forced into the seat in the center of the room. A bench of nine justices sits in judgment of me. These men are old and revered, each handpicked by the King, to mete out justice on this land. Above us is the great painting of the stars, from which this chamber takes its name.

Above me is a round window: a circle of light that stabs through the gloom of candles and dusty scrolls. Dust motes float in the beam and land upon the leg-irons and my blood-flecked tunic. The light from that window seems like a ghostly shape to me, an angel that hangs over all of us, silently judging every truth, every lie.

Yet one corner of the room is in darkness, shrouded by a heavy curtain. Someone is hidden there: my accuser, veiled and unknown to me. It must be the one the guards spoke of, the one of noble provenance whose accusation brought trial. Without that need for a hearing, I would already be dead.

Who could it be? The swarthy man who claimed to serve Lord Bellecort? A follower of the Earl of Hereford, still on the path to ensure his vengeance be done? A monk from the Cluniac monastery, a friend of the Abbot?

It is not the Knight, for as I was led in, I saw the mass of people waiting in the galley. And in that crowd, I saw Sir Phillip Gaumont. He sits behind me now.

The Magistrate leans forward, his heavy face catching the light as the other eight justices watch him close.

"You are brought here, before this Court, in order to clarify our findings and to explain the provenance of these writings. We have heard already from Sir Phillip Gaumont, who spoke on your behalf, and declares himself convinc'd of your tale."

I cannot help my mouth from dropping open: I had thought Gaumont a Judas, and instead he testified in my defense.

The Chief Magistrate sits back in his chair wearily, as if he has asked me a question.

I fear I have not understood. "Your Grace," I murmur. "I beg to know if you have read the letter of the Abbot."

"Yes, we know of this letter," says the Chief Magistrate slowly. "But the letter from the Abbot tells us only of the deceased monk, and the history he brings to the Tower's library. We do not care to speak of that."

A spike of anger rises in my breast. They do not care. They do not care that my friends have most probably been killed in the Tower, that my son has been murdered, that all I have has been taken away by force. They do not care. I will never able to fulfill my promise to my mother. And I have nothing left to lose.

I lift my head and stare along the long bench of justice—the word itself a mockery to me.

"Your Graces all, you say do not care?" I begin softly. "My companions and myself journeyed many miles to bring such a missive to this Tower, only to be told you do not deign to see it?"

Then I stand tall in my leg-irons, my voice high and rising. The nine Justices rear back in their seats, surprised. "You do not care?"

I shout. "Is it merely that you have not understood the story that has been beaten out of my mouth? What exactly do you not care of, Your Grace? You do not care, and yet my friends are dead, and I have suffere—"

"Be still!" The Chief Justice leans ahead and points at me. "I will ask the questions here!"

He stays in that erect posture, his wide-open eyes glaring at me as he speaks, as if willing me to silence. "The letter does nothing to correborate your story, except to establish that the Cluniac brother Moten was authorized by his abbot to travel with you. It does not establish any noble bloodline for your son, or for yourself or any of your companions. You are still therefore at the tender mercies of the Court, as vagabonds and willful violators of the Law of Interment. And some of the Chamber here believe you to be a murderer of those you bear hither."

"Murderer?" I lick my dry lips. Still they will prosecute me for this crime undone.

There is a murmur along the bench. The Magistrate pauses as the old men mutter. Finally, a thin, tall man leans forward and speaks softly in the Magistrate's ear. The Chief Magistrate listens and blinks his reddened hound-like eyes.

"Ah yes," he murmurs. Then to me: "You will tell us every step of your journey. You will tell the truth, or you will die on the rack. You are accused. Such an accusation carries much more weight when it comes from the lips of one who sits as the representative of a noble house recognized by the Court." He gestures to the figure behind the curtain. "Therefore, we summoned you."

Who could it be? Lord Bellecort? An heir of the Earl of Hereford, who fought Edward?

I lick my lips. I remind myself, I have nothing left. My voice is strong and fearless. "Your Grace, if I may ask, which House is represented here? Which House comes forth to make a statement against my own person? A cowardly act and an—"

The thin justice slams his fist down on the wooden bench with an echoing bang. He shouts at me, spittle flying across the room. "You are *not* of noble blood! You have no standing before this Court! How dare you! The House of Doncaster is a noble one, fully worth our support and belief in every—"

"You forget yourself, Thomas." The Chief Magistrate lifts a heavy hand and pushes the thin justice back in his chair. "We have read this monk's notes, and it would seem to me that his statements in that history require us to ask further of the relationship concerning—"

"No, this is but bilgewater and bodkins!" the thin justice says. "Lies and hearsay! We should throw the monk's notes in the fire, and this common harlot with them!"

Then the two of them are arguing. But I am caught by something that slipped. The House of Doncaster. The Lady who traveled with us on the road, accusing me? She did not even remember me, or know anything of my story. And the guard said it was a "noble gent." Could it be someone else from the house of Doncaster? Something niggles at my memory.

The Chief Magistrate sits back heavily in his seat. His face seems even more aged than before, and now he closes his eyes. But now a third justice shifts in his seat, the rotund and grizzled man sitting to the Chief Magistrate's left.

"Ah," he says in a wheezing voice. "But if we were to do as you recommend, Thomas, then we would be countermanding the request conveyed to us by the Cluniac abbot's own letter."

"The letter is but a meaningless nicety," says the thin justice. "Nothing of substance."

"I would beg to differ," remarks the Chief Magistrate, opening his eyes once more. "The Abbot's letter tells us of this Brother Moten, and describes in particular the history he has written—the book before us now. The Abbot states that this is a great record of the Cluniac monastery over the last twenty years. Over two hundred pages—one entry for every month of the monastery's history."

I am weary. My limbs ache with beating. My heart sinks as they continue their learned dialogue. Such empty words on Moten's many pages will not help me: the dry records of feast days, visitors, and ecclesiastical discussions. My eyes close and my mind wanders far away. *Where is my son's body now? Where is Cole and all that I fought for?*

"Speak when spoken to!" The guard cuffs me. "Your life is at issue!"

My eyes fly open once more. The nine justices all stare at me. "Well?" says the thin justice. "What is your answer? Have you read this book? Why are you named in these pages? Why did this Brother Moten write of you in this history?"

"I . . . I do not know," I stammer. "I have read but little of those pages. I would think I am but a footnote in the monastery's history."

The Chief Magistrate speaks kindly. "How did you set off on your journey? Begin with the fire that night."

The thin justice countermands him. "I do not care of some rumored fire—what secrets are hidden in this harlot?" He drags Moten's manuscript in front of him and turns some leaves, planting his finger on a page at last. "The monk wrote of a noblewoman. Of the arrival in the year sixty-five of someone claiming to be the secret lover of Prince Edward. Do you know who that person is?"

"I am that person," I say softly. "And so I claim'd to Moten, for it was true. I am Miriam Houmout."

"Ahh," sighs the grizzled man on the left. He seems satisfied at my answer. "There it is," he says. "That name, that word!"

"Hush," replies the thin man. "You would do well not to prompt the prisoner."

"Well," says the other. "This famous Brother Moten, the chronicler of this history, spent quite a number of pages upon your incidents and your life. And yet you did not know he did this. Curious."

Finally, the Chief Magistrate leans forward ponderously. "And he is attested to as a reliable chronicler by his own abbot."

A voice booms from behind the curtain. The voice is strong and deep. "I did not find him to be so. He is not reliable—a tale-teller, a story-spinner."

I know the voice, although I cannot place it. *Where have I heard it before?*

The Chief Magistrate turns his heavy eyes toward the curtain. "With permission, kind sir, I must say that you knew him for a lesser degree of time than his abbot. And the Abbot writes—"

"Do not badger our witness. Letters can be forged," scoffs the thin justice.

"Unbroken wax seals are difficult to forge," says the Chief Magistrate mildly. "And it is signed in the Abbot's own hand. André de Bottoun was once in cloisters with me. I know his hand."

The thin justice scoffs once more, but his scoffing is subdued now, as if out of habit.

"Therefore," continues the Chief Magistrate, his deep eyes revolving around the room, nodding slowly at each justice in turn. "It follows according to rationality that we also may believe the evidence given by this monk in his chronicle. And this evidence directs us to rely upon this text in turning our questions to the witness once again."

I am the witness he means. But I am confused. What do they want me to tell them? Moten did not know me in the village, and he wrote little during our journey, so how can my story be proved true by his words?

The Chief Magistrate leans forward into the light, as if to see my face more clearly. "Please," he says kindly. "Describe to us gathered here today what you knew of the late Prince."

"What I knew of Edward?"

The justices nod gravely.

I reach to my neck and undo the tattered remnants of my tunic. I reach for the chain around my neck. I grope a moment and then remember that the ring was taken from me. I let my hands drop to my lap, empty and fruitless.

"He gave me a ring," I say to them. "A token of his esteem."

The second one—the burning one—snorts and guffaws, as if I have said something ridiculous. Then he leans forward and speaks in a mocking tone. "Rings can be stolen. Rings can be mislaid. Such signet rings, I am sorry to tell a commoner such as you, can even be given by a king or prince to a favorite parlor maid. A ring of this nature says nothing of a prince's esteem."

But the Chief Magistrate does not acknowledge the other's objections. Instead, he holds out his hand. In his palm rests my ring, on my silver chain. "This ring?"

I nod.

He holds up the ring. "Yes, there is this. But if you wish to establish the particulars of your story, you must tell us more than your mere possession of a ring."

That spike in my chest becomes an overwhelming wall of thorns, sending prickles of anger and loss through my flesh. Everything is gone, everything except my memories of a life where I was loved, where I was someone with a future, instead of someone with only a past.

I raise my voice now. And I tell them what I know—all that is true that I can remember. I relate everything that Edward and I shared. I speak of where I came from, of my village of Houmout, and I tell them that Edward made promises to me, promises still unfulfilled.

"What promises?" The rotund man is looking down at the manuscript Moten wrote, his lips moving as he reads silently. I glance upward and am surprised to see that all the justices are leaning forward, their eyes intent.

I blush under their attention, and start to go mute again. "Ed… Edward… he promis'd me…"

"Pray continue," prompts the Chief Magistrate.

I blurt it out. "Edward promised me that he would be buried with me in the catacombs. When he gave me the ring, he promis'd me that. But it doesn't matter now, since he is dead..."

"Pray continue. We have not bid you cease."

I sigh. "Edward once told me, when we visited my village of Houmout, that he relished my name. He said that he would use the name of my own birthplace on the coast. That he himself would be called *Houmout*, as a name of his House. This never happened, of course." I give a short and bitter laugh.

The Chief Magistrate's eyes have grown wider yet, and he is stroking his bottom lip with one fat forefinger, as if caught in a moment of deep thought.

The thin justice beside him stares at me, his eyes sharp as daggers. "And you claim that you have not read this book, these pages from the Priory of Saint Mary Magdalene? You say you can actually read?"

"Yes, I was trained by Simon Sudbury. That is true," I answer simply. "But I have not read Brother Moten's journal."

"A lie!" The thin man clenches and unclenches a fist. "Any child knows that—"

The Chief Magistrate holds his hand up. "If these things are lies, she has been lying about them for over ten years, for this monk wrote them all down."

Was the book itself the thing that Moten was told to take to London? Could this be it?

He points at Moten's manuscript. "This monk has faithfully used the new anno Domino chart of days and months. Each of his months corresponds to the previous. There can be no doubt here that such a book was written over time, as a chronicle of events that are true in their particulars. This much, at least, his abbot already tells us, and this we must believe."

The Chief Magistrate looks from side to side. His voice is very weary but precise. He lifts up the tattered pages of Moten's book.

"Therefore, once we declare that the witness of this book is truthful, why we must by logic state that this woman before us has known all these proofs for years—since long before His Grace Edward the Black Prince was taken from this world."

"I still say she lies! There are other proofs!" The thin justice points to the closed curtain. "Why do you not let our witness from Doncaster speak again? What of this strong and forceful witness?"

The Chief Magistrate carries on. "I come now almost to my final ruling. I would venture to say that Edward himself, the Prince, is our final witness. There is proof that he did indeed love this woman, and if so, then her issue would be beloved and embraced by his Estate."

A voice is cleared behind the curtain. There is a nervous cough. The Chief Magistrate pauses as a loud voice speaks. "If I may, your gracious lords."

It is a voice I know, a voice that haunts my dreams.

CHAPTER 46

THE DEEP, MELODIOUS baritone rolls across the room. The voice rings out strong, a herald's cry. Now I recognize it clearly, for underneath that silver tongue is a lilting accent, the rough brogue of York and the northeast. It is a country voice underneath a layer of fear. There is some faint and anxious edge here: this man fears facing me.

"Your Graces, however much it pains me to admit, this person before you is a fraud. During all the time I have known this . . . woman . . . she never once spoke of Edward."

"Quite right, quite right," chimes in the thin magistrate.

"And furthermore, Your Grace, I would tell you true that . . ."

The deep and lovely baritone, all these smooth tones tuned to lies and accusations. He has a voice to fall in love with, a lordly voice that would deceive you to your death.

I know who this is.

"You never heard me speak at all!" The strength of my shout surprises even me. "You never once heard my voice until we came close to London. How could I speak of anything? For my voice was locked in my breast from my great grief!"

Although the guard approaches, I shout even louder still.

"How could you hear me? How could you judge me? You are a coward, who lurk behind that curtain. And you have not the courage to face me, a woman! You are afraid of women, even me!"

"I am no coward!" comes a quick retort. "I was brave enough to survive the river, to make my way to London before you, and to accuse you of what you have most unjustly done! You have murdered our children, every one!"

A hand sweeps aside the curtain, as if to prove his bravery. It is Salvius, come back to life, one arm in a sling.

I should have known that he could be alive, as I myself had been left for dead. Somehow, Salvius managed to survive his fall. He got himself to London, and he used the noble livery of Doncaster and his own lordly ways to convince the Court to accuse me of this crime.

"I indict this self-styl'd lady." Salvius points at me, haughty as ever. His voice now mirrors a lord precisely, and he acts as noble as his tone. "This one, she took upon herself to murder these children in devilish rites of a most foul sort, and then to bring them to the King, to infect him with her twisted spells. This is the truth!"

I see the trial with new eyes. It is the word of this inveterate liar against something that Moten wrote down all those years ago, when I first visited his monastery. One argues from the grave, telling my story for me. The other will say any words to see me hang, and he yet lives. All that I hoped for in this long journey now hangs upon a thread.

The pockmarked guard is at my side, moving to strike me a rough blow.

But the Chief Magistrate holds up a weighty hand. "Not now, Gerit, not when we have almost proven that this very same woman was once beloved of our sainted Black Prince, Edward. Would you wish the Prince's consort to strike you from the book of life?"

The guard steps back.

"Oh, strike her—I beg of you!" exclaims the thin man, standing from the bench in his rage. But the guard does not move again.

"A pox on this hearing!" cries the thin justice. "You cannot claim such a provenance for this whore. She has made these stories up. Let us discover what she knows. First, when did you discover that Edward, the Black Prince, was dead?"

"One week ago." I cannot look at Salvius. I fear the lies he has planted, the falsehood he has wrought.

"And do you know the manner of Edward's requested burial?"

"No." I am puzzled. What does Edward's final resting place have to do with me?

"Do you know what words are written now on his tomb?" My head whirls. How can such answers save me, or any that I love? I seize truth as my only answer, for it is the truth that Salvius will not say.

"No," I say again.

But at this last No, the rotund, grizzled justice shouts out with excitement. "See, if she knew, she would tell us now. She would tell us, in order to prove her claims. She has not done so."

"No." The thin man glares at me. "I will admit, she has not. But it could be a ruse."

"A ruse to what purpose?" the Chief Magistrate says.

"I tell you, this indeed is a ruse!" Salvius's voice comes ringing out triumphantly. If I did not know him, I too would believe him a lord in every way, for he mocks their manners perfectly. He has found a way to twist the world to his purpose once more. "It is a ruse to deceive you. She is a murderer and liar!"

At that moment, there is a jangling of chain mail as the guards at the rear of the room struggle to keep the door shut against a pounding fist.

"Your Graces all," shouts a voice. "I have a message from Doncaster, Your Lordships!"

The Chief Magistrate turns his sad deep eyes toward the door. "I will hear him."

The guards grudgingly allow the messenger through the gallery. He wears a red and gold livery, a nervous exactness in his poise. He bows from the waist. "Your Honors, all, I have come from Doncaster, as I was bid. The Lady of Doncaster, she replies to your missive with the answer that she has sent none of her House to this Court, and that none of her House was sent to testify here. So says milady."

"Ah," says the Chief Magistrate slowly. He turns his eyes back to Salvius.

"This messenger lies," Salvius asserts. "I have never seen this so-called messenger before in my life. I swear to you, the murderer before you has planted bribes. She has turned the truth to her own evil ends. Even as we were deceived by her all those years. When she lived in our village, she was a liar even then—a demon-infested liar."

The Chief Magistrate stares, alert, into the alcove. I am reminded this time of a hunting dog, a scent in front of him.

"Sir," he commands. "I question your veracity. You have told this Court that you encountered this woman—Miriam—on the road a mere fortnight ago, as part of the company of the Lady of Doncaster, and that the Lady sent you on the road in order to tell this very Court of their most foul murder of these children. What is this village you speak of?"

Salvius hesitates, but then plunges in. "Well, in a village we pass'd through, I have seen her at it, at her lies—and she has done it long! Yes, I am of the House of Doncaster. And I know that even before the Lady met her, yes, this one before you was at her deviltry even then."

The Chief Magistrate glances down at a page of parchment, and then fixes Salvius in his penetrating gaze. "You assert again that you are of the Lady's house and company. As such, you may not leave her company without leave. And this messenger bears the Lady's ring, so I am inclined to believe him. So tell us, I pray thee, how did you come to know this Miriam before your own Lady of Doncaster met her? Pray tell."

Salvius's mouth bulges a moment, with unspoken anxiety. Then I see his color change. He goes quite pale. Salvius has been caught in his own traps.

The Chief Magistrate gestures to the guard. "Take him away. This man's lies tie him in knots. This common miscreant is contemptible in my sight."

Salvius shouts in sudden panic, his voice shifting now out of a lordly tone. "But sir… Your Honor… Your Rever'd Grace… I beg of you…"

Not a one of the justices listen to his cries. The pockmarked guard seems to take some pleasure in seizing Salvius and taking the livery of Doncaster from off his chest. Finally, he is dragged shouting from the room.

After Salvius is gone, the Chief Magistrate looks back at me, and there is a strange tenderness in his tone.

"Your Ladyship," he says. "You have prov'd your provenance here today. And in that, I am ashamed of your treatment, for I must tell you now that Edward did in fact fulfill every aspect of his promises to you. In his will, he granted you much by inheritance. You are proclaimed the Lady of Ashcroft, according to his will, with lands and title all."

The Chief Magistrate glances across at the thin man beside him. "The ring he gave you—that was quite telling to me. Yet we were bound to test the holder, to see if it was the very one whom Edward named who still held this ring, not an impersonator of common blood and thin repute."

The thin magistrate looks down at the paper, his lips tight but un-speaking now.

"Further proofs are present in the fact that Edward's will stated that he would not be buried in Westminster Abbey with his fathers, amidst the crowned heads of state. Edward requested in his will to be buried in the catacombs of Canterbury."

Edward would lie with me, even in death. A quiver of glad surprise sweeps over me, covering my skin from my neck to my feet.

"And carved upon Edward's tomb even now are these words *Ich dien Houmout.'* What this means has been a mystery, for we know he 'served,' but not what or whom he served. We thought long it was a reference to an old battle, or a secret society now forgotten. Perhaps you yourself are the only one who would know all that this means."

Houmout.

He loved me.

But the magistrate is not done. "Finally, my Lady, during your incarceration, we sent messages to Canterbury. This Star Chamber of Justice found one old woman remaining there who still knew the truth—she said that you were told a lie when Edward last left you at Canterbury. And so was Edward himself. He was told that your child had come early, and that both you and the child had perished in the birth. He was told you were dead."

But I barely hear this explanation. Still, my skin is shivering with gladness.

Edward loved me.

He loved me beyond death and the grave.

My leg-irons are loosened, my bonds removed. The ring on its silver chain is placed around my neck. Someone settles a thin new cloak upon my shoulders.

"You are free to go. This Court grants you freedom, and license to travel in the kingdom as you will, slave to no man, and bound to no other than his Royal Highness, and His Grace the Prince Regent, John of Gaunt."

I sit stunned, unable to move. I had never expected such a drastic turn, such grace to be given to me ever. How can this be? The great wheel of Fortune turns, and with it all our lives.

The Magistrate repeats, "You are free to go."

I do not move.

"Ah," he says at last. "You have concern for your companions?"

And at this mention of my friends, my heart leaps once more. I had forgotten them entire amidst my shock and surprise.

"When the Abbot's letter was brought to us," says the Magistrate. "This Court stayed the death of your companions until the truth was found. It is now with our grace they will be granted freedom."

The Chief Magistrate continues. "Your companions will be set free. Your son will be disinterred from the commoners' pit and buried with honor in the courtyard of the king's second sons and consort children."

"And one last judgment I give to you—you are hereby commanded to attend the Prince Regent and the King at Court at the sixth hour— Sext—on the morrow."

The Star Chamber adjourns. The Court empties. A lady-in-waiting patiently stands at the back, to escort me.

I stand, and still that song of truth resonates in me, that reality, those holy notes.

Edward loved me, Miriam Houmout.

Edward loved me.

CHAPTER 47

A BEVY OF LADIES-IN-WAITING are ready for my arrival in the private rooms of the Tower. They look aghast at my condition. As they help me take off my soiled clothing, they stare at the strange and tortured landscape of my bruised and variegated flesh. Finally, the eldest of the ladies thinks to bring in a barrel and water heated from the fire. She pours mint-scented water into that great tub, hot and steaming, and urges me to disrobe down to the skin.

"A bath," this one says to me, a voice of authority. "Such as the Romans did. You will find it not so evil as the common people say. A bath for those who are royal parents I would advise."

And so I scrub the soilings of our journey from my flesh. I wipe away the thick layers of soot from my face, I rub off the last remaining drops of blood from my false plague, and I remove the stink of Salvius from my nose. Warm water soothes the sting and throb of my many welts from the prison, and I lave water over those wounds given me by Cole. I scrub off the darkened, corroded streaks that have stained my arms since that lost girl's distant birth. I wash away every bit of dirt and stone that clings to me.

There is a sea sponge here in the tub, floating amidst the water and the steam, and with it I clean even deeper. Gone is the encrusted scab that has lasted long upon my wounded foot. I scrape away each graved rune on my skin. Gone is that faint scent of apples that Moten left behind. Gone is the musty odor of scriptorium and catacombs.

And then I wash my head. It is still tender from that cudgeled blow given me by Cole before I fell over the lip of the riverbank. My hair is finally clean of gnats and fleas alike. I rub lavender and mint again between my thinning brown locks. I close my eyes, and inhale the subtle scents and think of Nell.

In the lodging where they put me is a gown of cream and white. When I emerge from my bath, a waiting tailor fits me most carefully, cautious of my bruises and welts.

"You will wear this on the morrow, Your Ladyship," says the tailor. "It has been brought here for you at great expense. The great Prince Regent, John of Gaunt, he paid for it to be made in honor of his brother Edward. Above the noble gown goes this coat here, to protect it from the common folk."

Dressed in this finery, the scene here seems lifted from my memory of a former life. I am given an evening meal of cold meats, white bread, and winter beets. My legs still ache, but I must stand as I eat so as not to soil that pristine gown.

Ladies-in-waiting curtsy to me, and I in turn bow down. All of them wear rich brocaded gowns, and headdresses the like of which I have never seen. I ask after my companions from the road, and I am told they will be at Court on the morrow. But we are no longer of one party, for they are commoners, and I am now called noble.

The ladies leave me in my room, alone at last for the night.

I stand before a polished silver mirror and hang around my throat that silver chain and Edward's signet ring. I think on my mother: what would she think to see me garbed in such splendor, standing in such luxury?

The world is open before me now. I have heard that Simon Sudbury still welcomes those who would study at Canterbury, both men and women, both of the cloth and Court. If I wish to study books again, and know my Latin, Greek, and Hebrew, I am permitted such fancies. What would it mean to Christian, to see his mother thus clothed and embroidered? What would it mean to take up quill and book again?

Who am I now? I ask myself. And who am I to be?

I wake before the Lauds bells chime, a dream still fresh and strong as saltwater on my lips. I rise from my bed.

I will not be everything I am—I will take my mother's secret to the grave—but I will not go to Court with utter falsehood. I will come closer to the truth. So I will tell them plain of all that the peasants suffer, all of the darts and pains that are put upon them in such a life. I will tell the Court and King the story of our journey to the Throne.

So I do not garb myself in the new great gown that has been fitted to me. I put on my old peasant clothes. They have been washed but still remain the same. They are stained and spotted, full of rips and tears. But I put them on my fresh and new washed flesh.

I do all this early in the morning, before the dawn, before the serving women can attend me. Then I work on my auburn hair, covering it with a hat of Court. I carefully cover every inch of my roadworn clothing with the rich brocaded cloak provided for my comfort in the dawn. By the time the serving women arrive, I am ready for Court, in my own eyes. And I do not allow them to touch or move a stitch of what I wear.

I come to Court attended by six women and a guard. Already, my companions have been brought; they are waiting in the crowd. We will receive some of the justice we seek, we bearers of a fallen prince. Honor and pride are to be meted out in Christian's name, a noble lad felled in his prime.

The Regent—that great man John of Gaunt—calls me forth, his eyebrow crooked in grave intent. And when I stride upon that inlaid marble floor in front of the assembled lords and ladies of Court,

I see that sitting on the throne is a small lad who bears the same bright eyes as Christian, the same waves of auburn hair. Richard II, the child king, advised by the Regent, John of Gaunt. There in Richard's face, I see my son again, in all but name. But this time, he holds a sceptre, and wears a long ermine-edged gown.

I stand, I bow, and then up I reach. Slowly I remove my hat, revealing my hacked short hair.

The crowd around me gasps, and noblewomen touch their hats as if in fear. A woman should not have her head uncovered, her long hair being her glory and her life. Then I open my rich cloak and let it fall to the ground. I stand alone and silent in my gray-and-brown stained peasant clothes. The Regent to the King steps forward, his hand on sword pommel, his face twisted with concern. But none can argue with me, for as I bow again to that young man on the throne, I lift up the great proof of love given to me by his father—Edward of Woodstock—all those years ago. I hold it high, in token and acclaim.

I bear the signet of the Black Prince in my hand. I have fought for the blessing of him who wears the crown, and I hold that ring now with assurance and with pride. I will not be moved.

After a long moment of muttering, a hush falls over this great and noble crowd.

Then I call forward my companions from Duns. They are commoners, every one, but here I name them with proper names as they emerge from the crowd—and I give each of their dead sons a name as well. I bless them and I thank them as a Lady of the Court. Then I give a greeting to this young King, alongside these my companions.

And I open my mouth.

I tell our tale.

EPILOGUE: TWO YEARS AFTER

APRIL COMES TO us with her showers sweet. I wake to the cries of little birds before the light comes across the heath. They wait all night with open eyes. Now, with the rain at dawn, their voices make melody.

I turn back the rich brocaded cloth of gold on my bed and walk to my glazed casement window. I imagine my mother calling to me in the plaintive voice of the wood fowl, her words echoing across the years.

My heart is restless though I live in comfort, cosseted in the manor house of Ashcroft. I wrap myself in a Moorish robe of intricate design and gaze beyond my solitary window. Raindrops speckle the costly glass as darkness lifts from the horizon.

Every night, I slip into the empty winter land of memory. In my dreams, I am not wealthy and landed, but in a strange and secret place. I grasp my long-gone mother's hand, tense with fear.

At aurora light, I open the casement, and the scent of lavender drifts in. A gentle rain sweeps across the fields. Then the clouds part with the sun's rising, and the birds raise their clamor anew.

Sunlight strikes across my room, bringing to light the gilded tapestry given me by the young King, in token of the bond we share. The tapestry gleams with the images of Edward in armor, and his great battle at Crécy. My lost love's deeds are recorded for all time. But I have not yet accomplished my great quest, the fulfillment of my secret charge.

In spring, many folk long to go on pilgrimage. Yet I have a different wilderness to wander than those who worship at shrines like Canterbury.

So on that morn when I wake to the brisk melody of fieldfare and plover, I decide. I will leave my life of luxury once more, to undertake this quest. Deep in the hidden recesses of my heart, I vow that I will not rest, not now, not this time. I will fulfill the promise that haunts my dreams, my mother's dying plea.

I lift the bell that lies near at hand and call my servant in. She dresses me in all my courtly finery and paints my face with oil and with scent. Then I order her to gather my household together and organize my retinue for travel. We will go on the open road this very day.

By the hour of Terce, at midmorning, we have already sent a messenger ahead to prepare our way.

✠

In the spring of our journey, the gods breathe lovely inspiration across the land. As we leave my estate, I wait on the pinnacle of a hill. Tender shoots of green have come forth from every dark holt, spreading across each dire heath until the world is in blossom once again. A young bright sun runs with the Ram, high in the sky.

It is now more than two years since my ordeal in the wasteland, and I feel my life renewed once more, the chill draughts of the past wafting away.

Behind and before me, my powerful retinue of bright mailed men stretches. Twenty-nine of us travel——enough to withstand most any bandits who dare approach. The men-at-arms know only that I travel to Court, to present myself before the King once more. I must guard my secrets, for it is perilous to do this thing. The only one I trust utterly and with my whole heart is my adopted son, Cole. He is tall and strong now, with coal-black hair and striking dark eyes. He is not the son I began my journey with, but he has become as close to me as Christian was.

A fortnight later, we come to London. Now I carry out my plans. The day fades as we enter the city. Dusk approaches. I have timed our journey well, for my secret errand is best done in darkness.

I send near half the men to lodgings, and most of the rest on duties related to my appearance at Court. I choose three of the most trusted to come with me and my son, as Christ chose his few trusted fellows to follow him to Gethsemane.

We pass the White Tower of London and turn a corner, wending our way toward the abandoned district I seek. My few trusted companions wait in the rear, watching for any who might follow.

Behind me, I have guards. Ahead of me, empty paths. Yet still I quake with fear, for even Christ's companions failed to open their eyes to danger.

My son and I turn our horses sharply as darkness falls across London. The smoke of many fires thickens and embitters the fog. We pull our hoods low and double back across the twisting maze of cobbled streets, so that any pursuers would find their way confused.

We leave the last of my men behind at the Seven Dials crossroads, to watch for any prying eyes. Cole and I take a narrow path through which a horse may hardly fit. Alone we are, finally, exposed and vulnerable.

I remember the corkscrewing turns of the map, the buildings with their signs. I head toward the Cripplegate. The night is late, but I hear revelry at the center of the town, men laughing drunk and loud. At a butcher's house, there are the cries of animals being slaughtered, and along every street, there are farm carts hauling goods to market.

I turn a corner at Red Cross Street. Then another at Aldergate, Cole at my side. We enter the maze of turning corners and cobblestones.

I grip Cole's hand.

There are people here on the cobblestones who look as bedraggled as the man I once was. They lie in the street, overcome by drink or weariness. These forgotten peasants lie here in the stinking refuse, far from the villages of their birth.

The fog swirls around us, and now I feel so very far from Court and from my home. Against my skin, I can feel the lines of my rich clothes. Yet I can still feel the scars on my skin from my long winter journey. There are scars on me made from weapons and from fists, from fear and hunger as well. I know I am no better than these wretches in the street.

At night, I find myself uncertain in my feather bed. Sometimes, I feel that a wood shed back in Duns is where I properly belong. Inside my skin, I still am a peasant through and through.

I have heard that my companions from Duns returned safe and sound to the village, escorted by Sir Phillip and other knights of the realm. Liam and Geoff and Tom and Benedict received food for the winter, and gold to better their houses—in token of the King's thanks for their shelter of Miriam, now Lady of Ashcroft, the mother of an heir and consort to a prince. I have not heard of them since.

I glance back at the dark windows of the Tower. No candlelight flickers—no one is awake. I point my nose toward the outer boroughs, where the buildings have been long abandoned. I enter a district mean and burned.

As I tread the moonlit cobblestones, I find my way through the maze. I turn the last corner, and there ahead of me, they wait. I have found the place marked on the map. The garden of my people. Leyrestowe.

Here, I find a building with three golden balls. The structure is broken and old. But it is a sign that I can fulfill my oath, at last. After all these years, I will help her spirit go free.

I close my eyes here in supplication. I remember my mother's face. She whispered to me. "Promise that you will say Kaddish for me. You will say Kaddish and bring me peace."

She held her hand out and grasped me tight.

"But you must wait to say them. You will go where there are other Jews, find them in London—you must find ten of them. Together, you must say Kaddish for me. It will save me, in the afterlife. These words will lift my soul to heaven."

Over the years to come, as I grew up in Canterbury, I searched for these special words. I found mention of the Kaddish here and there in secret books I read, the ones confiscated from murdered Jews by Simon Sudbury. I discovered that the Kaddish was the holy prayer said only by Jews at the end of our lives, the prayer said to unite us, to bring us to paradise. But always the texts said that one must say those sacred words among the family, joining hands with others of the same blood: with other Jews, as one community. I found ways to learn more of the Hebrew tongue, as scholar and as assistant to the Abbess. And I taught these words to my son Christian in his turn.

Always, I searched for Jews, but the records showed the Jews were all gone. Every district I visited was desecrated, dark. Here and there I heard a rumor of one, like poor Sophia, bereft of everything in her heritage, hungry and alone. But never did I hear of a group of them again. I thought if they still lived in England, they must be buried deep. Like me, with buried voice, buried life, buried tongue.

Now I have come to them at last.

They are in front of me. My people have gathered here, the remnant, altogether, in the Jews' Garden at Cripplegate. I lift my eyes to the distant moon that shines over our earthly sphere. I stare around at the field in front of me, the nine-branched candelabrum etched over the archway, the dark gray stones ranked together in rows, the brambles overgrowing this secret shadowed place.

This is the closest I will ever come to finding my people. It is the last graveyard of my people in London.

I stand here, under the moon and the menorah arch, and I begin to speak:

> Glorified and sanctified be God's great name throughout the world, which He has created according to His will. May He establish His kingdom in your lifetime and during your days, and within the life of the entire House of Israel, speedily and soon.

And I know the ancient words, in the old tongue, from all my long years of study. I whisper the Hebrew. I say Kaddish for my mother's soul:

> Yitgaddal veyitqaddash shmeh rabba,
> Be'alma di vra khir'uteh, veyamlikh malkhuteh
> Veyatzma' purqaneh viqarev qetz meshi'eh,
> Be'ayekhon uvyomekhon,
> Uv'aye dekhol bet yisrael, be'agala uvizman qariv ve'imru.

I close my eyes. My mother is walking in the spring, in the morning of the year. Oh, always when that season with sweet showers pierces through the chill draught of March, I can feel the sweet liquid of joy in me.

In this new spring come to earth, I look in my mother's eyes and I give her release at last.

> God who creates peace in His celestial heights, may He create peace for us and for all Israel... May there be abundant peace from heaven, and life, for us, and for all Yisrael; and say, amen. He who creates peace in His celestial heights, may He create peace for us and for all Yisrael. Oseh shalom... Amen, amen.

I say Kaddish twice. Once for my mother. Once for my lost son.

Cole holds my hand as the tears fall down. I bow low, praying for these departed ones— for rest, for peace at the end.

In the darkness, the silent ones speak to me, the dead whisper back:

> Amen.

ABOUT EDWARD THE BLACK PRINCE

EDWARD the Black Prince, the eldest son of King Edward III of England, died after illness in 1376 and never took the English throne. Thrust by his father into the role of warrior as a very young man, Edward became a powerful strategist and leader on the battlefield.

Edward was known to have several lovers prior to his marriage to Joan of Kent, who was thought by many to be an unsuitable bride. With Joan, Edward fathered two legitimate sons: Edward, who died at six, and Richard of Bordeaux, who later ruled as Richard II. Edward also fathered at least two illegitimate sons prior to his marriage, both of whom were granted titles and lands in his last will and testament. Other secret lovers have also been rumored.

In his will, Edward made the strange request that he not be buried beside his family and the crowned heads of England in the upper shrine of Westminster Abbey. Instead, he wished to be buried in the crypt of Canterbury Cathedral. This request was briefly honored, and his coat of arms and an image of his face are still inscribed in a chantry deep in the crypt.

The bodies of Edward and his wife, Joan, were subsequently removed from his desired resting place to be deposited in the upper shrine of nobility.

Edward also requested that the cryptic phrase *Ich dien Houmout* be inscribed on his tomb. This inscription remains a mystery to historians of the English crown. The first words can be read as "I serve," but no definitive interpretation has been found for the last word "Houmout"—although it may be Hebrew in derivation. Edward's secret went with him to the grave.

ACKNOWLEDGMENTS

Words cannot begin to thank my family for their encouragement and patience as I've spent my time deep in the fourteenth century over the past years. I owe you everything, Jill, Kate, and Nick.

I also offer my deep appreciation to Manek Mistry and Matt Haugh, who gave me brilliant insights that helped me craft the best story I could tell. Many thanks for their hours of reading, critiquing and story suggestions. Most of the best ideas in this novel can be credited to Manek and Matt. Thank you!

Artist Nikki McClure's early reading, encouragement, and marvelous illustrations have been an inspiration to me, and I appreciate her contributions profoundly.

On the publishing front, I extend my gratitude to my editors, Elizabeth Johnson and Kyra Freestar; proofreader extraordinaire Barry Foy; publishing maven Linda Marus; book publicist Mary Bisbee-Beek; book designer Sara DeHaan; and the rest of the staff of Campanile Press who helped to shape this book. I also thank agent Jenny Bent, who advised me on this story.

I acknowledge the assistance of the following early readers who helped tremendously: Christine Gunn, who gave me one of the best early critiques and helped me to find the heart of my main character;

Sheri Boggs, who gave me my first big encouragement; Beth Oshiki, who provided many helpful notes; Bianca Davis, who read faithfully until three in the morning, and then critiqued my work thoughtfully; Dean Bonnell and Larry Clark, who have both been faithful early readers for many years; and the accomplished medieval scholar Miria Hallum. Thank you all!

And the South Sound Algonquins writers group, who listened graciously, and helped the story to improve. I am especially grateful to Dolly Harmon, Mark Henry, Liz Shine, Chris Dahl, Tom Wright, Monica Britt, and Megan Pottorff. Doug Sugano and Victor Bobb of Whitworth College taught me my craft, and I appreciate their tutelage.

Finally, I thank both Jim Heynen and Jim Lynch for their continued encouragement in the writing journey.

AUTHOR'S NOTE

THE careful reader will note that I have included phrases and moments from various medieval texts, including lines from the drama *Everyman*, the allegorical poem *Piers Plowman*, and several stories that are lifted straight from Geoffrey Chaucer's *The Canterbury Tales*, with the conceit that these stories were part of the fabric of the time (as some Chaucerian scholars believe). Of course, I also paraphrase and cite Chaucer throughout the book. Also included is an entire scene from the *N-Town* Plays, the mysterious medieval drama that is called "N" only because no one can determine what village or town was the origin for this unusual and interesting medieval play cycle. (Doug Sugano first introduced me to these texts, and his contemporary rendition of the texts is wonderful.) The players who enact the *N-Town* scene are in fact the same players featured in Barry Unsworth's novel *Morality Play*, and I hope that I do Barry's memory an honor by showing his characters still at their art in the same era, albeit in a new story.

I have, of course, included actual citations from work by Thomas Aquinas, Augustine, and other notables from medieval theology, as their thinking on the topics of divine versus earthly dominion, and the pressing question of the burial of the dead were very much of the fabric of the time. Readers interested in these topics and in feminist readings of medieval spirituality will want to read Caroline

Walker Bynum's masterful works on these subjects. One recommended book is her *Fragmentation and Redemption: Essays on Gender and the Human Body in Medieval Religion*. Also of interest would be Thomas Aquinas's original works, which remain surprisingly readable and pertinent to our age. For a more general overview, Rik Van Nieuwenhove's *An Introduction to Medieval Theology* or Williston Walker's classic work *A History of the Christian Church* are both recommended. As always when I write of the medieval era, I am indebted to Barbara Tuchman's *A Distant Mirror*, to whose title I owe the name of my main character: Mear.